"I'VE NEVER LIED TO YOU, DANA."

"Maybe you haven't lied, but you sure don't tell—" She yelped as bullets impacted the vehicle.

In one smooth motion, he grabbed the back of her neck and bent her, shoving her below the window while punching the gas. The car lurched through the gate, which scraped along the passenger side, flicking sparks.

To her credit, she didn't struggle. "You think they're shooting at you or me?" Her voice was muffled against her legs.

"Good question." Trusting her to remain down, he released her to put both hands on the wheel and zip out to a main traffic artery, searching for the enemy in the rearview mirror. "I think they shot from the bushes at the exit. Hopefully no vehicle near."

A black truck swerved around the corner behind them, its headlights cutting through the darkness. He'd spoken too soon.

She partially lifted up to look over her shoulder. "You have a gun?"

"Where would I put a gun in this outfit?" He wouldn't be able to lose the truck in this small vehicle.

She snorted, her eyes wide, her face pale. "How are you so calm right now?" Her soft voice rose to almost shrill.

"Training?"

BROKEN

REBECCA ZANETTI

ZEBRA BOOKS
KENSINGTON PUBLISHING CORP.
www.kensingtonbooks.com

ZEBRA BOOKS are published by

Kensington Publishing Corp.
119 West 40th Street
New York, NY 10018

All Kensington titles, imprints, and distributed lines are available at special quantity discounts for bulk purchases for sales promotion, premiums, fund-raising, educational, or institutional use.

Special book excerpts or customized printings can also be created to fit specific needs. For details, write or phone the office of the Kensington Sales Manager: Attn.: Sales Department. Kensington Publishing Corp., 119 West 40th Street, New York, NY 10018. Phone: 1-800-221-2647.

Zebra and the Z logo Reg. U.S. Pat. & TM Off.

First Printing: June 2020
ISBN-13: 978-1-4201-4585-4
ISBN-10: 1-4201-4585-1

ISBN-13: 978-1-4201-4586-1 (eBook)
ISBN-10: 1-4201-4586-X (eBook)

10 9 8 7 6 5 4 3 2

Printed in the United States of America

*This one is dedicated to my mom,
who's the strongest person I've ever met.
I love you*

ACKNOWLEDGMENTS

My heartfelt thanks go out to everyone who helped with this book:

A HUGE thank you to Tony Zanetti for thinking it was a good idea, years ago, for me to change careers from law to writing. Not many husbands would have been so supportive, and I've never forgotten that moment.

Thank you to our kids, Gabe and Karlina, for the love, support, and all-around good times. I'm in awe of both of you, every day.

Thank you to my editor, Alicia Condon, and my agent, Caitlin Blasdell, for their encouragement, support, and insightful advice on this and every other book we've worked on together.

Thank you to Jim Dorohovich, who came up with the perfect name for this series.

Thank you to the Montana Tech gang for the ideas and fun: Josh and Jamie Beggerly and John and Angie Prendergast. Mermaids, Truly Spiked, and King Pins forever.

Thank you to the rest of the Kensington crew: Alexandra Nicolajsen, Steven Zacharius, Adam Zacharius, Ross Plotkin, Lynn Cully, Vida Engstrand, Jane Nutter, Lauren Vasallo, Lauren Jernigan, Kimberly Richardson, Erin Barker, and Rebecca Cremonese.

Thank you to Jillian Stein for her incredible creativity, strong work, and for being such an amazing friend.

Thanks to my fantastic street team, Rebecca's Rebels, and their creative and hardworking leader, Minga Portillo. Thanks also to Margarita Coale for her insights and great advice, as well as for her help at signings and with the Rebels.

Thanks also to my constant support system: Gail and Jim English, Kathy and Herb Zanetti, Debbie Smith, Stephanie West, Jessica Namson, Lexi Blake, Joanna Wylde, Asa Maria Bradley, Boone Brux, Kristen Ashley, MJ Rose, and Liz and Steve Berry.

Chapter One

Clarence Wolfe strode up to the entrance of the super-secret sex club as if he had done so a million times before.

Down the street and partially hidden by the branches of a sweeping cherry tree, Dana Mulberry ducked lower in her car and pressed the binoculars to her face so hard they pinched her skin. What in the world was Wolfe doing at a Captive party?

She swallowed. Her heart rate, already thundering, galloped into the unhealthy range. It had taken her weeks to find out about the club and track down the location of the newest party, and yet another week to finagle an invitation to the casual play night as a guest. And the ex-soldier, the beyond hunky badass who'd relegated her immediately to the friend zone, was walking inside like he owned one of the coveted million-dollar memberships?

She shook her head. Twice. When she could focus once more through her binoculars, there Wolfe prowled, clear as day in the full moonlight.

He'd followed the rules for the night, too. Male doms were to wear leather pants and dark shirts, females any leather outfit, and subs were to wear corsets and small skirts if they were female and knit shirts and light pants if they were male. Apparently, Wolfe was a dom. Figured. She had assumed she'd chuckle at seeing guys in leather pants, but there was nothing funny about Wolfe's long legs, powerful thighs and tight butt in those pants.

In fact, he looked even more dangerous than usual, and she would've bet that wasn't possible.

Where in the heck had Wolfe found leather pants? Was he really some sort of dom who went to clubs? He didn't *like* people enough to spend time with anybody in a dungeon. She giggled, the sound slightly hysterical, so she cleared her throat.

What now? She looked down at her tight green corset and a black skirt that was as short as she dared go. At least it covered the still healing knife marks on her upper thighs that she hadn't told anybody about. Not even her doctor. The guy who'd cut her had been killed in jail, so why did it matter?

Forget the nightmares. They'll go away soon.

Her more immediate problem was that Wolfe had just walked through the front door of the mansion housing the latest Captive party. The man she needed to find was inside that place, and she'd spent a lot of time gearing up for this.

Would Wolfe blow her cover?

She'd been sitting in her car for an hour watching people arrive. Okay. She might've been gathering her courage. This was so outside her experience. She hadn't even known sex clubs existed until that movie came out about BDSM.

But her boss at the national newspaper where she used to work, had once said she'd do anything for a story, and he'd been right. Well, mostly. Okay. She could do this. In fact, why not look at the fact that Wolfe was inside as a positive? His presence gave her unexpected backup.

Yeah. That was the idea. Forget the fact that the sexiest man she'd ever met was in a sex club right now. Yep. Good plan. She slid from her car and pulled her skirt down as far as she could, which still barely covered her butt.

Her heels tottered on the uneven sidewalk as she clip-clopped alongside a high stone wall that no doubt protected another zillion-dollar mansion. Then she crossed the street, her head high, shivering in the chilly breeze as she reached the front door and knocked.

"Hello." A man in full tuxedo opened the door. He was about six feet tall with curly blond hair, and he was built like a linebacker. "Can I help you?"

There was no way anybody could get by this guy if he didn't grant access. She handed over her gold-foiled invitation.

He accepted the paper and held up a small tablet to scroll through. "Ah. Miss Millerton. I see that you answered the questionnaire and have signed all of the necessary documents." He focused on her, still blocking entry. "A couple of quick questions."

She forced a smile, feeling way too exposed in her scant clothing. Hopefully the questions weren't about her cover ID. "All right."

"What's your safe word?"

"Red," she said instantly.

"Good. If you need help, who do you yell for?" His voice remained kind but firm.

She paused, thinking through the documents she'd read online. "For anybody, but especially the dungeon monitors." The words felt foreign in her mouth. Should she ask him about Albert? Or was that taboo? She didn't want to get kicked out before she found her source.

"Good." The guy stepped back to reveal a rather ordinary-looking front vestibule with another wide door directly across from them. "Go ahead and have fun, sweetheart."

Fun? She nodded and tottered on her heels across the

dark marble to the door, which, somehow, he reached first and opened for her.

"Thank you," she murmured, instantly hit by a wave of noise and heat. Music blasted from the ceiling, and in front of her, a palatial living room had been set up with a dance floor on one side and a full-length bar on the other. Bar. Definitely bar. She could have a drink and maybe chat up the bartender. A quick glance around the darkened room, highlighted by deep purple lights from far above, didn't reveal Albert's location. She didn't see Wolfe, either. Good.

She made her way through a crowd of people in leather and other gear, finally reaching the bar.

A six-foot-tall female bartender wearing a full leather outfit leaned over, her full breasts spilling out of the tight V-neck. "What can I get you, hon?"

"Tequila. Shot," Dana said. Should she ask for a double? No.

"Sure thing." The woman poured a generous shot and pushed it across the inlaid wood. "You a guest tonight?"

Dana tipped back the drink, sputtering just a little as her throat heated. "Yes."

The woman grinned, revealing a tongue piercing. "You new?"

"Yes." Dana coughed.

"I'm Jennie." She tilted her head and poured another shot. "Mistress Jennie."

Oh yeah. Dana had tried to memorize the appropriate lingo from the online sites. She accepted the second shot, her hand shaking. "Thank you." Was she supposed to add the "mistress"? The website hadn't said.

"You bet. Just have some fun and remember you don't have to do anything you don't want to do. The playrooms are all over the house, and if there's a red sign on a door, it can't be closed. You can just watch if you want," Jennie said, moving down the bar as somebody caught her attention.

Good advice. Definitely. Dana took the second shot and let the alcohol warm her body.

"Hello." A man appeared at her elbow. "We haven't met."

She partially turned. The guy was about fifty with shrewd eyes and an iron-hard body. He wore leather pants and a red leather vest that showed muscled arms. "Hello. I'm Dana," she said.

"Charles." He held out a hand to shake and kept hers longer than necessary. "You here to explore a little bit?"

Oh, crap. "I'm just here to ease my way in." She tried for a flirtatious smile, but her lips refused to curve. "In fact, I was looking for my friend Albert Nelson. Any chance you know him?"

Charles slid closer, his pupils dilated. "No. But I could make you forget him." He took her hand again, and she tried to pull back, but he just smiled. "How about we check out some of the rooms? I could show you around."

"No, thanks." She forced a smile in place as panic began to rise.

"Come on—" Charles began.

"She said no." Charles's hand was instantly removed from hers, and he was tossed toward the dance floor, barely catching his balance before he collided with two people slow dancing.

Dana gulped, tasting tequila on her lips as she looked up, knowing the voice well. "Wolfe." Only training kept her from blanching at the raw fury in his bourbon-colored eyes.

He leaned in, his full lips near her ear. "What the hell are you doing here?"

She shivered and dug deep for her own anger. Then she pressed her hands to her hips. "What are *you* doing here?" she snapped back.

His gaze swept from her revealing top, down to her toes, and back up to her blazing face. "Subs don't use that tone, baby. One who does ends up over a knee. Quickly."

Oh, he did not. She glared. "I am not a sub," she whispered.

"You're dressed like one." His dark T-shirt tightened across his muscled chest as he leaned closer again. His buzz cut had grown out to curl a bit beneath his ears, giving him a wild look.

"There weren't many options," she hissed.

"Wolfe." A man also dressed in leather, his brown hair slicked back, moved up beside Wolfe. He was about forty with tattoos down one arm. "I see you found a friend. Finally going to play?"

Wolfe didn't look away from Dana, his gaze going from furious to calm in a second. How in the world did he control himself like that? "I'm normally not a public player, as you know."

What did that mean? Dana began to ask, but Wolfe subtly shook his head.

The man held out a hand. "In that case, I'm Master Trentington. How about I show you around tonight?"

"That's kind of you." Dana shook his hand, her lip trembling annoyingly. "I was actually looking for a friend named Albert Nelson. Do you know him?"

Trentington reluctantly released her. "I do, but he's not here tonight. I'd love to be your guide in his stead."

"No," Wolfe answered before she could, angling his body closer and partially blocking the other man. He glanced over his shoulder at Jennie. "Spare cuffs?"

Jennie grinned, reached under the bar, and tossed over a pair of bright pink wrist cuffs.

Wolfe snagged them out of the air and snapped them on Dana's wrists before she could blink. They were fur lined and soft, but felt restrictive nonetheless. "We've already reached an agreement," he murmured.

"Well. In that case, have fun." Trentington moved to leave.

"Charles was being pushy again," Wolfe said quietly. "It's time you kicked him out."

Trentington sighed and turned toward the dance floor. "Thanks."

Dana looked down at the pink cuffs. She kind of felt like Wonder Woman. "Why did you—"

"They show ownership," Wolfe said, clipping the cuffs together easily.

Her abdomen rolled, and her head snapped back. "Excuse me?" She tugged hard, but they wouldn't separate, effectively binding her wrists together. She eyed his shin. With her heels, she could do some damage.

He chuckled, the sound low and dangerous. It slid over her skin, burning her from within. "Right now, you're playing a sub, no doubt for a story. But I'm playing a dom, and if you kick me, I'll toss your ass over that bar and beat it."

His words slid right through her to pulse between her legs. For Pete's sake. That scenario was not sexy. The idea of Wolfe's hand anywhere near her butt sent her already sensitive body into hyperdrive. Oh, she'd handle him later. For now, she had work to do, so she shook off all emotion and leaned closer. He'd said "playing." "Are you on a job?" she whispered.

"Yes." He glanced around. "Who's Albert Nelson?"

"Someone I need to talk to," she said, looking again. "I scared him off last week, but I know he's a member of Captive, so I came here to ask him questions." She planned to pressure him into answering all of her questions this time. She no longer cared about subtlety. Finding out who'd killed her friend was all that mattered. "Your job?"

"Confidential. You know a guy named Clarke Wellson?"

"No, but I could do a background check later," she murmured. They'd helped each other with cases before.

Wolfe glanced down at her, his gaze warming. "You look incredible."

"Thank you." It was nice he'd noticed, although the outfit wasn't really her style. She was more a jeans and flannel type of girl. She shuffled uneasily in her heels. That way he had of switching topics had thrown her ever since they'd met. "Okay. I'm going to mingle and ask questions. You?"

He smiled, the sight daunting. "I just cuffed you. No dom would allow a sub to mingle."

Allow? Oh, heck no. She blinked. "Then uncuff me."

"No. Last time you didn't have backup, you nearly died." He crossed his arms, somehow scouting the entire room while also watching her.

Her back teeth gritted together. "You're not in charge here, Wolfe."

"The cuffs say otherwise," he said, angling his head to take in the dance floor.

She couldn't help it. She really couldn't. Full on, she'd chased this story, and now she was pretty much tied up because of a guy who only wanted to be her friend. She kicked him, as hard as she could, right in the shin.

He stiffened and rapidly pivoted, and both hands went to her hips to lift her. She was in the air, halfway to the bar, before she even thought to struggle. A heavy thud sounded from behind Wolfe. A woman screamed.

Wolfe dropped Dana to her feet and shoved her behind him, angling toward the dance floor. He looked up to a balcony high above.

Dana craned her neck to look around him, staring down at the dead man on the ground with a bullet hole in his head. His eyes were wide open and frighteningly blank. Her stomach lurched, and she coughed. "That's Albert," she whispered.

Wolfe looked over his shoulder at her. "Well, shit. That's Clarke, too."

Sirens sounded in the distance. Wolfe grabbed her bound wrists. "We have to get out of here. Now."

Chapter Two

Holding Dana tight, ignoring her sweet orange blossoms scent, Wolfe ran past the gaping onlookers to the vestibule, where Thor with an attitude tried to stop him. Not halting his stride, Wolfe lifted the moron beneath the neck and tossed him against the far wall. The fancy wooden paneling cracked, and the guy dropped to the marble floor.

Dana gasped but kept pace with him as he charged out the front door and into the street, scouting for threats. "Where's your car?" he asked.

Trembling, she pointed down the quiet street to a compact lime-green bug.

His steps faltered and then quickened again. "Where did you get a tiny green car?" he snapped.

"Rented it," she panted, her eyes wild. "Figured it'd be tough to trace me if something went wrong."

It was freaking easy to trace a properly rented car if she had used her real ID, which no doubt she had. "Good idea," he rumbled. Why scare her even more than she already was? Or maybe he should. When he'd turned around and seen her at that sex club party, his head had almost exploded—and not just because of the danger she seemed to hunt like a bluetick hound. That outfit should be illegal.

He opened the passenger-side door and settled her inside, lifting his head. The skin of his neck prickled in warning. Slamming her door, he ran around and tried to force his six-foot-six body into the driver's seat. Groaning, he reached down and pushed the seat all the way back, which still wasn't far enough, then slammed the door, wincing as his knees pressed the steering wheel up. He turned the key, impressed she'd left it in the ignition.

The car bucked, and he punched the gas.

"Hey." Dana stabilized herself with her hands on the dash. "Slow down."

He didn't bother to answer, settling both hands on the steering wheel and taking a turn on two wheels.

Sirens trilled, rapidly approaching.

Going on instinct, he turned down another residential street in the subdivision, heading for the rear entrance. The emergency vehicles would use the main entrance. He hoped. "Put on your seat belt," he said, increasing his speed.

"Wh-what if we need to jump out?" she gasped.

"Seat. Belt." He didn't have time to argue.

She did as he ordered, mumbling something and no doubt rolling her spectacular green eyes. "You need to release these damn cuffs."

Without looking, he reached over and freed the clasp before taking another turn, swiping some rich person's rosebush. "I like you bound."

She snorted, tearing off the cuffs and tossing them in the back seat. "Don't flirt if you can't follow through."

He swallowed down a retort, because she was right. He had no intention of dragging her into his disaster of a world, because he knew, without a doubt, that she deserved much better than he'd ever be able to offer. "Want to tell me why you were at a sex party undercover, without backup?" One of the many skills he'd learned in the military was to keep his voice mild when his temper was spiking.

"Oh, no," she said, stabilizing herself by grabbing the *oh shit* handle above her head. "I'm not giving you a thing until you spill it all. Not this time."

Darn stubborn woman. He slowed the car as he caught sight of two kids tossing a football in front of a well-lit mansion. Shouldn't they be in bed? It was after midnight.

She cleared her throat. "When you picked me up after I kicked you—you weren't really going to . . ."

He sped by a cul-de-sac and headed for the exit, hitting the brakes as the gate slowly started to open. "I said I would." They'd both been undercover, and he'd provided warning. "Have I ever lied to you?"

"Probably," she returned, her voice a mite snappy. "You have no idea what hell you would've unleashed."

Amusement flitted through him like a ghost of the sense of humor he'd had years ago. He turned to face her, his gaze dropping to the sexy corset. "You don't think I could spank you?"

A startling pink flushed up from her breasts to her face, catching his attention as her cheeks darkened. Then her eyes sparked. Fascinating. Absolutely fascinating. He focused back on the infuriatingly slow gate. "I've never lied to you, Dana." He never would, either.

"Maybe you haven't lied, but you sure don't tell—" She yelped as bullets impacted the vehicle.

In one smooth motion, he grabbed the back of her neck and bent her, shoving her torso below the window while pressing hard on the gas pedal. The car lurched through the gate, which scraped along the passenger side, flicking sparks.

To her credit, she didn't struggle. "You think they're

shooting at you or me?" Her voice was muffled against her legs.

"Good question." Trusting her to remain down, he released her to put both hands on the wheel and zip out to a main traffic artery, searching for the enemy in the rearview mirror. "I think they shot from the bushes at the exit. Hopefully no vehicle near."

A black truck swerved around the corner behind them, its headlights cutting through the darkness. He'd spoken too soon.

She partially rose up to look over her shoulder. "You have a gun?"

"Where would I put a gun in this outfit?" He wouldn't be able to lose the truck in this small vehicle.

She coughed, her eyes wide, her face pale. "How are you so calm right now?" Her soft voice rose to almost shrill.

"Training?" He ripped around another corner and had to swerve to avoid a woman walking a poodle. Why wasn't anybody in bed at the damn late hour? "I don't feel things like other people do, not anymore." The truck was getting closer.

"As much as I like you opening up, maybe we should talk about your emotions later? After we get rid of these guys?" she gasped.

"Good point." One of the advantages of his lack of emotion was that the adrenaline flooding his system focused him. Keeping calm and rational was the only way they'd get out of this. He drove up the on-ramp to the interstate just as bullets grazed the back of the bug. If one hit a tire at this speed, the car would roll. "Hold on." He swerved in and out of traffic, ignoring the blaring horns. An elderly lady in a massive Buick missing a headlight flipped him the bird and he moved onto the shoulder, increasing speed. The truck followed.

At the last second, he veered across multiple lanes of traffic and shot down an off-ramp, barreling through a red light and swerving onto a busy street.

He skidded, hit the brakes, turned the car, and accelerated again.

Dana sat fully up, her blond hair flying over the back of the seat. "I should've brought a gun," she muttered.

"Why?" He turned the wheel and drove the car to the rear of a fast-food joint, whipping around to face the main street. The VW was partially hidden behind the building and foliage as well as the darkness of night.

"To shoot," she muttered.

He kept his hands light on the wheel. "You can't get into a shootout on a busy street. This isn't the movies."

She rolled her eyes. "Do you have to be so literal all the time?"

He mulled the question over. "Yeah. I think so." Several minutes passed without any sighting of the black truck. He tugged his phone from his back pocket, wincing as he caught his fingers in the tight leather of the pants. Hitting speed dial, he waited until Angus Force, his boss, picked up.

"What?" Force snarled.

Great. He was in another mood. "Have someone drop off my truck at . . ." Wolfe flipped open the jockey box to pull out the rental agreement and read quickly. "Squishy's Car Rental on Third Street." He clicked off before Force could ask questions, turning to face Dana. "We'll get rid of the car, fetch your things, and then you can come home with me."

She faltered. "I'm not going home with you."

"Sure, you are." Sometimes things were so clear to him, he truly couldn't understand how anybody else could be confused. "Either those guys were shooting at you—"

"Or maybe you," she countered, her fragile chin lifting.

He nodded. "Or maybe me. In which case, they surely got the plates of this thing and will investigate the hot blonde in the passenger seat. Even though it's dark, their headlights were bright enough to get the license plate and your hair color. The guys after me wouldn't hesitate to go through you to get to me."

She rubbed her nose. "What guys are after you? I mean, besides the guys in the black truck, who could be after me and not you."

There were too many guys after too many people. He had to take care of his problems sooner rather than later, and he needed to ensure her safety first. "I like you." The words rolled out, surprising him.

She drew back, confusion clouding her emerald eyes for the briefest of seconds. "I like you, too."

"I don't have many friends, Dana." It was hard to find the right words, especially when dealing with someone who used words all the time in her work. She was an excellent journalist and writer, and he knew he wasn't putting this right. "You're my friend, and I can't let you get hurt." There. That made sense.

Her shoulders relaxed. "You're my friend, too, but I've been taking care of myself for a long time, Wolfe. I'm on a story, one that matters to me, and I'm not letting up."

Her tenacity and dedication had impressed him from the beginning of their friendship. Oh, if she were tough or hardened, they would've taken it temporarily beyond friendship. But she was sweet and soft and kind . . . and he was none of those things. Probably never had been. "Would you please relocate to my place while we figure out what's happening with both of our cases?"

She blinked. "You just said please."

"Yeah." He was the muscle for his unit, and when it

came to safety, he usually gave orders. She wasn't his to protect unless she allowed it. Although, if she said no, he'd camp outside of her apartment out of sight. But she didn't know that.

She sighed. "If I don't go with you, you'll just skulk around my apartment complex and scare people."

Maybe she did know him better than he'd thought. "I don't skulk." The idea was a little insulting. He started the engine and drove sedately out onto the main road, turning quickly to use back roads to the car rental place, which took longer than he'd planned. By the time they reached the business, his truck was already waiting on the front curb, gleaming beneath the streetlight.

"Angus Force sure gets things done," Dana mused.

True. Wolfe parked the car, tossed the rental agreement and keys in the after-hours box, and once again took Dana's hand to lead her to his truck. Her hand was small and her skin soft against his, and he tried not to notice. He really did.

She hesitated at his truck, pulling free. "I'm not sure I should stay with you."

He turned to face her, knowing exactly what she meant. Even if he had it in him to be coy, he wouldn't be with her. Her green eyes glowed in the dim light, matching the corset that pushed up her breasts, creating enticing mounds. Her legs were bare to the heels, and somehow, even her knees were sexy. She was the girl next door, the ambitious professional, the sweet woman who'd befriended him when she'd had no reason to be nice. Somehow, she brought out a side of him he'd thought had died on a dusty road a million miles away, along with his teammates. With her, and only with her, he wished he could be different from the man he'd become.

Worse yet, she had a penchant for barreling headfirst

into danger, and everything about *him* spelled danger. He felt the draw between them, and he'd fought it since day one.

He swallowed as desire hit him so hard he couldn't speak for a moment.

Her eyes darkened and she shifted her weight, knowledge tilting her lips. "So. I stay at my place and you stay at yours?"

It was a smart plan, except for the fact that she might be in danger. "I'd rather have blue balls than you dead, sweetheart. Get in the truck."

Her face flushed. "Wolfe. Geez. You're not supposed to say everything that pops into your head."

He reached for her arm, assisting her into the truck. "Hazard of a brain injury, I guess." He waited until she settled and then gently shut the door, wishing he could shut down his attraction for her as he crossed in front of his vehicle and jumped into the driver's seat. Once he'd ignited the engine, he drove away from the curb. He'd already survived the closest thing to hell he could imagine, but something told him the next few days with her at his house would be worse. He needed to find the guys after them and take off their heads, now.

"Wolfe. Geez."

Crap. He'd said that out loud. Yep. This was going to be tough.

Chapter Three

By the time Dana had packed her clothes and research files and returned to Wolfe's truck, she was starving, and still uncomfortably turned on, or maybe her breathlessness resulted from the aftermath of the car chase. An image of Wolfe in those pants flashed through her head. Nope. Turned on, for sure. At least she'd had a chance to change into worn jeans and a comfy flannel shirt. As she retook her seat on the passenger side, he slid his phone into the cup holder between them.

"Force just called and I need to drop by the office," he said, starting the engine and pulling the truck out of her lot.

She glanced at the clock on the dash, frowning. "It's one in the morning."

Wolfe shrugged. "We work when Force wants to work, and that's usually late. I didn't see any activity around your building, so you're safe for now."

Her adrenaline had finally ebbed so she could think clearly. She shivered. Getting shot at shouldn't be in her wheelhouse, but it was happening more frequently. "Who's after you?" she asked, plucking at a string on her jeans.

"Nobody who matters." Streetlights and darkness took turns highlighting and shadowing his strong face as he sped toward his office outside of D.C., his voice deep and unemotional.

"That's not true. You're hunting them, too." She knew him well enough to understand he was on a mission of his own, one that had him often disappearing for a day or two at a time. "We help each other with cases." When she'd been in trouble before, she'd called Wolfe, but he'd never confided in her. Yeah, it hurt a little. A one-way friendship didn't appeal to her—even though he did. At some point, she was going to have to get a grip and move on if he didn't let her in. "Why won't you let me help with this case you're on? I know you're not letting your team know or provide backup."

"I don't need help." His tone didn't invite discussion.

Her temper boiled up faster than her mom's pie filling in a cast-iron pot. Her taste in men sucked. Without question. She was also getting tired of him thinking she wanted a white picket fence and that she wanted it with him. What an ego. Why did she keep getting involved with impossible men? As if on cue, her phone buzzed.

She sighed. Yep. It must be after midnight. Without looking, she reached into her purse and declined the call.

Wolfe didn't look over. "Who was that?"

"I don't need your help," she retorted, taking an admittedly immature pleasure in tossing his words back at him.

He turned then, those incredible bourbon-colored eyes catching her off guard once again. "We bring different talents to our friendship. I take care of problems."

The guy truly underestimated what he had to offer, but it wasn't her job to fix him. Not by a long shot. "And I do . . . what?"

"You do research and . . . let me take care of problems." His grin was intriguing in that it failed to soften his face in the slightest. "I've noticed your phone ringing at weird hours, and I've also noticed that you tense up in a way that shows you do not want your phone to ring at weird hours. It's time you told me what's happening."

She rolled her eyes. "That's a two-way street, my friend."

He pulled into a '70s-style office building in the middle of nowhere, parking near the door and away from the one flickering streetlight. "We're not finished with this discussion."

She faltered. "I can stay in the truck."

He turned again, his dark eyebrows rising. "That's silly. Why wouldn't you come inside?"

She rubbed both hands down her jeans. "I'm a freelance reporter, and your team works for the government. Nobody wants me there." They were good people on his team, but most feds didn't want a journalist snooping around their offices.

For answer, Wolfe jumped out, shut his door, and appeared at her door in a second. "You're part of the team, Dana." He helped her out, strong and sure, and butterflies once again zinged through her lower body. Not noticing, he ushered her through the darkness to the old door, which opened easily to reveal a dingy hallway with a couple of closed wooden doors down the way. "You've helped on cases."

Yeah, but she wasn't part of the team. The smell of pizza caught her attention, and she perked up, heading for the rickety elevator that accessed the basement. "Well, I could eat." Her stomach growled. If she'd known there was food, she wouldn't have tried to stay in the vehicle outside.

"Me, too." Once inside, Wolfe leaned against the elevator wall as if he could hold the entire contraption together, and his sigh of relief as the doors opened below was heartfelt. "Someday we're gonna get stuck in this thing."

"Nah. It'll just drop and land hard." She stepped out into

the vestibule of the depressing basement space, her gaze immediately caught by the German shepherd bounding her way. "Roscoe." She dropped to hug his furry neck, discreetly wiping marinara sauce off his coat, since he'd obviously snuck a piece of pizza somehow. Then she stood and moved forward, smiling at the two men in the main room, illuminated by old yellow buzzing lights in the ceiling. "Hi."

Angus Force, the leader of the ragtag unit, and Malcolm West, their best undercover operative, sat at the four-desk pod in the center of the room with two pizza boxes in front of them. It looked like they'd both healed after the last assignment several weeks ago, in which everyone, including her, had been injured. Neither answered, their gazes squarely on the man behind her.

Force spoke first, his chiseled jaw going slack. "Are you wearing leather pants?"

Malcolm snorted, chuckled, and then shook his head. "Please tell us you were at a costume party."

Force's gaze then turned to Dana. "Or is there something kinky going on?" He nudged the pizza box toward her.

Heat flushed her face, but she moved toward the box. So Wolfe's team had no clue what he was doing. Figured. "The leather pants weren't my idea, and his phone gets caught in the back pocket, so don't ask me what he was thinking."

Malcolm reached down and brought up two beers, tossing one to Wolfe and sliding one across the desk to her.

Force shook his head. "Wolfe? Leather pants?"

Heat suffused Dana's back as Wolfe moved closer, reaching around her for a piece of pizza, the underside of his arm brushing hers. "The lady at the department store said they made my butt look good. So I bought them," he drawled, his breath heating the nape of her neck.

"She lied," Force drawled, his eyes narrowing. The guy was a former FBI profiler, one of the best before he'd gone off the rails, and he could probably see past Wolfe's good ol' boy facade. To his credit, he didn't push. Yet, anyway.

Dana pulled out a chair and sat, munching happily on a slice of pepperoni. Someone had sprung for the good stuff from Palozzi's.

Wolfe took the only other vacant seat. "Where's the rest of the team?"

Malcolm took a big swallow of his beer. "Raider and Brigid are up north with her dad for the next few days, and our shrink is—"

"Right here." Nari Zhang clip-clopped in kitten heels from case room two, her hands full of manila file folders. Her black hair swung around her shoulders, and she'd dressed for the evening meeting in dark jeans and a pale yellow silk shirt, which made her dusky skin glow. "I've been going through these and have added notes and profiles where necessary." She handed the stack to Force and leaned over to secure a piece of veggie pizza. "I think a lot of this is busywork."

Force nodded, his jaw hardening. "Yeah. We pissed off our Homeland Defense handlers last month, and apparently they're trying to get even." He sighed, tossing a couple of folders toward Wolfe. "We all have assignments, and for now, we're going to have to play nice."

Wolfe tapped his finger on the top folder. "I don't play nice."

"Agreed," Force said, pushing more folders toward Malcolm. Then he grinned. "The good news is that, with this caseload, I said you needed a research assistant, and we can actually pay Dana to work with you this time. She's been a valuable asset and hasn't sold us out, so we're happy to have her onboard." He winked at her. "Welcome to the team. Oh. You have to sign a nondisclosure agreement. You know, since you're a nosy journalist and all."

Dana sat back, amusement taking her. The desire to belong to the team, just for a little while, caught her off guard. Working alone did get lonely. "I accept. So long as I can write a story once we're finished, with your approval."

Malcolm chuckled. "I told you she'd say that."

Nari nodded, her black eyes twinkling. "Yeah, you did. Also, Dana, everyone who works in the unit has weekly sessions with me. I assume you're okay with that?"

Dana stiffened. "I don't need a shrink."

"Amen, sister," Force muttered beneath his breath.

Dana caught her words and hastened to add, "Not that there's anything wrong with counseling. It's just that I'm fine."

Nari smiled. "Then our hour a week will go fast and we can just chat. The requirement is nonnegotiable." Her eyes hardened as she glanced sideways at Force. "For almost everybody, anyway."

Dana took another bite of pizza, chewing thoughtfully before turning toward Wolfe, who'd just finished his third slice. "Do you attend counseling once a week?"

He tipped back his beer, drinking the entire bottle, his throat moving in a way that was blatantly sexy. Finishing, he set it down and accepted a second one from Malcolm. "Yeah. Since I'm fine and don't need shrinking, Nari and I talk about fashion, the Kardashians, and sometimes the royal family. I'm betting little Archie will be a fantastic polo player."

What a smart aleck.

Nari drew a chair over from its perch against the dented yellowed wall and sat. "I took that bet. I'm going to win."

Okay. Two smart alecks.

Wolfe twisted the cap off the bottle. "Oh, and Dana is moving in with me for a short time while we handle a story that might've put her in danger. It's her story and not a Deep Ops case, and I'll call you in if we need you. Right now, we don't. Figured you gossips would like to hear it from me first."

Nari sat forward. "What kind of story?"

How interesting that Wolfe didn't mention his own case. Dana cut him a look but didn't rat him out, as he no doubt trusted her to keep silent. She'd agree for now, but if he didn't let her in, she wouldn't cover for him indefinitely with the team. Well, probably. She did feel a sense of loyalty to the guy, considering he'd saved her life from a psycho ex-senator the previous month. "I'm not at liberty to discuss it quite yet," she said, a little primly.

Force narrowed in on Wolfe. "Does the story explain those ridiculous pants?"

Frankly, they were kind of sexy on the hard-bodied soldier, but Dana didn't argue.

Wolfe nodded. "Yeah, and get used to them. Dana and I might have to go undercover in a couple of sex clubs for her story. Wait until you see her outfit. Meow, as they say."

Her jaw dropped open. Plain and simple. She whirled on him, her breath catching. "Are you serious?"

"Yeah. Tonight was just the beginning." His eyes gleamed in a way that made her lungs want to stop breathing altogether. "You have another corset, right? If not, we can go shopping. I bet the lady at the leather pants store will give you a deal."

She swallowed. What had she just gotten herself into? "Forget the corset. Maybe I'll go full leather and get my own whip this time."

Wolfe chuckled, the sound low and dark, sliding across her skin. "Not a chance. In this game, we go with our strengths. I'm the dom, baby."

Everything in Dana flushed hot, head to toe, her body totally betraying her mind. She couldn't find a word to say, and suddenly her clothes became too tight. She tried to give him a glare, but his face was inscrutable, the look in his eyes one she couldn't identify but felt in inappropriate places.

Nari pressed her lips together in a terrible attempt to hide a smile. "Well, now. Maybe we will have something to talk about in our sessions, Dana."

Chapter Four

Wolfe led Dana into his kitchen through the garage, quickly resetting the alarm system he'd installed the previous week. "The code is 1156, and you have to punch it in within twenty seconds of walking into the kitchen, or the noise is frightening." He gestured her toward the living room. Should he tell her where all the weapons were hidden? "Do you know how to shoot a gun?"

She dropped her folders on the round kitchen table that had come with the quaint house. "I can shoot a shotgun, but I haven't practiced much with handguns."

So, no. She didn't need to know where all the guns were hidden.

"How about knife fighting or hand to hand?" The woman took chances all the time in her job; surely, she'd gotten some training to protect herself.

"Not really. I took a couple of self-defense classes in college, but I've never fought with a knife." Her smile kind of ticked him off.

He crossed his arms and leaned back against the fridge. "When you choose a dangerous type of work, you have a responsibility to look at all the things that could go wrong." In fact, everyone in every job should look at the dangers around them, for Pete's sake.

"I'm still standing," she said, surveying his house. "I like your place."

The home felt different with her in it. More welcoming and somehow brighter. She'd only been there five minutes, and already the rooms seemed warmer with the sweet smell of orange blossoms hanging in the air. He had to shut down that kind of thinking right now. "When we get the chance, I'll teach you some knife moves. Also, you should learn how to shoot a gun at some point."

"Sure. Sounds like fun." She yawned and covered her mouth with her hand.

Shaking her would be rude, so he tamped down his irritation. He pointed toward the master bedroom. "Why don't you get some sleep? The room is yours."

She paused and glanced toward the other bedroom and its closed door. "I'm not sleeping with you, Wolfe. The guest room will be fine."

He smiled. Man, she was cute. Her blond hair was all ruffled around her shoulders, and her soft green eyes were glazed over and sleepy. She looked as sexy in the worn flannel and jeans as she had in the tight corset. He cleared his throat. "I know. I turned the other bedroom into an office, so I'll bunk out on the sofa. I end up falling asleep there most nights, anyway."

A plaintive meow caught his attention as a miniature kitten strutted out of the master bedroom, his damaged ear twitching. He blinked one green and one blue eye, saw Dana, and beelined to rub against her ankle. They were old friends.

She picked up the white fur ball and rubbed him against her cheek. "Hey, Kat. I wondered where you were hiding."

Lucky cat. Wolfe had rescued him from a park near the office, cleaned him up, and let him pretty much do what he wanted. As he grew, his eyes had gone from all blue to just one blue and one green. It was pretty cool. His food bowl was full, as was his water, so he was content. The little bastard probably would sleep with Dana, so the kitten was one lucky feline.

"He's almost too big for my jacket pocket, but not quite." Wolfe's leather jacket had hand pockets that were wide enough for the kitten to burrow into, if he so wished. Wolfe tossed several case files onto the table next to Dana's research.

Her phone buzzed from her purse, and she sighed, reaching in to stop the noise.

His patience was close to an end, but he kept his voice mild. "Who is bothering you?"

"Nobody." She stretched her neck, the movement both stubborn and sexy—an intriguing combination.

Heat ticked down his back. "I could take your phone from you, you know."

Her eyebrows rose, and challenge filled her intelligent eyes. "But you won't."

She was correct. He wouldn't take her phone because he didn't have the right to do so. She wasn't his, and she never would be. "I want to help."

"If I need help, I'll ask." She turned for the bedroom, taking the kitten with her, that sweet butt swaying. "Good night, Wolfe."

"'Night." He watched her go, his hands feeling way too empty. When the door shut behind them, he quickly texted information to Brigid so she could track down the two guys in the black truck. As soon as Wolfe took them out, Dana could go back to her safe apartment and his house could go back to being empty and too quiet. Good plan.

Now what?

He looked around the comfortable home, which had come furnished. He'd purchased it from Malcolm when Mal had moved into the house next door with his girlfriend,

Pippa, who was an amazing cook. In fact, wasn't there some leftover apple pie in the fridge? Being Pippa's neighbor came with definite perks.

He moved toward the refrigerator just as an ominous ding came from a kitchen drawer. He went cold and then moved to it, taking out the untraceable burner phone. "Wolfe," he answered.

"Hi, buddy. Rumor has it you're looking for me."

Freezing claws raked Wolfe, and he leaned against the counter, forcing his heart rate to stay normal. "Who dis?" He drawled, nearly choking on the words.

Gary laughed, the sound slightly off. "Cute. For old time's sake, I'm gonna give you one chance to fuck off and stop the hunt."

"Never." He'd wondered if Gary Rockcliff would call the phone, the one from their time in the unit, so he'd kept it charged.

Gary sighed. "We both know I could find you before you find me. I'm better at this."

"I'm motivated, Rock," Wolfe said, listening for any background clues that would tell him where Gary had holed up. Had he been paid from the sale of his stolen drugs yet? If so, shouldn't he be on an island somewhere drinking rum?

"Move on, Wolfe." Gary's voice turned serious. Deadly. "You keep this up, and I'll tear through everything and everyone you love before you get a bead on me, and then it'll be too late. I trained you. You're not that good. Don't lose everything I haven't already taken."

Rage burned through Wolfe's throat. "Do you have any regrets? Those men trusted you. I trusted you." Sometimes fury could be colder than ice.

"No. They, and you, made the mistake of getting involved with something you shouldn't have. If they hadn't pursued me, they'd be alive. Take a lesson from that, or I'll take it all."

"Well now, there's the rub." Wolfe straightened. "I don't have anything else to lose. Don't love anybody or anything."

Gary's chuckle scraped Wolfe's nerves raw. "That doesn't sound like you."

Wolfe blew out air to keep calm. "Why don't you stop being a coward and just meet me? The two of us? Get it over with."

"You and me to the death? You want to beat me until I stop breathing?" Gary almost sounded amused.

"Yeah."

"What if we kill each other?"

Wolfe rolled his neck. "Okay." He'd figured that would be the result, anyway.

"I guess I haven't taught you everything, then." For a moment, there was a heavy silence on the line. "Death is easy. Living can be hell. The game is on." He disengaged the call.

Wolfe inhaled and lifted his head. "Finally," he muttered, sliding the phone back into the drawer. He glanced toward the closed bedroom door. If Gary didn't know where he was, Gary couldn't have been the one who'd killed Clarke Wellson/Albert Nelson, unless Gary was just messing with his head. Wolfe should just think about the dead guy as Albert from now on. Wolfe had been involved in other missions that might have made him enemies, so he wasn't positive yet that the guys in that black truck were involved in the Albert Nelson case. It was more likely that Dana's story had prompted the bullets, so he needed to take care of the threat to her and then get her safely out of his life.

Gary was coming. Finally.

Now what? It wasn't as if Wolfe could sleep, especially now. He moved to the fridge again and then caught sight of Mal out on his back porch through the window. Wolfe instantly pivoted and headed out his glass sliding door, punching in the alarm code as he went. The two homes shared a fenced backyard, and that suited him just fine. He strode across the grass and dropped into a cushioned chair next to Mal, who flipped on the fire in a new patio table.

"Nice," Wolfe murmured, kicking his feet out.

"Pippa bought it yesterday," Mal said, handing over a glass of whiskey and keeping one for himself. It was summer in Cottage Grove, but nighttime got chilly once in a while, which made for good sleeping if one slept.

Wolfe took the heavy crystal and inhaled deeply. Ah. The good stuff. "Is Pippa asleep?"

"Yep. It's three in the morning. Why aren't you sleeping?"

"Why aren't you?" Wolfe returned. Neither one of them slept much, so why dick around about it?

Mal silently contemplated the flames for several moments. "You seemed more jazzed than usual. What's up?" When Wolfe didn't answer, he grinned. "Ah. Pretty girl in your bed and you're here with me. No wonder."

Wolfe let him think what he wanted. No way was he telling Mal about Gary Rockcliff. "I need a favor."

"Okay."

It was that easy, and that was the reason Wolfe had to keep this new team safe. "Can you reach out to any of your old contacts on the force who might have a line on the heroin drug trade out of Afghanistan? My guess would be southern route." It was the only way Gary could've gotten the stolen drugs transported across the world.

Mal stared at the fire. "Off the books?"

"Yeah. For now." Wolfe lowered his chin. "Keep it under the radar. No ties."

Malcolm nodded. "I can do that. How much heroin and when?"

"A shit ton and it would've been transported between two and six months ago." They sat in silence for a while, but tension still emanated from Mal. "What's on your mind?" Wolfe asked.

Malcolm twirled his drink in his hand. "You think it's odd that Force wants to hire a journalist to assist you with busywork?"

Wolfe rubbed his chin, scratching his palms. When had he last shaved? "Not really. Dana has worked with us before and is great at research, and with Brigid gone for the week, we need the help." Brigid, their computer expert, could hack any system. "Why?"

"I don't know." Mal took another sip. "I think we're all chess pieces and Force is moving us around. The guy almost seems like a matchmaker sometimes, you know? Deep down, the grumpy drunk is a romantic."

Huh. "He didn't want you with Pippa in the beginning. Well, until we figured out she was a good guy and not a bad one." Wolfe took a deep drink, letting the expensive Scotch heat his stomach. He didn't have the words to express himself, but these times drinking with Mal, just the two of them late at night, or rather early in the morning, made him feel human again. Like he was part of something and not a damaged leftover. He tried to communicate as best he could. "Dana and I are just friends."

"I know, but you'll be working with your friend a lot, and now she's sleeping in your house." Mal grinned, settling his muscled bulk farther into the chair. "Temptation."

Not something Wolfe could give in to at this point. "She's a nice girl, and she takes too many chances. If anything happens to me, promise you'll look out for her."

"I promise. What's going to happen to you? Level with me."

Now that was temptation. Wolfe had already lost too

many friends in this fight, and he wasn't putting this one in danger. "When I need help, I'll ask." Yeah, he was using Dana's words. Hopefully they wouldn't piss off Malcolm like they had Wolfe when she'd said them.

Mal reached over and poured them each more whiskey. "Doing any job without backup is a mistake. Keep that in mind."

Letting his team get killed—again—would be a bigger mistake. "What else?" Wolfe asked. Mal only poured a second glass when something was on his mind.

"Angus Force. He's getting more and more obsessed with his search for Lassiter." Mal swirled his liquor in the tumbler, watching the liquid catch the firelight.

"Are you worried he won't find him?" Wolfe took another drink and grinned.

Mal jerked in a laugh. "No. I'm worried he will. So far, there hasn't been any real evidence that Lassiter is alive. If we get even one lead, I'm not sure what Force will do."

Wolfe sighed as the whiskey hit his belly. Force had shot and killed a serial killer named Lassiter about five years ago, but now he believed the man wasn't really dead. They had no concrete proof, though, and it was driving Force nuts. "I'll keep an eye on him," Wolfe said, finishing his drink and handing over the glass. For now, he had a woman to protect in his house. First things first—he needed to find out if those shooters were after her . . . or him.

Either way, they were going to bleed.

Chapter Five

She was back in the Senator's office, strapped to the chair, and he'd cut her arms and the tops of her thighs with a sharp knife. He laughed, enjoying the moment. She kicked out and screamed.

Dana sat up in Wolfe's bed, gasping for air, holding the covers to her chest, knocking the framed picture by the bed to the floor and scattering research notes, which she'd been trying to decipher before falling asleep.

Wolfe burst in the door, gun in hand, pointing it at the window. He looked around, dodged into the bathroom, scouted the closet, and then set the gun on the dresser. "Bad dream?"

She gulped and nodded.

The kitten hissed from the top of a tall bureau, where he'd obviously jumped.

She wiped a tear from her face. "Kat. I'm sorry. It's okay." She spoke soothingly, trying to reassure the frightened animal.

Wolfe stayed away from the bed.

She focused on him and then wished she hadn't. His broad chest was bare, showing hard-cut muscle along with a couple of bullet holes and what looked like knife wounds. A military tattoo of some type covered his left bicep, and that massive chest narrowed down several roped abs to loose sweats. His hair had grown out a little, curling over his ears, and thick scruff covered his rugged jaw. But those eyes. Light brown and brilliant and masculine, they missed nothing.

The kitten gave a soft meow.

Wolfe went to him, lifting him up and setting him on his right shoulder. "It's okay, dude. Everyone has bad dreams."

The huge man and the small kitten were such an obvious contradiction that she could only stare as Kat rubbed against Wolfe's chin and started purring.

"The kitten and the wolf," she murmured, forcing her hands to stop clutching the bedcovers.

"Sounds like a nursery rhyme." All fierce grace, Wolfe moved to sit on the bed, reaching down and replacing the photograph on the bed table. "What was the dream about?"

She took a deep breath. Wolfe had rescued her when an ex-senator had kidnapped and tried to torture her, so there wasn't much to hide from him. "I was back in the Senator's office," she whispered.

"Thought so." Wolfe covered her hand with his broad one. "That monster is dead and gone. He can't get to you ever again."

"I know." The senator had been killed in prison by another prisoner in a fight over a tomato, oddly enough. That made no difference to the nightmares. Wolfe's hand was warm and firm, and nothing in her wanted to move her fingers out from under his. Friends held hands, right? It was okay to take some comfort from him, since he was offering it. "I'm sorry I woke you up."

"I don't sleep much," he said, smelling like whiskey and male.

Her mouth watered.

Kat jumped from his shoulder and landed in Dana's

lap, stretching his back and clawing the comforter. He kept purring. At least the animal had forgiven her. She looked for somewhere to focus other than on the sexy male sitting too close but not close enough. Her gaze landed on the picture of him in his early teens, his arm slung around a girl with the same brown eyes, both standing in front of an elderly woman with a soft smile. "Is this your family?"

"Yeah." He exhaled. "My sister, Karen, and our grandmother, who raised us. Well, mostly."

"You have a sister?" Blinking, she turned to look at him again. Wolfe had a sister?

"I had one," he said softly. "She was killed at fifteen, when I was thirteen. Joined the wrong chat room and ended up chatting with the wrong guy. She thought he was seventeen and met him at a mall one night, without us knowing, of course. We found her body a week later. He's in jail, serving a life sentence."

God, how painful. "I'm sorry."

He nodded. "Me, too. Grams died four years later, after talking me into joining the military. Thought I could use structure and a purpose. She was usually right."

The night closed in, the silence cocooning them. Memories of her own childhood, of happiness untouched by tragedy, filled her heart. Why had Wolfe lost so much, and what was driving him so hard now? It wasn't fair. "Parents?"

He lifted one powerful shoulder. "Father took off a month after I was born, and saying our biological mother was unfit is an understatement. We were lucky Grams stepped in."

"I'm sorry, Wolfe. I really am." There weren't any words that could help.

"I know. You're a sweetheart, Dana. Soft and kind."

There was an obvious warning behind the murmured

words. She shook her head. "I'm pretty tough, and you know it. If life hits me, I'll get back up." He had to stop pushing her away.

His chin lifted, but he didn't answer.

She looked at his scarred chest. "You've seen some serious fights."

He released her hand and stood, withdrawing. "Yeah." He moved for the door, revealing a broad, strong back—along with more healed wounds. The bullet holes were obvious, as were the knife marks, but a couple of burns down his right side were a surprise.

What had he endured? She swallowed, feeling small and vulnerable in the big bed that smelled enticingly of him. "Why won't you trust me?" Why the heck had she asked that question?

He turned at the doorway, leaning against the jamb, one eyebrow rising. His lips twitched. "You're in my house, in my bed, with my kitten on your lap. I gave you the code to my alarm system. Why in the world do you not feel trusted?"

How could he not understand? "You don't tell me anything. You don't share. I don't know you." The words burst out before her mind could kick into gear. "You always say we're friends, and you are there any time I need you. You even saved me from a madman with a knife. But you don't let me know you."

Indecision crossed his face—an expression different from any she'd ever seen on him. Apparently making up his mind, he moved to his perch on the bed again, the heat from his body instantly washing over her. "There isn't anything else." His voice remained low and calm, deep with a certainty that seemed to lack regret. "You're searching for a depth that just isn't there. Doesn't exist."

She tilted her head, reading beneath the surface when

he'd just told her not to bother. "Do you really believe that?" Her voice softened along with her heart. Oh, this wasn't good. Not at all. Distance. She should draw back.

"Yes." His chin lowered, and his gaze ran down her tank top and back up, his eyes darkening to the color of topaz gems hiding their brilliance. "My whole life has been about survival. First as a kid in a rough neighborhood and then in the military, where I thought I'd found family." His nostrils flared as he exhaled slowly. "When my whole team died, all that was left for me was to seek justice. Maybe revenge. I don't really care which."

She barely moved, not wanting to spook him. He'd never told her this much before. "Revenge? That's why you were looking for Clarke Wellson? I mean, Albert Nelson?"

He nodded. "It took me nearly six months to tie Nelson to my case. All I had was his picture and his affiliation with Captive; I didn't even have his correct name. Never even got a chance to question the guy."

Nelson had been a pretty shady guy, so he'd probably had plenty of enemies. Dana remained still. "How did your team die?"

His head lifted, and his gaze shuttered. "That's the question, isn't it?"

"Wolfe, I—"

He startled her into silence by cupping her jaw, his touch warm and firm. Then he leaned in, all intent.

Her breath caught, and excitement winged through her abdomen.

He came an inch closer. "I'm not gonna let anybody hurt you, and that's all I have to give."

Amusement infiltrated the desire she couldn't seem to banish. "You'll jump on a grenade for me?"

His lips tipped, and he released her. "Yeah. Gladly. I'll help you get your story and keep you safe in the process.

But then we're done. The job I have to do . . . I can't have any distractions."

Distractions? Why did that tickle her ego? Wolfe always seemed so focused, that was probably a compliment. It hit her then. When she was in trouble, when she was in need, she called Wolfe. He came. But he was telling her that he had other things to do, and she was taking advantage of a truly good guy. It wasn't right. "I'm going back to my apartment tomorrow," she said quietly.

One of his dark eyebrows rose. "It's not safe."

Maybe it was, maybe it wasn't. But she had to get out of this situation before she did something really stupid and kissed the guy. "I'm not yours to worry about." Yeah, they were friends, but it was pretty much a one-way situation with him giving and her taking. That needed to end now. "I hate ultimatums," she murmured, not meaning to give him one.

He blinked. "Me, too. I've had enough of those for tonight."

She tilted her head. "What do you mean?"

He shook his. "Nothing."

Ah. Once again shutting her out. She took a deep breath. "We're either friends who share our problems or we're not. Let me help you like you've helped me."

A muscle ticked in his jaw. "Dana, stop whatever you're thinking right now. You can't help me, and you sure as hell can't save me. Trying is only going to get you hurt."

His mouth was so close to hers, she could almost taste him. Whiskey and male and Wolfe. She blinked once and then again. Wait a minute. Fix him? He was warning her off? Again? "I'm a big girl and I can take care of myself." She edged away and let herself feel the sorrow of losing something she'd never had. "Believe me. When a man tells me to stay away, I'm not dumb enough to want to change him." The ego on the guy. He was just too much.

"Good." Quick and graceful, he stood and stalked to the doorway. "Oh. I have a call in to Captive to see if the annual party next Tuesday is still on or not. If it's on, I'm going. You can come if you want, but you'll have to act as a sub so I can keep you safe. Have a nice night, Dana." He shut the door behind himself.

Her jaw dropped open, and she snuggled the kitten closer. "Can you believe that?" she muttered, her body uncomfortably tingly.

Kat snorted and bit her ear.

Males. Seriously. Males.

Chapter Six

The woman looked a mite grumpy in the morning as she walked out with the binder she'd had on the bed the night before. Wolfe fought to keep his face stoic and quickly poured Dana a cup of coffee, shaking the whipped cream bottle he'd bought earlier and spraying generously before nudging a fresh pan of cinnamon rolls across the table. "Pippa brought these over." He'd already eaten three before running quickly to the store.

Dana took the coffee, inhaled deeply, and then drank. "Thanks." She'd donned another pair of faded jeans with a green striped button-down shirt that somehow hugged her curves. Her hair was up in a ponytail, and with no makeup, she looked about sixteen. He really liked the freckles across her nose. Did she have them other places?

Damn it. He had to stop thinking of her as anything but a friend. When he'd almost kissed her the night before, he'd realized he had to get a grip. "What are your plans for this Sunday morning?"

She took a seat and eyed the cinnamon rolls. "Well, I'll probably eat one of those, regret it, do some research, compare notes with you, and head home."

So she was still on that track. "You need to stay here."

"No, I don't. I'd also like to work out, but I can do that later tonight."

Yeah, she had nice muscle tone but was still curvy. Not that he'd noticed. "I turned the garage into a gym. Feel free."

Her eyebrows rose. "Thanks. Also, we need to compare notes and figure out why we have two different names for the same dead guy." She looked up, her green eyes clear. "Care to explain why you think you'll be invited to another Captive party after you scattered last night the second the body dropped to the floor?"

He lifted a shoulder. "That's easy. Half of the people there made a run for it once the cops were on the way. It's a BDSM club, and many of the members want that part of their life to remain private. There were some influential people there."

Her frown wrinkled her forehead. "They think you're influential?"

He grinned. "They think I'm a mercenary who founded my own business and became a millionaire. Some of it's accurate." Should he have another roll? If so, he'd need to jog a couple extra miles tonight. "But not the millionaire part."

"Huh." She sipped her coffee, her lips a pretty pink against the cup. "I'm surprised they're having another party so soon."

He nodded. "Yeah, I think they're looking for leads on who murdered Albert Nelson. I checked with the local cops, through Angus Force, and there are no leads. The cops are frustrated at the lack of cooperation on the part of witnesses."

She nodded. "Who do you think killed Albert Nelson?"

Wolfe had his suspicions but wasn't ready to speculate. "That's what we need to find out. Let's eat and then we can share our case files and strategize for the next party." He knew her well enough to assume that she was all in, even if it meant wearing a skimpy outfit.

She bit her lip. "If we're really going undercover at a sex club party, we'll need to get some rules in place."

Man, she was cute when blushing and being bossy. Obviously she'd been giving it some thought since he'd dropped the challenge on her the previous night. He sat back, enjoying his second cup of java, although he'd only bought whipped cream and forgotten the sprinkles earlier. He'd have to go to the store again. He was out of dish soap, too. "All right. What rules?"

She picked at a piece of roll. "If there is a party next Tuesday, we both go as guests. No cuffs and no touching."

"No." He calmly took another sip. Yeah. Definitely needed sprinkles.

She coughed and then sputtered. "Excuse me?"

"The next party is members only, and they're courting me for membership, so I'll barely get in. The only way you get to go is as my sub." More importantly, that meant she'd stay near him, where he could keep an eye on her.

"How about you find me a different date?" She gave in and took a roll.

The idea of her playing with another man awoke something dark in him. Something deep that he had to quell. "Another man who thinks you really want to be a sub for the night?" His tone came out a little grittier than he'd intended. "You sure you want to go that far undercover?"

She was having a hard time meeting his gaze. "Good point. I'm not exactly the submissive type."

"It's up to your dom to get that from you." Yeah, he was having a good time messing with her.

She frowned. "Are you—I mean, I have no problem with alternative lifestyles, but are you really a dom?"

Was she scared or interested? Either way, he wasn't going to start lying to her now. "No. I'm undercover, looking for a source, and you of all people know I don't like clubs or group activities." He took another cinnamon roll. Why not run extra miles? "I also don't like labels. Or rules." He chewed thoughtfully. "Or contracts that govern intimate relationships."

She finished her breakfast. "I think the contracts are necessary when you're talking trust and pain."

"Oh. I also don't like pain. Giving or receiving it." He pushed the pan closer to her. "However, if I eat another one of these, punch me in the nose."

She chuckled.

He cleared his throat. "You don't have to come to the party. I can do enough investigating for both of us." Although, as a sub, she'd be allowed in different areas than he, and she could talk to other subs.

"Oh, I'm going." Her chin lifted. "I just wish I could wear flannel." Her smile jolted electricity through him.

He had to stop looking at her lips. "I'd pay to see you in a flannel corset," he murmured, meaning every word. He had no doubt she'd conducted extensive research before going to the first party, but she seemed uncertain. "Do you understand the dom/sub dynamic, these types of parties, and Captive in general?"

"Yeah, I understand how clubs like Captive work and the appeal to some folks. I'd rather take a date fishing or rafting down the river, you know?" She sipped at the coffee.

He couldn't agree more. Peace and quiet with few people around was his idea of a good day. It was too bad he was damaged and probably going to get killed taking out his enemy. Why couldn't he have met Dana before the explosion that had sent his life to hell? He shook his head. Even as a kid he'd known not to play the *what if* game. Reality was reality, and he couldn't change it. "Let's talk about your story. Why were you looking for the dead guy?"

Her face got that stubborn look that perversely turned him on. "Oh, no. You first. Why were you at the party in the first place, and how did you know the dead guy?"

He considered what he could tell her. "On my last mission, somewhere I can't tell you about, my unit was hunting for a group smuggling drugs. It turned out somebody close to us was a traitor. Five out of seven of us were killed, and I'm going to find the Judas and take him down. Albert Nelson was my connection to somebody who might know where Rock is."

"Rock." Dana pounced on the name like a hound on a quail scent.

"Yeah. Nickname. We all had them, and it won't help you to find him. The military has been looking for six months, and even the top intel folks can't find the guy." Wolfe grasped her wrist, needing to get through to her. No way would he give her Gary's full name. "Leave him alone. No research, no calling in favors, no nothing. You will not do anything to make him aware you even exist. Promise me."

She surprised him by asking, "What was your nickname?"

He shrugged. "Wolfe. It's easy and it's my name. People have always called me that."

"Tell me more about Rock." She tapped her fingers on the table.

"He's a trained killer, one of the best, and I'm fairly certain he's a sociopath who actually enjoys the killing more than the endgame." Wolfe had spent too many restless nights trying to figure Rock out, trying to understand how he'd blinded everyone to his true nature.

She tilted her head, those intelligent green eyes studying his face. "Is Rock better than you?"

"We're about to find out that answer to that question." Lacking empathy or any sense of loyalty just made the bastard all the more dangerous. "Your turn."

She visibly tried to banish emotion as she told her own story. "I was friends with Candice Folks, who worked for the *Times*."

Wolfe frowned. "The journalist who disappeared?"

"Yeah, and I believe she was murdered. There was a lot of blood in her apartment, and there's no way Candy would just disappear and not stay in touch with her elderly mother. She was a business reporter, usually covering the stock market, upstart businesses, and so on." Dana licked whipped cream off her lip.

Wolfe's groin tightened.

Dana went on, having no clue she was killing him. "Candy was working on a series featuring up-and-coming corporations owned by women, and according to the few notes I've been able to decipher, Albert Nelson was one of her sources."

Wolfe took another drink. "You think he had dirt on one of the businesses?"

"I have no idea. Candy doesn't usually follow dangerous stories, so this is confusing." Dana rubbed her hands down her jeans. "I met with Albert once, and he was sketchy. I knew he had more information." Her voice hardened. "I conducted a deep dive, discovered his affiliation with Captive, and was going to expose him unless he told me everything he knew."

None of that sounded good. "Any chance your friend is still alive?"

Dana pressed her lips together. "I've been interviewed by the police detectives a couple of times, trying to give them a lead or two for Candy, but I just didn't know anything. They shared some of the facts of the case the way they would for any friend of a missing person. The blood in her apartment was identified as belonging to her, and there was enough that the doctors said no way could somebody survive losing that much."

"I'm sorry," Wolfe said. Not just for the deceased journalist, but for the fact that Dana wouldn't stop until she found out who had taken her friend, regardless of the danger.

"Me too," Dana murmured. She patted the now closed binder on the table. "I also stopped by the newspaper where Candy worked; her assistant had already made me a copy of her notebook before handing the original over to the police. We're old friends, too." She flipped open copied pages that had been placed in a binder. "It's all in code, and I haven't been able to figure out how to break it, yet. Her assistant has no clue, either. Candy was secretive that way."

Maybe Brigid could help when she returned. Wolfe made a mental note to give her a call. "I don't suppose you'd agree to just go home to your parents' house in Tennessee for a couple of weeks and let me handle this?" he asked.

Her snort was kind of cute and not a surprise.

His phone buzzed, and he looked down to read a text from Brigid. Finally. "I have a line on the guys who shot at us from the black truck."

Chapter Seven

The house was on the outskirts of D.C., in an area of town that Wolfe had never been. Lawns were small and burned, porches sagged, and paint peeled. A drug deal went down at the far corner, and feral cats fought near an overturned garbage can across the pothole-riddled concrete.

Clouds hung low and dark as if the sun didn't dare to enter the neighborhood.

He drove by the address Brigid had given him, peering for a good alleyway to hide his truck. "I'm not comfortable leaving my truck around here." The tires and wheels would be gone in seconds.

Malcolm nodded from the passenger seat, sliding a clip into his gun. "We could just park at the street and make a run for the door in a shock and awe, but that'd give them time to grab weapons." He angled his head and studied the dismal street. "Plus, how good is your intel? I'd rather not burst in on an elderly couple having a late breakfast."

"No kidding," Wolfe returned, still not sure about having Mal along for backup. Not that he'd invited Malcolm. The guy had seen Wolfe leaving and had jumped in the truck, somehow knowing Wolfe was going hunting. "The intel is from Brigid."

"Then it's good," Mal said. "Though I'd still like to peek into the garage to see if it holds the truck you saw the other night."

Yeah, double-checking was never a bad thing when guns were involved. He drove a mile out of the neighborhood and parked in the front of a gas station/mini mart, running inside to pay the kid behind the counter to watch his truck. Then he jogged back out as a slight rain began to fall.

Mal stood near the truck. "How much did you give him?"

"Fifty now and a hundred if my truck is in one piece when I get back." Wolfe zipped up his sweatshirt to hide his gun and then pulled the hood over his head. "Ready?"

"Sure." Mal looked dangerous in his dark hoodie with unnecessary sunglasses hiding his eyes, but he'd fit right in as they jogged back to the house.

Wolfe took off at a fast pace. "You didn't have to come— I can handle this."

"Right. These solo missions you've been doing are stupid." Mal kept pace, his tone more thoughtful than sharp.

"Yeah, I know." Wolfe had been trained well, and backup was always a necessary precaution. It felt good to have Mal along.

Mal hunched his shoulders and slid his hands into his pockets. "The other day you mentioned a job dealing with sex clubs."

"No, the job is tracking down a guy who went to sex clubs. Now that he's dead, I have to figure out who he was, who killed him, and why." The club was just coincidental, and he certainly didn't want to see Mal in leather pants, backing him up at a club party.

Malcolm's gait slowed. "Did you really go to a sex club?"

Wolfe grinned. "Yeah. A BDSM one."

"Huh." They moved silently for a while as the rain increased in force.

"You ever been to one?" Wolfe asked, keeping the conversation going.

"Nope. I make no judgments, but I'm more of a private type of guy when it comes to romance." Mal's boots splashed water up from holes in the sidewalk.

Wolfe stepped over a pile of fast food wrappers. "Ditto."

"Was Dana really there?" Mal chuckled.

"Yeah, and she was barely dressed. I stopped breathing for almost two seconds." Which was a long time for Wolfe to forget to watch his six.

"So the two of you—"

"No." Wolfe increased his pace. "Just friends." Why was it when a guy found love, he assumed everyone else would, too? Some guys, like Mal, found that happiness. Guys like Wolfe did not.

Mal stiffened as the sound of yelling came from one of the homes. A woman screaming at a lazy, no-good bum. "Sometimes romance sneaks up on you."

"Nothing sneaks up on me." Wolfe slowed his pace near the correct house, keeping out of sight of the narrow front window that was caked with mud and bird poop. He moved to the side of the garage, barely squeezing in between the worn siding and a rough chain-link fence, and then cautiously approaching an oval-shaped window. Weeds made his boots and jeans wet. After wiping grime off the glass, a lot of it, he peered inside. Satisfaction ran through him faster than a good latte. "It's the truck," he whispered.

Mal slid his sunglasses up on his thick hair, his intelligent eyes piercing the haze. "You want front or back?"

"Front." Wolfe slid out of the way to the front of the garage. "On ten?"

"Ten." Mal sucked in air and inched by the fence to the backyard, his chest barely making it through the narrow path.

The neighborhood was quiet, and if anybody was watching through a window, they probably wouldn't call the cops. Wolfe started counting in his head, keeping his back to the garage door and pulling his gun free of his jeans. He arrived at eight, ducked his head, and ran full bore at the front door, breaking it wide open with his right shoulder.

A half-dressed man jumped up from a torn sofa and Wolfe shoved him back down with one hand, his gun sweeping the room.

From the kitchen, Mal prodded another man in front of him toward the sofa. "Sit." He then turned back and made quick work of the rest of the small house. "Clear," he called out.

Wolfe smiled at the two staring defiantly up at him. The first guy was around thirty with dirty blond hair, bloodshot eyes, and open sores along his neck. The second was maybe around twenty-five years old, and was a tall guy with darker skin and a bruise on his cheekbone who had the shakes. Definitely needed a fix. "I'm going to ask this once. Why did you shoot at me?" Wolfe kept his gun pointed low, not wanting to freak them out too badly. Yet.

The blond sniffed and then shrugged. "No clue who you are."

The other guy shook harder, his dreadlocks moving over his bony shoulders.

Mal returned to the room. "Drugs and guns in the back room. I put everything in this duffel." He tossed a dirty duffel on the floor and decided to point his gun at the guys.

The shaky guy sat up, his gaze planted on the duffel. "You can't take that."

Wolfe sighed. "We can do pretty much anything we want." These guys were pathetic. "Just tell me who hired you and who you meant to follow or shoot, and we'll leave you and your drugs alone." He was taking their guns, though. Anybody who shot at him deserved to lose their weapons. That seemed fair.

The blond guy looked over at his buddy.

Mal stepped forward, his expression pissed. "Listen. I have no patience for this shit. Talk now, or I'm going to start hitting people."

Okay. Wolfe didn't usually play good cop, but what the hell. "You guys want out of this? Believe me—talk and we'll leave."

Mal growled. "Let's just kill them. They don't know anything, and I'm hungry."

"I saw an IHOP a couple of blocks over," Wolfe offered. "I guess we could just shoot them and go, but that'd probably make a bunch of noise."

Mal pursed his lips. "We could go for blunt-force trauma. There's probably a baseball bat around here somewhere."

"Knives would be better," Wolfe said thoughtfully. "Did you see any when you came in through the kitchen?"

Mal winced. "That's so messy, and this is a new sweat-shirt. Strangulation?"

The blond drooled and sucked in air. "Wait a minute. Just wait a minute."

"One chance," Wolfe said, letting the predator in him show.

"There isn't much to tell." The shaky guy exhaled, his thin body shuddering with the movement. "Some guy hired us to follow the pretty blond chick. Gave us her address. We've been watching her for about a week. Got the text to take her out after the party in the mansion."

Heat rolled through Wolfe. It had been Dana in danger? He'd known it was a possibility, but he'd truly thought the guys were after him. The tweakers pressed back on the sofa as if somehow sensing his mood had changed.

"You've been watching her for a week?" Wolfe asked.

The shaky guy nodded, the movement a painful-looking jerk. "Yeah, kind of. We've staked out her apartment building and followed her a few times, but we've lost her a lot."

Probably when they stopped to shoot up drugs.

"But you caught her scent when she went to the party last night?" Malcolm prodded him.

The blond guy's face brightened. "Yeah. We followed her cab to the car rental place and then to the mansion, and man, that outfit she was wearing was something else. Thought about—" He caught himself and made a strangled noise, heeding too late his sense of self-preservation.

"Thought about what?" Wolfe asked, his tone dropping to deadly and his hands starting to twitch with the need to punch through the asshole's face to the sofa.

The blond gulped and shook his head, his breath turning shallow. If he passed out, he'd stop talking, darn it.

"Somebody texted you to kill her?" Wolfe asked, enunciating each word and trying to keep his calm in place.

The blond winced. "Yeah."

"When did you get the text?" Wolfe snapped.

"Right before she ran out of that mansion with you. I'm sorry," the blond whined.

"Why her?" Mal asked, his gun remaining trained on the duo.

The shaky guy bit his lip and a little blood welled. "Nobody said."

This was getting worse. Whoever wanted Dana dead might have nothing to do with the death of her friend, considering some of the stories she'd pursued through the years. Wolfe tamped down on his anger and tried to concentrate.

"Who hired you?" Mal snarled.

The shaky guy shrugged, his dreadlocks sliding over his shoulders. "Dunno. It's common knowledge we're available for odd jobs. Cash, instructions, and a phone came in an envelope. Right to the door. More money was supposed to come after, but it never did."

What morons.

"There's nothing more here," Mal said quietly. "Where's the phone?"

The blond pulled a phone off the filthy carpet. "It's a burner, and I'm sure he used one, too."

Wolfe grabbed up the duffel. "I'm taking it all—even the drugs." He'd pour them down the toilet. Wait. Wasn't that causing animals drinking from rivers to get high? Hmm. He'd have to figure out a way to dispose of the drugs later. When the blond started crying, he felt marginally better. Not much. Who was after Dana?

He led the way outside, his mind on the pretty journalist and not his surroundings. When the first bullet pierced his flesh, he was more surprised than hurt.

The second bullet whizzed by his ear.

He dove into some dead bushes as a volley of shots splattered against the house and splintered the front window into deadly projectiles. Quiet descended, and then the sound of screeching tires echoed from a street over. He peered over the bushes to the other side of the door, clamping a hand on his bleeding arm. "Malcolm?"

His friend didn't answer.

Chapter Eight

Dana finished typing the intro to her story, trying to ignore the remaining cinnamon roll on the table. Pippa could sure bake. Dana had never experienced much success in the kitchen, but she'd never really tried, either. There was always another story to chase, and this one mattered.

She paused. It was time to diagram some of the information. Standing, she stretched her neck. Wolfe had said he'd turned the guest room into an office, and hopefully he had a notepad in there she could borrow. She hadn't realized hers was full. Just as she turned, her phone buzzed. She read the screen and then lifted it to answer. "Hi, Mom. What's up?"

"Hi, honey. Your dad wanted me to call. He's out fishing early on the river." Her mom's voice was distracted.

Of course he was. Dana turned away from the tempting treat. "I hope it's a good catch." Her dad was a river and fishing guide.

"Me, too." Dishes clinked across the line. "Anyway, somebody has been calling here for you. A man saying he has information for a story, and your dad told him to go fall off a cliff. But he keeps calling, so we thought you should have the number. Now, don't call him. Or if you do, use a pay phone."

Dana tried not to chuckle, although her instincts had started humming. "I'm not sure there are any pay phones around anymore, but I'll be careful."

"Is this for a story?"

Hopefully, but probably not. "Sure. Isn't it always?" Dana forced humor into her voice, even though her stomach began to ache.

Her mom rattled off the number.

Ah, crap. It was Mike's phone number. The guy just wouldn't give up, and now he was harassing her parents? She needed to take care of him and soon. "Thanks, Mom. I'm sorry my sources are bugging you. I'll handle it."

"I'm sure—just be careful in case this has to do with one of those dangerous stories you like to investigate. By the way, Lissa and the musician broke up, thank goodness. Katie won't fill me in on her dating life, and I believe Charlotte is dating someone, but she's being very mum about it. Quite annoying, if you ask me. How about you? Have you had any interesting dates lately?"

Did running out of a sex party with a hot ex-soldier count? "No. I've been working a lot." What would her mom think about Wolfe? Not that it mattered, because he was just a friend. Still. It'd be funny to see her petite mother order Wolfe around. She needed to change the subject. "How's your knee?" Her mom had fallen down a riverbank and pulled ligaments months ago.

"It's good. I finish with physical therapy next week, and I should be able to raft again in a few weeks." Her mom chuckled. "Before I forget, do I need to alter your dress for the wedding next Saturday?"

Dana winced. There wasn't much that could be done with that dress. "How about you burn it?"

"You sound just like your sisters, and you need to knock it off. You'll look beautiful, and you know none of us thought your cousin would ever get married. She's, well, a lot."

It was just like her mother to find a silver lining. Sally wasn't a lot. Sally was the drama queen from the third realm of an entitled universe. "Uh-huh." Dana pushed the cinnamon roll across the table. "The dress should still fit me. Haven't changed much. Um, I am in the middle of—"

"A story? You're always in the middle of a story. This is your cousin's wedding, and you're being honored as one of the bridesmaids." The perfect amount of motherly guilt infused her mom's chipper tone.

Really? Dana and her sisters were Sally's bridesmaids because the whiny wench didn't have any friends. It was revenge, darn it. She and Sally had never gotten along, but there was no excuse for that puke-green, puffy-sleeved dress. Plus, it was tight in the wrong places and wide in the others, which made her look like a waddling rotten kiwi. "I'll be there, Mom. When is the rest of the gang getting in?" She missed her three sisters, and Katie definitely owed her a call. It had been a week, and they never went that long without talking, but things had been crazy.

"The twins arrive Thursday, and Katie gets in about the same time you do on Saturday morning, which really is cutting it way too close. Dad will pick you up at the airport. Also, I think I might've mentioned the Mulvaney boys are in town and will be attending the wedding." Before Dana could protest, her mother continued, "Your dad is coming up from the bank with a lot of fish. I have to go, honey."

"Bye, Mom." Dana shook her head as she disengaged the call. "The Mulvaney boys. Right." She quickly sent a group text to her three sisters that their mom was planning on matchmaking at the upcoming wedding and to be ready.

Various emojis and gifs quickly blew up her phone, ranging from eye-rolling to a giraffe vigorously shaking its head.

She smiled and turned again for the guest room. What had she been doing? Oh yeah. She needed paper to start diagramming the connections in her research because it wasn't coming together for her. She rolled her shoulders and sucked in her stomach. The dress would still fit, right? Of course. Shaking her head, she strode around the sofa just as Kat leaped from a hiding spot behind the television. He landed on her shoulder and bounded off, rolling down the sofa and plopping on the far pillow with a soft meow.

She looked down. "You're as crazy as Wolfe is."

The kitten blinked pretty eyes, sneezed, and then started licking his paw, effectively dismissing her.

All righty, then. "As soon as he gets back, I'm going home," she told the kitten, who still didn't look up. She grinned and then pushed the door open. Fumbling for the light, she stepped inside, the carpet soft on her bare feet. Then she stopped cold, looking around. "Wow," she breathed.

Guns and knives—all types of them—were mounted on the wall to the left, floor to ceiling. The next wall held a matching set of antique armoires that stood tall on either side of a window, underneath which was a short shelving system holding a laptop, printer, and various supplies.

It was the final wall that held her attention. She blinked several times at a wide, green glass magnetic board that took up the entire wall. Pictures, diagrams, notecards, and notes covered the surface with lines drawn between them. She'd never seen an evidence board so precise—and full.

Albert Nelson's picture was taped over to the right with one thick line drawn through it.

She swallowed. Who were the other people? A group of seven young soldiers in the desert, smiling at the camera, caught her eye. Wolfe was in the middle, and he looked . . . lighter. Happier. Then her breath caught as she moved to the next picture, which showed five coffins in an airplane hangar, all covered with the United States flag. Another picture, this one blown up, showed one of the guys from the team picture. Various lines connected his picture to other pictures, notecards, and documents. "You must be Rock," she murmured. Just as she stepped closer for a better look, the front door banged open.

"Dana?" Wolfe bellowed.

She jumped and ran back through the living room, where Wolfe was helping a bleeding Malcolm West to sit at the kitchen table. Blood flowed down Mal's face from a cut along his temple. Her stomach lurched. "What happened?" Her legs trembled, and she looked up at Wolfe's hard face, not seeing the blood dripping down his arm for a minute. It caught her eye as red splotches fell onto the tile. "You're injured, too." Without thought, she reached for his wrist.

He pulled away and strode to a drawer by the door to the garage, returning with a first aid kit and clean towels. Even though he moved toward her, he felt miles away, and his gaze remained on Malcolm.

Dana hesitated, oddly hurt.

Wolfe handed an orange striped kitchen towel to his friend. "I'm sorry, West."

Mal rolled his eyes and pressed the material against his head. The cotton quickly turned a deep red. "Unlike you, I wasn't even shot. Glass from the window cut me."

"You were shot?" Dana breathed. "Those guys in the truck shot at you again?"

"No," Wolfe muttered. "Somebody else—who was probably there to take care of those morons."

Mal grimaced. "I'm not sure we provided a public service by warning them to get the hell out of town."

This was getting worse by the minute. Were those guys after her or Wolfe? Had they been attacked because of Albert Nelson and Candy's story? Or because of Wolfe's super-secret case? Questions zinged around in her head, but she had to make sure both men were okay before getting down to business. "Did you see who shot at you this time?"

Wolfe shook his head. "No. They just scattered bullets and then got out of there. We had to run to the truck, which was a few blocks away."

They'd run bleeding like this? Dana ignored the way the room seemed to be swirling around her. "Are you two injured anywhere else?"

"No," Malcolm said.

"You were knocked out, Mal." Wolfe's eyes had gone a deep hue, and his movements were stiff. Though he stood near them, somehow he seemed far away. "It's my fault."

"No, it isn't." Mal wiped his forehead off, leaving a smear of blood across his eyebrow. "How bad is it?"

Dana turned and bile rose up her throat. The deep cut ran from his temple to above his eye, and it was still bleeding. Honestly, it was pretty ugly. She couldn't see bone, but there was no way a bandage would keep that skin together. "You need stitches."

Wolfe sighed. "Let's get you to the doctor."

"No. You stitch it up." Mal pressed the bloody towel to his head again. "After you take off your shirt so we can see how bad you've been shot. We can go to the doctor for you, if you want."

"I'm fine," Wolfe all but snarled.

That was it. Just plain and simple it. The room smelled like blood and dirt, and she couldn't take any more. Adrenaline raced through her veins, and her heart rate would not slow down. One or both of them could've been killed, and they were acting like it wasn't the big deal that it really was. "Take off your damn shirt, Wolfe," she ordered, pressing her hands to her hips. "You have two seconds. Do it, or I'll do it for you."

He turned then, stepping into her space, his body vibrating and his eyes ablaze. "Try it."

Chapter Nine

Wolfe kept his stance wide as Dana's pupils widened and then contracted. Her curvy body settled in for a fight.

"Wolfe?" Mal said mildly, slumped in the chair, blood matting his left eyebrow. "You're being an asshole."

"I'm aware of that fact," Wolfe returned, unable to move away from Dana. An invisible force kept him in place, his muscles tight, his chest heated. He didn't like himself at the moment, and that regret could later join his constant guilt when he regained control. The fact that he'd gotten Mal shot was yet more proof that everyone around him was in danger, and that definitely included the angry journalist trying to stare him down.

Her nostrils widened and she reached for the bottom of his T-shirt, her gaze daring.

He began to step back, and she tightened her hold, the soft pads of her fingers brushing his bare abs. A jolt shot through him, and he may have growled.

She sucked in air and her delicate jaw tightened. She yanked him toward her with the cotton and pulled it up, giving him no choice but to duck his head so she didn't choke him. Oh, the stubborn woman was asking for it. What, he had no clue—but everything in him wanted to give it to her.

The shirt came over his head, and then she gentled her movements, making a sound of distress as his wound was revealed.

The soft noise pummeled straight to his heart and he shut his eyes against an unwanted wave of warmth. As soon as he made sure she was safe, he had to distance himself. Completely, even though she was a good friend. Temptation was a killer.

Then she held a towel to his arm. Pain centered him, and he took a deep breath, opening his eyes to survey the wound. "The bullet cut along my bicep but didn't go in."

"You need stitches." She gulped and then looked up. Her eyes were the color of a spring meadow against her suddenly pale skin. She wavered.

He grasped her arm just as Mal kicked out the adjacent chair, and then he settled her down. "You're okay." Sometimes he forgot that not everyone was accustomed to blood and bruises. "Honest. I'm fine." After making sure she was steady in the chair, he glanced down at his arm, which ached but wasn't that bad. "A couple of stitches should do it." He didn't even need Mal's help with that. "First, are you sure you don't want to go to the doc, West?"

Mal nodded. "Just stitch me up, slap a bandage on me, and I'll tell Pippa it's no big deal."

Oh. He was worried about frightening Pippa. Of course. "Stitches are stitches, so what's the problem?" Why not have a doctor do it?

Mal swallowed and the blood on his throat cracked. "There's a difference between having to go to the hospital and just having you bandage it. She won't worry this way."

Man, Wolfe really didn't understand women. "You're messing with your pretty looks," he warned.

"What's one more scar on my face?" Mal sighed, his

torso too wide for the quaint kitchen chair that had come with the house.

Wasn't that the truth? Wolfe rolled his shoulders and tried to focus, when all he wanted to do was go for a long, hard run. He hadn't given Pippa a thought when he'd reluctantly agreed to let Malcolm provide backup, and look what had happened. Steadying his hands, he reached for the stitching kit he'd put together in the first aid box, pausing to check on Dana's color. Still pale. "You need to look the other way."

She blinked, tried to argue, and then just turned to stare out the window.

Kat meowed and rubbed against Wolfe's leg before jumping into Dana's lap. Her smooth hands instantly started to pet him, and his purr filled the room.

As the kitten and the woman provided each other comfort, Wolfe painstakingly stitched up Mal's skin on his forehead, trying to keep the ends as even as possible. Maybe the scar would be very small or even fade completely. His friend shut his eyes and breathed normally, his body relaxed the entire time. Finally, Wolfe spread antibacterial gel across the stitches and gingerly planted a bandage in place. "I did my best." He stood back and made sure the bandage was even.

Mal stood, almost eye to eye with him. "I'm sure it's perfect. Now let me stitch you—" He paused, swiveling back toward the sliding glass door.

A light footstep on his patio caught Wolfe's attention. "Pippa's coming." He glanced at the bloody towels. "Go, now. I'll take care of the mess."

Mal paused for a second and then nodded, already moving to the door. "If you need me to stitch you up—"

"I don't," Wolfe interrupted. "A couple of stitches is nothing new." Unfortunately, true words.

"Copy that." Mal slipped outside, heading off Pippa, their voices quiet as they returned to their house. Wolfe shuddered. What had he been thinking to take Malcolm to that area of town?

"It wasn't your fault," Dana said, once again looking his way.

Sometimes he thought she could read minds. Nobody had ever seen him so clearly before, and that wasn't a good thing. Her words were so blatantly wrong that Wolfe didn't bother replying. Instead, he took Mal's vacated seat and reached for another clean needle.

Dana audibly swallowed. "I can do that if you want."

The woman would probably pass out. "That's okay. Not my first time." He took a lot less care with his skin than he had with Mal's, then slapped on a bandage and faced Dana. "The men in the truck were after you, not me, and I think you should lie low until we figure out why." Risking her wasn't an option.

She blinked. "You're giving me orders? After being shot at—again?"

He stiffened, his skin prickling. The world was closing in and he was losing control. That could not happen. "Did you not hear me? They were after you."

"Then I'm getting close." Her chin rose. "That's a good thing."

He took his time exhaling, trying to manage his emotions. From the second those bullets had crashed through the glass, and he'd realized he'd put another one of his team into danger, he'd been on edge. "You don't want to argue with me today, sweetheart." He gave her the full truth.

She stood and gathered the bloody towels. "The heck I don't. Bring it on, Wolfe." Her exit was stalled by her phone going off on the table. She sighed, lifted it up, and declined the call.

Oh, he was too close to losing it. Way too close. "Who keeps calling that you're ignoring?" Focusing on this problem, for a moment, gave him a needed reprieve from the shit show his life had just become. "Dana?" He didn't like the irritation in her eyes.

"Nobody." She turned again, and the phone went off again.

Smoothly, he snaked out a hand and grabbed the phone from her. He was being an ass, but at this point, he just didn't care. He pressed the speaker button and set the phone on the table.

Dana's glare could melt concrete. "Hello?" she muttered.

"Dana. It's about time you answered my calls." The voice was male with what sounded like a Northern accent. Maine, probably.

She shook her head, her gaze leveling Wolfe. "I didn't mean to answer. Stop calling me, and definitely stop calling my parents to find me. We're done. Got it?"

Wolfe cocked his head. When he'd met Dana, she'd been home covering a story about river guides. Hadn't somebody mentioned that she was just out of a relationship with a guy she never should've dated? Was this the guy? If so, he didn't seem to be getting the hint.

The guy sighed loudly through the phone, raising Wolfe's hackles. "Listen to me. I'm sorry about what happened, and I really would like to apologize in person. Please forgive me."

"You're forgiven, Mike," she said, shuffling the bloody towels to her other arm.

Wolfe sat back and crossed his arms. It was that easy? What the heck was happening, and what did good ol' Mike do in the first place?

Even Mike seemed taken aback. "Well, okay. Thanks, then. When can we get together?"

Dana drew air in through her nose. "Never. You're forgiven and all of that, but I'm not going back. So please move on and stop calling me."

"Now that's just silly," Mike said, his voice turning charming. "I'm going to be at Sally's wedding next weekend, and she wouldn't have invited me if there wasn't still a chance for us. Maybe I can finally meet your parents."

Pink bloomed across Dana's cheekbones. "Sally invited you because she doesn't like me but loves drama. Don't come." At Wolfe's raised eyebrows, her own rose. "Or come, if you want, but you have to know that I'm going to be busy and have no intention of going out with you again. Though I do wish you well." The last was said on a rush.

Mike's chuckle was like bone scraping bone. "Come on, Dana. You have to at least save me a dance."

"No, she really doesn't," Wolfe said quietly. "Believe me. Her date won't like it."

Dana's lips snapped together, and she whirled on him. "You just couldn't be quiet, could you? Everything was going fine, and I was handling it, but you just couldn't sit there."

"Sorry," Wolfe said, totally not sorry.

"Why do you do that?" She waved her free hand through the air. "You act like a boyfriend, but you're not. You try to take over, but you know you shouldn't." The pink in her face blossomed into a lovely rose.

Wolfe uncrossed his arms and leaned forward, his own temper still barely banked. "I'm acting like a friend who doesn't appreciate this asshat bugging you. Apparently, your attempts to ignore him haven't worked, and I feel like taking a different tack. It's a free world, you know."

She sucked in air, her eyes widening. "My world is my

world, and when I want your help, I'll freakin' ask for it."
Anger turned her stunning eyes a fascinating emerald.

"Um, excuse me?" Mike snapped through the phone
line. "Who the hell is this?"

Wolfe and Dana both turned toward the phone on the
table. Wolfe had forgotten the jerk for a moment. "Name
is Wolfe and I'll be Dana's date for the wedding." He knew
he was pushing it, but no way would he leave Dana alone
to fend off this guy. Plus, food at weddings was usually
delicious and there wasn't much he wouldn't do for cake.

Dana sucked in air. "You're crazy."

"Probably," he agreed. "Head injury makes a good
excuse."

Mike cleared his throat. "Uh, Dana? Are you in danger
there with a guy with a head injury who thinks he's a wolf?
Should I call the police?"

Dana rolled her eyes so hard she had to have seen part
of her brain. "I am not in danger and, yes, this guy is nuts,
and frankly I believe he might be more wolf than man."
She tossed the bloody towels onto the table and lifted her
chin. "I have not asked you to be my date."

Wolfe stood then, gratified when she took a step back.
"You don't think I could get you to ask me?" His voice was
grittier than he liked.

She visibly swallowed, tilting her head to meet his gaze.
She was a good five-foot-eight, but he was over six-six, so
there wasn't much else the pretty woman could do. Except
reach over and disengage the call, cutting Mike out of the
equation completely. "If we're going to have this fight, I
don't need a witness."

"I like cake," Wolfe returned.

Her chin lowered. "Don't try to be cute with me,
Clarence."

He barely kept from wincing. The world had gotten

way too out of control, and he couldn't escape the sense of panic he'd felt when Malcolm had been injured. It had been Wolfe's fault. Besides that, Dana's orange blossom scent was too tempting in the small kitchen. "Okay. I need some alone time, and then we can argue about where you're staying the night tonight." Without waiting for a response, he strode into his office and shut the door, facing his whiteboard.

The dead stared back at him.

Chapter Ten

Dana finished typing more notes, sitting at Wolfe's kitchen table and purposely ignoring the email from her cousin about the wedding. Why did the bridesmaids have to be ready for pictures five hours before the wedding? She looked, once again, toward the closed door of Wolfe's office. He'd disappeared inside hours ago, obviously needing some time by himself, but darkness was beginning to fall, and she was hungry for dinner.

Should she just rummage in the fridge? After being ignored all day, searching through Wolfe's stuff held little appeal.

He'd almost been shot—again. She'd been kidnapped, cut, and then right when life had started to normalize, she'd been shot at and chased by guys in a truck who'd wanted to hurt her. Life was too short to wait on the sidelines. She was done waiting.

Enough of this. Shutting her laptop, she stood and stretched her back, gathering her courage. Then she walked past the sofa. Kat looked up, blinked his eyes, and meowed softly as if in warning.

She frowned. That was odd. "I'm talking to him," she said to the cat, feeling only a little silly as she moved forward and reached the office door. Her knock was more forceful than she'd intended, and she winced.

Nothing.

She pressed her ear to the door.

No sound.

Huh. Had Wolfe somehow left when she had been in the bathroom earlier? She twisted the knob and stepped inside, her steps faltering on the soft carpet.

Wolfe sat with his back to her, facing the whiteboard, his gaze seemingly directed at the photograph of the smiling young soldiers. His shoulders were rigid and his body unmoving. Tension cloaked him, erecting an invisible barrier that electrified the air around him.

Her mouth opened and closed. A chill slid down her back, and she hunched a little, her instincts blaring for her to run.

How long had he sat in that position? All day?

That couldn't be healthy. She swallowed over a lump in her throat and edged closer to him, reaching out with one shaking hand.

"Don't." His gravelly voice was a stark warning.

She paused and her lip trembled. Her lungs filled with something other than air, something akin to panic, and she breathed shallowly. Too shallowly.

"Go, Dana." His stillness was nearly preternatural.

She should go. Run and leave him to this . . . whatever this was. But she couldn't. Why, she'd figure out later. "Clarence." Fighting every biological survival instinct stamped into her DNA, she reached out and set a hand on his rigid shoulder.

When he didn't jump and bite off her arm, she settled closer, everything inside her wanting to comfort him. A hint of the wild emanated from him—primitive and dangerous. There was no doubt Wolfe was as dangerous as a man got, but he was hurting, and she'd never been able to turn away from an animal in pain.

Especially this one.

Her other hand settled on his other shoulder, and she bit back a grimace at the hard knots against her palms. His head had to be killing him. If there were words for her to offer, she couldn't think of them. Instead, she began to knead the roped muscles beneath her palms, digging deep with her thumbs, finally giving herself permission to touch him.

She worked some of the tension out of his neck, her own body aching in response. He held perfectly still, his hands on his jean-clad legs, the arm bandage stark against his tanned skin. For one fraction of a second, his shoulders relaxed. "What are you doing?" he rumbled.

"Providing comfort."

He stiffened again and, without warning, planted a hand over hers, drawing her in front of him.

She reluctantly released his shoulders and stood between his legs, looking into his hard face, feeling unbalanced and warm. Intimacy surrounded them. "Wolfe?"

"I don't want comfort." He tipped his head back, his eyes a tumultuous brown.

She'd never seen anybody more in need of comfort than Clarence Wolfe. "Why not? Everyone needs comfort."

"Don't want it and don't need it," he said, the sides of his thighs bracketing hers, giving her a feeling of being trapped. The look on his face and the tone of his voice were all the more frightening for the lack of feeling in them.

She couldn't reach him. This was something new, something scary, and she didn't know what to do. So she grasped the sides of his shoulders and leaned in to press a kiss to his nose, just like her dad had always done for her when she'd felt lost.

Wolfe sucked in a breath, his eyes narrowing and finally

focusing on her. He was back. Temptation lurked there and something darker . . . something deeper. A glint—raw and male—zeroing in on just her. All of her.

Words died in her throat. She couldn't move, held in place by that look and his hard body.

His gaze dropped to her breasts.

Honest to God, they started to tingle. She still couldn't breathe, and her adrenaline was flowing as if she'd run ten miles being chased by a grizzly bear.

His hands, rough and calloused, warm and firm, slid up her arms.

This was wrong. Not fair. He'd been in a bad place, he'd been vulnerable, and she would be taking advantage if she let this go where it was headed. Well, where she kind of hoped it was headed. She couldn't do that to him. So she started to step back.

And was shocked when his thighs clamped against hers, easily holding her in place. His hands slid to her wrists and tugged her down, flattening her palms on his incredibly hard legs, partially bending her toward him. "Wh-what are you doing?" she whispered.

For answer, his gaze lifted to her lips and then her eyes. His hands flattened over hers and slid them up his thighs. "You are not listening to me, Dana."

"I think you're wrong," she said quietly, keeping her balance while she bent toward him. "You do need comfort, and sitting here all day staring at these pictures is not good for you. I might not be a shrink, but even I know that much about the demons that haunt people."

"You have no idea."

"Oh yeah?" There was no denying the attraction she felt toward him, and she was tired of trying. She leaned closer, gratified by the way his eyelids lowered to hide his surprise. Oh, she could read him, whether he liked it or not. "I'm tired of the friend zone, Wolfe. I'm breaking the caution tape." As she said the words, they felt right. Finally.

His shoulder jerked. "Excuse me?"

"I want you." There was no reason to lie, considering she was having trouble breathing and her hardened nipples were clearly outlined beneath her shirt.

The hardness of his face contrasted with the hot liquid glide of lust that darkened his deep eyes. "I'm not just trying to keep you safe. Some of it, maybe most of it, is that I can't be distracted from what I have to do and who I have to be to take Rock on. I'm all in on this fight, and there can't be anything else in my life right now. Anybody else."

Honesty was sometimes a pain in the butt. "So I'm a distraction?" The idea warmed her even more.

"Hell, yes." Frustration coated his words.

Good enough. She leaned even closer, until her nose almost touched his. "I don't want forever, and I don't want a white picket fence." Not right now, anyway. "I want you, and you want me, and the way we're going, one of us will probably be shot within the week. So, why not?"

"Not a good idea." His nostrils flared and he almost vibrated with tension. "You wanting to provide comfort with your body."

Was that judgment in his tone? "No. I *want* an orgasm," she snapped. Now she was both turned on and pissed off. "Unless you're incapable of providing one."

His eyelids lifted, his gaze glittering.

Oh. Oops. Well. She should say something, but all sound died in her throat. Her lungs froze, much smarter than her brain. Challenging Wolfe was a mistake she'd never made. Until now.

"You want to take that back?" he rumbled, one eyebrow lifting.

The memory of how quickly he'd picked her up and

headed for that bar the other night sent heated air into her lungs. "No." Her voice wavered, but her gaze remained on his. "If you're not up to it, just let me know."

Yep. She had completely lost her mind.

"You think I'm that easy to manipulate?" His voice remained steady, but the tension rolling from him choked the space between them.

"I think you're as tired as I am of fighting this, whatever it is, that's between us." Her hands were still on his legs and she dug in with her nails. "Come on, Wolfe. You know you want it." She let her voice lower to a croon. While she'd never been a temptress, she was enjoying this. If one of them didn't make a move, they'd both go to bed alone, sleepless, and unsatisfied. "We should enjoy life while we have it." Unfortunately, a true statement.

"Nothing is going to happen to you." He growled the words, his hands lifting to her hips, heated and firm. His fingers flexed, hinting at restrained strength. Ruthlessly controlled power. "I've been as honest as I can be. I can't promise you a damn thing, but I'm done pushing you away. You sure about this?"

Anticipation licked through her as if she were at the start of a race, right before the bell rang and the gate swung open to free the horses. "I'm sure."

He stood and lifted her at the same time, tossing her over his shoulder. She landed with a muffled *oof*, laughing and trying to shove her hair out of her face. This side of Wolfe was new, and her body felt electrified, the shoulder beneath her stomach solid rock.

She might have taken on more than she could handle.

He strode into the kitchen, reached for the whipped-cream can still on the table, tossed it in the air, caught it, and headed toward his bedroom, his steps even and sure, his strides long and purposeful.

"Whipped cream?" she gasped, the blood rushing to her face as she turned her head to the side to breathe, her cheek resting against his broad back.

"We're gonna make a sweet memory," he murmured, reaching the bedroom and kicking the door closed with the back of one foot. It slammed shut, the sound amplified by her too-aware body and mind. He flipped her over, then stood, towering over her with heat and strength, his gaze hungry and a mite intimidating. "Take off your shirt."

There was only one possible answer. "No."

His slow smile awoke every girly part she had. "We're doin' this my way, green eyes."

She bit her lip, contemplating his rock-solid body. "Who says?"

"Well?" He shook the whipped cream can. "Is this going to end up with me inside you, probably covered in sugar, making you scream my name?"

"Hopefully," she croaked, her knees wobbling. Had she ever been this aroused?

"Then it's my way." His smile widened, giving him a boyish look she'd never seen on him before. Her heart just flipped right over and submitted. He finished shaking the can. "Now. This is going on you. That's a pretty shirt, and I'd hate to get it messy. You have two seconds to take it off."

Humor bubbled through her arousal, torturing her. "Fine." But she wasn't going to make it easy on him. Keeping his gaze, she slowly, very slowly, released each button, her breath catching as his smile disappeared and he looked even hungrier. "You look like a wolf about to eat," she whispered, dropping the shirt and revealing her white lacy bra.

"I am a wolf about to eat." He ran a knuckle along the tops of her breasts, his breath catching, his gaze heating even more. A smooth flick of his fingers released the front clasp, and the bra, too, dropped out of existence. Then he sprayed her, over her breasts, causing flecks of whipped cream to pepper her face.

She laughed, protesting. "Wolfe—"

His head dropped, and his mouth found her breast. Heat surrounded her, and he sucked. She gasped, her hands instinctively clutching his shoulders so she didn't fall. It figured Wolfe would go all in with no hesitation. He licked the other breast with a happy hum and then lifted up, his mouth taking hers.

Wolfe didn't kiss—he consumed. A sharp nip to her lip made her gasp, and he took advantage, his tongue sweeping in, tasting like whipped cream and spice. The demanding thrust of his tongue was accompanied by both hands on her breasts, the whipped cream letting him slide tantalizingly over her skin with a hint of bite.

She moaned and yanked on his shirt so he'd duck his head and let her toss it free. A sigh escaped her, into his mouth, when she finally settled her hands on that solid torso. Frantically, she caressed each bullet hole, knife wound, and ripped muscle.

He overwhelmed her, and she grasped his jeans, unzipping them.

Releasing her mouth, he ran his slippery palms down her arms and then gracefully dropped to his knees.

She protested, her hands now over his shoulders.

"Dana." One word from him had her growing still. His hands were sure and gentle as he tugged down her yoga pants and panties, cool air brushing her skin.

He froze.

She blinked. Oh, crap. She'd forgotten. Caught up in his seduction, she'd completely forgotten the marks still on her upper thighs from the crazy senator and his sharp knife.

Wolfe jerked as if he'd been punched in the gut. Gingerly, he reached out and rubbed a gentle finger along one of the many still healing cuts. "Why didn't you tell me?"

She tried to concentrate. "I didn't want you to kill him." It was the truth. "You saved me before he could do any more damage."

"I would've killed him." Wolfe glanced up, looking dangerous and big, even on his knees.

Yeah, she knew.

"I'm sorry." He leaned forward and kissed each mark with a gentleness that nearly undid her. "These will heal. And I'll make you forget." The whipped cream suddenly sprayed across her lower part, and his mouth found her right where she ached for him.

"Jesus, Wolfe." Fire lanced through her, and her thighs trembled. She grasped his shoulders, trying for balance.

Laughing against her core, he grasped her hips and tossed her on the bed, his mouth working her the entire time, his tongue lashing her clit as if he couldn't get enough. It was too much. She gasped, trying for control, while sparks uncoiled inside her faster than she could track.

An orgasm took her, spiraling from nowhere, shaking through her. She closed her eyes and rode the waves, shocked at the height of them. When she was finished, he stood up. There was whipped cream in his hair from her hands.

"That was so fast," she gasped.

His eyebrows rose. "Want another one?" He moved to bend down.

"No." She held up a hand. "I want you. All of you."

His eyes darkened, and he shoved his jeans off, freeing himself.

She grinned, her body on fire for him. "Glad to see you're in proportion." Truth be told, the guy was huge.

"Smart-ass." He leaned over and drew a condom out of the bedside table.

She sat up, reaching for him.

"Later. Want to be inside you now." He quickly rolled it on and moved her up the bed, covering her.

This was too good to be true. She explored his chest, the whipped cream starting to dry and get sticky. "Your bed will be a mess."

"Then let's make it good." Somehow, he found the can and sprayed more whipped cream across her chest.

She laughed, widening her legs; she hadn't expected Wolfe to be fun, just mind-blowing.

He pressed against her, sliding the head of his cock through her wetness, and she stopped laughing. Even after her orgasm, she was tight, and her body tried to resist his size. Pleasure and pain caught her, and she panted, then held her breath.

His gaze kept hers, dark and intense, as he pushed inside her inch by inch, filling her until she wasn't sure where she began and he ended.

Finally, he stopped, deep inside her. Fully taking her. This was more than fun and more than friendship, but she couldn't land on the right feeling.

As if sensing her sudden vulnerability, he caressed her jawline. "Deep breaths, baby."

She took a deep breath, and the craving inside her intensified, pleasure overtaking the pain.

"There we go." Shadows deepened the strong hollows of his face, and his eyes blazed as darkness finished falling outside. He moved within her, and she bit her lip against a moan at the delicious friction.

He eased out and pushed back in, watching her closely. She dug her nails into the rigid muscles of his arms, his movements increasing in strength and speed and rocketing need through her body. The room smelled like whipped cream and male, and she held tighter, each thrust of his powerful body pressing him against her still engorged clit.

Pressure built, live wires uncoiled, and he hammered harder, his concentration almost intimidating. She had to shut her eyes and just let the colors take her away. Spasms of raw pleasure burst from her core, spreading throughout her body, making her toes curl. She whispered his name, overtaken, shocked by the intensity.

He kept powering into her, faster and even harder, and then came with a husky groan. His head dropped to her nape, and his chest panted.

Whoa. She tried to breathe normally, overwhelmed. This wasn't just sex.

He lifted his head and slowly licked whipped cream from her collarbone to her ear. His voice was a pleased rumble. "You're all sticky. Let's take this to the shower."

She blinked. "We're not done?"

"Not even close."

Chapter Eleven

Well after midnight, Dana snuggled into Wolfe's side, his heartbeat steady and sure beneath her palm. They'd gone three times, and her body was done. She'd barely helped with changing the sheets. "You're not sleeping," she murmured, her eyelids closing.

"I know."

"Do you sleep often?" She tried to hide a yawn, her body shutting down.

He didn't answer and instead played with her hand on his chest.

She sighed. "Tell me you're not regretting tonight." Did she have the energy to get upset? Probably not.

"I'm not regretting tonight." His voice remained steady and thoughtful, not giving away his thoughts. "Those marks on your thighs won't scar. I'm glad."

What was going on in his head? She tried to track his reasoning when all she wanted was to sink into his warmth and relax. "Your wounds won't?"

"No. There's a place inside you, one you never even knew existed, that can be broken. There's an actual sound when it happens, and then your whole body is like a puzzle that doesn't go together any longer." He rolled them over and spooned his body around hers, offering comfort whether or not he realized it.

She relaxed against him, even as her heart hurt for him. "I don't have the right words, but I think the puzzle you've put back into place is a good one. I trust you. It can't be easy, but anything broken can be fixed."

He hugged her closer. The gesture was all the more special for its brevity. Then he gentled his hold. "The final configuration can be unstable, though, and I can't risk that with you—with anybody—and that's final."

"We've already gone over this." If he hadn't sounded so serious, she'd mess with him a bit and tease him about getting married or something. Instead, she tried to follow his mood, which seemed a little off, though she couldn't pin down what was bothering him. Was it about earlier that afternoon? "It wasn't your fault Malcolm was hurt."

"Yeah, it was."

Ah. So that's what was happening.

His phone buzzed.

She jerked against him. "Who in the world would be calling this late?"

"Dunno." Keeping her in place, he stretched an arm to his bedtable and pulled the phone to his ear. "Who the hell is calling so late?" he answered.

He listened, his body warm beneath her touch. "Oh, yeah. I forgot I told you to call any time. What do you want?" Then he paused "Yeah? What's the consensus?" He listened for a while, and then shook his head. "Absolutely not. We signed an NDA, remember?"

Whoever was on the other end of the line replied with something Wolfe didn't like, if the stiffening of his torso was any indication. "Right. Who do the cops think killed him?"

Dana lifted her head from his chest to watch his reactions during the call.

A muscle twitched in Wolfe's jaw. "Is that right? Absolutely nothing, huh? What about the party on Tuesday?" He listened, remaining still in that odd way he had. "Is it private with no cops?" A male voice echoed slightly over the phone. "Good. I'll be there, and I'm bringing a sub. And Trentington? I want full details on who the dead guy was and why the hell he was murdered at one of our parties— as well as any leads." He clicked off.

Dana played with his chest. "Did Trentington have any information?"

"No. He said the police had no idea who killed Albert Nelson, which was his real name, by the way. Besides the Clarke Wellson identity, he had several aliases. I'll have to get to the club records to see what he put down on his application." Wolfe kissed the top of her head in what felt like a good-bye. "The cops want to talk to anybody who was at the party."

Well, that wasn't good. "I used a fake name. Didn't you?"

"Of course."

Her body felt a little tight. "So they're having another party on Tuesday night? Despite the murder?"

"Probably because of the murder," Wolfe said, seeming to be miles away all of a sudden. "I wouldn't be surprised if Trentington is working with the cops to find out who killed the man with too many names. This party will be at Trentington's house, which is where all of the member records should be. Hopefully."

She bit her lip. "What if there are cameras? For the police?"

"It'd be a contract breach and betrayal of the members' privacy, so I doubt it. But, since Tuesday's event is a costume party, we'll find a way to hide who we are."

Wolfe was too big to hide, but Dana didn't say anything as she waited for him to say whatever he had to say.

"I don't want you to be there." Yeah, he'd said it.

"Too bad." She wasn't going to let Candy down. She was going to find her friend's killer no matter how nervous she felt about going undercover, and no matter how unsettled she was after sleeping with Wolfe.

He was silent long enough that she almost fell asleep. "I'm going out for a while. I'll make sure Malcolm is watching the house while I'm gone," he finally said.

No cuddling into the wee hours, then. She understood his need to get away and think. "Okay."

He stood and dressed, pausing at his doorway. The bed felt cold without him in it. "I won't let anybody hurt you, Dana. No matter what. You have to believe me."

She did. No outside threat would get to her with Wolfe around. But every second in his presence drew her closer to him, and if he wouldn't let her in, she wasn't sure her heart would recover. Ever.

And she had nobody else to blame but herself.

Wolfe was putting his life at risk every time he descended in the rickety elevator at his sorry office building. After leaving Dana, he'd decided to work instead of run, tonight. His brain didn't need free rein after the night they'd just shared. How could he keep his distance from her? The woman was a siren to him, and he wanted nothing more than to go right back to bed with her.

The silence of the office building on Sunday night usually soothed him, but he still couldn't calm down. He often spent weekends and even nights at the office, which was pathetic. It wasn't that he was so dedicated to the job but rather that he didn't have another place to go.

Bars didn't do it for him, and neither did places with, well, other people.

So here he was. Again—with a couple of lattes covered in whipped cream and sprinkles that he'd drink through the night. Now every time he saw whipped cream, he saw it covering Dana's generous breasts. His mouth salivated.

The elevator doors opened, and the buzz of the ancient fluorescent lights provided a strange sense of comfort for him.

Then the German shepherd pranced out of the shrink's office. Wolfe caught his breath. Not again. "Roscoe."

The dog smiled around the shredded red high heel dangling from his mouth, his snout covered in what looked like mauve-colored paste. He snorted, dropped the shoe, and danced around in a circle, somehow shaking his butt and tail in the opposing directions.

Oh, so not good. Wolfe set the coffee cups down on his desk, stalked into Nari's office, looked around, and slapped his head. A desk drawer had been busted open, revealing the remains of a gold-plated lipstick with bite marks on it. The colorful hue was smeared over several papers on the desk and across the white leather chair. No doubt the makeup had been expensive. "She'll kill you." Then he caught sight of the other damaged shoe in the far corner, which Roscoe had bitten right through. Wolfe looked up to the top of a bookcase to see everything scattered across it as if the dog had somehow jumped from the desk, hit the books and potted plant, and knocked much of it down. The shoes had probably been up there. "Why didn't you just wear them?" The dog seemed to have a shoe fetish, both wearing and eating them.

Roscoe snorted and reclaimed the second shoe, flopping down and munching happily. He burped.

Wolfe straightened and turned, studying the pooch. "Tell me you're sober," he ordered.

Roscoe hiccupped.

Damn it. Wolfe dropped to his knees and lifted the dog's head to stare into murky brown eyes. The dog had a drinking problem and had been to the vet several times, but he apparently had the liver of a ninety-year-old miner. "Booze is bad for dogs," Wolfe murmured, patting Roscoe's head. "I wonder if you'd be better off around people who weren't so screwed up."

Roscoe sneezed and sent the shoe flying.

Wolfe sighed. This wasn't good. He stood and angled his neck toward the enclosed office in the back of the depressing space, which was situated between the two case rooms. Only silence came from the office.

Roscoe followed his gaze and whined.

Wolfe rubbed the ache between his eyes, took a deep breath, and nodded. "I've got it, buddy. Just stay here and sober up."

Roscoe set his face on his paws, sneezed again, and then shut his eyes. Snoring commenced almost immediately, interspersed with a whimper or two. Then the dog let out a stream of farts that punctured the silence with loud pops.

Wolfe stood to grab the lattes before striding around the pod of desks to the rear office. "Force?" He poked his head in to see Angus sprawled, face first, across a worn leather sofa against the wall, his arm hanging off near an empty bottle of Jack Daniels on the floor.

Wonderful. Wolfe set the lattes on the paper-strewn desk and grasped his boss by the shoulders, flipping him around to a sitting position. "Do you need to throw up?"

Force wobbled and then blinked, his eyes so bloodshot

it hurt to look at them. "Wolfe. It's Sunday," he slurred. "What are you doing here?"

"Thought I'd wait here until my church services started," Wolfe drawled, releasing his hold on Force's shoulders once the man seemed semi-stable.

Force snorted and kicked out his legs. The bottle rolled across the floor to hit the desk. "Where's Roscoe?"

"Sleeping it off out in the main room. You gave him booze?" Wolfe tried to keep from sounding judgmental but failed.

"No." Force looked around, blinking. "I thought I'd finished this bottle, but maybe not." He dropped his head into his hands, a massive man with guilt pouring from him. "Lassiter is out there. He's killing and we're not finding him, so he's killing more. I just know it." His voice was gritty, tortured.

"There's no proof the guy is alive." Wolfe reached for a latte and nudged it against Force's hand.

"I know he is." Force lifted his head and took the sugary drink, downing half of it in one gulp.

Wolfe nodded, working his way through his own whipped cream. The stuff didn't taste nearly as good as it did on Dana's skin. Damn it, he needed to focus. He trusted Force's instincts almost as implicitly as he did his own. "If Brigid hasn't found a line to Lassiter, there isn't one. Is he really that good?"

"Yeah." Force finished the drink and then winced. "He's that good, and I'm not the man I was five years ago. Not even close."

Wolfe could see that. "You have a good team this time, though. Together, we'll find the guy." If he was alive.

Force wiped a sprinkle off his bottom lip. "That's a lot of sugar."

"Only the best for you." Wolfe drank his latte more slowly, feeling back in control, finally. "Have you, maybe, thought of talking to Nari about everything?" The shrink was smart and often helpful.

Force stiffened and sat up straighter. "No."

Okay. Well, then. Wolfe had learned at an early age not to try to run through a brick wall, so enough of that. "This isn't good, man. You have to stop with the Jack." And the Johnny, Bud, and Jose.

Force nodded, looking green. "Yeah. Got it."

Enough of the lecture. "Thanks for bringing Dana on board." Was Force trying to matchmake?

Force nodded. "I figured you'd need her with Bridge and Raider gone, and frankly, she's pretty darn good at research. Are you two fuckin' or what?"

"Mind your own business," Wolfe returned.

Force sighed. "What a disaster."

Wasn't that the damn truth?

Dana tugged her blouse into place, sitting in the passenger side of Wolfe's truck on the way to work. He must've returned sometime during the night but had slept on the sofa. Nope. She wasn't hurt by that at all. Ugh. "I can get my own ride to work, you know?" She eyed the way-too-sweet latte already waiting for her in his cupholder.

He banked left and drove around a hearse. "I know, but I figured you'd want support for your first Monday morning."

There probably wouldn't be a lot of Monday mornings, and she knew him better than that. "I appreciate your playing bodyguard, but if our friendship is temporary, then I shouldn't start to count on that, right?" Yeah, she might be sounding a little snippy.

"Our friendship isn't temporary, but our close proximity is, because it needs to be." He sounded oh so reasonable and back in control this morning. He also looked fresh and ready to rumble in dark jeans and a light green T-shirt, but there was stubble along his hard jawline.

She sighed. "Don't act all distant and weird because we burned up the sheets last night."

He didn't glance her way, but his lips twitched. "You do have a way with words, and I'm not acting distant and weird. Well, maybe weird, but that's normal for me."

"You said you didn't regret it, and I don't regret it, so knock it off." She was starting to feel like a dork, and she'd had enough of this. "You're lucky, in fact." It wasn't as if she went around sleeping with guys. Who had the time?

"I know. Very lucky." His smile flashed straight white teeth.

She watched the traffic go by outside the truck. It seemed like the guy had the world on his mind. "Are you worried we just complicated everything?"

"Oh, we definitely just complicated everything." He edged around a semi carting fruit. "Drink your latte. It's getting cold." He jerked his head toward the melting whipped cream.

She took the coffee and sipped gingerly, letting the syrup slam into her system. Why didn't somebody tell Wolfe to take it easy on the sugar? He seemed to get so much enjoyment from providing the sweets that even she couldn't say anything, although she was feeling a mite prickly with him right now—and not just because she'd gained five pounds since starting to hang out with him. "I appreciate your concern. I am capable, you know."

"Very much so." He turned off the interstate and wound

down the quiet road toward the '70s-style office building. "No matter how capable you are, I would want to protect you if you were mine."

Whoa. "I'm mine," she retorted. "Even if we had decided to take all of this to the next level, which we did not, I would not be *yours*." The warmth spreading through her limbs was irritation, not desire. Yep. Definitely.

"Sure, you would be." He pulled into a spot between two faded yellow lines and cut the engine.

"Wolfe," she protested, waiting until he partially turned to face her. "It's not the nineteen hundreds."

One of his dark eyebrows rose. "Dana, I'm the muscle for the Deep Ops Unit because I'm good at it. It's my job to protect and defend and diffuse. You're nuts if you think I wouldn't protect my woman with everything I have, especially my life."

His woman. She shook her head, even though her heart rate seemed to be perking up considerably, and not from irritation. "I think you're behind the times here."

"Maybe," he allowed. "But it's a dangerous world, and you and I know that better than most. In this world, we give ourselves to the people we care about, and with that comes responsibilities. I'm all for independence, equal pay, and all of that, but a man's job is to protect women and children, and that reality transcends any time." Kat took that moment to jump from the back seat and land on Wolfe's shoulder. "Animals and the elderly should be protected, too," Wolfe added, opening his door and somehow jumping out without dislodging the kitten.

"How does somebody argue with that?" she muttered as she exited the truck without waiting for him to open her door.

He shrugged. "Why would you argue? However, if you

someday end up with a guy who doesn't agree with that sentiment, you've ended up with the wrong guy."

"Like you care who I end up with," she said, stepping lightly over a puddle.

"Well, I'd hate to have to kill him for not protecting you." Wolfe patted the kitten, slowing his stride to match Dana's.

It was sometimes difficult to tell if Wolfe was joking or not. "Discussions like these throw me off kilter," she said.

"Why?"

That was a good question. Maybe because part of her wanted to be *his*, even though she didn't like the terminology. Or a part of her wanted to know why he was so sure his next mission would be his last and he wouldn't be around afterward. Or maybe because if his mission was dangerous, she wanted to help and make it sure that it *wasn't* his last one. "I want to help you take Rock down without dying yourself."

His jaw tightened, making the scar stand out. "No."

Her hackles rose. There was no way he was working alone on this, and the idea that he wouldn't let her in kind of hurt. "I'm sure you have Brigid trying to track him with bank or military records."

"No, I don't." He opened the door and waited for her to walk inside the dusty hallway.

She stumbled and quickly righted herself. "Why not?" Brigid was the best.

"He can't be found," Wolfe said, pushing the elevator button. "There's no trace of him for Bridge to follow. The game isn't played that way."

A chill slithered down her spine. "Game?"

"Oh, yeah. Rock is all about the game." The elevator door opened, and Wolfe gestured her inside. "He knows

I'm looking for him, and now that he's engaged, he'll come to me."

She leaned against the worn paneled siding, her mind spinning. "Wait a minute. You've sent out some crazy guy challenge?"

"Yep. I have a little time, but I'm gonna need to start making a trail that leads away from the team." He pushed the button, and the elevator rocked twice before descending, creaking loudly with a protest that hurt her ears.

She needed to get through to him. "You're crazy."

"Wrong. I'm bait."

Chapter Twelve

The smell of dust combined with the scents of pepperoni and whiskey made the bullpen area of the office smell like home. Wolfe kicked back and flipped through the manila file folders of the cases assigned to him as Dana worked away in Brigid's computer room, conducting basic research.

The ability to manipulate people wasn't one of his talents, unlike going through doors or dodging bullets. However, he'd do what he had to do, and by the end of the workday, he'd have Dana agreeing to stay at his cottage and take care of Kat, even if he had to go hunting Rock. Yeah, he was using the kitten as a pawn, but the house, located at the end of a cul-de-sac with a very armed and capable Malcolm West as a neighbor, was safe.

He'd learned early on that getting Dana to think something was her idea was the best way to gain her cooperation. Stubborn woman.

Force had shut the door to his office as he worked, and Roscoe snored quietly at Wolfe's feet, no doubt sporting a doggie hangover from the booze. Malcolm worked through files silently at his desk, occasionally sipping the latte Wolfe had brought for him. He looked up. "I made inquiries about the heroin pipeline around six months ago, but it's going to take time."

"Thanks," Wolfe said. That kind of inquiry always took time, and Gary Rockcliff had probably covered his tracks well. Wolfe settled back, relaxing as much as he could. Office work wasn't his thing, but this was kind of nice. Peaceful, even, with Nari typing a mile a minute in her office, Kat sleeping on her desk, and the door open. The shrink must have some serious work to catch up on, since she'd barely scolded Roscoe for his foraging through her office the previous night.

The typing stopped. "Guys?" she called out. "I'm printing out the reports from the last op. Would you look them over and make sure I added everything I need and didn't add anything that might hurt us with our HDD handlers? They're not happy with us, and I need a couple extra sets of eyes on this."

"Sure," Mal said, not looking up.

"Yep," Wolfe said. Unlike the other members of the unit, he didn't mind being the outcasts of the Homeland Defense Department who had handlers to try and keep them in line. So far, Angus Force still had enough juice with the HDD to keep the team alive, but if he didn't climb out of the bottle soon, that would end. Wolfe needed to find Rock before that happened. "Why do you have to send reports to the HDD, anyway?"

The printer clunked to life in the corner. "It's the only way we keep our funding," she called, starting to type once again.

"What funding?" Mal asked before Wolfe could.

Wolfe grinned and took another deep gulp of his latte. "Do you have anything interesting in your pile of busy-work?"

Mal pushed a folder toward Wolfe. "Not really. Securities fraud, computer hacking, and possible political extortion. You?"

Wolfe shook his head. "Not even remotely. A couple of money laundering possibilities and a blond bank robber who has somehow kept her face from being recorded."

"Blond, female bank robber?" Mal's eyebrows rose.

Wolfe nodded. "Yep. Hits only safety deposit boxes, and it turns out a lot of them are owned by some pretty shady criminals."

"Let her rob them, then." Mal opened one of his files and then rubbed his left eye. "This is just busywork because the HDD is pissed. Without Brigid here this week, we don't even have a hacker for the computer cases."

The crank of the elevator reverberated through the room.

"Is Pippa coming by?" Wolfe asked, sitting up.

"Nope." Malcolm straightened and drew out his desk drawer.

Wolfe did the same, resting his hand on his Glock.

The door opened, and a man stepped out. Wolfe categorized him instantly. About six-foot-three, graceful movements, intelligent brown eyes behind modern rimmed glasses. A six-o'clock shadow covered his jaw and went perfectly with his mussed dark blond hair. The satchel slung over his shoulder was half open and revealed several textbooks. "Hello." The accent was British.

Wolfe kept his hand on the gun. The newcomer might look like a college professor, but he'd unobtrusively scouted the entire room, noted the lack of exits, and settled his stance in a way that looked casual but was far from it. "Can we help you?" Yeah, his tone wasn't all that helpful.

Force's door opened. "Professor. I wondered when you'd finally arrive."

A slow smile tugged at the professor's full lips as he focused beyond the hub of desks. "Angus, my friend. You look like shite."

"You look like you're undercover at a college," Force returned, his eyes bloodshot but his smile genuine. "Chasing coeds these days, are you?"

"Hardly. Just teaching them," the professor returned easily.

Malcolm cleared his throat.

Force nodded. "Dr. Jethro Hanson, please meet my agents, Malcolm West and Clarence Wolfe."

Malcolm nodded, but Wolfe decided to remain still. If this guy was a professor, Wolfe was a perfume salesperson. "Doctor in what?" Wolfe asked. They could actually use a medical doctor around if he was an M.D.

Hanson unslung his bag and set it against the wall. "Philosophy with emphases in ethics, moral theory, decision, game, and rational choice theories."

"As well as doctorates in psychology, criminology, and last I heard, string theory," Force drawled.

"One does hate to brag." Hanson straightened back up. "You still tilting at windmills, Force?"

Angus sighed. "I wish."

The glimmer in Hanson's eyes faded. "I can't go down that road with you again, mate. It leads nowhere." The accent rolled out smoothly, but his voice roughened.

"Lassiter is alive," Force said, leaning against his doorjamb.

"Ah." Wolfe cut Malcolm a look. So the guy was there to help Force chase the elusive, possibly dead, maybe alive serial killer who, as far as they knew, hadn't killed anybody since Force had shot him dead. Well, mostly dead. Maybe all the way dead. Wolfe lifted his latte and downed the rest of the contents, keeping everyone in sight.

"You shot and killed Lassiter." Hanson's face softened. "You have no proof that he's alive or you would've contacted me with more than a text."

Roscoe snorted awake, rolled to the side, and bounded halfheartedly toward Hanson.

Hanson crouched down and petted the animal with both hands on the sides of his furry face, looking into his eyes. "Ah, chap. You've been into the bottle again, eh? Haven't you learned your lesson yet?"

Roscoe panted and wagged his tail.

Wolfe shut his drawer in unison with Malcolm. No need to shoot the guy if Roscoe liked him.

Heels clip-clopped, and Nari emerged from her office. A wide smile curved her lips, and she moved toward the elevator. "Jethro. How nice to see you."

Jethro stood and hugged Nari, his hold visibly gentle. "What in the world are you doing in this dive?"

Nari chuckled and leaned back, patting Roscoe on the way. "You know I like adventure."

"You've met?" Force asked, his calm voice giving away everything.

Wolfe bit back a grin. Oh, he wasn't wading into this one, but it was fun to watch Force hold himself together.

"We consulted on a case," Nari said, turning again as Dana walked out of the computer room. "Ah, good. Dana, it's time for our session."

Dana's steps hesitated and then her shoulders straightened. "Oh, all right."

Hanson cocked his head. "Hi. I'm Jethro."

"Hi." Her smile was way too cute. "Dana."

Wolfe set his cup down. The new guy had to go. Definitely.

Dana settled herself in the one guest chair in the minuscule office, facing Nari across a short desk. A wide picture of an outdoor scene, a pretty lake, took up the entire wall behind the psychologist. "How did you end up with the closet for an office?"

Nari rolled her eyes. "Angus took the only office; the other two spaces are larger case rooms." She tapped one red nail against her lips. "We do have two interrogation rooms to the left of the elevators, but we've needed both a couple of times, so oh well."

"Kat likes it in here." Dana nodded at the kitten sprawled across the keyboard, snoring softly.

Nari slid her chair to the side and away from the computer. "How has your first day been?"

"Fine. This morning, I conducted some research and compiled information on a bank robber. I'll hit the case on securities fraud next. I'm nowhere near as good as Brigid on the computers, but I do have some decent contacts." Dana crossed her legs and sat back in the chair.

"You're not here to be a hacker," Nari said, smiling. Today the shrink had worn a light pink blouse, dark slacks, and very pretty gray and black sandals, with her black hair tied up in a messy bun. "How are you doing working with Clarence?"

"So far, so good," Dana said. "I've been in the computer room, and he's been out working with Malcolm, so I can't really say we've collaborated much." Not that Wolfe was much of a collaborator.

"Tell me about this case you and Wolfe are working that involves leather pants." Nari leaned forward, her brown eyes sparkling. "That was quite a sight."

"I know," Dana said, her voice hushed. "Could you believe it?"

Nari laughed. "No. What's the case about?"

"I can't tell you." Dana didn't have enough about Candy's story to share, and she wasn't going to betray Wolfe's confidence, either. "Sorry."

"It's part of the gig," Nari said.

"My story isn't a case for the unit." Dana reached down and tied her shoelace. The previous month, they'd been attacked and Nari had fought like a warrior before Dana was taken. "I've been wondering. Where did you learn to fight?"

"My mom," Nari said. "She owns a jewelry store in L.A., but she has always trained. It's something we did together as I was growing up."

That was so sweet. Dana chuckled. "My mom taught me to fish and play the piano."

"Cool." Nari neatly stacked purple file folders on her desk. "I'm worried about Wolfe and think I could assist with whatever case you two are working."

Dana straightened. "Why are you worried?"

Nari patted the files. "I'm afraid I can't get into that."

"Then we're at a stalemate." Dana liked the shrink, but work was work. "When are you and Angus going to get together, anyway?"

Nari blushed. "That's crazy."

There was a lot of that going on these days, it seemed. "Why are you in this office, Nari?" Dana asked.

"What do you mean?"

Right. "You know what I mean. This is the HDD's Island of Misfit Toys. You seem to have your act together." The journalist in Dana couldn't let the question go. "Oh, I understand you report back to the agency about the group, and the unit knows that, but why you?"

"I wanted a challenge."

That wasn't the full truth. Dana's investigative instincts awakened. "There's more, I can tell." She smiled. "I love a good story."

"As do I," Nari said softly.

Dana perked up. She and Nari had hit it off right away and were quickly becoming friends. "Is that a challenge?"

Nari's dark eyes gleamed. "Oh, you bet. I'll have the info long before you will."

"I don't see how." If she didn't talk, and if Wolfe didn't talk, there was no way the shrink would figure out their case. "I, however, do have connections in HDD."

Nari reached out and gently stroked Kat. "Okay. The bet is for lunch at Gerviani's in D.C."

Dana blew out air. "Wow. You've got it." She looked at the shrink's expensive blouse. "You must do all right with the HDD."

Nari chuckled. "Government salary? No. But I did invest well a few years back in a beverage company that partnered with a cannabis company to create drinks for the states where cannabis is legal."

Dana's mouth dropped open. "No kidding?"

"Yep. Has been quite lucrative." Nari scratched behind Kat's ears, and his purring got louder. "The company does a great job, and someday will probably be bought out. My stock should provide a good retirement."

"Good for you." The thrill of the challenge went through Dana. "Maybe we should bet for more than lunch."

Nari's smile widened. "Lunch is enough." She sobered. "Seriously, though. Be careful with Wolfe. He's lost a lot."

Dana cleared her throat. "Is that advice from a shrink or a friend?"

"It has to be from a friend," Nari said. "As a shrink, I can't talk about him. As a friend, I can tell you that you'd need to be all in or all out with him. After everything he's lost, he won't know any other way."

In other words, don't play with the hot ex-soldier. Dana nodded. "I read him that way, too. I mean, not right away, but after I got to know him." Her first impression was of a fun-loving, flirty hottie who just wanted a good time. His mask was good, but that wasn't Wolfe. He had depths that still surprised her. Although, even though they'd taken the step and had gone full on in bed, they still weren't together.

"Fine." Nari's eyes twinkled again. "If you go undercover at a sex party, you might want to remind yourself that you're just friends."

Friends with benefits, but Nari didn't know that. Dana relaxed again. "Isn't that the truth?" She shivered. The next party was the following night. She could do this. She had to—for Candy.

Chapter Thirteen

"You're going to have to leave the trench coat in the car," Wolfe said calmly as he drove an older BMW expertly through traffic after their second day working together. They'd already solved the securities fraud case with three arrests.

"I know." Dana sighed, really not wanting to remove the protective coat. Why couldn't subs wear cardigans, for goodness sake? She fought another yawn. She'd slept at Wolfe's the previous night, but neither of them had made a move, and she'd been too tired to worry about why.

She glanced sideways at her partner for the night.

Wolfe wore those devastating leather pants and a long-sleeve black shirt that covered the bandage on his arm and somehow made his chest look even broader than usual. After going through two toll roads and exiting the interstate, Wolfe drove by a river and then into a gated community with mature trees, perfectly manicured lawns, and expensive streetlights that showed it all off. "Tell me about Trenting-ton," Dana murmured. The guy was obviously loaded if he lived here.

"Interesting guy," Wolfe said, driving through the sub-division and scoping out each side cul-de-sac. "Grew up on the West Coast; both folks were in the movie industry.

Trentington took a small family fortune and turned it into a colossal one by investing in start-ups ranging from computer programs to independent films, as well as some real estate. He seems to have a knack."

Dana crossed her legs, acutely aware that they were way too bare. "All legal?"

"Seems like it. I asked Brigid to do a deep dive off the books, and she didn't find any red flags. Let's park here and walk." He maneuvered the car into a nicely treed area by another gate, this one leading to a quiet street.

Dana released her seat belt. "Where'd you get the car, anyway?"

"Stole it."

"Seriously?" She turned to look at him.

He opened his door and stepped out, sighing as he stretched. "Yeah. We'll leave it somewhere nice later tonight so the police will find it. No worries."

She glanced at her watch. Nearly eleven at night, so the party would be going strong, and hopefully people would be engaged and not notice their arrival. Yet she didn't move. Yeah, she should've insisted on going undercover as a dom, because the sub outfit was way too revealing.

He opened the passenger-side door. "The coat, Dana."

Look who was already turning bossy. Her tummy wobbled. "I know." She took his hand and stepped out on the tall heels, glancing around the peaceful, quietly austere neighborhood with mansions hidden behind stone walls and perfectly manicured shrubbery. She'd streaked her hair with bright pink and had a sequined mask to wear, but she still hesitated.

"You can stay in the car," Wolfe offered, surveying the area.

"No. I have to do this." Steeling herself, she released the belt and dropped the coat into the vehicle.

Wolfe sucked in air, his gaze raking her from head to toe. "Uh, well."

Amusement and feminine pride tickled her. How rare to see Wolfe taken off guard. She looked down at the bright pink corset. The tight material pushed her breasts up, giving the illusion of a lot more cleavage than she really had, and the flimsy skirt barely covered the tops of her thighs. "What? You don't like it?" It was difficult not to grin like an idiot.

"I'm going to feel your image in my left pocket for a long time." His smile was rare, and all the more special for it. "Let's make sure you don't get grabbed up instantly." He reached beyond her for the glovebox, removing a bag.

Curiosity kept her still.

He pulled out a necklace—a choker, really—with a delicate wolf pendant attached by an emerald on the small circular chain. "Here, it's called a collar. Later, you can keep it and wear it as a choker or just a necklace."

He was giving it to her? "Why?" she asked, her abdomen doing a funny flip-flop.

"To remember me. You're probably the best friend I've had in a long time, and you've made this last op more fun than it should be." The smile had long since disappeared, leaving his solemn look in its place.

She swallowed and partially shook her head. "This isn't your last op." From the beginning, she'd had the feeling he was barreling toward a rough ending, and everything in her wanted to save him. For a smart girl, she sure had some dumb ideas sometimes, but that was life.

"We'll see."

"It's beautiful," she breathed, taking in the white gold, charmed although she didn't want to be. "But way too expensive."

He shrugged and settled it around her neck, expertly

fastening the chain in the back, his fingers warm on her skin. "I thought the design was pretty and you'd like it. Plus, it works for this op."

The jewelry was light but present, encircling her neck with a feeling she couldn't quite identify. To cover her confusion, she peered in the sack, needing to regain some control. "No cuffs this time."

"Agreed. You need your arms free in case we have to fight our way out. The collar shows enough ownership that no dom will bother you." He tossed the bag back into the car and gently shut the door, his gaze warm on the necklace. "The wolf really does suit you."

Ownership? "Whoa. Wait a sec."

One of his dark eyebrows rose. "It's fine if you can't go undercover, but it's all or nothing here. You're in or out."

For the first time, doubt ticked through her determination. She had friends who lived the lifestyle, and she understood why it worked for them, but it wasn't her thing. Instead of letting doubt take over, she lifted her chin. "I've been undercover before, and I can do this." Sure, last time she went under was as a swim coach to bust a circle of boosting athletes, but still. How hard could this be?

He lowered his head, settling his black mask over the top part of his face. "If we go in that house, I won't let either one of us blow the op. You need to understand that."

She set her sparkly pink mask in place, making sure she could see. "I'll play my part, Wolfe." What that entailed, she wasn't sure. As he took her hand, his warm and callused, the first shiver wandered down her back.

Wolfe couldn't get rid of the itch at the base of his neck as he led Dana into the stark white great room, where a woman wearing pasties and nothing else handed him a menu listing locations and activities. He glanced down to read. "Fire play after midnight, huh?" Keeping his gaze impassive, he glanced back at Dana. "Maybe we should try that."

To her credit, she kept herself from rolling her eyes. Her pink lips twitched in almost a smile, and it hit him that she wasn't remotely afraid of him or this op. Smart girl when it came to him, not so smart when it came to the fact that somebody had tried to kill her the other night. That fact didn't seem to be registering with her. At the thought, something must've settled on his face, because she lost the amusement and the sub at the door took two steps back. Good.

He kept his jaw hard and then turned to survey the environment.

Like at the last party, the main floor had been cleared to provide a place to dance, and several couples were gyrating to a hard, rhythmic song, one couple pretty much going at it against the far wall. His ears heated as if someone had a scope on him.

A sharp slap echoed from a room upstairs and then a cry. Maybe of passion or maybe not.

Dana jumped, and her hand tightened in his.

They definitely shouldn't look in on the fire play later. Her hand trembled slightly, and Wolfe paused to see if she wanted to leave, but movement toward the back door caught his eye. A couple he'd never seen was snuggled up on a duvet in the corner, but the guy seemed to be scoping the place behind a plain green mask. The tat peeking out beneath his collar was of some sort of crest. Interesting.

Wolfe made a mental note to find out more about the guy and then looked through a sweeping archway to a darkened kitchen with low blue mood lighting, "Let's check out the bar." He needed her calmer than she was to get through this, but they both had to keep their faculties.

The mask over his eyes was bugging him, but in case there were cameras, he needed to keep it on. Mask or not, anybody he'd met before would recognize him because of his size, but he didn't want to be recorded.

She tottered on her high heels but quickly regained her balance as they wound through the crowd to the bar. He clocked an exit to the north that led to a backyard and a side door to the east that no doubt went to the garage. The counters had been wiped clean to leave room for bottles and glasses, so no knife block. Experience told him knives would be in one of the drawers near the sterling-silver high-end range with dual oven doors. The thing probably cost more than he made in a year. He ordered two beers from the buxom bartender. "I'll open them," he said.

She reached down and then plunked two bottles on the counter. "Glasses?"

"No." He reached for the bottles and twisted off the tops.

Dana edged closer, leaning up to whisper, "I don't like beer."

"I know. Don't drink," he replied, handing one of the bottles to her. The itch at the base of his neck was getting more irritating, and they had to be ready to run or fight.

"Wolfe." It wasn't a surprise when Trentington angled his way, recognizing him even while wearing a mask.

"Nice place you've got here." Wolfe settled his hand at Dana's nape.

Trentington, wearing a furry mask that made him look like a tiger, ordered a Scotch. "Thanks. It's nice to see you with such an intriguing lady. I love the pink mask."

Wolfe leaned against the side wall, hopefully looking

casual. "I'd hate to risk her safety, considering somebody was shot at the last party. What do we know?"

"Not much. Whoever shot him went out the window, scaled down a drain, and then disappeared." Trentington accepted his drink, his gaze scouting the party.

"Why would anybody want that guy dead?" Dana asked. Wolfe tightened his hold on her nape.

Trentington took a big gulp. "Albert Nelson had some shady dealings, I'm afraid. I knew he'd broken the law a few times in the past, but when we conducted a background check for membership, he came up clean." He smiled at Dana. "I can assure you we have plenty of security in place, and that whoever wanted Albert Nelson dead was after him specifically."

Ah. That explained the guy on the sofa. "The police are here, aren't they?" Wolfe muttered. No wonder they were having a second party so soon after the murder. "What time is the roundup?" There was one good way to question everyone in a private organization and that was to get them all together in the same place.

"I've been promised no roundup." Trentington switched easily into telling the truth, didn't he? "They're cataloging people, license plates, and planning to make contact next week."

Wolfe sighed. "You handed over the membership documents."

"They had a subpoena, Wolfe." Trentington took a big sip.

"So the police will make contact next week, threaten to go public, and get folks to cooperate." Wolfe would need to make sure Brigid had his cover ID all up to snuff. His name was Zeke Warrington, but Wolfe was his nickname from his hunting days. Or something like that.

"Most folks aren't ashamed of their BDSM lifestyle,"

Trentington murmured. "We're practically mainstream these days." He nodded at a stunning redhead in pasties walking his way. "Though you might want to take full advantage of tonight's party because we may have to take a break until they solve Nelson's murder."

Wolfe set the bottle back on the counter. "Good advice. For now, do you have a lounge or somewhere where subs have lockers?" It was standard practice.

Trentington nodded. "Yes. The guest suite on the other side of the living room has been set up with lockers and a quiet place for subs."

"Good." Wolfe rubbed Dana's neck. "Go lose the high heels, sweetheart. I want you barefoot tonight." So she could run if necessary.

She paused. "Wh—"

He tightened his hold.

Irritation flared in her eyes, but she held her tongue. It was all he could do not to grin. "Now." He removed the beer from her hand.

She nodded and turned to go through the crowd.

Trentington chuckled. "You'll have a tough time taming that one."

Wolfe watched the sway of her curvy ass. "It's a good thing I don't want her tamed, then."

Chapter Fourteen

Dana chose a locker in the gold-gilded bathroom, angling her head to see if the toilet was gold, too. Nope. Regular porcelain. She left her shoes and exited the bathroom, nearly running into a voluptuous brunette struggling with a corset in the ostentatious guest room, complete with mirrors on the ceiling. "Help," the woman said, partially turning, her mask a sparkling aqua.

"No problem." Dana swiftly tightened the drawstring at the back. "You were tangled."

"Got a little busy playing in the upstairs office," the woman said, turning. "Next I'm hitting the dungeon downstairs. Lilia said there's a couple of crosses down there. I'm Julie."

Dana shook her hand. "Dana." She studied the woman's sparkling blue eyes as the hard rock thumped through the closed door. "You look familiar, even wearing that stunning mask."

"I'm an aide with Senator Locombe. We've been in the news a lot lately with the new farm bill." Julie brushed her hair away from her face. "Man, I needed a relaxing time tonight."

Dana nodded. "Yeah, me too. Sometimes the pressures of work take over, and it's good to just let go for a bit."

"Amen, sister. It's the one place I can just be me without having to make a decision." She leaned toward Dana. "I saw you with Wolfe. I've been trying to catch that guy's eye for a month. He is such a hottie. I bet he knows how to spank a girl properly."

Dana choked and then quickly regained control. "Yeah, he's gifted." If Wolfe tried with her, she'd break his hand. But she did understand the desire to let go and just relax with somebody else making decisions. "I initially came to hang out with Albert Nelson because my friend knew him, but . . ."

Julie's eyes widened. "I know. I wasn't here last time, but I heard all about him being shot and falling right to the ground. Do you know anything about it?"

Dana shook her head and leaned in. "Not really. You?"

Julie looked around and then back, her voice lowering. "Just the usual rumors that if you wanted drugs, he was the go-to guy, or if you wanted connections, he was the guy to ask."

"Connections?" Dana murmured.

Julie nodded. "Yeah. Like if you somehow ended up with jewelry or a painting or whatever that you needed to get off your hands, then Albert Nelson was the guy to call to find the right people who could get it done." Her voice dropped lower. "I only know that because I was playing with Ralph, the big blond guy, and he got really drunk one night and talked a lot about getting rid of an ex-girlfriend's designer purses without her knowing."

Ralph. Wasn't that name in Candy's notes? Dana perked up. "Is Ralph here tonight?"

"Haven't seen him, but I've been up playing." Julie straightened.

In the office. Were there records in there? Dana

moved toward the door. "Hey. Does Trentington know about Albert?"

Julie pursed her lips. "I doubt it—especially the drug part. Trentington has a no-drugs policy."

Anybody could've killed Albert Nelson, apparently. She opened the door, her breath catching at the sight of Wolfe leaning against the fireplace, waiting for her. With the dark mask covering his eyes, he looked like a roadside bandit determined to kidnap some helpless female.

Dana's body tightened, awakening, and she padded on her bare feet across the smooth marble to reach him. Without her shoes, she felt even more vulnerable. "Happy now?"

"Watch your tone, sub," he said gently, grasping her chin.

Her heart dropped to her stomach. His fingers were warm and firm, and for the briefest of seconds, she forgot she had a part to play. Before she could think of an answer, he turned her toward the staircase and released her chin. "Let's check out the playrooms upstairs," he murmured.

She was suddenly thankful she'd tossed the high heels since her legs felt wobbly. "I heard there's an office up-stairs to play in."

"Ah. One of my favorite fantasies," he said smoothly, leading the way up a grand staircase. "Over the desk in an office."

The image of Wolfe bending her over a desk flashed into her mind, and her breath quickened. The staircase curved to the left at the top, with bedrooms spaced down a long hallway leading to a wide window with a reading alcove beneath it.

She swallowed and peered in the first room, which had been set up with a bed big enough to be two kings pushed together. Several people were in the middle engaged in var-ious forms of sex. She blinked and took a step back, her eyes widening. Another step, and she collided with Wolfe.

He gently turned her. "Need to check out the rest of the rooms," he said.

She blanched. Too much flesh. Way too much nakedness. "Does that turn you on?" she whispered.

"Sex with a bunch of people at the same time? Hell, no. Not my thing. I don't judge it, but I'm more of a one-on-one type of guy." He kept her to the side and poked his head into the next room, quickly withdrawing. "Nope." Before she could look, he tugged her farther down the wide hallway.

The next room was western themed with saddles, whips, and even hay spread around the floor. A couple was having a good time over a bench, the man working hard.

Wolfe grabbed her hand and drew her farther down the hallway. Her adrenaline surged as she took in a vacant room with a desk, complete with a laptop. She stepped inside and instantly began opening drawers, which were all empty. "Shoot. This is just a prop room."

Wolfe looked at his watch. "Beyond the living room downstairs on the main level is a cordoned-off area. That has to be his actual office."

Loud voices caught her attention, and three couples stumbled into the room. The first woman, a dark-skinned beauty in a silk negligée, smiled up at Wolfe. "Hi. We were going to play corporate tycoon. Would you like to join in?"

Wolfe reached for Dana's wrist. "Thanks, but we thought we'd check out the dungeon downstairs."

Her companion leaned in, his brown eyes dilated. "Unless you're into knife play, stay away from the room at the far end of the dungeon." He shook his head.

"Good tip." Wolfe drew Dana out of the room and headed swiftly back the way they'd come.

"Knife play?" Dana asked, wincing. "Do people really cut each other?"

Wolfe shrugged. "I guess. To each his own, but I've seen enough knife fights in my life."

The cold marble chilled Dana's feet, but she followed Wolfe down the stairs and over to the cordoned-off area. He pressed her against the wall, his hands at her waist, his body warming hers. "What are you doing?" Her entire body heated.

He dropped his mouth to her bare shoulder. "Look around and tell me when nobody is watching us." His breath brushed her skin, and she shivered.

Concentrate, damn it. Nobody seemed to be paying attention to them, most people watching two women dance together, removing clothing as they did so. "Um, now would probably be a good time." Her voice came out garbled.

"Okay." Swift as a thought, he ducked beneath the rope, grabbed her hand, and tugged her through to another hallway. "My guess is the master bedroom is the far door, and this first one is an office." Wolfe twisted the knob, shoved open the door, and yanked her inside.

It had all happened so quickly.

He flicked a light switch to reveal a gentleman's study, complete with cherrywood desk, cigar area, and trophies on a shelf.

She headed for the trophies. "Bowling championships?" Not in a million years would she have considered Trentington a bowler. "Interesting."

Wolfe moved to the desk, pulling out drawers. The thump of the music from the living room rattled a snow globe on the desk. "Check out the file drawers in the credenza."

She pulled off her mask, dropping down to tug open drawers. The first two opened easily, and she looked through them, only finding Trentington's business records.

The third drawer was locked. "Bingo." She ducked down more and inspected the lock, biting her lip.

Wolfe reached her in a second, crouching with a bent paperclip. "Let me." Quick movements had the drawer opening.

Dana breathed, reaching for the neatly labeled manila files. "Here's yours."

"Here's Albert's, also known as Burt or Clarke." Wolfe drew it out and opened it, angling his watch toward the pages and pressing the side of it.

Dana leaned in to see better. "Is that a camera?"

"Yep. Agent Frost got it for me. She's got a talent with gadgets. Works with us sometimes when HDD lets her." He flipped pages, quickly taking pictures.

Dana brushed through the files, not feeling jealous of the woman with the cool name who Wolfe thought was talented. Nope. Not at all. "I don't see a membership list here." Shoot. They needed that.

"Figures." He was quick and efficient with the watch, and soon they had everything.

She replaced all the files and stood, quietly shutting the drawer.

He drew off his mask. "Okay. Let's get out—"

The door started to open.

Strong hands grabbed her hips, and Wolfe lifted her, pivoted, and planted her butt on the desk. He grasped her neck, pressed his hips between her thighs and moved in. Wild and commanding, he kissed her, going deep and sure. Desire blasted her, and she grabbed his shirt for balance, kissing him back and closing her eyes.

He took her over, plain and simple. Electricity arced between her nerves, sending her senses spiraling. There was only Wolfe and his mouth on her, his hands on her. All of him over her.

A throat cleared.

Wolfe pulled away, his hands remaining tight on her hips, and looked over his shoulder. "We're busy."

Dana couldn't breathe. Her body felt pliable and needy. The desk was cool beneath her nearly bare butt, and her thighs were warm on either side of his legs. She blew out air, trying to calm her rioting heart, embarrassed by her very vulnerable position.

"This isn't a playroom," Trentington said, his voice hard.

Wolfe tugged her up and partially turned, finally releasing her. "Sorry. Office fantasy, and the one upstairs was occupied."

Trentington looked around the room. "The rope should've been your first clue." Suspicion darkened his eyes.

"Sorry," Wolfe repeated, reaching to help Dana off the desk and pulling her mask back down to shield her features.

She wobbled for a moment and then took his hand, trying to slow her breathing so her breasts didn't just pop over the top of the corset. So much for their one night of sex taking the edge off this unreal desire for him.

"It's midnight and time for a toast." Trentington moved back. "Get out of my office."

"Sure thing," Wolfe said cheerfully, leading Dana out and ducking them beneath the rope, his mask back in place. They reached the living area, where the music had softened to light jazz. The room was packed, with people spilling into the kitchen area and up the stairway.

A woman in pasties handed them champagne glasses before handing one to Trentington, who emerged next to Wolfe.

Another woman, also in pasties, followed and poured champagne into their glasses before moving through the crowd. Trentington lifted his glass. "To all of our friends. May our nights be filled with fun, pleasure, and consensual kinkiness. To Captive."

"To Captive," the crowd said, turning and clinking glasses.

Wolfe clinked her glass and then Trentington did the same. Dana took a drink. Whoa. Delicious and definitely the good stuff. She took another drink as Wolfe did the same, sipping and looking around the gathering for any sort of clue for who'd shot Albert Nelson. Another woman in bright pink pasties collected glasses on a tray that looked like a shield.

Then the crowd started to chant Trentington's name.

He rolled his eyes, grinned, and headed for a grand piano in the far corner. "It's good luck to dance to our song," he tossed over his shoulder, his eyes still unpleased.

"Then we'll dance." Wolfe grasped her hip and swung her around. He leaned down, his mouth near her ear. "Dance with me, and I'll maneuver us toward the doorway."

She nodded and leaned into him, reminding herself this was a job. Her body didn't care. Her bare thighs brushed his, and her nearly bare chest rubbed against his rock hard one. Maybe they should try to burn the edge off the attraction with just one more night. Why not? She closed her eyes and gave in to the feeling, trusting him to get them across the room.

The bodies were packed close together as Trentington started to play and sing with a surprisingly good baritone. The song was a melody with heart and humor, and she let it take her away for a brief time.

That song turned into a wilder one, and then another, and they were almost at the door. It had taken nearly half an hour, but she didn't care. Life was good.

She leaned back and focused, surprised at the clarity of colors all around her. "Oh, Wolfe. It's all so beautiful."

"Yeah." His knuckles rubbed across her cheekbone. "You're beautiful. You glow."

The words touched her as deeply as his gentle movements. In the back of her mind, way back, an alarm clanged. But the splendor of the newest song dug deep inside her, making her one with music and with Wolfe and with the world at large.

Life was perfect. She wanted him again. Now.

He took her hand. "Let's get out of here. Life is beautiful."

Yeah, it was. The warning alarm disappeared, chased away by a feeling of perfection. "I want you," she whispered, needing him, almost frantic but not understanding why.

"You've got me." He led the way through the door into the stunningly magical darkness of the night.

Chapter Fifteen

A pounding on the door awoke Wolfe, and he sat up in bed, his head spinning. "Shut the hell up," he slurred, looking frantically around. Where was he? Where was his gun? He shook his head just as the door burst open, and Malcolm West flew through, his hands up and ready to fight.

He stopped cold, looked at Wolfe, and then glanced to the side. "Oh, shit. Sorry."

Kat tiptoed in behind him, rubbing against his ankles.

Huh? Wolfe frowned and then glanced sideways to see Dana sleepily sitting up on the bed. The covers dropped to reveal bare breasts, and she yelped, tugging up the comforter. Light bruises were visible on her biceps.

Confusion clouded her eyes and her hair was wild around her face. She'd left pink streaks on the pillow, but plenty remained in her hair. "Wh-what happened?"

A pit opened up in his gut. His jaw felt like he'd been punched several times, and the room kept spinning. He pressed his fingers against his eyes, trying to catch a thought. He was in his bed, with a naked Dana, and his body hurt. He glanced down at scratches on his arm. "What the fuck?"

Mal cleared his throat. "Sorry. You guys must've tied

one on. I saw the weird car in the driveway, checked it out, and noticed it had been hot-wired."

Wolfe coughed, his lungs protesting. "What car? A BMW?"

"No. Old Chevy," Mal said, frowning. "What's going on?"

Wolfe stretched his legs beneath the sheet, not surprised to find himself buck naked. The room smelled like sex. "We need a minute, Mal."

"Sure." Mal turned to go, plucking up the kitten. "We'll be in the living room." The door closed softly behind him, hanging haphazardly.

Wolfe wanted to puke. He sucked deep for fresh air and partially turned. "What do you remember?"

She swallowed, too pale for his liking. "Um, not much? We were at the party, found the files, and started dancing?"

Images, more like snapshots, filtered through his mind, but it was like trying to catch mist. Images of Dana over him, under him, all over him. The scent of her, her laughing, her smiling.

Her green eyes were huge and bewildered in her pale face. "I don't understand."

He had to ask. "Did we . . . I mean?"

She bit her lip and nodded. "Yeah. Definitely."

That's what he'd thought. He reached for the phone on his nightstand and speed-dialed Force.

"Force," Angus answered.

Wolfe cleared his throat. "Can you get a drug test done unofficially? I don't want it in our medical records, but I need to know what Dana and I were drugged with last night." It had to have been in the champagne, damn it.

Dana gasped.

Silence came over the line. "You were drugged?" Force finally asked.

"Had to be. Can only remember snapshots of what happened and have no idea how we got home. Except I apparently hot-wired a car and somehow drove." Now that his head was clearing, fury and guilt started to build, making his ribs feel like they were about to burst wide open.

"Yeah. I can make it happen. I'll be there in half an hour," Force said, disengaging the call.

Wolfe set the phone gently down to keep from ripping it completely apart. "I'm sorry."

Her knuckles were white on the sheet as she held it against her breasts. "You think we were drugged."

He nodded. "Yeah." This was his fault. "You have bruises on your arms, probably from me. Where else are you bruised?" His voice emerged garbled and gritty as he wrestled with the rage beginning to consume him. The idea that he'd hurt her tore him in two.

Dana pushed her hair away from her face, leaning back to stare at his shoulders. "Um, it looks like I scratched you. A lot."

His stomach lurched. "You were probably fighting back." God. Had she been willing?

She frowned. "Um, I don't think so. I do remember willingly taking your pants off." She gently reached out to touch his arm.

He flinched. How could she even sit next to him? "I'm so sorry," he repeated.

"No." She tightened her hold. "Listen. We were both drugged, it seems. Even drugged, I don't think you'd do anything to harm me." She sighed. "Wolfe. I remember feeling euphoric and in love with the entire universe. I wanted another night with you. You were the same."

Yeah, he did remember the sky sparkling at him. He shifted his legs, and pain flared along his thigh. Gingerly angling to the side, he lifted the covers and looked down. "Oh."

"What?" She didn't try to look.

"Nothing." He settled back down, trying to keep his hands from closing into fists.

"Wolfe," she said, turning more fully toward him.

He scratched his chin. "You, ah, bit my thigh." He might wear the mark forever, since she'd broken the skin. Images flowed through him of her taking him in her mouth, humming happily, fully engaged.

"Oh." She blushed. "Yeah. I kind of remember that. Sort of." She cleared her throat. "I'm sure I was willing."

His head snapped back. "We were drugged. Neither of us were willing, and I promise you I'll rip the fucking heads off of whoever did this."

For the first time that morning, she looked scared instead of confused.

He immediately dialed it back. "It's okay, Dana. I'll make it okay." He had no clue how he would do that.

She inched from the bed, taking the sheet with her and standing. "I, ah, am going to take a shower."

"Wait." He held up a hand. "In case you want to, um, have a kit done."

She blinked. "Why would I do that?"

"Because you weren't in any state to consent. You should have evidence in case you want to file suit against me." Of course, he'd just confess if she wanted.

Her brows drew down. "You need to knock it off."

What the heck? "Huh?"

"We were both drugged, both participated, and that's the end of it." She looked small and vulnerable with the sheet wrapped around her body. "If you're not filing suit, neither am I." She sighed. "Truth be told, I would've not only consented but probably initiated something tonight, even if we hadn't been drugged."

"That doesn't matter. Somebody drugged us, and that's criminal," he reminded her, feeling it to his gut.

"I know." She turned for the bathroom, pausing at the doorway, not facing him. "Unlike the other night, I don't see any evidence of condoms. Um, I'm clean. Had a checkup last month and haven't been with anybody for eons."

"Ditto," he responded. "Totally clean." Another thought occurred to him, and his chest pounded. "Are you, well, on . . ."

"No. My mom beat breast cancer in her early forties, and the doctors have advised me to stay away from hormones just in case. I'm not on the pill or any other form of birth control." She moved into the bathroom and shut the door.

Dana sat at Wolfe's kitchen table, thumbing through Candy's notebook, once again. "Maybe 'dialysis' means some sort of corporate espionage? Theft?" The symbols and weird words kept blurring in front of her eyes, and the over-the-counter painkiller wasn't working on her headache. She'd slept with Wolfe the night before and could only remember bits and pieces.

Worse yet, he was like a thundercloud—full of anger and barely contained violence, pacing back and forth in the living room. He'd showered as well and dressed in his usual jeans and faded T-shirt, his wet hair a little spiky.

Even though she trusted him, she was still feeling vulnerable after being drugged. She remembered making the move with Wolfe, and images of her participating with him, but everything was so fuzzy. Whoever had drugged them would pay, for sure.

The back slider opened, and Malcolm delivered a couple of sandwiches. "Pippa made extra for lunch." His sharp gaze took them both in. "How are you two doing?"

"Fucking great," Wolfe growled, peering out the front window.

"Dana?" Malcolm asked, setting the plate down.

The smell of fresh turkey wafted closer. "I'm fine," she said, lying only a little.

"Good. What can I do?" Mal asked.

Wolfe stopped moving. "Would you mind scrubbing down the Chevy and getting rid of it? Leave it somewhere it'll be found, but stay away from cameras."

Mal's expression smoothed out. "Love to. I'll take care of it." He was gone within a second, making a quick exit.

The kitten jumped onto Dana's lap and snuggled in with a soft purr.

"Finally." Wolfe let the curtains drop and yanked the door open.

Roscoe was the first through the door, making a beeline for Dana to scratch his ears. She leaned over and petted the pooch, wanting all of a sudden to bury her face in his fur. She cleared her throat.

Angus followed, along with the British guy and then a gnarled bald man, around sixty years old, wearing a white lab coat and holding an old-fashioned doctor's bag.

"Ah, shit," Wolfe muttered, slamming the door. "You brought Doctor Crazy?"

"You said to keep it quiet," Angus replied, moving toward Dana and halting a few feet away. "Are you all right?" Concern glowed in his deep green eyes.

She forced a smile, trying not to freak out any more

than necessary. Nope. "I'm fine. Wolfe is blaming himself, and he needs to stop it right now."

Angus sighed. "This is Dr. Georgetown, and he often does work off the books for us."

The doctor gave a half bow. "Happy to be of service." He shoved wire spectacles up his nose. "Angus filled me in on the way here, even though the British chap drives like a bat out of, well, heck."

Jethro eyed the sandwiches. "It's not my fault Force can't find his truck and you all needed a ride."

Angus flushed. "My truck is in the shop."

"Uh-huh," Jethro returned.

"You can have my sandwich—I'm not hungry," Dana said, nudging the plate toward him.

Jethro dropped into the adjacent seat. "Perhaps we could split it." He neatly tore it in two and leaned to the side. "What were your symptoms?"

"Euphoria, arousal, and then missing memory," Dana said, accepting the other half.

"Hmmm." Dr. Georgetown set his bag down on the table. "We'll do a blood test and not worry about urine since there should still be time to get everything we need from your blood. I'm dating the medical director of Lambert Hospital, and he's a board-certified pathologist. I'm sure he'll do us this favor since you were both dosed." He drew out a syringe and several vials. "Any other symptoms?"

Wolfe leaned against the fridge in an obvious attempt to appear casual. "Nausea and an aching jaw."

The doctor pushed his spectacles back up his nose. "Aching jaw? Interesting. With the euphoria, I was guessing GHB, but with the jaw aching, it'd be MDMA."

Dana held out her arm after making sure the syringe had been in its original wrapper. "I don't know what those are."

"Liquid X and Ecstasy," the doctor said, smoothly withdrawing blood after using a rubber tourniquet. "I'll have Donald check for those as well as a few other drugs that could've been slipped in your drinks."

Had they finished their drinks? Dana couldn't remember exactly, but she didn't think so. "Long-term effects?"

"You're coherent, and this was a one-time thing, so I'm not concerned about long-term. However, you should consider making a police report."

"We'll handle it," Wolfe said.

Dana winced as the doctor settled a Band-Aid over her vein. Handle it? What in the world did that mean? She stared at Wolfe, but he wouldn't look at her. The doctor finished with her and turned to Wolfe. "Was there, ah, sexual activity?" he asked.

"Why?" Wolfe growled.

"Because MDMA would possibly make you tired or lethargic, so I'd rule it out except for the jaw tightness. GBD can cause sexual arousal, which would make sense if you so engaged." The doctor drew the tourniquet around Wolfe's arm. "Also, as your doctor, I'd have to recommend STD testing."

"We're both clean," Wolfe said, his words clipped and his jaw rock hard.

Dana remained quiet.

The doctor turned to her. "I can get you a morning-after pill, if you'd like."

She blinked. "No. Thanks, though."

Wolfe just watched her, no expression on his face.

Dana turned back to the pages in front of her, wanting to make the men in the room disappear. She turned the page and found more hieroglyphics.

Jethro sat up. "What's all this?"

"My friend, who's missing, used a code when she worked on sensitive articles," Dana murmured. "I can't decipher it."

Jethro rubbed his whiskered chin, leaning over to look. "Fascinating."

Dana lifted her head. "Are you any good with codes?"

He frowned and pulled the notebook closer. "Not really. I'm more of a philosophical interpreter of data, if you know what I mean."

She didn't, but with his British accent, it sounded intriguing.

Angus drew out a vacant chair and sat. "I know a code breaker. Well, she's a lot more than a code breaker, but she consulted with us on a couple of cases when I worked for the FBI Behavioral Analysis Unit. I could give her a call, if you like. What's this about?"

Dana pressed her lips together. Thank goodness they were talking about work again and not drugs or sex. "This is about my friend Candy Folks."

"The journalist who disappeared?" Angus asked, looking toward Wolfe. "This is the case you've been handling on your own?"

"It's my story," Dana said before Wolfe could answer.

Angus leaned over and scratched Roscoe between the ears. "What's *your* case about, Wolfe? I'm done with being left out of it."

Dana's eyebrows rose, and she turned toward Wolfe. Would he let the unit help him find Rock at this point?

Wolfe looked at her, then at the doctor, and then at Angus. "Considering how things have changed, I'll think about it. First, we have a visit to make."

"Visit?" Dana sat up.

"Yeah. You with me, Force?" Wolfe asked.

Angus studied him and then slowly nodded. "If that's how you want to go about it, I'm with you."

Dana's breath caught. "What things have changed?"

Wolfe's gaze held a look she couldn't decipher. "Everything has changed. We'll discuss it later."

Chapter Sixteen

Moonlight beamed down, highlighting the homes of the rich and super rich, although clouds were starting to gather and reduce its power. A sense of tension filled the air as the storm drew near.

Wolfe leaned against the side of a tree adjacent to Trentington's mansion, his gun tucked safely at his waist and his knife at his boot, waiting for the British man to disengage the alarm. "You sure you trust this guy?"

Force nodded. "Yeah. He won't be as quick as Brigid, but he'll get the job done."

Jethro whistled from the darkness.

"Alarm deactivated," Force said. "This is your op."

Yeah, it definitely was his op. Wolfe circled the tree and strode down the imported stone driveway to the front door, picking the lock and then twisting the knob. It opened easily, and the night remained silent. Okay. The British dude did know his alarm systems. The guy jogged around the area by the garage, his movements economical.

"Thanks, professor," Force drawled.

Jethro crouched by a hydrangea bush. "Last time, Force. I left this life behind me."

Wolfe slipped inside the entryway and let his eyes

adjust to the darkness. Moonlight streamed in through gauzy curtains, caressing a white leather sofa with matching chairs near the fireplace. The room smelled like a fresh breeze off the ocean. The cleaning crew had done a good job.

He motioned for Force to take the upstairs and Jethro to head downstairs. Then he silently strode down the hallway, past the office, and right through the double doors to what had to be the master bedroom.

Trentington slept on his stomach, one arm flung out, next to a lush blonde.

Wolfe crept toward him, taking out his gun and pressing the barrel to Trentington's forehead. He'd rather use a knife, but he had to get the man out of there without awakening the woman. He pressed harder.

Trentington jumped, and his eyes opened. Wide.

Wolfe gestured for him to get out of the bed, and he did so, barely moving the comforter. Maybe the man cared about the woman next to him. They walked out of the room, and Wolfe shut the door. "Office," he whispered.

Trentington, dressed only in gray boxer briefs with a hole in the left butt cheek, walked silently into his office and waited until Wolfe had shut the door. "Your membership is hereby revoked, jackass." He moved to one of the chairs in the cigar area near another stone fireplace.

Wolfe tucked his gun back into place and reached down for his knife. "You might want to lose the attitude. I'm pretty pissed right now."

"I can see that." While Trentington's arms and hairy chest were muscled, his gut had started going to fat. "Problem?"

"Yeah. My champagne was spiked last night, as was the drink of my guest. You have three seconds to tell me how that happened before I start cutting pieces off you." Wolfe twirled the knife and made sure it caught the light.

"Drugged?" Trentington's eyebrows rose. "You're kidding."

"Do I look like I'm kidding?" Every instinct in Wolfe yelled that the guy was lying. "I'm gonna have to hurt you, aren't I?"

The door opened, and Force entered, followed by Jethro.

"I don't need witnesses for this," Wolfe muttered. He lowered his chin, letting his anger finally take over. "You made sure we toasted with you, and you made sure we had champagne." His memory was too fuzzy to remember the face of the woman who'd poured his glass. He'd been off balance from kissing Dana right before that, and he hadn't paid attention. "You knew we'd be dosed."

"That's ridiculous. I had no idea," Trentington said, his eyes spitting.

Wolfe looked over his shoulder at Force. "I think he's lying."

Force nodded. "Yeah, that's my take. How about you, J?"

Jethro leaned back against the door. "I might have a degree or two in micro-expressions, and he's definitely lying to you. He's also scared and doing a marvelous job of hiding it."

Yeah, Wolfe had already clocked that. "Maybe I should ask the blonde if she poured the booze for me."

Trentington's eyes widened and then relaxed. "You may be good with a knife, but even I can read that you wouldn't harm an innocent woman."

"If she dosed my drink, she ain't innocent," Wolfe returned, his grip steady on the knife. "You're right, though. I want to hurt somebody bad right now, and I'll sleep better if it's you and not her."

"Me too," Trentington said.

"Okay." Wolfe moved for him.

Trentington lifted a hand. "Wait." He sighed. "Fine. An associate, not a close friend, asked me to make sure you and your date were there to share in the toast. I figured he wanted a look at you, not that you'd be drugged. I truly had no idea about the drugs."

"Name?" Wolfe asked, not backing away.

"I can't tell you." Trentington leaned back in the chair, away from the knife.

"Did he mention me or my date or both?" Wolfe had to know who the target was, damn it.

"Both." Trentington jumped up.

Wolfe swatted him back down with one hand at the neck. He squeezed. "There were bruises on my date this morning, and I'd like to return the favor to you." He squeezed harder.

Trentington's eyes bugged out, and his face turned red. He clawed at Wolfe's hold.

Jethro cleared his throat. "He can't talk if you kill him, mate."

Wolfe lightened his grip a fraction. "Name," he bit out.

"Frank Spanek," Trentington gasped out, his eyes filling with tears. "He's been a member of Captive for years."

"Was he friends with Albert Nelson?" Wolfe snarled.

Trentington coughed. "Um, I think so. In fact, I believe Spanek sponsored Nelson a decade or so ago. I'd forgotten all about it," he rushed to add.

Wolfe released him. That was almost too easy, and he hadn't gotten to hit the idiot. "Do you know Candy Folks?"

Trentington frowned. "The journalist who has gone missing? Why would I know her?"

"Do you know her or not?" Wolfe twirled the knife again.

"No. Never met her."

He still couldn't figure out if they'd been drugged because of Dana's story or his hunt for Rock. The anger inside Wolfe hadn't abated. Even if Gary Rockcliff had started playing games and drugged him, there was no way he'd revealed himself to Trentington, so asking the question with Force standing behind him would be a useless move. "Who was the woman who poured my drink last night?" He still couldn't get a bead on her face. Why would Spanek and the woman want him drugged? Or was it Dana they'd wanted?

"I don't know. She was Spanek's guest, but she had a mask on." Trentington glared. "Now get out."

"Oh, I will, after you print me out a list of your members. The real list with phone numbers and addresses. Then I want a list of anyone who attended or worked the party last night." Wolfe leaned in, letting his fury show. Thunder bellowed outside in tune with his mood. "Please say no."

Dana tried another algorithm on Candy's notes. This one she'd found on the Internet, and it had been somewhat helpful. So far, she'd partially deciphered a list of female CEOs who also ran nonprofits and were key to Candy's story. The first was Margaret Jones, who ran a makeup empire and donated to cancer causes. She was out of the country for the next three months. The second woman was Phyllis Donald, who was a real estate mogul who donated to causes that benefited the elderly, and she was busy for the next two weeks. The final lead was to Theresa Rhodes, who was the CEO of a sporting goods company that spent tons of money on female start-ups. Dana called to set up an appointment with her and discovered the woman was out of town on sabbatical for the rest of the month.

Apparently the rich and very rich didn't spend much time in the office. There was probably a lesson to be learned there.

She sat on Wolfe's sofa with the kitten next to her and the dog at her feet. Roscoe chased something in dreamland, kicking and snorting every once in a while and completely ignoring the summer storm going on outside.

Rain slashed against the windows, and thunder rolled high and loud.

She couldn't sleep, and she didn't want to go back to Wolfe's bed. Everything had just gotten too weird. She glanced at her phone and almost picked it up, but it was after midnight, and her mom would be asleep. Plus, what would she say? That she'd gone to a BDSM sex party with a friend, had gotten drugged, and then had had unprotected sex with the hot ex-soldier she'd been crushing on and had already had safe sex with?

The phone could stay in place.

Then it buzzed, and she leaned to read the face. Enough already. She clicked on the speaker. "Mike? Stop calling me." Then she ended the call and turned off the phone. He had to knock it off.

Grumbling, she stood and walked into the office to stare at the whiteboard. She took a picture of Candy out of the file folder she'd set up and placed it on the board, drawing a line to Albert Nelson. Several lines cascaded out from him to different sources. She and Wolfe might as well work together since they shared Albert as a person of interest, even though their cases went in completely different directions.

The front door opened, and she stiffened.

It closed, and heavy footsteps sounded before Wolfe stood in the doorway. "What are you doing?"

"Connecting Candy to Albert," she said, wanting to shuffle her feet. "What did you find out?"

"Guy named Frank Spanek had us drugged."

She frowned, running the name around in her head. "Never heard of him. Why did he drug us?"

Wolfe lifted one powerful shoulder. "That's the question I'm going to ask him the second I find him. I already called Brigid and asked her to do a deep dive, even though she's kind of on vacation." Something buzzed, and he drew his phone out of his back pocket. "The doc has answers and wants to know if we're awake."

Ha. Like she could sleep. "Call him."

Wolfe pressed a button and then set the phone on the desk.

"Howdy. Figured you wouldn't be sleeping," the doctor said, his tone cheerful.

"Well?" Wolfe asked.

Papers rustled over the line. "I found a combination of MDMA, GHB, and ketamine in both of your systems," the doctor said thoughtfully.

Dana's knees weakened, and she leaned against the wall. "What is all of that?"

"Ecstasy, Liquid X, and Special K are the street names." The doctor's voice came over the line tinny.

Wait a minute. Dana's head ached, but she focused in. "Aren't a couple of those date-rape drugs?"

"Can be," the doctor affirmed.

"I thought those drugs made people calm and lethargic," she said, trying to remember what she'd read about them.

"They can, or they can have other effects such as euphoria and sexual arousal," the doctor said. "They combine differently in different people, and the two of you are lucky to be breathing."

Tension cascaded through the room, coming off the man

staring at the phone three feet away from her. "Then we can assume the purpose was to kill one or both of us?"

"Maybe. Or the purpose was to kidnap one or both of you," the doctor said. "It's hard to tell, to be honest. Neither of you can remember if you only had a few sips or if you drank your entire glass down." More papers shuffled. "Since you reacted by leaving the party, perhaps the person who drugged you didn't get a chance to grab you."

"Or they wanted us dead," Wolfe said, his voice gritty.

"That could very well be the case," the doctor agreed. "I think you should file a police report."

Wolfe shook his head, finally looking at Dana. His topaz eyes had darkened to glittering fury. "No. We need to keep this under wraps."

"That is your decision, but I want to recheck your blood in a week," the doctor said.

"Fine," Wolfe said. "Since we ingested the drugs, there are no other concerns, right?"

The doctor sighed. "Right. Well, except for the unprotected sex. I don't need to tell you—"

Wolfe cut off the call.

Dana ran her hands through her now blond hair, pulling near her scalp. "We're both clean, so stop worrying."

"That's not what I'm worrying about." Wolfe tucked the phone away.

She shook her head. "Don't borrow trouble." She wouldn't even go there in her mind.

"When will we know?"

Man, she missed the fun-loving, goofy Wolfe. This guy was too serious, too intense. "It doesn't matter," she said.

"Dana."

"Fine. In two weeks, but I'm not worried about it." She turned and strode into the living room, stopping at the sight of the sleeping dog. "Force didn't take Roscoe?"

"No. Roscoe stays with you until I find this guy." Wolfe turned off the office light and shut the door. "Things have changed. We're in this together, and Roscoe is part of that."

Lightning flashed outside and she jumped. Then she turned to face him, her head hurting more. "You're being crazy."

The muscle beneath his jaw visibly ticked. "This guy used me to hurt you, and that changes things."

Sometimes she couldn't follow his logic. "Hurt me?"

"Yeah. Having drugged sex that you can barely remember definitely hurts you." Wolfe growled the last words.

"Then somebody used me to hurt you, too," she countered, her chin lifting. "Frankly, since it was you, I'm not all that hurt. Sure, I'm mad somebody did that, and we'll make them pay. But I trust you, and none of this is your fault." He seemed so far away.

"Yeah, it is my fault, and I'm going to fix it. Until I do, if I'm not with you, then Roscoe is, and Mal will watch from his place." Wolfe's face showed no give. None. His shoulders went back. "For now, why don't you get some sleep? You can have the bedroom. I'm going to get some work done, and we can talk more tomorrow." He moved past her, went back into the office, and shut the door.

Anger roared through her, followed by exhaustion. Sleep was a good idea, but no way could she do it. Maybe Wolfe would stop being so angry in the morning. She retook her seat on the sofa and grabbed up Candy's notes. If she couldn't crack Wolfe's hard head, maybe she could crack this code.

Chapter Seventeen

Wolfe couldn't think and he couldn't breathe. He'd been in his home office for an hour, and his mind wouldn't work. Grimacing, he left the office and stopped cold.

Dana had fallen asleep on the sofa, with the dog at her feet and the kitten near her head. Her silky hair was spread out on the cushions, and even in sleep, dark circles marred the pale skin beneath her eyes. She was a tall woman, a curvy one, but lying there on his sofa, she looked fragile. Vulnerable and defenseless.

He'd been an ass to her earlier, but the anger wouldn't leave him alone. It was eating him from the inside out.

Using all his stealth, he moved into his bedroom and changed into sweats and tennis shoes without making a sound. Then he returned to the living room, gently removed the papers off her stomach, and lifted her from the sofa. With a murmur, she cuddled into his chest, remaining asleep.

Trusting him completely.

She sighed and sliced his heart in two. He carried her into the bedroom and set her in the bed, turning as the dog padded into the room.

"Watch her," Wolfe ordered, grabbing his phone and striding from the room.

The first text he sent was to Malcolm so that he would watch the house for the next couple of hours. He sent the second text because he'd promised he would.

Then he stepped into the stormy night and made sure to lock the door behind himself. A light flicked on at Mal's house, and he nodded, moving into a jog and then a full-out run. Heated rain splattered against him, quickly soaking his T-shirt. He let the water run down his face, taking the punishment and running down the forested road even faster.

Emotions coursed through him along with the pain in his ankles and knees. He took the pain and tried for more.

Images clicked through his head, moments with Dana the night before. Fury choked him, making breathing difficult, but he didn't relent.

He ran for almost two hours, along back roads, his tennis shoes splashing up mud. A couple of houses came into view and then a few businesses. The diner stood at the end of a dirt road, only two miles from the interstate and somehow only known by locals and a few truckdrivers. He slowed when its lights glowed into the wild night, walking the last several yards to the front door.

The bell clanged when he shoved it open.

Without halting, he turned and walked to the booth in the far back, his shoes squeaking on the cracked tiles and leaving a wet trail.

Nari Zhang took one look at him, slid from the side of the booth facing the door, and took the seat across from it. He claimed her vacated seat. "We'll work on putting your back to the door some other night." She crossed one leg beneath her and then dug a beach towel out of her bag. "Saw it was raining."

He took the towel and wiped down his head and face. "I don't want to practice my Mandarin tonight." The shrink had been teaching him to speak one of her languages, but he wasn't in the mood.

"I figured." She retook the towel and shoved it in the beach bag. "We haven't done this in a while."

His skin went numb after the run. "I don't like doing it." But he'd promised her if he was ever in that state, the purely angry one, he'd text her and meet here after running.

"I appreciate you keeping your promise." She sipped a cup of coffee.

The waitress sidled up, her orthopedic shoes spreading the water he'd dropped. "Wolfe? It's a weird night to run." Janice pulled an old-fashioned order pad from her faded green uniform. "You want the usual, hon?"

"No. Not hungry," he said, trying to calm his voice for the seventy-year-old.

Nari nodded. "Bring him the usual. Thanks."

"You betcha." Janice turned on one shoe and made her way back to the kitchen.

Wolfe didn't have the energy to fight with the shrink. "Fine, but you're eating some of it this time." He looked at her and guilt swamped him again. She'd dressed in a white button-down shirt and dark jeans, her black hair up on her head and no makeup on her pretty face. She was Chinese, and even without makeup, her dusky skin glowed. Her dark brown eyes were bloodshot. "You should be sleeping," he murmured.

"Sleep is a luxury," she returned, her small hands around her coffee cup. "I heard about the drugging. You must be pissed."

That's why he let her be his shrink. She got him and

didn't try to be all intellectual. "Yeah. Anger is like acid, and it's eating through me."

She blew on her coffee and then took another sip. "Any flashbacks?"

"Just to the night with Dana." He rolled his neck, feeling the muscles tighten anyway. "I'm sure I'll have more if I try to sleep." Facing the day his team had died was never easy, and a nightmare in his current mood would be a disaster.

"How about the hyper vigilance?" Nari asked.

"I'm not looking over my shoulder, but I want to lock Dana down to keep her safe." Unfortunately, Dana wasn't a woman who would be locked down.

Nari leaned back. "Deal with right here and right now and with what you can control. The rest will come."

It was good advice. "I just want to kill whoever put that drug in our drinks," he admitted.

"Sure, you do." Nari nodded, her gaze soft. "Somebody either tried to kidnap or kill both of you, and they forced you two to take a step you hadn't intended to take."

"We'd already had consensual sex, but that doesn't make this okay," he said.

Nari's eyebrows rose. "Ah. Okay. Well, you're right. The choice was taken away from you both in this instance, and you have every right in the world to be furious." Nari leaned toward him. "That's a normal and healthy reaction, Wolfe. Stop being so hard on yourself."

Janice plunked down a cup of coffee with whipped cream and sprinkles for him. "Be right back with the food."

He took the drink and sipped. "I made myself a target for someone from my past, which means I need to stay the hell away from Dana so she doesn't get caught in the firefight. But now somebody has drugged us, and I've learned she's a target too. I need to stay beside her to protect her." He was being pulled in two directions, and even his ribs hurt.

"That is a conundrum." Nari eyed his whipped cream.

He nudged his cup to her. "Why don't you just order your own?"

She grasped her spoon and took several scoops from his to put into her cup. "Thanks." She hummed happily as she licked off the spoon. "How's it going with your great plan to protect the team without getting emotionally involved?"

"Shrinks aren't supposed to be sarcastic." He looked down as Janice delivered his veggie egg-white omelet with a side of fresh fruit.

Once again, amusement lit Nari's eyes.

"Shut up," Wolfe said mildly, reaching for the hot sauce at the end of the table near the salt.

"Didn't say anything. Except it's hilarious that you're actually a health food nut—except for the latte treats." She wiped whipped cream off her top lip.

Wolfe unfolded his paper napkin. "I need to be in top shape and nutrition is part of that. Besides, everyone deserves a treat sometimes."

"That's just it, Wolfe." Nari leaned toward him. "You've made connections, you've shared your treats with the team, and you didn't want to, but you have connected. Stop pretending otherwise." She shook her head as he dug into his healthy meal. "I know you've lost a lot, starting with your sister. Even so, you can't shut yourself off for the rest of your life."

"I'm more worried about people being sad they lost me," he said thoughtfully. "Though talking to you about Karen has been good, I think." Many of their nightly talks had centered around his geeky, adorable, lost sister. In fact, one of the reasons he'd opened up to Nari so quickly was that she reminded him of Karen. He liked the shrink and considered her a friend.

"Then try not to get lost." She dug into his fruit with her fork. "You're stronger with a team behind you, so let them help with whatever you have going on. Let me help. We can beat whoever you're chasing."

He'd run some of the anger out, but he still kept an eye on the other diners, even though they were few and far between. A threat could come from anywhere. "This guy is a sociopath who will instantly take advantage of any weakness."

"Your team isn't a weakness."

She just didn't get it. Wolfe shook his head. "If they're killed to hurt me, they're a weakness." As was Dana. The idea of Rock even finding out about Dana made Wolfe lose his appetite. He pushed his plate away.

"Not if you work together. You've become a team, Wolfe. We all have."

Last time he'd had a team, they'd all died. "You and I both know that the second I let my guard down and believe the team will last, I'll start holding on too tight and freak everyone the hell out." He took another drink of the brew, letting it warm his chilled stomach.

"Right. You care about Dana?"

"Of course. Feel responsible for her." That didn't mean anything.

Nari finished the fruit. "Who's protecting her right now?"

Wolfe rolled his eyes. "Roscoe is a dog. Dogs don't count." Though it was a nice try.

"Hmmm. What's Malcolm doing?" Nari set her fork down.

Wolfe opened his mouth and then shut it.

"Who went with you to the mansion to confront Trentington?" She finished off her coffee.

Force and the new guy. "I get your meaning," Wolfe said. He needed to stop relying on people who would just get killed. "You don't know this guy—the one from my past. He enjoys killing, and he's damn good at it." Though Wolfe didn't like arguing with the shrink, he was feeling marginally calmer.

"What are the odds that this mysterious guy somehow found you two and had you drugged last night?" Nari asked.

Wolfe had already considered the idea. "Zero. It's not his style. He would've just bombed the entire party and then enjoyed the chaos and destruction. Drugging us is too . . ."

"Distant?" Nari asked. "From what you've said, this guy likes to get his hands bloody."

Wolfe nodded. "Exactly." He drew bills out of his pocket to leave beneath the plate. "I'm gonna miss these talks."

Nari gathered her belongings and scooted from the booth. "What do you mean?"

He waited for her to stand and precede him to the door, waving a good-bye at Janice on the way. "Just what I said."

Nari pushed open the door and winced at the heavy rain outside. "How about I give you a ride home?"

"No." Wolfe escorted her to her compact car, checked the back seat and underneath the vehicle, and then opened her car door. "I'll wait until you lock it, and please drive carefully." He'd followed her one time, making sure her route was safe. She had an attached garage in her rental house outside of D.C., and she'd wisely driven inside and shut the door before exiting the vehicle. However, she hadn't realized he'd followed her, so that was a concern. "Be safe, Nari."

She looked up from her car. "Wolfe? I don't understand.

Usually I can read you, but I'm lost. We're not finished meeting up once in a while."

"We are." If anything, their comfortable chat had shown him how close he'd let himself get to this team. He could never let Rock know what they meant to him. "I've challenged the past, and he'll be coming soon. It's too late to stop."

A line formed between Nari's brows. "I don't understand."

"I know." She was an excellent psychologist, but sometimes evil just existed. There was no analyzing it.

Wolfe shut her door and planted his hand on the window.

She frowned but started the car and then drove carefully over the potholes in the parking lot.

Wolfe watched her until the taillights disappeared into the storm. "Bye, Nari."

Chapter Eighteen

Dana sat at the middle hub of desks in the Deep Ops dismal basement, researching Frank Spanek on her laptop all morning. Why would that man have wanted to drug either her or Wolfe? Did he want them dead? If it was because of her, then she was getting closer to deciphering Candy's story. If it was because of Wolfe's search for Rock, whoever he was, then she had no idea why. Also, had Spanek killed Albert Nelson? If so, why?

Wolfe had given her the silent treatment on the way in to the office, and even the super sweet latte he'd bought for her on the way had failed to lighten her mood. There was something up with him, and it wasn't good.

He'd dropped her off, along with Roscoe, and then had gone to run errands. Whatever the heck that meant.

Angus Force worked quietly in his office, and Nari was in hers, so Dana had the hub to herself. Apparently Malcolm was out on a case.

The room was too quiet.

She looked up to find Angus watching her, leaning against the doorjamb of his office.

"How are you feeling?" he asked.

Sometimes she forgot he could be such a nice guy. "I'm fine." It was more or less the truth.

Angus ruffled a hand through his thick hair. His green eyes were sharp and focused today, and his broad shoulders took up most of the space in the doorway. Like Wolfe, he was all muscle. Lean and strong. His face was sharper, more angled, than Wolfe's rugged one. "If you need to, talk to the shrink. I've heard she has some good advice."

"Okay." They had enough hotties on this unit to make a calendar. Dana grinned.

"It's good to see you smile." Angus straightened, and a second later, the elevator's gears ground loudly.

Dana pivoted, her heart rate accelerating. Was Wolfe back?

The door opened, and a woman stumbled out, her hands full of papers. Her curly black hair was cut in a blunt bob, and a fine smattering of freckles spread across her nose and cheeks, a shade darker than her russet brown skin. She wore cargo pants, tennis shoes, and a T-shirt depicting the Starship Enterprise being swallowed by a black hole. The woman's gaze caught on Angus, and relief filled her face. "Angus. This is such a dump."

Angus smiled, a genuine one. "Serena." He maneuvered around desks to reach her, picking up her falling papers. "Thank you for coming." Grasping her arm, he drew her closer to Dana. "This is my friend who's good with puzzles. Dana Mulberry, meet Serena Johnson."

"Hi," Serena said, crouching to scratch Roscoe's ears.

The dog perked up, rolled out his tongue, and then froze. He growled and jumped up, grabbing Serena's handbag with sharp teeth and running around the desks.

"Roscoe!" Dana pushed her chair back and stood. "Stop it."

He growled and shook his head, tearing the purse. It looked like cloth with an argyle pattern of purples and blues across it. The fabric ripped apart.

Dana went one way and Serena the other, both trying to hem the pooch in.

Angus whistled, but the dog ignored him. Dana's breath panted out, but she nearly caught him. In a smooth leap, he jumped onto the desks, skidded across, and landed on the other side. With a doggie burp, he dropped the wet, shredded mass to the ground.

"Huh," Serena said, looking down at the ruins of her bag.

Angus sighed. "I'm sorry. He has a problem with argyle patterns. We believe there was one on a vest nearby when we took that shrapnel overseas, and he freaks out every time he sees it."

"Is it the colors or the actual x pattern?" Serena asked.

"I think it's the pattern," Angus said, shaking his head.

With the argyle safely destroyed, Roscoe padded up to Serena and nudged her hand. The woman patted him, staring down at her ruined purse. "Well, I guess it's good news I forgot my wallet before leaving the apartment. He only ruined some tissues, gum, and my favorite lip gloss."

"Man, you have issues," Dana murmured, staring at the happily panting dog.

"I'll buy you a new purse," Angus said, whistling for the dog, grasping his fur, and leading him to the office in the back. "Get in there and take a nap."

Roscoe rolled his eyes and padded inside the office, brushing by Angus with a twitch of his head. The phone rang from somewhere inside the room, playing a tune about lost boats. "Excuse me." Angus shut the door and disappeared.

"Hi." Dana tilted her head, retaking her seat, trying to calm her breath as she studied the newcomer. "You're good with puzzles?"

Serena pulled out Malcolm's chair and sat. "I like a good puzzle."

"So do I. Are you a journalist?" Dana asked.

Serena shook her head. "I have PhDs in physics and applied mathematics with a focus on quantum cryptography, measurement-based quantum computation, and of course, methods for entanglement verification."

Of course. Dana grinned. "I don't know what any of that means."

"It means that I like puzzles." Serena shared her smile. "I consulted with Angus on a case several years ago where a serial murderer was sending coded messages to the press. It took a while, but I saw the patterns in them, and we figured it out from there."

"Like with a computer program?" Dana had used all the ones she'd found on the internet.

"It's more intuitive than that initially." Serena shrugged. "Patterns are everywhere, and I can recognize one if it's there. Once I can see how everything figures together, then we can develop a computer program to decipher it, if we need to. Sometimes a good code just unravels."

The elevator protested loudly again, and Dana sat up. This had to be Wolfe.

It opened, and the British guy stepped out.

Serena's head snapped up. "What in the world are you doing here, Professor Hanson?"

Oh yeah. That was his last name. Dana's ears twitched. Tension zinged between him and Serena. Oh, there was a story here.

The professor, satchel slung across his surprisingly fit body, strode inside. "Sometimes I like to slum it." He turned his intelligent brown gaze on Dana. "I mean the building, not the company. The company is lovely."

Serena snorted. "I doubt the unit needs to dissect the philosophy of crime and punishment or good and evil."

"Love, there's always time to dissect good and evil," the

professor returned, his jaw cleanly shaven today, showing very hard angles.

What was his first name? Dana searched her memory, but the last few days kept fuzzing.

The office door opened, and Roscoe bounded out, kicked out his back leg, and then shook his fur. With a happy yip, he trotted toward the professor, rubbing against the man's jeans.

"Jethro?" Angus appeared in his doorway. "Do you have your old notes?"

Oh yeah. Jethro. Cool name. Dana continued to observe the tension between Serena and the professor. What in the world was up with the two of them?

Jethro tugged the wide strap of his satchel over his head and strode around the desks toward the first case room. "I have my notes, but I don't see how any of this will help since Lassiter hasn't made a move, if he's even alive. I do think we should discuss the possibility that he's dead. Sometimes evil does lose."

Angus followed him into the case room and shut the door.

Roscoe flopped back down, this time lying across Dana's tennis shoes and giving a short whimper.

"Ha." She reached down to pat his head. "I'm not dumb enough to wear high heels around you, buddy." They'd be instantly snatched away. She pushed the notebook toward Serena. Why not? "These are copies of notes my friend Candy made about a story she was working on. She's the journalist who disappeared two months ago."

"I see." Serena opened the binder and flipped through the pages. She shut it and looked up, stretching out in the chair. "So. Tell me about Candy."

Dana stilled. "Those are her notes."

Serena smiled, and a dimple winked in her left cheek.

"Did you think I'd look at the pages and then have a *Good Will Hunting* moment?"

Well, yeah. "Maybe a *Beautiful Mind* one," Dana admitted.

"Or a Daniel figuring out the *Stargate* situation?" Serena laughed, leaning back and plopping her tennis shoes on the desk. She wore one yellow and one blue footie that barely peeked above the shoes, somehow looking right on her. "Tell me about Candy, so I can get into her head a little bit. Like, how did you meet?"

"Same journalism class at Columbia," Dana said, remembering fondly. "She's a city girl, I'm a country girl, and we both love words. We worked together on several projects and became good friends." In fact, one of her best memories was of taking Candy fishing one weekend when they visited Dana's family. The city girl had done all right, although she just wouldn't take a fish off the line to save her life.

"What three words would you use to describe her?" Serena asked, intelligence shining in her eyes. This close, specks of green and gold were visible in the brown.

It hurt to think about her friend, but she persisted in using the present tense. Chances were that Candy hadn't survived the attack, but Dana had to keep some hope. "Three words? Hmm." She thought for several moments. "I'd say organized, adventurous, and tenacious." She'd never give up on a story, much like Dana. "She's interested in how businesses work and how people can infiltrate them and cause problems."

Serena nodded. "All right. Who are her favorite authors?"

"Steve Berry, Nora Roberts, Lexi Blake, and Stephen King," Dana said instantly.

"Favorite animals?"

"Well, I don't know that she had a favorite. She didn't

have pets." Dana chewed her lip. "As for her family life, she had a brother she lost to a car wreck in high school, and they were raised by a single mom who died of breast cancer shortly thereafter." Dana breathed out. "I kind of adopted her into our family during college and dragged her home for holidays. She enjoyed that, I think." Then they'd gotten busy with work and their adult lives. It had been a while since they'd vacationed together.

"What kind of people did she date?"

"Very smart men," Dana mused. "Past boyfriends include an inventor of some computer program, a theoretical physicist, and a quite successful stockbroker."

"How about you?" Serena asked.

Dana chuckled. "Lost causes seem to be my type. How about you? What's up with you and Professor British accent and cute butt?"

Serena rolled her sparkling eyes. "Uptight academics who have lived their whole lives in the ivory tower just bug me."

Dana hadn't tagged the professor that way. "And?"

"He stole my office." Serena frowned. "We both work at D.C. University, and we were up for a very plush, in the corner, perfectly situated office, and he got it. Butthead." She reached down and rubbed between Roscoe's ears. "I mean, I was new at the university, and I guess he had some seniority, but that was the empty office when I agreed to teach there and I assumed it would be mine."

"Well, then. You should teach him a lesson," Dana said.

Serena straightened up. "Go on." Her tone was both interested and encouraging.

"I don't know, but your revenge should have something to do with the office, you know? Like fill it with confetti or foam or something." Dana leaned back and set her shoes on her desk. "Candy loved practical jokes. I mean loves.

She loves practical jokes." The levity disappeared with her slip of the tongue.

Serena sobered and opened the binder again. "Okay. Let's see what we have here." She read through the notes. "Is there a wall or a whiteboard I could use to tape these pages up?" She clicked the binder open.

"Yeah." Dana's feet dropped to the floor, carefully missing the dog. "We can use case room two. I think it's clear for now."

"What's in the first case room?" Serena asked, glancing toward the three doors at the back of the office.

Dana winced. "The Lassiter case."

Serena pulled her legs back and set her feet on the floor. "I worked with Angus before that case, but I heard it destroyed him."

Dana nodded. "Yeah. I think it did."

The elevator creaked, groaned, hitched, and then opened.

Wolfe stepped out, a stack of dark brown folders in one hand and a tray of whipped-cream-topped lattes in the other.

"Wow," Serena whispered.

Amen to that. The ex-soldier wore jeans that emphasized his long legs, a ratty T-shirt that showed off his broad chest, and a pissed-off expression that somehow made him seem even more handsome and yet unapproachable.

He set the folders and drinks down. "I have copies of the police files for Albert Nelson and Frank Spanek, as well as the entire Candy Folks case file. Don't ask me what I had to do to get them." He handed a latte to Dana and then one to Serena. "I'm Wolfe."

Serena blushed a light pink beneath her darker skin. "Serena."

"Nice to meet you." He took a latte, focusing on Dana. "Yours is decaf."

Irritation swept her, and she set her first latte down, definitely not needing the second one. "Knock it off, Wolfe."

Serena looked from one to the other and then sipped her whipped cream before glancing down at her deconstructed purse, still in a wet heap on the cracked floor. "This is sure an interesting place to work."

Chapter Nineteen

The pizza sat in a lump in Wolfe's stomach, even though he'd eaten the veggie one with less cheese. "Stop staring at me," he muttered to the dog while pulling his beer bottle closer to his opened laptop on the conference table in case room two.

Roscoe barked once, whined, and blinked several times.

Wolfe sat back. "Tell me you're not batting your eyes at me."

The dog's eyes widened, making him look pretty freaking adorable. He panted, his tongue rolling out, his tail wagging across the torn tile. "Woof."

Dana came into the room, followed closely by Serena. They seemed to be having some sort of mild disagreement about the original *Star Trek* versus *The Next Generation*, but he didn't really care.

Serena returned to her half of the wide wall board, where she'd taped rows of Candy's notes. "Hmm." She took a page from the bottom and exchanged it for one at the top, seeming to forget there were other people in the room. Wolfe kind of liked that about her.

Dana drew the chair out next to him, and the tantalizing scent of orange blossoms tickled his nose. He had no idea if she used a lotion that smelled like that, or if it was just her, but for the rest of his short life, he'd think of her every time he saw an orange. "Are you ready?" she asked.

He started and then covered by sliding his yellow pad filled with notes toward her. "Yeah. You?"

"Yeah." She wasn't meeting his gaze, and he didn't much blame her.

He looked at the board in front of him, where he'd pasted pictures of Frank Spanek, Albert Nelson, Trentington, Candy Folks, Dana, and himself with lines between points of contact. He'd gotten the pictures of almost everyone from their police files.

She frowned. "Is that you?"

He nodded. "Yeah. Didn't have a picture, so I drew me." It looked like a stick figure drawn by a drunk moron, but he'd placed a misshapen and rather chunky wolf next to it.

Her lips pressed together. "Is that a wolf?"

Of course it was a wolf. "Drawing isn't my specialty," he said, feeling oddly defensive. Yet when she gave in and smiled, a weight lifted off his chest. "I can try to draw you, if you'd like."

"No. That's okay." She held up a hand. "Please don't."

Fair enough. He tuned out the mutterings and tape-ripping noises of Serena in the corner. "What did you find in Candy's file?"

Dana exhaled and drew her notes out from under the file folder. "The police have been very diligent and have talked to pretty much everyone they could. They think her disappearance is associated with her current story, as do I. Their guys haven't been able to decipher the code of her notes, either." She looked pale.

Wolfe clenched his fist on his jean-clad leg to keep from reaching for her to offer comfort. "What else?" he asked instead.

She pushed her notes toward him. "I diagrammed the people they've talked to."

"Is Frank Spanek one of them?" he asked, wondering if there was a connection to the guy who'd had them drugged.

"No." Dana smoothed her hair away from her face. Today she'd worn nice jeans and a short-sleeved green shirt that brought out the color of her eyes. The dark smudges beneath her eyes did nothing to detract from her beauty. "The police estimate that Candy was missing for almost two days, maybe more, before anybody knew."

Guilt. He recognized it. "That's not your fault, Dana."

"I know, but I'd been meaning to take her to lunch, and we both just got busy." Even Dana's lips were pale.

He had to get her into bed to sleep, as soon as they finished this debriefing. "Anything else?"

"They're still looking at Candy's current boyfriend, Brett Sawyer, who's an investment banker. He doesn't have an alibi for the time they think Candy was taken, and supposedly a neighbor heard them arguing a few days before that." Dana scrubbed both hands down her face. "I find his involvement doubtful. I figure this is bigger than a domestic dispute. Not that domestic disputes aren't big, but you know what I mean."

Wolfe nodded. "I do. This feels less personal and more businesslike, for some reason. But we should check out Brett, anyway."

"Agreed. Let's do that tomorrow." She sat back, partially turning toward him. "What did you discover?"

He tapped his fingers on the Captive membership list. "I'm about a quarter through members and haven't found much of interest, yet." Leaning to the side, he tugged another list his way. "I've done a breakdown of the caterer and entertainment for the night, and we'll research the employees and talk to the owners of the club soon. So far, I haven't found the woman who served us the drinks, or how she relates to Frank Spanek and ultimately Albert Nelson. It has to all be connected, and my guess it all stems from Candy's story and her disappearance. It makes more sense that way." He'd looked up pictures of everyone he'd researched so far, using social media.

"Do you remember what the woman who drugged us looked like?" Dana asked.

"Kind of." The woman had dark hair, blue eyes, and light skin, but the mask had covered a lot of her face. "The hair may have been a wig, but I think I'd recognize her eyes if I saw her again." More memories were coming back to him all the time. "I'll need another day or even two to finish researching both lists." There were some high-up government employees on the membership list that he'd need to be careful in approaching.

"All right." She pushed the chart out of the way and tugged the two case files closer. "There's some good stuff in here."

Wolfe closed his laptop. "Like what?"

"The police were investigating both Albert Nelson and Frank Spanek for distribution of heroin, but couldn't find enough to make charges stick," Dana said.

Wolfe went cold. His throat closed. "Heroin? When?"

"The police started investigating the two men a couple of years ago, and from these files, it looks like the investigation heated up around three months ago," Dana said, pulling out another notebook and not catching his tension.

Three months ago. "Are you sure it was heroin? How did they know? What kind of evidence did they have?" Wolfe rapid-fired the questions at her, simultaneously reaching for the police case files.

She paused and turned toward him. "What's going on?"

Serena pivoted. "Did you say heroin?"

"Yeah." Wolfe's pulse started to beat too fast, and he took a deep breath to control his body. "Why?"

Serena looked up at the ceiling as she thought. Ignoring him, she turned back to the papers, muttering under her breath and tapping her foot.

One issue at a time. Wolfe flipped open the first case file, his skin suddenly feeling too tight. The timeline fit with Rock's drug dealings as well as his possible connection to Albert Nelson, but if the police had been investigating Nelson and Spanek for years, they probably had many enemies in the drug trade. Even so, Rock was getting closer, he could just feel it.

"Wolfe?" Dana asked, placing her hand over the page he was reading. "What is happening?"

Too much was happening. A boulder dropped into his gut with a force he felt to his toes. What had he been thinking sleeping with Dana? All of a sudden, the world came unexpectedly falling down. What if Rock had been working with Nelson and Spanek? Had he now put Dana on Rock's radar? Although Rock would never go for a drugging. It wasn't his style. Even so, a cold sweat broke out on Wolfe's forehead, and his chest tightened.

"Hey." Dana leaned toward him, somehow sounding far away. "You okay? You just got really pale."

Was he having a heart attack? Wait a minute. No. This was a fucking panic attack. He hadn't had one in so long that he almost didn't recognize the signs. It was out of the blue, like usual, and he couldn't stop it. He dropped his head into his hands, gasping for breath.

Fur instantly pressed up between his palms, and a rough tongue licked his chin.

His chest shuddered, and he pressed his face to the

dog's fur, sucking in air. *Calm. Be calm. It's all right.* He ran the litany through his head, finding comfort in the animal, his legs shaking as he slowly came down. An instant headache blasted him between the eyes, and he winced, willing it away.

Roscoe sat patiently, steady next to him, offering support.

Heat roared into Wolfe's face as reality returned, leaving him hollow. He wanted to crawl under the table with the animal, but that wasn't how he faced life. He lifted his head, even though it weighed about fifty pounds. "I'm sorry."

Dana reached over and kneaded the back of his neck, her eyes soft and concerned. "Take a deep breath. It's okay."

Her touch soothed him, easing the pain exploding through his head. Even his ears heated. Talk about losing control in front of people he'd just met. He looked over to apologize to Serena, but she was facing her board, moving back and forth, and muttering a bunch of science-sounding words to herself.

Dana leaned in, her mouth close to his ear. "She didn't even turn around. I'm not sure she knows we're in the same universe with her. I like how completely she focuses, don't you?"

Yeah. Especially right now, since the woman hadn't seen his breakdown. If only Dana hadn't seen it either. "I haven't had a panic attack in ages," he whispered. "I don't know what happened, and it definitely won't happen again." Well, it probably would, but hopefully he'd be alone next time. Yet another reason why he shouldn't enter into a relationship, even if he wasn't about to battle to the death.

"Don't worry about it," Dana said softly, her touch bringing more ease than any run. "I've had a couple since my run-in with the Senator, and I understand. Yours passed quickly."

Was she trying to build him up? Laughter tickled his throat, and he smiled. "Okay. I'm fine, now."

She leaned back. "Good. How about you tell me why you suddenly went into a panic attack?"

There wasn't any rhyme or reason to why, but when an attack hit, he knew he was dealing with anxiety. The woman was about to lose that sweet look on her face. "I want you to go home, to your parents' house, for a couple of weeks." He kept her gaze and wouldn't release her.

She pulled away from him. "No."

"Yes." Before she could argue, the door opened and Angus stood there, his gaze somber.

"What?" Wolfe asked, his body tensing.

Angus focused on Dana. "I'm sorry. The police think they've found Candy Folks. You're listed as her emergency contact, and the authorities need somebody to identify the body."

Chapter Twenty

The rain splattered almost gently against the windshield of Wolfe's truck, breaking through the humidity of the evening in Washington, D.C. Dana watched buildings and streetlights slide by outside as if the night was normal. "Do you think there's any chance the police are wrong?" she asked.

"Doubtful." The lights and shadows played across Wolfe's knuckles on the steering wheel. "I can do this for you."

"No. I need to do it." She'd never believe Candy was dead without seeing for herself.

Wolfe turned into a parking area near a large stone building and stopped the vehicle. "Force pulled some strings so you could do this tonight and not wait, but maybe tomorrow would be better? Are you sure you're up to this?"

"Yes." She opened the door and jumped down, letting the heated rain wash over her face. The air closed in, full of moisture. She shut the door and walked around the front of the truck, where Wolfe grasped her elbow and hurried her toward the steps.

A woman wearing jeans and a blue blouse waited just inside, opening the door for them. She had to be around sixty years old, with kind brown eyes, short brown hair, and ebony skin with laugh lines along her mouth. An ID badge had been clipped at her waist. "You must be Dana."

"Yes." Dana shivered, even though the air-conditioning wasn't set too high. Her stomach hurt, and her temples ticked with pain.

The woman held out a hand. "I'm Betty Williams, and I'm a social worker with the coroner's office." They shook, and then Betty shook Wolfe's hand before turning and starting down a long, clean hallway with cream-colored tiles and pictures of nature scenes on the walls. The building felt vacant at this late hour.

She led them into a small conference room with a wooden table and two orange chairs on each side. "Please take a seat."

Wolfe pulled out Dana's chair, waited until both women were seated, and then sat next to her.

Dana bit her lip, her chest hurting. "When do we go to the morgue?"

Across the table, Betty smiled. "We don't. Identifications aren't like on television." She reached to the side of the table, where a manila folder had been set. "I have a photo of the victim the police have found, and I'll hand it to you facedown. You can take all the time you need to turn the picture over."

Dana swallowed, her throat bone dry. "I don't understand. There's no body or sheet or anything?"

"No." Betty shook her head. "This is how we do identifications. You'll see a picture of Candy's face with blue blankets around her. I have to warn you that there is damage to the right side of her face and skull, so please prepare yourself if you can before you look."

Dana glanced at Wolfe, who wore no expression. He took her hand beneath the table, offering strength and reassurance. Even though they hadn't been on the same page lately, she leaned closer to him. Thank goodness he'd insisted on driving and sitting next to her during this.

Betty drew out a small clipboard with a picture attached to the top, facedown. She set it in front of Dana. "There is no hurry. I'm happy to stay here all night. Make sure you're ready. I often recommend people take several deep breaths first."

The AC switched on, blowing quietly from a vent in the ceiling.

Dana stared at the back of the picture. Maybe it wasn't Candy. "How was she found? We haven't heard any details."

"I don't know," Betty said softly. "I'm sure the police will want to speak with you, and they can give you all that information once we know for sure it's Ms. Folks."

Wolfe released Dana's hand and put his arm around her shoulders, pulling her into his warmth. "I can look for you, sweetheart. I know what Candy looks like."

She was tempted. So tempted. Instead, she reached out and turned the picture over, staring at her friend's face surrounded by a blue blanket. A jolt of shock was followed by a numbing buzz and a chill through her body.

Bruises covered the right side of Candy's face, and it looked like her hair had been arranged in a way to hide more damage to her head. Her skin was stark white, and her lips were tinged blue. Dark eyelashes spread out beneath her closed eyes, hiding the green that Dana remembered. "That's Candy Folks," she said hollowly, the words sounding as if they were far away from her mouth and this room and reality.

Wolfe pulled her closer to his body and reached out to turn the photograph back over. "Remember her from the good times," he rumbled.

Dana nodded, tears pricking her eyes. "Is that all?"

"Yes," Betty said, tucking the picture back into the folder. "I have a list of resources available to you, both short and long term."

Dana shook her head and stood, letting Wolfe take some of her weight. "Thanks, but I already have a shrink. I'll talk to her."

Betty stood. "All right. If you need anything, don't hesitate to call our office."

Wolfe turned Dana, and she let him. As she stumbled next to him, the hallway tilted to the right, and the air felt like cement. "What happened to her face?" she asked, her ears starting to ring.

"I don't know," Wolfe said, holding her as they walked through the building and out into the rain. "I promise I'll find out."

Her knees gave as they exited the building, and Wolfe swept her up, striding through the rain and opening his door to sit in his truck. With the door shut, he cuddled her close.

She took a deep breath and broke.

Feeling helpless, Wolfe held Dana tight as she sobbed against his chest. Helplessness quickly turned into anger, but he held her lightly, careful not to bruise her. Rain continued to pound through the muggy night, splattering on his windshield, making the windows fog. He let her cry and patted her hair, trying to be soothing.

When the heat became too stifling, he gingerly started the truck and switched on the AC.

Still, she cried. Her entire body shuddered, breaking his heart. No matter what happened, he'd avenge her friend.

Finally, Dana's tears subsided, and she rubbed her

cheek against his chest. She looked up, her eyes the color of a misty meadow, tears streaking her smooth cheeks.

"I'll find whoever did it," Wolfe said, his voice throbbing with the anger beating like a club in his heart. "I promise."

Dana nodded and gingerly moved off his lap as if she were a hundred years old. She pushed her hair off her wet face and fastened her seat belt, looking wounded and fragile on the large leather seat. "We need to find out how she died."

Wolfe put the truck into drive. "Force is already trying to get updates and should have more information tomorrow." He didn't much care what kind of favors their boss needed to use.

He made a couple of turns and drove by a fast-food place. "You hungry?"

"God, no." She looked out the window, huddled in the seat.

Four vehicles behind him, twin headlights followed, and had since they'd left the medical examiner's office. He reached across Dana and drew his gun from the jockey box, setting the weapon on the seat next to him.

"What's happening?" Dana turned to look at him, her eyes weary.

"Probably nothing." He turned onto I-395 and merged with traffic, heading toward I-95.

The headlights followed.

Okay. He checked to make sure Dana's seat belt was positioned correctly. "I need you to face front and put your hands in your lap."

She did so without argument. "Want me to shoot?"

"No. Just keep your body aligned in case they hit us from behind. They're in a car and we're in a truck, so the impact shouldn't do too much damage." He maneuvered in and out of traffic, looking like he was in a hurry but not like he was running from anybody. The car kept pace behind him, not getting any closer.

"They're not bad," he murmured, looking around for a second vehicle. Nothing stood out.

Dana kept in position but glanced at the passenger-side mirror. "Are you sure they're following us?"

"No." He merged onto I-95 S, not surprised when the car followed suit—along with tons of other traffic. "I'm going to exit in about ten minutes and drive fast, so get ready."

She swallowed audibly. "You're already driving fast."

Yeah, he was. He angled to the right.

"What do you think they're waiting for?" She whispered, for some reason.

"Fewer witnesses." His instincts were humming, and he trusted them. "Or maybe they're hoping to follow us home?" This sucked. He had to be careful with Dana in the car, damn it. "Hold on."

She reached for the dash.

He took the exit at the last second, barreling down the road and making a fast right.

Horns honked behind him, and the car swerved across three lanes to follow him. "Thought so," he said grimly, reaching for the gun. "When I tell you to duck, you do it."

Gulping, she nodded, her eyes wide.

He punched the gas and sped through a quiet, rundown commercial office area, yanking the wheel and zipping around a darkened dental office to the parking area in the back. "Get in the driver's seat, get down, and get out of here if I yell." He opened the door, jumped out, and ran toward the side of the building, where the car had just turned in.

Lifting his hand, he squeezed off three rapid shots, continuing to walk forward. The first bullet hit the windshield above the driver's head, shattering the glass. The next one hit the engine block, and the third the right front tire. The car veered to the left and drove over bushes and a nicely manicured lawn to smash into the glass front door. Its horn blared continuously.

A building alarm instantly blasted through the rain.

Wolfe ran to the car and ripped open the passenger-side door, yanking a bleeding man out and throwing him on the ground. He leaned in to find the driver slumped unconscious over the steering wheel.

He flipped the guy on the ground over and set a knee in his chest and a gun in his face, searching him for weapons and finding a high-end Ruger SR, which he slid into his waistband with his free hand. "Who are you?"

The guy was about thirty with dark hair and tattoos down the side of his face. "Screw you."

Wolfe punched him in the nose, and cartilage crunched beneath his knuckles. "Try again."

Blood spurted from the guy's face and he put a hand over the wound, tears filling his eyes. "Fine. You have no idea who you've messed with. I'm C-Spike from the Seventh Street Warriors."

Great. A gang was after him. "What do you want with me?" He pressed the gun close to the guy's no-doubt aching and broken nose.

The guy turned slightly to see his buddy still passed out in the car.

"You can tell. He can't hear you, and if you don't tell me, I'm going to kill you." Wolfe meant every word.

C-Spike spit out blood. "It's a contract on the blonde. We were told she'd be at the medical examiner's tonight or tomorrow morning. When she showed, we were to follow her and take her out somewhere discreet."

Ice-cold fury settled into Wolfe. "Who hired you?"

"Don't know. I swear. The order came from high up." His words were slurred through the blood as rain pelted them without cooling off the night in the slightest. "I don't even know her name."

"Make sure you never do." Wolfe hit him in the temple, knocking him out.

Sirens sounded down the road. He stood and ran to his truck, motioning Dana back to her seat. "Let's get out of here."

Chapter Twenty-One

Well after midnight, Dana fluffed her hair with a towel after a long shower and then padded into Wolfe's bedroom dressed in shorts and a cami. The splattering of rain echoed all around, tinging against the wide skylight in the master bathroom. Even though it had been raining for hours, the air still hung heavy around them. The whir of the AC came on, and she lifted her head, breathing deep. The image of Wolfe calmly grabbing his gun and striding into the storm to confront those bad guys wouldn't leave her mind.

When she was with Wolfe, she always felt safe. Protected.

Roscoe looked up from the foot of the bed, where he was not supposed to be. He gave her a look, snuggled his nose into his paws, and started snoring again.

She left the bedroom to find Wolfe on the sofa, his bare feet crossed at the ankles on the coffee table. He'd changed into gray basketball shorts and a black tank top, and his hair was still wet from the rain. A case file lay open across his chest, and his head was back with his eyes closed.

So this was how he slept.

Whiskers covered his rugged jaw, giving him the look of a rebel. She let her gaze wander over his thick cheekbones, straight nose, and scar down the side of his face.

"What are you doing?" He didn't twitch.

She jumped. "Looking at you."

He opened his eyes, and they appeared more topaz than brown in the darkened room. They swept her, head to toe, and her breasts actually tingled in response. His gaze moved back up, lingered on her chest, and finished on her face. "Have you been crying again?"

She nodded, her throat thick. "In the shower." It was a good place to cry, actually.

"Come here." He held out an arm.

She hesitated for half a second and then walked over, sitting next to him on the sofa and leaning against him. He tucked his arm around her and kissed the top of her head.

She licked her lips, her body humming. "Wolfe—"

"No." He set his head back again and shut his eyes.

Huh. "You don't know what I was going to say." Heck. Even she wasn't sure.

"Yes, I do," he said, his heartbeat steady beneath her cheek. "It's been a rough night and you're feeling both vulnerable and happy to be alive. There's this thing between us, we both feel it, and it'd be easy to fall in. It ain't gonna happen again."

She couldn't find the energy to drum up irritation at his confidence. "I believe that's arrogant." Except it wasn't—not from Wolfe. A tear leaked from her eye. "I just don't want to be sad any longer." Why couldn't they escape for another night?

"If you're sad, you feel sad." He lifted her with one arm and settled her on his lap. "It's okay to cry."

She didn't want to cry. His lips were close, but rejection would sting. He was so solid around her. "Do you feel things like other people?"

His eyelids opened. "No. I'm not sure I ever have, but

definitely not after the explosion." A vertical line showed between his eyes.

She chewed on her bottom lip. "Do you have feelings?"

His right eyebrow rose. "Yeah. I haven't turned into a sociopath or anything. My feelings are kind of under the surface and usually not as bright as before, but they're still there. The numbness has made me a better fighter and a better soldier."

Was that true? It seemed that Wolfe cared about his team and about her, and loyalty was definitely a feeling. "I think you're selling yourself short." Her gaze dropped to his enticing lips again.

They curved; an amused Wolfe was better than a grumpy one any day. "My feelings don't matter."

"What does?" She placed her palm in the center of his chest, marveling at the hardness.

"Your safety." He planted his hand over hers. "It's time for you to go to bed, Dana."

Darn her curiosity, because she was probably about to get her feelings hurt. "Don't you want me?" She had to know.

His pupils narrowed, and he shifted his weight, moving her slightly back. An erection beneath his shorts, hard and strong, pressed against her left buttock.

Her mouth opened. "Oh."

"Yeah. Oh." Amusement now melded with need in his eyes. "I've wanted you since I first saw you in the forest outside of Hunter's cabin, and after having you one night, without question I want more. A lot more."

"You still owe me an umbrella." Her breath quickened, and heat rolled through her abdomen in slow motion. She'd been heading over to visit her buddy Hunter, and Wolfe had found her, dragging her to the cabin. Then he'd asked her out once Hunter had explained they were friends. The second she'd gotten to know Wolfe, he'd turned off the charm and had placed her in the friend zone. "You're not responsible for everyone around you. You get that, right?"

"Yeah." His minty breath, with just a hint of whiskey, brushed her cheek. "However, things are about to get bloody. You need to be away from the danger in a safe house. I'm having Force look into one for you."

Hurt sliced through her. So that's why he'd put her on his lap. With his arms around her, she couldn't move. "No."

"Yes." He leaned in, his gaze intense. "Somebody has taken a hit out on you. Even though I believe it was limited to those two morons tonight, you're in danger. I need to know you're safe while I take care of it."

"I'm a journalist, and I never get scared off a story." It was really difficult to argue with that hard-on right beneath her. "Plus, I made a promise that I'd figure out who killed Candy and finish her story. You wouldn't let anybody put you in a safe house."

"I don't care." For the first time, he dropped the gentle-manly act. "I'm done playing fair. You're going to a safe house, and that's final."

A laugh burst out of her before she could stop it. She clapped a hand over her mouth, struggling to regain control.

His lids half-lowered, giving him the look he'd had as an undercover dom.

Her amusement fled. She sobered. "I appreciate the concern, but I'm going to a family wedding on Saturday, and then I'm coming back and getting to work. You can't stop me." Okay. That was a childish challenge, and by the hardening of his already rock-solid jaw, he was about to pick it up. So she did the only thing a smart girl could do.

She grabbed the sides of his head and kissed him, full on, her lips against his.

Fire jolted through her at the contact, and she nibbled at his lips, giving herself free rein. He stiffened against her, his chest holding air, his body heated and tightened. Finally, she leaned back and released his head, disappointed but not surprised. "You have a lot of control."

His eyes had darkened and deepened. "Do I?" The dark rumble of his voice skimmed over her skin.

She shivered. "Um, yes?" Why couldn't she breathe?

He grasped the front of her neck, his large hand easily spanning the entire width. Gently, he drew her closer to him. "Dana? You have one second to get your ass safely to bed. I suggest you do it."

She couldn't move.

He lightened his hold so she could go.

She stayed in place, wondering. Curious. Not even remotely willing to get off his lap. "The second is up," she whispered.

For answer, his fingers tightened, and he jerked her to his mouth. Then he *devoured* her. The kiss was hard and carnal, deep and commanding. He delved deep, holding her in place, conquering with just his lips.

She sighed and kissed him back, planting her hands on his chest and slinging one leg across him so she could straddle him. They both groaned when she pressed down on his cock.

A pounding on the door had Wolfe standing and turning to drop her on the sofa. "Where's my gun?"

Wolfe scrambled for his gun, his mind fuzzy. "Get in the bedroom and lock the door."

"Wolfe? Open this damn door," Angus Force bellowed, pounding harder.

Wolfe's shoulders went down as Roscoe bounded out of the bedroom and barked twice in happy greeting. "I'm coming," he yelled. "Hold your horses." He turned to a wide-eyed and rosy-lipped Dana. "You're gonna want to go to bed, I think."

Her smile was a dare. "All right. You should join me later."

Sounded like a good plan. Why fight it? "Go. Now." He let her pass before striding over to open the door.

Force shoved him back two steps and stomped inside, his green eyes ablaze and darker than usual. "What the holy fuck are you up to?"

Currently Wolfe was trying to force his hard-on away, but it wasn't cooperating. He moved past Force and walked into the rain, noting the steam rising from his skin. It took several minutes, but he got his body under control. He turned back, went inside, and found Force sitting on the sofa petting his dog.

"All better?" Force snarled, no doubt having seen Wolfe's state.

Wolfe nodded. "Yeah. Your timing is actually excellent."

"Yours isn't," Force said, grinding his back teeth. "Did you, or did you not, get in a car chase ending with gunshots and two injured men?"

Wolfe stilled. "How did you know that?"

Force ripped a folded piece of paper out of his back pocket and tossed it over. "BOLO for a truck matching yours as well as a guy with a gun matching you."

"Huh." Wolfe scratched his head. "Didn't know anybody saw me." He'd checked the area for cameras and hadn't seen any, but he had been driving fast, shooting, and then smacking a guy around. "Guess I should store the truck for a little while. Am I on camera?"

"Not to my knowledge." Force set his jaw. "Why aren't you more concerned? Surely somebody got your license plate."

"Oh." Wolfe wiped rain off his forehead. "I bought the truck with cash and used a fake ID, so the title isn't in my name. The plates are stolen from a different state, and I'll switch them out right now."

Force's head jerked. "Well, now. Aren't we the careful criminal?"

"I try," Wolfe said dryly. "You quit drinking yet?"

Roscoe's ears twitched.

"No," Force said, scratching the pooch under the chin. "You offering?"

"Yeah." He dripped water on the carpet as he walked into the kitchen and poured whiskey into two tumblers. He returned and handed one to Force, looking the man in the eye. "Slainté."

"Slainté." Force tipped back a healthy swallow.

Wolfe dropped into the adjacent chair, which had come with the house. "Have you gotten your hands on Candy Folks's autopsy report yet?"

"Still working on it." The kitten dodged from behind the sofa and jumped onto Force's lap, digging his nails into his jeans. "Kat. Take it easy." He scratched the kitten between the ears. "I don't have connections in D.C. any longer, but Raider does, so he should have the report sometime tomorrow."

Wolfe let the whiskey warm his belly. "What about the safe house?"

"Not yet, but again, working on it." Strain showed in

the lines around Force's eyes. "We may have to put her with Jethro."

The hair on the back of Wolfe's neck stood up. "Absolutely not." The charming Brit would make a move, and he wouldn't know how to protect her from a monster like Rock.

Force swirled his drink in the glass. "If you're not interested, you shouldn't care."

"He's a professor, for Pete's sake." Wolfe shook his head. What in the world was Force thinking? This British dude had him confused.

Force tipped back the rest of the booze. "He's a professor *now*. Used to be MI6."

Wolfe drew up short. "No shit?"

Force nodded, stood, and headed into the kitchen to reach into the top cupboard for the bottle. "Yep. I'm sure he doesn't want that getting out with his fresh start on life and all of that, so keep it between us."

No problem.

Wolfe caught movement from the corner of his eye, and he partially turned to see Roscoe drop low and shimmy silently across the living room, stopping in the middle. That was odd.

"I'm not your girlfriend, but do you want to talk about Dana?" Force emerged from the kitchen.

A split second before it happened, Wolfe realized the dog's intent. "Force—" His buddy tripped over the sprawled canine, his arms windmilling as he started to fall. The glass and bottle went flying.

Wolfe jumped up and snagged the bottle before the dog could. He held it up high.

Roscoe yipped and sat on his haunches, his gaze on the bottle. The glass hit the carpet and bounced. Roscoe leaped for it, shoving his nose in and licking wildly before turning his attention to the carpet to suck up any remaining whiskey.

"Damn it, Roscoe." Force planted a hand on the coffee table and shoved himself to his feet.

Wolfe calmly poured himself another glass. "You really need to get that dog some help." He handed his glass over. "Oh, and Dana and I need the weekend off. Apparently, we're going to a wedding in Tennessee."

Chapter Twenty-Two

Dawn arrived hot and humid with the hint of another summer storm in the air. Wolfe sprawled on the sofa with the dog snoring on the floor, once in a while emitting whiskey farts. Wolfe had alternated all night between wanting to join Dana in the bedroom and *desperately* wanting to join Dana in the bedroom, but he'd peeked in on her, and she'd been sleeping peacefully. Finally.

He let his hand flop off the sofa to rest on the dog's head, his eyes closing for a short nap. He had to get a little sleep so he could function during the day, and he'd avoided it during the darker hours of night. Light peeked in through the blinds, so it was safe to let his guard down for a few minutes.

He could taste the dust before he saw the dirt road around their medium tactical vehicle. Behind them was an older truck that held four of his teammates. Rock had gone up ahead in a motorcycle to scout for mines, his specialty. Wolfe looked sideways at Billy, a good ol' Southern boy from Alabama who still had fresh bruises across his dark forehead and was one of the best intelligence gatherers in the entire service. "I'm not used to riding in the MTV," Wolfe said, itching to get on a motorcycle, speaking in Dari to keep fluent.

Billy snorted, and his hands relaxed on the wheel before he replied in the same language. "Rock got to the cycle first."

Whatever. Wolfe stared out the thick window as they passed by a village of brown mud compounds outside Khost city, wondering how many Taliban-affiliated families lived there. The barren hills around them promised more dust and heat as the day wore on.

He rolled his neck as the vehicle bumped over potholes in the barely there road.

Billy sighed. "Man, I'm still pissed. That boxing match yesterday didn't help with the anger."

Wolfe turned back toward his brother. "Yeah. I get that." Although he usually banked anger low and dealt with it when it exploded. "We lost two guys hauling in that heroin, and having it stolen is an insult." They had a line on a key player in the trafficking routes, and his unit specialized in hunting. "We're good at evidence collection."

Billy drove around a large rock. "Evidence collection. Man, I'm getting tired of our euphemisms. Evidence collection, wet work, the gray zone. Why don't we just say we're going to fight this guy and scare or beat the crap out of him until he gives up the information?"

"Because we're too classy," Wolfe retorted, straightening as Rock came back into view, riding toward them and giving an all-clear sign. He relaxed again.

There was a moment of silence before the world detonated.

An explosion rocked the truck behind them, and Wolfe instantly pivoted, trying to see what had happened. "Turn around. Fast."

Billy yanked the wheel and thumped off the road, hitting several rocks before turning and heading toward the burning truck and spirals of black smoke billowing into the sky.

Wolfe scouted the area, saw no one, and jumped out of the MTV, running toward the hissing metal. "Cover me."

"Got it," Billy yelled, already out of the vehicle, crouched near the rear, no doubt with his gun out.

Two men had been thrown free and were both lying against rocks to the north. Wolfe reached the truck and ripped open the door, burning his hand. Flames flashed down his side and pain flared, but he ignored it all and dragged Jack from the truck, shoving him to safety. Wolfe reached in for Booker and dragged his limp body, still burning, across the seat to safety.

He was turning to help them when a second explosion rocked the area. His ears compressed and his brain ticked in the microsecond before he was blown through the air, the light disappearing as he landed with a pain he could feel to his soul.

Night was falling when he awoke, parts of his body numb and parts in excruciating pain. Sucking in dust, he rolled over, biting his lip in agony. His team. Where was his team? He used his elbow to force himself to sit. His gut lurched and he turned to the side to puke into the dirt, his lungs and ribs screaming the whole time. He turned and saw Jack facedown in the dirt. Grunting against the pain, he crawled over to his friend and felt for a pulse.

Nothing, and Jack was cold.

The sound Wolfe made felt like it came from the depths of hell. He checked Booker, who was also dead.

Then he passed out for a while, waking to look at the stars. Blood dripped into his eyes, and he wiped it away, struggling to sit up and move toward the two men who'd been thrown from the blast earlier. His vision faded, and he fought against passing out again.

They were dead, too. Saul and Jose. Gone.

That left Rock and Billy. Where the hell were they? He

couldn't stand, so he crawled past the still burning truck toward the MTV, seeing a prone body. Billy? He'd been away from the explosion. Why was he down?

The world wasn't making sense, and an ominous ticking sound echoed between Wolfe's ears. He reached Billy to find a bullet hole neatly placed in the back of his large head. In the back? There hadn't been insurgents near—he would have seen them.

"Rock?" Wolfe croaked, looking for the motorcycle. It was gone. So was Rock.

Wolfe let the ground take him again, awakening briefly when troops arrived and then again in a medicopter. He wanted to tell them to leave him with his team, but his voice wouldn't work.

The dream morphed to the hospital in Germany where he'd recuperated. To the moment when the investigators determined that Rock had been the inside guy who'd stolen the heroin and killed the team. Anger had propelled Wolfe to heal and survive, at least temporarily. There would be justice.

The dream again changed direction, this time to images of Dana in the woods, in that pink corset, in his bed. An explosion rocked through his house, and she screamed as she was burned.

He sat up on the sofa, gasping for breath. Sweat soaked his chest. His hand trembled as he wiped his eyes.

Nothing would stop him from protecting her. Then, he would find justice.

Dana ignored her headache as Wolfe drove through the thick air to their office building. They'd both been silent on the drive in, and the inscrutable expression on the man's face hadn't encouraged discussion. This close to him, her body hummed with need, now that she had firsthand proof of how well he could handle that need.

He parked near the door and turned toward her. "We'll leave around three for Tennessee."

She paused in the midst of reaching for the door handle. "Huh?"

"For the wedding. We can drive about four or five hours today, stay somewhere in West Virginia for the night and get on the road in the morning. I'll have you at your folks' by noon, which is when your plane would've landed." He opened his door, his voice matter of fact. "The wedding is at five, right?"

She tried to make sense of his words, opening the door and stepping down. Heat blasted her. "What in the world are you talking about?" She shut the door and jumped over a puddle before reaching the cracked sidewalk.

"I need to be armed and don't have time to get permits to fly. Plus, I don't want a record of me flying." He opened the back door, and Roscoe bounded out, spraying water. "The dog is coming, too, and he doesn't like airplanes."

None of this was making sense.

She turned at the entrance, her mind reeling. "You don't need to go with me to the wedding."

He reached her, looking dangerous today in black cargo pants with a matching shirt. "We can argue if you like, but I am taking you to Tennessee if you're still going."

The mild headache turned into a pounding annoyance. "I'm not agreeing, but I don't have the energy to fight with you right now." She needed to drink the coffee he'd bought her.

"Okay." He opened the door.

Maybe the coffee and a few moments would get her back on track so she could focus. She held her breath in the elevator until it reached the bottom, waiting for Roscoe to run out before following him.

Serena was working at Mal's desk, mumbling to herself without looking up at them.

Wolfe slid a sugar-laden latte next to her before working his way toward the back room. "You can have my desk, Dana. I'll be in the second case room." Without looking back, he disappeared into the room.

Dana fought the very real urge to stick her tongue out at him and sat instead, tugging her laptop from her bag and letting Serena mumble in peace.

She worked for several hours, trying to track down Frank Spanek, using her cell phone to reach out to friends of Candy who might've known something about the story she'd been working on. Nobody knew a thing. She also tried to track down the three female CEO's, managing to interview two of them on the phone, which didn't help much. Theresa Rhodes was the only one on her list she couldn't reach, and the woman's assistant refused to give the location of her sabbatical. She'd much rather meet each one in person to gauge their expressions.

Dana's mind kept returning to her sleepless night and that kiss from Wolfe. Her cheeks filled with heat.

"You okay?" Serena asked, diagramming on a notepad while sitting at the unclaimed desk.

She nodded, surprised the woman had realized she was in the room. "Yeah. I'm fine." Not really, but she didn't know Serena well enough to confide in her.

Serena tapped her pencil on the desk. "I'm really sorry about your friend. Force mentioned your loss when I got in earlier."

Dana's throat hurt from crying during the night. "Thank you. We should have the autopsy results soon." She rubbed her aching temples. "You have any drugs? Advil?"

"Drugs?" Serena pushed away from the desk. "That's it. The symbols—the first part anyway—correspond to some sort of equation." She ran into the first case room, her tennis shoes squeaking.

Dana followed, her hand pressed against her left eye. This headache had better not turn into a migraine.

Serena moved to the taped-up notes. "That's it. Right there." She looked frantically around and then picked up a chewed pencil that Dana had forced Roscoe to drop earlier. "The code is quite elegant. Every symbol corresponds to a number, which corresponds to a letter minus three." She rapidly began deciphering the notes, jotting down letters beneath the symbols. "Smart woman."

Wolfe leaned back in his chair and kicked his massive boots up on the conference table, nudging thick case files to the side. Lines of stress cut into the sides of his mouth. "What is happening?"

Dana dropped her hand and waited for her aching eye to focus. Serena formed words beneath the symbols and letters.

Serena finished with one page and turned. "I have phrases in note form but no story. The phrases indicate a problem with Theresa Rhodes and her company."

Dana nodded. "I figured we'd find notes that she'd turn into a story when she was ready. That's how many of us write." She moved closer. "Did Candy find corruption at Rhodes's sports company? Maybe embezzlement or tax evasion or something like that?"

Serena frowned. "Well, kind of."

Dana read more. "Any other CEO's mentioned?"

"No," Serena said.

Dana leaned in closer. "The word 'heroin' is everywhere in Candy's notes."

Wolfe's boots dropped to the floor with a loud *thunk*.

Dana read out loud. "Heroin from Afghanistan?"

Wolfe stood to read over her shoulder. "More than ninety percent of illicit heroin is from Afghanistan's opium poppy harvest."

She glanced sideways. "Really?"

He nodded. "Yeah. What do you think I was doing in Afghanistan for so long?"

Her skin prickled. "How the heck should I know? You don't tell me anything."

"Fair enough." Apparently, Wolfe had returned to being reasonable. He leaned closer to read the deciphered page and then stiffened. "We need to find this CEO Theresa Rhodes."

"Yes." Serena leaned back and studied the entire wall. "I have a feeling this page is kind of a table of contents, so I'm assuming one of these other pages corresponds to her."

Wolfe rolled his neck. "What does a CEO of a sports company have to do with heroin?"

Dana looked at the many pages. "Well, let's decode them."

Serena grinned. "Ah, wouldn't that be nice? But, no. Your friend used a different code for each page. Now that I understand this one, I'll be able to extrapolate and crack the others, but it'll take me a little time. She was impressive—I wish I could've met her."

Nausea swirled in Dana's stomach. "Yeah, she was pretty amazing. You would've liked her."

Wolfe shook his head. "I'm so fed up with the drug trade. It's everywhere, even in your business stories. Enough is enough."

Dana nodded. "Yeah." But they were getting closer. "Let's have Brigid track down Theresa Rhodes. I don't care if she's on sabbatical. She's the only one, so far, listed in Candy's notes."

Wolfe grasped her arm. "It's time to go."

"No. We don't have the autopsy results yet." Dana couldn't leave without them, although she'd decided it'd be nice to have Wolfe on the trip home. They needed to talk.

"I read them. You don't need to." He turned for the door.

"The heck I don't." She set her feet. "Tell me, or I'm not moving an inch."

He sighed. "Fine. I'll tell you on the way." ·

Now she had to go.

Force came into view, irritation darkening his face. "I tried to buy you time, but the police need to talk to you about Candy again, Dana. They're here, and I sent them to interrogation room one. I promised you'd talk to them right now."

Dana sighed. "Might as well get this over with."

Wolfe's brows drew down. "If it goes late, we'll stay at my house tonight and head to Tennessee early tomorrow morning."

"It shouldn't go late," Dana said, sweeping by him. "Hopefully."

Chapter Twenty-Three

Dana's interview the night before had gone way too late, and Wolfe was still fighting irritation the next morning that he hadn't been allowed to go in with her.

The last thing he needed right now was to sit in a truck for hours when he should be hunting down Rock. The dream from the other night, a flashback really, stuck in him like a rusty blade he couldn't dislodge, so he'd had trouble sleeping again.

The interview had taken so long that they'd decided to stay at his house and head to Tennessee in the morning. They'd both gone to bed and pretty much passed out, and now they had to drive straight through to get to the wedding in time.

He controlled his emotions and drove away from his house at the crack of dawn, acutely aware of Roscoe staring at him from the back seat and Dana from his side. He'd left Kat with Pippa, and the kitten had meowed out of pleasure. There was no doubt Pippa snuck him treats.

"Well?" Dana asked, dressed in cutoff shorts and a plain heather-green T-shirt for the long drive. Her legs were long and tan, and his mouth kept watering, even though her eyes were exhausted and her face pale. "I let you be quiet last night after my interview. Now it's time you gave me the autopsy report."

"I left it at the office," he said, peering through the hazy day. It felt like another storm was coming.

"Wolfe," she snapped.

He had promised. "Didn't the police tell you anything during your interview?"

Her cute face scrunched up in pure irritation. "No. They seemed to think giving a journalist information was a bad idea." She slipped her flip-flops off and stretched her toes, her toenails painted a pretty pink. "Although they did give me a copy of Candy's will, which names me as Executor."

He should've forced his way into the room with her. "Did Candy have an estate?"

"Some money she wanted donated to a couple of charities, and she wants to be cremated and have her ashes scattered on Dogwood Creek, where we used to go fishing. I'm pretty sure that's illegal, but I'll take care of it next week after the wedding." Her voiced thickened.

There was nothing he could do to ease her pain, and his body tensed. He'd given her space the night before, when maybe he should've pushed her to talk, but he hadn't wanted to tell her about the autopsy. "What all did the detective ask?"

She rocked back and forth, still wearing her seat belt. "They asked the same questions as before, and I told them everything I knew."

His eyebrows lifted. "Even about Captive and Frank Spanek?"

"Yeah, but I left your name out of it all. They need a complete picture, and I want them to find out who killed her. Even if we find the killer, you and me, we're going to call the police, right?" She leaned down and reached into her bag, retrieving a band to secure her thick hair in a ponytail. "It's so muggy. When will fall be here?"

Not soon enough. He didn't answer her question, because he wasn't turning Rock into the police.

"The police wouldn't give me any details last night, but it all had to be in the autopsy report, right? So tell me everything. Where did they find Candy?" Dana asked, persistent as ever.

He normally liked that quality in her. Not so much right now. "Two hikers in a wooded area in rural Virginia found the body. She was probably killed at home and then dumped elsewhere."

Dana paled and pulled her knees up, wrapping her arms around them. "She'd been dead the whole two months?"

"Yes." The ME had done a good job with makeup and putty, putting her face back together for the picture. "She died from blunt-force trauma." There wasn't any need to go into more detail.

"Somebody beat her to death?" Dana's voice shook. "Was she raped?"

"No." He told the lie without flinching. In addition, she had been stabbed several times, which could have a sexual component. "A blow to the head, fast and hard, killed her quick." It was a blatant lie, so he had to make sure Dana never saw the entire report. Candy had slowly bled to death, and she had to have been in torturous pain.

Wolfe glanced at the defenseless woman in his passenger seat, one being hunted from too many directions.

The burner phone buzzed from the back seat.

Every muscle in Wolfe's body tensed as Dana dropped her feet and partially turned. "Pull the black phone out of my pack, but do not answer it."

She released her seat belt, gave him a look at the order, and then leaned over to unzip his pack. "Is this a burner phone? Why do you have a burner phone?" She grunted as she turned and settled back down, handing over the innocuous-looking phone.

Wolfe took it. "Don't say a word. Don't even breathe." He reached over and turned up the music, which was a combination of country and rock. He pressed the phone hard against his ear so she couldn't hear anything. "What?" he answered, the knuckles on his left hand turning white on the steering wheel.

"Hey, buddy. I didn't want you to think I was ignoring you." Rock came over the line clearly, anticipation bubbling through his voice. "Had a couple of things to take care of but am narrowing your location down."

"Are you, now?" Wolfe couldn't hear anything in the background on the other end of the line. Perfect silence. Not even the hum of an air-conditioning unit. "Somehow, I don't think you're very close. I'm getting kinda bored waiting for you."

"Then maybe you should learn to track and find me. You never were as good."

Not exactly true. They just had different styles, and Wolfe's style of patience usually won out. "I've found your contact and know exactly how you got the heroin here," he taunted, hoping Rock would bite and not catch that he was bluffing.

"Maybe you do know, but it's too late for me to worry about it. I got my hands on your military file, and boy, it looked like you had some trouble in that German hospital. Pain and outbursts and a whole lotta PTSD. Feeling any better?" Rock chuckled.

"Much," Wolfe said, hiding his instant irritation. "Guess that file didn't reveal where I'd gone upon discharge." He'd made sure the records showed him being discharged and not sent to the Deep Ops Unit.

"Nope. Just makes the game more fun. For now, get ready. I'll see you soon." Rock clicked off.

Wolfe drew in several breaths to calm his temper and then slipped the phone into the pocket by the door.

Dana crossed her arms. "Well? Who was that?"

"Doesn't matter." He had to get her to safety, because the clock was counting down. His hand twitched for his knife.

Dana stared at the veggie burger in her lap as Wolfe continued driving through the rapidly heating day. Why wouldn't he tell her more? She'd learned a long time ago that one way to get answers was to start guessing and see if she was close. "You do know that nothing is going to happen to you, right? You are not going to die in some final battle."

"We'll see." He lifted a massive shoulder. "Maybe not, and I'm certainly going to try to remain breathing, but it's nice to be prepared." His voice was calm and reasonable—even thoughtful.

So the person on the phone had been Rock. "Why won't you let me help against this Rock person?" Her temper detonated. Sometimes she wanted to smack him on his hard head and just see if she could knock some sense into him. "You absolutely drive me crazy sometimes. You want to live, right? I mean, you see you have people and things and life to live for?"

He pursed his lips, taking a right turn. "Lately, yeah. At first, after I was blown up, I didn't care if I lived or died. Then I found out about my teammate betraying us, and I wanted to live long enough to rip off his head. Now, I don't know. It'd be nice to live."

Nice to live? "That's all?" Her voice rose.

"I don't want to get your hopes up," he said reasonably.

Yep. She might just smack him in the head for the fun of it. "At least tell me that your obvious plan of mutual destruction and personal sacrifice with this asshat has changed since you've made connections with the team and, well, me." Yeah, she was beating her own head against a brick wall here, but the guy had gotten under her skin, and it wasn't just because of multiple orgasms. There was a lot more to Clarence Wolfe than muscle, and she wanted to know more of him. Wanted him to know more of her. That was enough for now.

He pulled into the parking lot of a restaurant with a stone facade and bright lights. "My plan has changed, and now I do care if I live or die."

Well, that was something. But apparently Wolfe wasn't done.

"I like you, and if I'm able to kill Rock, then I'd like to ask you out."

Ask her out? Somehow, it felt like they'd moved past that moment, but his honesty was sweet. "I don't believe in waiting for life to happen—I'm more of a make-it-happen type of gal." She cocked her head, studying him in the too warm morning.

"Yeah, no kidding." He released his seat belt and partially turned his bulk to face her. "I know you don't understand this, but I can't be thinking of you or Nari or Force when I go after Rock. It has to be just me, with no thought of the consequences to my relationship with any of you."

She swallowed. "You think what you're about to do will change you in our eyes?"

"Maybe. You've never seen that side of me, and I hope you never do." His eyes were stark, but his voice strong. "Some things in life change us, Dana. Whether we like it or not."

What would it be like to be on the other side of that wall he'd erected around himself? "Do you ever let anybody in?"

His chin lifted. "Be careful what you wish for. You might not like being in." He opened his door and jumped out, letting the dog bound into the parking lot and hustle over to a wide grass field.

She stepped down and grabbed her pack, shutting the door. "Please tell me you're not keeping distant for my own good? You're not that much of a dumb ass, are you?"

"I don't think so," Wolfe said thoughtfully, visibly scouting the entire area. "I'm just trying to keep everything locked down until I finish this op. It's how we were trained to conduct missions." He rubbed his whiskered jaw. "Complications are to be ignored until they need to be dealt with."

Oh really? Against all logic, she stepped right up to him, body to body. "Am I someone who needs to be dealt with?" Her voice dropped low. Husky.

He reached up, his thumb caressing across her cheekbone and down her face, his chest rising with a deep breath. "Definitely."

Well, at least that was something. "What now?" Her body tingled with warmth, ready for action, primed after just one touch from him.

"Now?" He dropped his hand. "Now we grab an early lunch, try to keep Roscoe out of trouble, and then head to a family wedding where I'll stick out like a serial killer who's chasing you."

She snorted. "You're not that big." In fact, he'd fit right in.

"If you say so," he agreed.

Chapter Twenty-Four

Wolfe drove through the Tennessee countryside, feeling like he was going into battle. He'd never been to a family wedding. There were norms he had no clue about. Dana watched the trees fly by outside, in a cheerful mood, anticipation turning her eyes a sparkling emerald.

His normal phone buzzed, and he lifted it to his ear after glancing at the caller ID. "Hi, Brigid. What's up?"

"Hallo. Force says you're on the road, and I wanted to update you." Her soft Irish brogue came through the line like a sound from home. Papers shuffled, and she continued. "I've done a deep dive on that fella Frank Spanek, and he owns several properties across the Northeast. I'm emailing you a list of properties as well as other police reports on him—most inconclusive. Several state agencies have looked at the guy."

"Did you find connections to Albert Nelson?" Wolfe asked.

"Yes. They're co-owners of properties and businesses. Just the two of them so far, but I'm looking for other associates or partners," Brigid said.

Wolfe slowed down to drive around a sharp curve.

"Thanks. I'll get on it tomorrow night when we're back in Cottage Grove. Dana says hi."

"Aye, no problem. Speaking of Dana, what's going—"

"Bye, Brigid. Thanks." He disengaged the call before she could get too nosy. "Brigid says hi," he told Dana.

"Turn left here," Dana said, pointing at the entrance to a golf course in Dogcreek Village. "The country club is up the lane, and supposedly the bridesmaids have a suite to get ready. Hopefully, the gods have interfered, and the bridesmaids' dresses were caught in a fire last night."

"They can't be that bad," Wolfe said, allowing himself some amusement.

Dana shook her head. "You'll just have to see for yourself, but believe me, it's bad. Try not to wince, okay?"

"No problem." The blonde would look pretty in anything. "Are you sure the gray suit we brought will be fine? I have a black one." They'd gone through his wardrobe, and she'd appeared pleasantly surprised that he had not only two suits but dress shirts and a few ties.

She scoffed. "No. Sure, it's at the country club, but we're in the country, and you'll see everything from jeans to maybe a full suit. That pinstriped gray suit with the lighter green shirt and darker tie are perfect. It'll be casual, Wolfe. Trust me—you'll see everything. My sisters and I even play wedding bingo at these type of things."

"Wedding bingo?" He drove past a row of cars and up to the wood-sided building with heavy oak doors.

"Long story." She pointed to the east. "Drive that way beyond the entrance to the second cabana. That's where Mom said I should go to get ready."

He followed her directions, noting possible sniper positions out of habit. He parked near a stone pathway that angled off a golf-cart path to a small bungalow surrounded by red flowers. "You think this is it?"

"Maybe?"

The door to the cabana opened, and three women ran out, all different versions of Dana.

Dana gave a happy squeal and opened the door, jumping out and colliding with another blonde and two curly-haired brunettes.

Good Lord. There were four of her. Wolfe's stomach flipped over, and it took him a moment to realize it was nervousness. Interesting. He hadn't realized he could get nervous. He slid out of the truck and opened the back door for Roscoe before walking around the front toward the rapidly chattering women.

The noise halted abruptly, and four pairs of identical green eyes turned his way.

"Holy moly," the nearest brunette said, her chin dropping.

Dana's blond sister nodded. "Wow. Hunkalicious."

Heat ticked his face. Was he blushing?

Dana, a wide smile brightening her already stunning face, grabbed his arm and pulled him toward the group. "Clarence Wolfe, meet my older sister, Katie." She pointed him toward the blonde, who was about an inch shorter than Dana and a little slenderer, with a scar across her right hand.

"Hi. I'm older by less than a year." Katie smiled, her teeth straight, and held out a hand.

"Call me Wolfe." He was über gentle with the shake. She seemed even more fragile than Dana, but he couldn't put his finger on why.

Dana partially turned him. "These are the twins, Lissa and Charlotte."

Lissa had long curly hair, three piercings in her left ear, and a smile that screamed trouble. She had to be around five-foot-four, no taller. Wolfe liked her immediately.

"How long have you been dating Dana?" she asked, a protective challenge curving her lips.

"Just friends." He shook her hand.

Charlotte then held out a hand, a serious light in her eyes. Her curly hair was in a bob, and she looked almost identical to Lissa, except for a small and faded scar beneath her jaw. "It was very nice of you to drive *your friend* all the way to Tennessee for a wedding."

Cute. He liked sarcasm. "I'm a very nice guy."

Lissa geared up, her shoulders going back, her mouth starting to move to ask him a bunch of questions—he could just tell. Before she could start, a woman appeared in the doorway and clapped her hands. "Girls! For goodness sake, you have to get ready."

Wolfe partially turned to see an older version of Dana, short and pretty with blond hair, standing in the doorway wearing jeans and a white blouse. Her gaze caught his, and she summed him up in a second with shrewd blue eyes. Then she walked forward, all grace, a pretty smile curving her mouth. "Well, hello. I hadn't realized Dana was bringing a date." Delight made her eyes dance.

He fought the very real urge to shuffle his feet. "Hi. I'm, ah, Clarence." He gently shook her hand.

"Wolfe," Dana said, helping him out. "Everyone calls him Wolfe because it's his last name."

"What a lovely last name." Dana's mom kept his hand. "You can call me Evie." She leaned in to him, smelling like fresh roses. "I will preemptively apologize for subjecting you to our crazy family en masse like this."

"I fit in with crazy, ma'am," he admitted.

She chuckled. "I'm glad to hear it. I rented Dana a room over the main clubhouse for the night, so you can have that. Dana can bunk in with Katie, who didn't bring a date and won't tell me a thing about her love life."

Wolfe kept perfectly still so as not to scare the nice lady. "I'll see what I can find out."

Evie patted his arm. "You're a sweet one." Her eyes widened. "And so strong." She felt his bicep.

"Mom!" Dana protested.

Evie rolled her eyes. "He just has nice muscles, and your father could use some help setting up the chairs on the lawn overlooking the river. Wolfe, do you mind helping?"

"Not at all." His collar felt too tight, even though he wasn't wearing one. Escaping was a good idea. "I'll, ah, check in with you later, Dana." He whistled for Roscoe, who'd disappeared in the flowers. Then he turned and almost ran toward the area near the river.

"Oh, my. I think we've already scared him," Evie worried in a whisper that followed him.

Dana's responding laugh immediately lifted his spirits and calmed his nerves. He slowed and looked at the dog. "I may have miscalculated here."

Roscoe snorted.

Dana looked at herself in the full-length mirror and then wished she hadn't. The odd shade of purplish green washed out her skin, and so far, makeup wasn't helping. The bodice was straight across, leading to puffed sleeves that made it look like she was wearing shoulder pads. The dress was tight across her stomach and then flared to end right below her knees. "Ug."

"Mom?" Charlotte yelled from the other room.

"She went to make sure Dad was changing into his nicer clothes," Dana yelled back. She studied her image, trying to find something positive about the dress, but nothing came to mind. When she moved, the shimmery material moved from an ugly green to an even uglier purple. "This sucks."

"Shut up," Lissa muttered, shuffling in from the bathroom. "At least you have several inches of height to lengthen the lines."

Dana turned around, coughed, and then clapped her hand over her mouth. Her younger sister looked like a green grape. She tried to hold down the laugh as tears filled her eyes, but her body shook anyway.

"I hate you," Lissa said, an unwilling smile tipping her lips. "Though you look like a bruised kiwi."

Dana let the laugh loose and then regained her control, only to lose it again when Katie stomped into the room.

"What hell did we ever unleash on Sally to earn this as retribution?" Katie snarled, the green dress with its puffy sleeves somehow flattening her size Bs.

"Well, didn't Charlotte steal her boyfriend in the sixth grade?" Lissa asked, trying unsuccessfully to pat down the sleeves.

"That was you," her twin reminded her, coming in from the other room looking as bad as Lissa.

"Oh yeah," Lissa said, giving up on the sleeves. "Charlotte? I can honestly say I've never seen you look so bad."

Dana shook her head. Charlotte was a health nut and had an incredible body, and it had to have been a personal challenge for Sally to find a dress that was unflattering on her. But Sally had succeeded.

Lissa tossed a ringlet over her shoulder. "I say we stage a rebellion."

It was surprising Lissa had waited this long to make

the suggestion. "I think you're mellowing in your old age," Dana observed.

"Being twenty-eight does come with responsibility," Lissa agreed. "Now. How about we cut off the puffs and shorten these skirts by about four inches to just above the knees?"

Dana glanced at Katie. "We shouldn't."

Katie was usually the voice of reason. "What would happen to the dress if we cut off the puffs?"

Lissa stood up on her tiptoes and played with Dana's left puff. "It looks like there's a fabric strip beneath the sleeve that's more like a halter. Did Sally have these stupid sleeves added to the dress? She would just do that." She dropped back down and turned for her bag, rummaging around and emerging with a pair of nail scissors. "Give me a sec."

Dana held still. "Hurry before Mom gets back."

"Okay." Lissa drew her to sit on an ottoman by the western-style sofa and then leaned down, gingerly cutting, her cheek close to Dana's. "It'll take me a few minutes to do all of these. How about we discuss Wolfe in the meantime?"

"Good plan." Charlotte flounced over and sat on the sofa. "Dana? What the heck? He's seriously hot."

"And big," Katie said, more gracefully sitting next to Charlotte. "He's taller than Dad, I think. If not, he's the same height."

"I wonder what's gonna happen when Mike sees him," Charlotte said.

"Don't tell me Mike actually showed up," Dana groaned, fiddling with the wolf necklace she'd just wanted to wear for a little while. "Could this wedding get any worse?"

Lissa nodded. "I ran into Sally yesterday, and she

mentioned he was coming and how nice that was. That maybe you two could get back together." She rolled her eyes. "Obviously she knows the guy is a tool, but he's friends with her fiancé, so there's that."

Charlotte nodded. "Total tool. Why did you go out with him, anyway?"

Dana shrugged. "I didn't know he was a tool until a couple of dates. It's not like I slept with him or anything."

"Wolfe is a big guy. Maybe when Mike spots him with you, he'll decide to keep a low profile." Lissa tossed the offending puff across the room and moved to Dana's other side. "You have always liked big guys. Is Wolfe solid muscle everywhere?"

Dana swallowed. "He runs and eats pretty healthy."

"Go on," Lissa said, pursing her lips and cutting.

"He kisses better than I can even describe." Dana tilted her head away from the scissors.

Charlotte leaned forward. "And?"

"That's all you're getting on the matter." Dana let out a breath as Lissa moved away with the puff. "He's on some dangerous mission that he thinks will either ruin him or get him killed, so he keeps everyone at a distance, even me."

Katie's eyebrows rose. "That's just stupid."

Charlotte nodded. "Is he a moron?"

"No, just kind of lost," Dana said.

"Weddings are romantic, and I'm sure you'll easily catch his attention," Katie said.

"You're not gonna be able to seduce Wolfe in this dress." Lissa motioned for her to stand. "Yet. Let's see what I can do." She knelt down and rapidly cut the shimmery fabric to right above Dana's knees. "Well, that's better." She stood and viewed the dress critically. "One more adjustment." She reached for the bodice and cut a quick v, tucking the edges into Dana's bra so that a nice amount of cleavage showed. "Your push-up bra is doing most of the work."

Katie stood. "So much better. Do me next."

Dana turned to look in the mirror, starting in surprise. Twin straps held the dress up and attached to the back, and without the extra material, the bodice looked sleek and not so tight around her torso. "It looks a zillion times better, even though there's nothing we can do about the color."

Charlotte leaned to the side of the sofa to drag out a box. "Did you guys see the shoes?"

Dread pooled in Dana's stomach. "No. How bad?"

Charlotte flipped open the lid to reveal a plain black orthopedic-type sandal with three thick straps across the top and a chunky heel. "Guaranteed to make even the slenderest of ankles look like cankles."

Dana burst out laughing. "Those are the ugliest old lady shoes I've ever seen." Knowing Sally, she'd bought them either too big or too small for everyone, too. "Maybe we should go barefoot?" Their mom would kill them.

"Ah, you'd have to go barefoot if I wasn't your sister," Katie said with a small smile.

Dana whirled around. "You didn't."

"I did." Katie gingerly pointed toward the television console in the corner while Lissa went to work on her hemline. "I hid them in there."

Dana beat Charlotte to the cabinet and pulled out four shoe boxes, tipping the first one open. "Oh," she gasped, pulling out a sparkling light-gold high heel with a winding strap across the front. "This is gorgeous."

"I figured the metallic gold would class up the outfit and play well off the green and purple." Katie looked down at her bare knees. "Also, I assumed we'd all wear our gold crosses and the gold earrings Great-Grandma May gave us for our eighteenth birthdays, so that'll tie it all together."

Dana grinned, feeling lighter for the first time in too long. She'd missed her sisters. "Oh, this is gonna be fun."

"Now." Lissa grinned. "Katie, fix Dana's makeup, would you? We need to get that slumbering wolf to wake up and howl."

Chapter Twenty-Five

Wolfe had helped with the chairs and then found his assigned hotel room, changing into the suit that Dana had said was perfect before heading back outside. He'd also shaved. Ties weren't his thing, but he could handle one for a few hours. He looked out over the wide swath of white chairs facing a gazebo in front of the winding river. Trees on the other side made for a nice backdrop. Many people had already been seated, and music played softly through speakers set unobtrusively around the area. A breeze wandered through, and with a slight cloud cover, it wasn't too hot.

He felt mildly guilty at locking Roscoe in his room on the second floor after sneaking the pooch up the back stairs, but dogs weren't usually allowed at weddings. He'd googled it earlier.

Where should he sit? Was there a spot for a kinda friend, not really date, of a bridesmaid who had unprotected sex with her after being drugged at a BDSM party? He doubted it.

"Hey." A gray-haired guy, broad across the chest and with Dana's green eyes, came up from the side. "I didn't get a chance earlier to thank you for helping with the chairs. The woman barking orders is my not-so-sweet sister,

Roberta, and we try not to piss her off." He held out a beefy hand. "I'm Mitch Mulberry."

"Clarence Wolfe." Wolfe shook, impressed by the man's strength.

Mitch released him and turned to look at the chairs. "My wife wants me to check you out. You have good intentions toward my daughter?"

"Always." Even though Dana and he might not agree upon those intentions.

"Good." Mitch slapped him on the back. "Why don't you come sit up front with me? You're a big guy. If things go south, you can block the way while I run." He tugged on his tie. "I hate dressing up. How about you?"

Wolfe followed him up the aisle to the second row, careful not to tear the flimsy material dotted with rose petals on the way. "I find it's difficult to get to the knife in my boot when I'm dressed up, but Dana said I can take the jacket off after the wedding."

Mitch took the second seat and left the aisle seat for Wolfe. "You have a knife in your boot?" His bushy eyebrows rose, and the smile lines near his eyes crinkled in his weathered face.

"Yeah." Wolfe settled into the seat, which was a little too small. "Don't you?"

Mitch grinned. "Buddy, I have four beautiful daughters. Believe me, I always have a knife close by."

Wolfe matched his smile.

Mitch reached into his jacket pocket. "Did anyone find you a bingo card?" he whispered.

Wolfe shook his head.

Mitch handed over a square sheet of paper. "I have an extra, but don't let anybody see it, especially my wife. Winner gets the pot." He paused. "Oh. Give me twenty dollars."

Wolfe handed over a twenty, which quickly disappeared

in Mitch's right pocket. Then he looked at the squares on his paper. "Ah. So I cross off what I see." Was this what families did at weddings? He hadn't seen a purple hat, someone's Spanx, or a flask yet. He read more. "What is a jortz?"

"Jean shorts on a man," Mitch whispered. "We have a couple of cousins that'll give you that square if they make it here."

"Not sure I want to see that." Wolfe tucked the bingo card away in his pocket, oddly touched to take part in the family bingo game.

"You fish?" Mitch asked.

Wolfe rubbed his now smoothly shaven chin. "I haven't but think I'd like it. I mean, if there weren't a bunch of people around also fishing."

Mitch nodded. "Exactly. A man fishes to commune with nature, not neighbors. We should go sometime."

A pang hit Wolfe dead center in the chest. "I'd like that." Chances weren't great, but who knew? Maybe he would live to learn how to fish. "Thanks for the thought." His voice had become gruff for some reason.

"Do you have 'flask' as one of your squares?" Mitch asked.

Wolfe nodded.

"Then I'll help you out." Mitch took a dinged metal flask from his other inside pocket, twisted off the cap, and tipped back a drink before handing it to Wolfe.

Wolfe was done taking drinks from anybody he didn't know, but Dana's dad had to be all right. He took a hit and let the pure Irish whiskey warm his body. "Thanks." He handed it back.

"You bet." Mitch scrambled to hide the flask as his wife moved down the opposite end of the aisle, waving and smiling at women in summer dresses and men in light suits before finally taking her seat.

She eyed her husband and then Wolfe. "What are you two up to?"

"Nothin'," Mitch said, his eyes wide. "Honest, Evie. We're just sitting here waiting for this shindig to start." He slid an arm around his wife. "You look even prettier now than you did in the pictures earlier with the girls."

Evie blushed a lovely pink that matched her pale dress. Her blond hair was curled, and her blue eyes sparkled. "Don't try to charm me."

Wolfe hadn't spent much time around married people with families; it looked like a good gig. His chest felt empty. Maybe some people weren't supposed to have that kind of life. Nobody related to him ever had.

Evie smacked her husband in the chest. "Those girls of yours. They completely altered their dresses."

Mitch's eyes danced. "I bet that ticked off the bride."

"You have no idea," Evie whispered, obviously fighting a laugh.

The music started, a soft melody, and the groom walked someone who must be his mom down the aisle, helped her sit on the other side, and then took his place by the minister.

When had the minister come out? Wolfe needed to start paying attention. The groom was about six feet tall with a cheesy grin. He looked as if a punch to the jaw would break it and maybe his whole face.

The music changed, and Charlotte started down the aisle with white flowers in her hands, escorted by a shorter, portly twenty-something boy who strutted rather than walked.

Wolfe's gaze flew right past the next two couples and landed on Dana. The breath left his chest faster than it had last time he'd ducked and rolled away from spraying bullets. She was glorious, her green eyes glimmering, wide in her beautiful face. The dress hugged her body, revealing a little cleavage that was a dangerous temptation.

Her gaze met his, and she smiled.

He rocked back as if he'd been punched in the solar plexus.

Dana finished her cake, unable to take her eyes off Wolfe. He was something in a suit, and when he'd discarded the gray jacket and rolled up his sleeves, her mouth had just plain watered. She pushed the plate away on the white-linen-covered table, laughing as Charlotte shimmied on the dance floor with their mom.

Wolfe turned her way, his smile genuine. "Have I told you that you look beautiful?"

About five times, but she loved it every time. "You might've mentioned it." She'd never seen him this relaxed. Not quite carefree, but as close as Wolfe would probably ever get. "So, we've survived the wedding, the toasts, the cake cutting, bouquet and garter tosses, and the first dances. I handled a temper tantrum from the bride about the dresses, and I kept Lissa from punching her. I think we're home free." She eyed the bouquet she'd caught, which lay on the table.

"Not quite." He stood and held out a hand. "We haven't danced."

She wouldn't have been more surprised if he'd suddenly taken off his clothes and jumped into the river. "Good point." Sliding her hand into his, she fought to play it cool. Katie must've done a really good job with the makeup.

"Excuse me. Dana, can we talk?"

Ugh. She'd managed to avoid Mike so far, but apparently

he'd gathered the courage to approach, even with Wolfe towering over her. "There's really nothing to talk about."

"Please, let me apologize." Mike wore a dark blue suit with red power tie, his dark blond hair swept back. "I drank too much, and I regret everything I said. Please forgive me."

Wolfe stepped right behind Dana, no doubt looking at Mike over her head. "What did he do?"

"Nothing," Dana said. "We went to a ball game, he drank too much, and then got handsy. I told him to knock it off, and he made some unkind comments."

"Handsy?" Wolfe repeated, his breath brushing her hair. "Do you want me to break his hands?"

Mike paled, but to his credit, he didn't step back.

It'd be nice to mess with the guy a little longer, but if she told Wolfe yes, he might actually do it. "No, but thanks for the offer." The song was winding down, darn it. The next one had better be a slow tune and not a hard rock one.

Mike held out a hand toward Wolfe. "Hi. I'm Mike. I own River Lake Realty."

Well, he and his daddy did.

"Wolfe." Wolfe reached around Dana to shake, and by the further whitening of Mike's face, he might've gripped too hard. "I'm not looking to buy a house."

Mike yanked his hand free. "If you don't mind, I'd like some privacy with Dana."

"I do mind," Wolfe said, his voice admirably mild.

Mike chuckled. "Good one. Okay, then how about you do me a favor and give us a second? We were rather close." His voice dropped. "So just a small talk."

Her spine straightened up. Irritation swept along her skin. "Wait a minute." She looked over her shoulder and had to tilt her head to look all the way up at Wolfe's face. "Did he just make that sound dirty? Like we were all intimate and everything?"

Wolfe nodded, his eyes burning. "Yeah, yeah, he did. I'd think you had sex."

She let herself laugh out loud. "Nope. We never had sex. A couple of dates, a few kisses, but frankly, I never really wanted it to go beyond that."

Wolfe's lips tipped. "I figured. Now can I break his hand?"

Yep. He looked serious about that. She winked and turned back around to face Mike with Wolfe a very solid force at her back. "No, let's leave his hands alone."

"Just one hand?" Wolfe asked. "How about the one that keeps dialing your phone late at night? I can make sure he stops."

Now, finally, Mike took a wise step back.

Dana pretended to think about it, and Wolfe started to set her to the side. "No," she hurried to say. "If he promises not to call any longer, don't break his hand."

Wolfe kept his hands on her upper arms, his body against hers. "Well?"

"Fine." Mike lost the amused look, started to say something, and apparently grew a brain and held his tongue. He turned on his loafer and headed toward the bar.

"What a tool," Wolfe muttered, sliding one hand down her arm to grasp her hand and lead her to the dance floor. Once there, he turned her and pulled her into him, setting one hand on her hip and scouting the other dancers.

"What are you looking at?" she asked, enjoying the freedom of being able to plant her hand on his hard body.

He focused on her upturned face. "I was looking for jortz."

Happiness bubbled through her and she stepped closer, enjoying the soft song as he moved them around the dance floor. "Sounds like you got a difficult bingo card."

"Apparently." His gaze landed on her mouth and heated.

Her blood sped up as if she'd taken a shot of whiskey.

"What happens if nobody gets bingo?" Wolfe asked, his head lowering toward hers.

Her mind fuzzed, and she tried to concentrate. "We meet for breakfast in the morning, and whoever has the most squares blocked out wins."

His lips were almost on hers when he straightened.

She looked sideways to see her parents dancing right next to them, her mom smiling at her. "Hi." Wonderful timing, darn it.

"Hi." Her mom swayed easily. "Oh, Wolfe. Before I forget. I ran up to our room to grab a wrap, and I heard your puppy whining in your room. So, I let him out. Dogs are allowed on the grounds here."

Wolfe stopped them cold.

Dana gasped. "Oh, no. Where is he?"

The bride shrieked from near the bar.

Chapter Twenty-Six

Wolfe grabbed Dana's hand, unwilling to let her go. He dodged through dancers and reached the tables nearest the bar. "Oh, crap," he muttered.

Dana halted next to him, grabbing his arm to keep her balance. "Whoa."

Roscoe pranced, his front feet in the bride's red-bottomed, high-heeled, and very sparkly shoes. He caught sight of Dana, wagged his tail, and shuffled toward her.

Dana audibly swallowed and looked over at the bride, who sat at the head table, her face red.

"I just took them off for a second," Sally said, glaring at Dana.

Wolfe fought the urge to stand in front of Dana to shield her from the meanness.

"Now, Sally," Dana said, edging toward Roscoe. "He just wants to be a little taller and he looks so nice."

Sally stood about five-foot-five and had blond hair and blue eyes. Her dress was white and sparkly, and she smiled a lot but didn't seem all that warm around Dana or her family. Wolfe hadn't yet figured out why she'd put Dana and her sisters in the wedding. "This is your fault," Sally spat.

He almost agreed until he realized she was talking to Dana and not to him.

"It's my fault," he corrected, edging to the left to grab the dog.

Sally put her hands on her slim waist. "Dana, you brought this crazy dog on purpose. You've always been jealous of me, and here I am getting married."

Dana turned pink, but she didn't argue.

"Wait a minute." Katie stepped up to her side, followed by the twins. "That's not true."

Dana partially turned. "It's her wedding. She needs her shoes."

Wolfe nabbed Roscoe by the scruff of his neck. "Drop the shoes and keep your mouth off them."

The dog snorted, growled, and then gingerly stepped out of first one and then the other shoe. Wolfe breathed out, his body calming. Roscoe then turned his head and ducked.

"No." Wolfe pushed the dog out of the way and snagged the shoes before he could get one in his teeth. He strode toward Sally. "I'm really sorry about this. Apparently, Roscoe was in a firefight with the FBI and somebody got blown up and he was injured and he had a problem with another dog being taller than him. Or something like that." Wolfe had never really paid attention to the story.

Sally took the shoes and gave him a brilliant smile. "Why, thank you."

The growl behind him was from Dana, not Roscoe.

The music started up again, and Wolfe took a step away from the bride. He looked back momentarily, turning to meet Roscoe's wide eyes. "Don't," Wolfe warned.

"Yip." The sound was pure joy as Roscoe bounded over the bar, snagging a bottle of Jack on the way and landing on the nearest table, sliding slightly on the soft linen. He sucked the whiskey down before Wolfe could get to him and then leaped from table to table, scattering glasses and purses.

The bride yelled again.

People scrambled out of the way. Roscoe landed on another table, set his mouth over a bottle of champagne, and tipped it back, gulping wildly.

"Holy shit," Mitch said, lunging off the dance floor.

"Go left," Wolfe ordered, heading to the right. They had to get the dog before he drank any more. Roscoe never knew when to stop.

"That's it," the bride bellowed, gathering her dress and storming toward the dog.

Wolfe held up a hand, trying to stop her. "Wait a sec—"

The dog jumped toward another table, but the ticked-off bride blocked him, throwing her shoulder into Roscoe. He spun in the air, and then everything happened in slow motion.

"No," Dana yelled just as Roscoe fell on the cake table, scattering frosting, utensils, and plates.

The music stopped. Everyone froze. Roscoe looked around at all the people, slid a little in the frosting, and then turned to view the remains of the cake. He struck fast, his entire face diving into the mound of frosting and cake, growling as he ate his way to the bottom. Then he lifted his head, licking his lips. White frosting and pink roses covered his nose and whiskers and most of his head.

Wolfe couldn't move. His entire body had been stunned into immobility.

"My cake!" the bride screamed.

Dana rushed for the dog. "It's okay, Sally. You already cut the cake, fed it to each other, and we put the top layer in the freezer for you to keep for your first anniversary along with the topper. It's all good." She reached the dog and tried to grab him, her fingers sliding through the frosting covering his fur.

Mitch snorted next to Wolfe, trying unsuccessfully to keep from laughing.

Sally ran forward and shoved Dana. "You bitch. You jealous bitch."

Wolfe started to move, and Mitch grasped his arm. "Hold it."

Dana's sisters came up on her side, and Lissa was having a difficult time trying to stop laughing. Dana held up a hand, keeping the other one on the happily panting dog. "Sally, this was an accident. Honest. We're sorry. We'll lock Roscoe up."

Sally moved toward Dana, and Wolfe tensed.

"Wait a minute," Charlotte said. "Everyone, relax and knock it off."

Sally swept her hand out. "Relax? Look at my cake."

Lissa laughed harder.

Sally glared and took another menacing step toward Dana.

"Shouldn't we do something?" Wolfe asked.

"No. Just hold on a sec. Don't worry," Mitch said, reaching for a beer on the table behind him.

Evie and Roberta marched up and quickly took care of business, sending everyone off to dance or drink. The music started again, and Wolfe made his way to Dana as the caterers started to clean up the mess. "I've got him."

She looked up, frosting on her cheek. "You sure?"

He gently reached out to wipe off the frosting. "Yeah. I'll go drop him in the river and clean him off." He whistled, and Roscoe jumped down to the ground, happily drunk and high on sugar.

Wolfe sighed. He wasn't sure whether he owed the dog gratitude or a dunking.

* * *

Wolfe twirled the whiskey in his glass, sitting bare-chested on the king-sized bed in his darkened hotel room, which was lit only by the moon's rays sneaking through the tall window. Roscoe was sprawled across the sofa, sleeping off the booze. The day with Dana's family had shown him a world he hadn't realized existed. He didn't belong in that world, but what a temptation it was. His mood remained unsettled at the thought.

Light footsteps pattered in the hallway outside, and he finished his drink, standing and setting the glass on the counter as he moved toward the door.

He opened it on the second knock to find Dana in another cute camisole and short set, her face scrubbed clean and her feet bare. She was sexy as hell and somehow adorable at the same time. The top barely covered her breasts, and her nipples were hard beneath the thin cotton.

There was no way he was strong enough to be smart for the both of them. So he shifted his weight to the side without a word. Surprise danced across her face and she moved past him, turning around feet from the bed.

He shut the door and locked it.

Her eyes widened, and her chest moved as if her breathing had quickened. "You owe me a kiss," she whispered, looking beautiful in the moonlight streaming through the window.

His body tightened, need raging through him. "If you stay, it's gonna be more than a kiss," he said, his blood starting to hum.

Her chin lifted. "Good."

"I can't promise you more than this." The vow he'd taken, bleeding and furious in the dust beside his slaughtered team, meant something. As did she, so he had to be honest. The pull she had on him was unreal, and his control was close to shredding. "I need you to understand that."

"I still understand that nothing has changed between us," she said softly, "but I'm not giving up on your survival or on getting you to let me help."

There was no chance he'd let her get involved in the fight with Rock, but she could hope for his survival all she wanted. Couldn't hurt. "I dream about you sometimes."

"Yeah?" Her smile held a feminine knowledge.

"Yeah." Oh, this was a mistake, but for the first time in his life, he didn't care. He crossed the distance between them, getting closer to her sweet scent of orange blossoms. The bruises on her arms had faded, and he needed to be careful not to leave any more on her. The smooth skin on her face called for his touch, and he traced along her cheekbone and down her neck to her clavicle, his fingers light. "Are you sure?"

Her dimples winked. "I'm here, barefoot, in the middle of the night, Wolfe." She looked around. "No whipped cream to play with this time."

"I ain't playin' this time." He pressed his thumb in that enticing dimple, the way he'd wanted to do for months. "I went gentle on you last time, and I also ain't feeling gentle right now."

She stepped into him, her hands sliding up his bare chest, teasing him with a light touch. "I never asked for gentle."

His cock leaped to life, pressing against his zipper. He smoothed down her bare arms with both hands, encircling her wrists and pulling them up so he could kiss each knuckle, taking his time to give himself control. "I can't get enough of you," he rumbled, opening her hand and placing a kiss in the center of her palm.

"Ditto." She freed her wrists and cupped his jaw, rising up on her toes to kiss him.

The feel of her soft lips against his sent a jolt of sparking electricity through him to land in his balls. He let her nibble for a couple of moments, enjoying the sensations, and then he took over. He cupped the back of her head, holding her still, and went as deep as he wanted.

She moaned and moved closer to him, her fingers curling into his skin, biting.

He kissed her harder, exploring her, running his free hand down her side to clasp her hip and pull her into his aching groin. The contact nearly undid him, and he groaned, tasting wine and frosting on her lips.

She kissed him back, moving against him, her hands flattening against his bare chest. Even her hands were soft on him. So delicate.

Never in his life had he wanted a woman so much. He released her mouth and leaned back to look his full. Her lips were rosy, her cheeks pink, and her eyes dark with need. With desire. For him. He'd done nothing in his life to deserve this, to deserve her, but he couldn't turn away.

Slowly, drawing out the anticipation, he hooked his thumb beneath a strap and gently drew it down her arm. Then the other one, and the cami fell to her waist.

He breathed out. Her full breasts were tight, the nipples a light pink that were beyond temptation, even without the whipped cream. "So pretty," he murmured, brushing his thumbs across both nipples.

She shuddered, leaning into his touch.

He yanked the top off her, tossing it over his head.

She gasped and smiled, leaning in to free his shirt. He let her and then tangled his fingers through her hair, holding her still for a kiss. The AC kicked on, but he didn't feel the chill. His heart started to thump with a hard-rock beat, and he went deeper, walking her back to the bed.

He grasped her hips and lifted her, intending to set her down gently.

She clamped her thighs onto his hips, clutched his neck, and kissed him ferociously. He tried to be gentle, tried to slow her down, tried to keep his mind in charge.

His control uncoiled and then shredded with a physical jolt.

Chapter Twenty-Seven

Finally.

Dana felt the change in him the second it happened. He stopped pretending to let her direct the kiss and took over, as in really *took over*. Somehow, she ended up on her back on the bed, all of that muscle and strength and raw heat over her, his mouth working hers like he was starving.

She was frantic, caressing his ripped arms, wanting to touch him everywhere.

In a move of easy strength, he rolled them, landing on his back and planting her on his groin. She pressed down and arched her back, biting her lip against the exquisite agony. She dropped forward, her hands flattened on his hard chest, nowhere near to covering all the muscle.

Finally.

She traced cords and muscles, her fingers dipping into healed bullet holes, knife wounds, and burns on his side.

He glanced down, his voice rough. "I've had a bit of damage."

"You're perfect." She meant it. Humming, rubbing against his erection, she leaned over and kissed his collarbone, nipping near his neck before sitting back up and gyrating against him.

He palmed her breasts, rolling both nipples and shooting lust straight to her core. "Slow down," he murmured.

"Not a chance." She scraped her nails down his abs, wanting to lick and count each ripple.

"Dana." He punctuated the word by tugging on her nipples with more than a hint of bite.

She stilled, sparks uncoiling in her abdomen, her gaze slashing to his. Dark hunger made his eyes glow like those of a tiger out for the hunt, watching prey, ready to spring. His impossibly ripped body pulsed beneath her, his power barely banked.

"We've gone slow enough," she gasped. If she didn't get him inside her now, she was going to lose her mind.

The muscles in his corded neck swelled. His biceps bunched, providing warning as he lifted her easily and set her on her back. He hooked his thumbs in her waistband, pressed her knees up and together, and tugged the remaining clothing off, leaving her completely nude to his gaze. "Ah, baby."

In one smooth move, he rolled from the bed to his knees, jerked her ankles apart and pulled her toward him.

Then his mouth found her.

He sucked. Hard.

She arched, crying out, clinging to the bedspread as Wolfe apparently decided to stop going slow. He went at her like a starving man, one hand palming both her buttocks and lifting her against his mouth, his tongue lashing her clit with unrelenting purpose.

Waves of pleasure pummeled her, spiraling out from his talented mouth. He played her body like he'd created it.

She frantically patted the bed, secured a pillow, and planted it over her face, biting the soft cotton. Her mind fuzzed, electricity zinging behind her eyes.

The orgasm swelled and then detonated in a blaze of

devastation, and she cried out, pressing the pillow to her mouth to try to diminish the sound. He pressed two fingers inside her, twisting them and prolonging the devastating ecstasy until her body went limp.

She gasped, sucking in cotton, and then shoved the pillow to the side so she could breathe.

Wolfe set her butt back down on the comforter and stood, his eyes glittering. The moonlight danced across the muscles in his chest, hinting at the power and strength she'd only just begun to tap. His hands went to his belt, and she shivered, her legs still trembling.

This was different from last time. More intense, as if he was giving her more of himself.

He unbuckled with a metallic clank, unzipped with a metal hiss, and shoved his pants to the floor with a swish that had her panting and ready for more.

Holy moly on a double cracker. Her memory of him was spot on. Sometimes a girl just got a gift from the gods in this life. He was hard and thick and long . . . totally in proportion to his spectacular body. Knife wounds, healed and white, dotted his left thigh, while healed burns ran along the other one, next to the perfect bite mark from her mouth. Oh yeah. She'd forgotten about that.

He rummaged in his bag and drew out a condom, which he quickly rolled into place. Then, his hold surprisingly gentle, he clamped her hips and lifted her, turning to set her the right way on the bed.

Finally.

"Now we're gonna go slow." He maneuvered his body into place, held himself with one hand over her, careful not to crush her.

"Nope." She bent her knees and manacled his arms, pressing up for just one touch.

"Yes." He obliged her, sliding a hand between her legs, driving two fingers inside. Easily. "Just making sure you're ready."

She pressed her lips together to keep from begging. "I nearly choked on a pillow trying not to scream a second ago. I'm ready." She was wet, her body primed.

He did that crisscrossing thing with his fingers that he'd done earlier, and she whimpered. Actually whimpered.

The sound made his eyes glitter, open and clearly hungry. Nothing veiled and nothing held back. There was no doubt few people in the world had ever seen that look on Clarence Wolfe's face.

"Now, Wolfe. Please." Being polite wasn't exactly begging.

When he removed his fingers, her body felt empty, unfulfilled, until he guided the head of his cock into her.

Finally.

"Yes," she breathed, digging her fingers into the sleek skin at his waist. "More."

He rocked against her, sweat dotting his forehead with the strain of going slow. Another inch inside, and he groaned, the tension between them almost too much. "You okay?" he grunted.

Her heart rolled over and filled up with him. "Yes." Her voice thickened. This close to being all the way inside her heat, with his body so hard and tense it had to hurt, he still paused to make sure she was safe. "Though I'd be better if you'd get a move on." She opened her legs wider, her feet sliding on the bedspread.

He rocked back and forth, in and out, giving her a couple more inches. She stretched around him, gasping, her clit firing again as if awakened from a long slumber.

Maybe an entire lifetime of sleep. "I can't wait any longer," she moaned, pulling at his hips with all of her strength.

"That's unfortunate." He dropped his head to the crook of her neck, his voice gritty, the tone pained. He kissed her jugular and reached under her, palming her entire butt again and lifting her against him.

Thank God.

She arched, taking more of him than he'd intended and feeling victorious.

He growled against her neck, sending vibrations through her skin to zing her breasts and zap her whole body. "You are not in control here."

She dug her nails into his flesh, more than willing to leave scratches. "Fine. You be in charge but get all the way inside me. Now."

He lifted his head, his eyes piercing. "Are you really arguing with me right now?"

Her eyes widened. "I wouldn't be if you would just shove—argh." She yelped as he powered all the way inside her, groin to groin, stretching her in every direction.

He stopped moving, holding her tight, the hand on her ass firm. "Happy now?"

She had to take a second to find out. He more than filled her, pulsing against her internal walls, owning her body in a way she never would've imagined. "Yes. I'm much happier now," she admitted, smiling as the pain slid right to pleasure with an edge. "Now you can start moving."

His lids lowered. "Dana? You've pushed enough."

"Then you start pushing." She tried to clamp her knees to his thighs, but she was spread too wide by his hips. At the realization, a shiver took her, landing hard right where their bodies connected.

"Now you're getting it." He lowered his forehead to hers.

"I want more of you," she breathed, going on instinct.

He lifted up, his gaze boring into her, his body taking hers. "Then I'll give you more. On my terms."

"I'll battle you for that." She lifted against him as much as she was able, which wasn't much. "You can spank me later. For now, let's do this." Her voice was breathy, almost husky.

His eyes flared. "Oh, that's a date, then."

Wait a minute. What had she—

He slid out and then powered back inside her, watching her expression carefully. When she didn't flinch or gasp or do anything but glide her hands up his chest, he did it again, this time with a little more force.

"Yes," she moaned.

He powered into her, no longer going slow, and all she could do was hold on. Faster and harder, longer and deeper, he took her, his gaze an intense promise she couldn't decipher. Energy uncoiled inside her, deeper than before, and her legs started to shake with an intensity that ran down to her feet.

She fought the orgasm, wanting to prolong this time as long as possible.

His jaw hardened and he tilted his hips just enough to pummel her clit. She exploded with a rough cry she couldn't stop.

His mouth took hers, stifling her cries, kissing her deep enough she could only moan as she shut her eyes and let pleasure surge through her, taking her into a moment of raw feeling with no thought. Ecstasy ravaged her, leaving her gasping for breath even as her body relaxed into a marshmallow.

But he wasn't done.

"Fuck," he murmured, holding her tighter.

She held on to him, taking all of him, wonder filling her. His body tightened even more, the cords in his neck straining. He hammered faster and then held her against him, shuddering with his own release. He groaned, dropping his head to the safety of her neck again, his breath harsh against her skin.

One more grunt, and he paused, not moving.

She could feel his heartbeat slamming against hers. "Wolfe." Hot, heated, slick skin filled her palms as she caressed up his flanks to his shoulders, rubbing soothing circles on the way.

He lifted his head, his eyes soft. "Are you all right?"

She laughed, feeling free. "I'm better than all right. How about you?" He was still inside her, lightly throbbing, his weight held off her by his elbow.

"Yeah, I'm good," he said softly, brushing the hair away from her face in a gentle touch that nearly brought tears to her eyes. "There's water in the fridge if you want some."

Her chuckle emerged naturally. "I'm not thirsty." Yet.

"You will be." The promise in his eyes stole what little breath she had left. "It's gonna be a long night."

Her body woke right up again. "Is it?"

"Yep. Now, about that spanking you mentioned . . ."

Chapter Twenty-Eight

Wolfe finished his egg-white omelet, sitting between Dana and her dad at a long table with Evie, the three sisters, and a bunch of other relatives. The bride and groom had taken off for their honeymoon, and the bride's mother wasn't around, so it was a boisterous affair. Dana's sisters had sent him knowing smiles, and her parents had been polite and friendly, no doubt not wanting to dwell on thoughts of what he'd done to their daughter the night before.

There wasn't much he hadn't done.

His limbs were relaxed, and his chest felt like he'd let it expand for the first time in years. Next to him, Dana chattered happily with Katie, and he got the sense of why his buddies had fought for family back home. This was everything.

Dana leaned over him to talk to her mom, her breast brushing his arm. "Hey, Mom? I forgot to ask why Hunter, Faye, and Miss A weren't at the wedding last night."

Wolfe partially turned to face Evie. He'd met Hunter and Faye while on leave with his buddy Raider not too long ago. The three had been raised by Miss A in a foster home. Of course, that's also when he'd met Dana. He'd found her in the woods and had tossed her umbrella in the river when she'd tried to stab him with it. He grinned at the memory.

Evie delicately wiped her mouth on her napkin. "Hunter and Faye took his brother, Jackson, to some space camp in Florida. While there, I'm hoping they start ring shopping, as is Miss A." She winked at her husband. "Miss A had another wedding up in Boston for one of her foster kids. I think she was acting as mother of the groom, and rumor has it the bride was a total bridezilla."

"Miss A will handle her," Lissa said, tipping back a mimosa across from him.

"Wish I could see that," Katie agreed, reaching over to steal bacon from Charlotte's plate.

Good idea. Wolfe snagged a piece of whole-wheat toast from Dana's plate, munching quietly. For the first time, he tried to think of a way to take out Rock without getting injured. Chances weren't great.

He liked Dana. A lot. Maybe she really would date him after all of this was over. She had to appreciate that he'd kept himself from breaking Mike's hands the previous night, when he'd at least wanted to twist a thumb or something. And she didn't seem to mind Kat being around or Wolfe being too blunt, so maybe there was a chance. It was hard to be anything but hopeful when surrounded by the Mulberry family.

Mitch looked more at home dressed in ripped jeans and a worn T-shirt today. He pushed his plate away. "Okay. Now we get down to business."

The table grew silent.

Wolfe leaned back to better see everyone, realizing his hand was playing with Dana's hair. He dropped his arm. The woman had just dug right into his heart and planted her stubborn blond ass. What in the hell was he going to do now?

Mitch pulled his bingo card from his back pocket with a flourish. "I have fourteen squares marked out."

Cards instantly appeared on the table with shouts of numbers, and when things settled down, Charlotte had twenty marked out. Lissa peered over her shoulder to read the card. "You cheat, you know."

Dana elbowed Wolfe. "Where's your card?"

He shrugged. Let Charlotte win this one. The brunette was smiling triumphantly at her sisters.

Mitch elbowed him from the other side. "She does cheat. Where's your card?"

His ribs weren't going to survive sitting between these two. Wolfe reluctantly drew the card from his back pocket, sliding it to Mitch.

"Whoa. Twenty-four squares." Mitch clapped him on the back. "You were one away from the entire card. Great job." He laughed and tossed a mushroom at Charlotte. "And I know you cheated. Nobody did the tango last night."

"I got Lissa to do it in the bedroom," Charlotte countered. "Rose and everything."

Lissa rubbed her nose. "I might've had a bit too much champagne, but I think I rocked it."

"Had to be on the dance floor, and you know it." Mitch reached in his pocket and handed cash to Wolfe. "Four hundred bucks. Don't spend it all in one place."

Wolfe took the bills, his ears heating. A thought occurred to him as he counted heads at the table. "This should cover breakfast." As well as a very nice tip for the harried waitress, a forty-something woman with an excellent memory.

Mitch clapped him again, this time harder. "It certainly should. That's mighty kind of you."

Evie leaned around her husband. "That is very nice, Clarence. Thank you so much."

His ears heated more, and he just nodded, fighting the temptation to slide right into the warmth offered by these kind people. He got the feeling that whoever won bingo usually bought breakfast. Thank goodness his brain was working this morning. Dana leaned over and pressed a quick kiss to his cheek, obviously not caring that her family was watching.

She accepted him so completely and openly. He didn't deserve that, but he wasn't sure he could let her go any longer. He needed some time and distance to figure all of this out.

Lissa's eyebrows rose. "Oh. I forgot to ask how your dog is doing this morning."

"He's hungover," Wolfe said, relieved to be talking about anything but himself. "I sent him down to the river to dunk his head, and he's probably asleep in the sun now."

Katie worried her lower lip across from him. "Doesn't alcohol kill dogs?"

Wolfe shook his head. "Most dogs but not that one. The vet can't explain it, but Roscoe always survives. We try to keep him away from the booze, but accidents happen."

"Especially when there is cake involved." Mitch started laughing, and his wife slapped his hand.

Conversations started up again around them, and Wolfe turned toward Dana. She'd come to breakfast in a pale yellow summer dress with her long hair back in a ponytail. Her pretty pink lipstick made her mouth shimmer and all but beg for a kiss. Her eyes were a clear, happy green, and although she'd moved a little carefully this morning, she seemed relaxed.

He gave in to temptation and reached out to knead her nape. "How are you doing?" He kept his voice low.

"Great." She sipped her orange juice, a muted pink tinging her cheekbones. "A little sore but in a good way."

Yeah, he got that. The scratches on his arms and chest were light and would fade, but he liked that she'd left her mark on him, at least temporarily. "Your family is pretty great."

"Thanks." She leaned into him naturally, and he tried not to think beyond this moment. "I know we have to get on the road soon, so when it's time, just let me know."

The desire to stay another day with everyone caught him by surprise, since he'd usually rather be alone. Oddly enough, he didn't feel out of place here. But he and Dana had cases to solve, and he needed to keep an eye on Force and make sure he wasn't killing his liver. "We have a few minutes." He tugged on her ponytail, and she smacked his arm, laughing and then rolling her eyes at Lissa, who was openly grinning at them.

Was it possible for him to have a real relationship with Dana? There were a lot of people to protect in this family, but he was one of the best. He settled his hand against her nape, stopping the kneading. "I was thinking—"

"No," Dana said, her smile remaining firmly in place. "I am not staying with my family while you solve all of the world's problems on your own."

Well, then. That wasn't exactly how he'd planned to word the suggestion, but she'd caught his gist. He could appeal to her father, but something told him that would get him punched in the gut. It'd probably tick off her sisters, too. "Hey. I forgot to ask about that scene with the bride last night. It had looked like she was actually going to hit you. You weren't really going to fight, were you?"

She shrugged. "No. Lissa would've tried to jump in, and Katie would've stopped her, and it would've been a mess if the moms hadn't arrived in time. But nobody would've gotten hit. Well, probably."

Okay. The Mulberry sisters were nuts. He should probably be careful not to piss them all off at the same time. "I'm glad the moms stepped in," he muttered.

"Me too." Dana speared a piece of melon and plopped it in her mouth, chewing thoughtfully.

"Have you ever been in a physical fight?" Wolfe asked.

She shook her head. "Not unless you count fighting over the television remote control with one of my sisters."

"I don't," Wolfe said.

"Then, nope. Never been in a fight."

He needed to teach her how to fight. Not that he wanted her to fight, but those skills were necessary in their work. Even in her work as a journalist. "You should know how to protect yourself," he said.

She snorted. "You know I could help you on your case, right?"

He wasn't going to argue with her in front of her family. "You are not on my case, and that's the end of it." He kept his voice low, but nobody seemed to be listening to their conversation, anyway.

She patted his jean-clad thigh. "We can talk about that on the drive home. Either way, I'm on the payroll now, remember? We have actual assignments."

That was fine, but his fight with Rock could get her killed. During this escape from reality, he'd been able to banish the images of Candy Folks's autopsy, but soon he'd be back at his crappy office searching for the guy who'd killed her while also preparing to either kill Rock or die trying.

Dana brushed his arm, and the scent of orange blossoms wafted over him. "Congrats on winning bingo. Beginner's luck and all."

"Thanks." A chill clacked down his spine, and he stiffened, going on alert. He scouted the room, landed on a couple of kids eating pancakes in the corner, and then kept going to a window facing the golf course.

Gary Rockcliff stood framed in the window, looking right at him.

Chapter Twenty-Nine

Wolfe's muscles tightened, and ice flowed through his blood. Gary Rockcliff jerked his head to the south and then disappeared. Barely keeping his cool, Wolfe set his napkin on his plate. "Excuse me."

Dana's eyebrows rose, but everyone else kept up their conversations.

His knife was in his boot. Oh, he'd end up in jail and probably be banished from all future Mulberry breakfasts, but if he got the chance to kill Rock right now, he was going to take it. All sound disappeared as he strode through the restaurant and outside to the club grounds, spotting Rock lounging in an outdoor seating area next to a board set up for tournaments.

Wolfe counted the civilians in the area as well as the avenues of escape, his gaze never leaving his enemy. Heat and humidity swam around him, making his shirt too tight.

Rock sat in a lounge chair at one corner of an unused outdoor fireplace and gestured to the seat across from him. "Please."

Wolfe reached down for his knife.

Rock lifted his right hand, showing a detonator with a green blinking light. Coils of some kind attached the device to his hand, so that nobody could take it away.

Wolfe's gut clenched. "You wired the place."

Rock smiled, revealing his too long left canine. "I do love things that go boom."

Fuck. The happy group in the restaurant behind Wolfe had no idea. He started to turn back, to run, to do something, when Rock whistled. "Just sit."

Was there a choice? Wolfe turned back around, pulled out the chair to sit, staring at the man he'd once considered a brother. Rock had let his buzz cut grow out, but his eyes were as sharp and blue as ever. The beard was new. Today he wore a gray golf shirt and khaki pants that showed muscle and brute strength. Wait a minute. Was that a hickey on Rock's neck? "How did you find me, Gary?"

"What? No nicknames any longer because I killed a couple of morons in the desert?" A scar down Gary's throat moved, right beside the hickey, when he talked.

"No. You don't deserve a nickname." Wolfe would never call him Rock again, and he deeply regretted holding that throat wound together on a mission until they could get help. "How?"

"The gods favor me, as you should know by now," Gary said.

Wolfe forced his body to remain relaxed when all he wanted to do was leap over the fireplace and break Gary's neck. The detonator no doubt had a dead man's switch, so if he tackled Gary, the bomb or bombs might explode. "How so?" he asked, wanting confirmation.

Gary looked past him to the restaurant. "Luck. It always finds me."

Wolfe sat quietly, his mind spinning. Luck? If it was luck, then Gary hadn't been looking for Wolfe. So the only way he could've found him would've been through Dana? The pit in his gut now made sense. "Heroin," he murmured, the puzzle still not quite fitting together.

Gary focused on him again. "What about it?"

Candy's notes. The drugging. Albert Nelson's ties to Frank Spanek. The missing CEO—Theresa Rhodes. Heroin tracked over the southern route. Serena's deciphering of Candy's notes and finding heroin in them, in a story about Theresa Rhodes Ah, crap. The pieces all swirled around, hinting at the danger of the ticking explosives as everything dropped into place. Finally. "Nice hickey."

Gary studied him. "Thanks."

The cases were combined. His and Dana's and poor Candy's. There was no doubt Rock would detonate the bomb and enjoy watching Wolfe react, so there was only one option. Hopefully he'd get the facts right. Time to bluff. "I know about your woman. Have a friend on her right now, watching through the scope." Wolfe went with his gut, faster than his brain at the moment.

"Bullshit," Gary retorted.

Jackpot. All right. Wolfe dealt with the facts, shoving emotion away for now. He'd freak out later. "Oh, come on, Gary. You thought I'd miss the clues? You hire Frank Spanek as a middleman, who also somehow, just coincidentally, is a connection to both Albert Nelson and Theresa Rhodes?"

Gary sat back, his gaze shuttering.

But Wolfe knew him. There it was. A fleeting reaction. "So your pretty CEO has been, what? Running drugs through her sporting goods company and associated nonprofits?"

No response.

"Through her nonprofits that help women." Wolfe tsked, forcing amusement into his tone. "Candy Folks tracked down that story, no doubt tugging the strings from money laundering to the heroin market. You used Theresa

Rhodes and her connections with Nelson and Spanek to get your heroin out of Afghanistan, and Candy figured it out. Shit, Rock. Did you kill an innocent journalist?"

Rock lifted a shoulder, his hand steady around the trigger. "She put up a good fight. Nothing close to what I assume your blonde would give. If she lives, that is."

Wolfe showed his teeth. "If I don't make the phone call within the hour, your CEO dies. Do you care?" It was a bluff, because there was a good chance Gary didn't care about the woman. About anybody.

"I care," Gary growled. "Should we let both of our women live or die today?"

Wolfe could deny it, or he could say they were just friends, but it was too late. Dana was already on Rock's radar. Gary's radar. Gary, damn it. But if Wolfe's involvement at the golf course was a surprise, then Gary hadn't found out about the Deep Ops team. That was something. "What do you want?"

Gary sighed. "Well, world peace would be a nice start." He shifted his weight, showing he'd been working out.

Wolfe remained silent.

"You never did have a sense of humor. Apparently being blown up hasn't helped any."

Wolfe barely kept his hands from curling into fists and instead adopted a slightly bored expression. "I always wondered. Why did you leave me alive?"

Gary chuckled, the sound grating. "I thought you were dead. You sure looked dead, and I was under a bit of a deadline."

That explained it, then. "How about we leave the women out of it and just go to it, you and me? I've offered several times, and you keep refusing. You think you'll lose?"

"No. I'd win, but what fun would that be? Over so

quickly?" Gary leaned forward. "Didn't you ever wonder? Who was better at the game—you or me?"

Wolfe shook his head. "I never considered any of it a game. We were on the same team, so it didn't matter who was better." It mattered that they covered each other's backs. "It sickens me that you killed one innocent woman and have been stalking another one. How long have you been following Dana?" He had to make sure Gary hadn't found the unit as well.

"I haven't." Gary grinned, leaning back as if they were two old buddies catching up. "Found out she was snooping around the story about Candy disappearing, had a buddy look her up, and guess what's plastered all over social media? Yep. This wedding. The bride is very energetic and so helpful. I arrived, found you, and got to work on the building after all of the nice wedding guests went to bed, including you."

Was he telling the truth? Seemed like it.

Bile rolled around in Wolfe's stomach. "This is getting tedious, and we're at a stalemate. We both need to walk away right now." So he could get Dana and her family to safety. The urge to do so rushed through his veins.

"Oh, I'm not quite done today." Gary stroked the detonator with his free hand. "What do you know about my operation?"

"Not enough. I was just on to Albert Nelson when he was shot in the head. You?" Wolfe asked as more of the puzzle took shape.

"Me," Gary confirmed. "It was an easy kill. Were you at the party?"

Wolfe nodded. "Yeah. Didn't feel you there." Was he losing his edge?

Gary scratched his beard. "I didn't feel you there, either. Interesting."

Wait a minute. "The second Captive party. Were you there?"

"No." Gary sighed. "I'd never dose you. Too easy, you know?"

Ah, shit. "It was Theresa." Now he remembered the woman wearing the mask.

Gary snorted. "She's a crafty one, and she did that on her own. Had a couple of men there to take Dana, and neither of us realized that you were there as well. Otherwise, Dana would've met me in person that night and told me all she'd discovered."

Bile rose in Wolfe's throat. "Great. You and a sociopath teaming up. What could go wrong?"

"The sex is amazing." Gary's eyes gleamed. "You should also be aware that you didn't feel me here last night. That was quite a spectacle with your dog, who is sneaking up behind me, by the way. Might want to stop him before I let go of this handy detonator."

Wolfe whistled, and Roscoe emerged from the bushes behind Gary. "Here, boy. Leave the psycho alone."

The fur stood up across Roscoe's back, and he growled low, moving past Gary to sit slightly in front of Wolfe, facing the enemy. "Good dog." Wolfe reached out and set a reassuring hand on the canine's head, rubbing his fur. Roscoe apparently had great instincts with people. His fur and muscles quivered as he kept himself from attacking.

"What else have you figured out?" Gary asked, his gaze on the dog.

"Nothing yet, but I'll get it all. I'm assuming you traveled from Afghanistan via the southern route?" Wolfe didn't really care how, but he wanted to know where.

"Maybe, but I'm a long-term thinker, you know." Gary tilted his head and looked past Wolfe. "Your blonde is looking out the window."

"She's not mine," Wolfe retorted.

Gary jerked his chin. "She is now." He smiled, his gaze lightening, giving away his intention. He couldn't help himself. The bastard was going to blow up the entire building, even if it meant Theresa died as well.

Shit. There wasn't a choice here. God, Wolfe hoped he was as fast as he used to be. He plastered a bored expression on his face and tugged on Roscoe's ear while standing, his leg muscles bunching. "I'm done with this."

Gary started to push from the chair, anticipation dancing across his broad face.

"Now," Wolfe ordered, leaping for Gary along with Roscoe.

They impacted, and Wolfe grabbed the detonator, uncoiling the wires, sliding his finger beneath Gary's and then elbowing him in the eye. Roscoe went for the legs. Gary bellowed, punched Wolfe in the neck and turned to kick Roscoe in the face. The dog yelped and rolled toward the bushes, springing up quickly and charging.

Wolfe rolled to the side, holding his finger over the button so it couldn't be depressed. Adrenaline flooded him.

Roscoe hit Gary mid-center, throwing them both over the bushes.

Wolfe jumped to his feet, his heart thundering, the detonator safe in his hands.

The dog yelped again, and Gary ran several feet to a ball washer, grabbing the attending kid and putting a knife to his neck.

Wolfe paused. "Roscoe. Come."

The dog instantly jumped his way, growling and snarling. The kid's eyes were a wide, terrified blue, but he didn't make a sound. He looked about seventeen, and his skinny arms hung by his sides.

Gary kept the knife in place and started to back up, taking the kid with him.

Dana came into view through Wolfe's peripheral vision. "Wolfe? What's going on?"

Gary smiled and kept backing up, dragging the kid to the parking lot.

Wolfe had to let him go for now. "Tell everyone to get out of the building and call the bomb squad. Now."

She gasped and turned to run back to the building.

Gary finally reached the parking lot and threw the kid into the side of the nearest truck. "We're just getting started, Wolfe." He jumped into a souped-up coup and zipped out of the parking lot, while the kid stood, rubbing his temple.

"You bet we are," Wolfe muttered, looking down at the innocuous detonator as people streamed from the restaurant. He needed to call Force. Now.

Chapter Thirty

Gary Rockcliff threw the keys across the luxurious living room, watching impassively as they crashed into the sliding glass door leading to the sprawling deck and down to the lake. It had taken him several hours to drive to the remote and very private estate in North Carolina, and his anger had grown with each passing mile.

"Problem?" Theresa Rhodes stepped out of the perfectly decorated kitchen, wiping her manicured hands on a hand towel. Not that she'd been cooking. The princess never cooked.

"No." He quickly banked all emotion and set his shoulders back. "Everything is going according to plan."

One of her perfectly plucked eyebrows rose. "Is that a fact? The news has been covering an interesting story out of Tennessee." She gestured toward the plasma television mounted above the large wooden mantel of the fireplace, beyond the white leather sofas that were harder than cement blocks.

He turned to watch the news, the sound muted, to see the country club he'd left hours earlier, where crime scene tape was stretched in overkill mode. Somebody had been bored. "So?"

"So?" She tossed the towel behind her, those intriguing blue eyes sparking. "Watch longer."

"Watch your tone." He turned, bored, and then saw his military ID plastered on the screen.

She stepped closer to him, her white linen pantsuit un-wrinkled and molding to her tight body. Even hanging out in one of her many corporate and impossible-to-find mansions, she wore high heels and matching jewelry. "What were you thinking?"

He moved out of instinct, wrapping his hand around her neck and shoving her against the wall.

She gasped, her eyes widened, and color infused her patrician cheekbones. Excitement had her tongue out and wetting her perfectly Botoxed lips. She reached up and clawed sharp nails into his forearm, drawing blood. "Let go."

He leaned in, every instinct inside him urging him to start squeezing until her eyes bugged out.

Her nipples hardened against the thin material, easily visible since she didn't wear a bra. "You want to play? We'll play, Rock. But don't think for one second that you're going to take your failure today out on me. We both know I have protection in place."

Yeah, the bitch had evidence on his holdings that'd be released at her death, enough that he'd never get free. Oh, he might elude the government for a time, but if that evidence got out, his time would be limited. "Maybe I don't care about your protection." He tightened his hold and leaned in to bite her bottom lip, drawing blood in turn.

Her sharp intake of breath coincided with lust flashing into her eyes.

Man, she was one screwed-up woman. Serious issues. His dick hardened, and he licked the blood off her mouth.

Her moan set him on fire.

"Any calls?" he asked, grabbing her top to rip it apart,

revealing perfectly created breasts. Her surgeon had been a damn genius.

"Forget calls." She purred and scraped her nails down his T-shirt, tucking them into his waist.

"Business first." He grabbed her wrists and ground them together.

She winced. "Two calls. One from Mexico, where they're cutting the product right now. A second from our supplier on the northern route, who will only talk to you." She pouted, her lip already swelling. "I'm an equal partner here."

She wasn't close to an equal partner. Despite her connections, she hadn't found all of his stash. Though he did need her pipeline, and she knew it. "You're too public, and they won't risk talking to you."

"Whatever." She glanced over at her many humanitarian awards stacked in a tall curio cabinet. "What happened in Tennessee?"

Clarence Wolfe had happened. Anger rushed through Rock faster than the lust had, and he held her tighter, fury beating into him.

She cried out and tried to pull free, failing completely. "I was just asking."

"Don't ask." Oh, he'd kill Wolfe, but first he'd make the bastard hurt. The game was going to take time, and he was going to cut off pieces of everything and everyone Wolfe cared about. The idiot had always gone with the heart.

Theresa moved into him, even though he still had her wrists. "We're together, Rock. You went to blow something up, and you were excited. I'm sorry it didn't happen."

"It's too late to appease me." He yanked her even closer.

Her breath caught and her nipples hardened even more. "You're mad." Her voice had dropped to a husky hush that did nothing but add to his fury.

"I am." One of these times, he was going to kill her. He

could control himself today, but he had to figure out a way to get that evidence she'd collected. Torture wouldn't do it, because she was too damn smart. She had given it to a friend, one he couldn't track down, with instructions that only on her death would it be released. Rock just had to find the friend. Theresa was almost as big a threat to Rock as Wolfe was. Not quite, and she had other attributes he quite enjoyed. He released her wrists.

She pulled back, rubbing them. "Wha—"

Then he grabbed her hair, yanking her toward the bedroom.

Her pained laugh filled the day as she grabbed onto his belt loops. "Rock? Do you care for me at all?"

The question caught him off guard, and he paused in the doorway, pressing her against the wall. If he cared for her, wouldn't he get her help? Or would he continue bringing out her darker side? "I care for you." Probably. He'd never met anybody like her.

For the briefest of seconds, she looked sweet. Even vulnerable.

"But I'm still going to hurt you." He threw her toward the bed, not surprised when she laughed.

Definite issues.

Chapter Thirty-One

Dana glanced at her bag in the back seat of Wolfe's truck and then waved as her parents drove by, heading home. The breeze of the day before had disappeared, leaving a sweltering heat laden with moisture. The bomb squad had arrived surprisingly quickly, followed by federal agents whom Angus Force had handled over the phone.

"Well. That was exciting," Dana murmured, her heart still pounding.

"Your folks took all of it pretty well," Wolfe murmured, starting the engine, his gun tucked into the side of his waistband.

"Dad was a marine," Dana said, shivering. "Those were real explosives? Not a bluff?" She'd watched, from a safe distance, as Wolfe had met with the bomb guys.

"Yes," Wolfe said, his voice clipped.

Roscoe sprawled across the back seat, his nose on his paws.

They both seemed out of sorts.

Okay. Something was so not right. Dana secured her belt, her hands trembling. Gone was the good-natured and finally relaxed Wolfe of the night before. Not that she could blame him. She remained quiet as he drove by the golf course and out of the club grounds, turning toward home.

The silence between them was nothing like what they'd shared that morning before breakfast, when she'd cuddled in his arms and just enjoyed being near him. This was hard and cold and distant.

She swallowed. "What all did you and Rock talk about before I came outside?"

Wolfe remained silent, his gaze on the shimmering asphalt through the window.

Irritation itched through her. She tried to remain calm, but he was freaking her the heck out. "I asked you a question."

For answer, he pulled off the road and drove to the first pump at a quaint little gas station, and then stopped the truck. "Give me your phone." He held out his hand.

She frowned. What was happening? Shrugging, she dug in her purse and brought out her cell phone. "I haven't called anybody." In fact, she'd forgotten to even charge it with the excitement of the night before. She looked down at the screen. "The battery is almost dead, and there aren't any messages or anything." Was somebody from the team supposed to call her?

"Phone," Wolfe repeated, his hand out and his tone lacking inflection.

She slapped the phone into his hand with more force than was necessary. "Don't you believe me?"

"Yes." He stepped out of the truck, his boots loud on the cracked concrete. Then he tore off the cover and removed the battery, tossing it toward the antique garbage can by the pump. He dropped the phone and stomped on it, sending plastic scattering.

Dana's mouth gaped. "What are you *doing*?"

He leaned down to pick up the pieces and then deposited those in the garbage as well. "Do you have any tablets or Bluetooth devices on you?"

It was like talking to a robot. She flipped her ponytail over her shoulder. "What is wrong with you?" she breathed. He had just *destroyed* her phone.

"Dana." One word, spoken in a voice with no give.

Had she dropped into an alternate universe? "No. I don't have a tablet or any Bluetooth devices on me."

He tugged his phone from his back pocket and hit a speed dial, pressing it to his ear. "Brigid? Hey." His eyes were hard and remote. "Yeah. Go into Dana's online accounts, any clouds, and delete everything, would you?"

Dana scrambled to release her seat belt. "Wait a minute."

Wolfe handed her the phone. "Tell her what you want to save. Pictures only. No data." He shut the door and moved to the back of the truck to pump gas.

Dana shook her head, her body going numb. "Um, Brigid?"

"Hi. What the heck is up with him?" Brigid burst out. "He sounds weird."

"Get the full story from Angus." Dana huddled over the phone, feeling like she should whisper. "He just broke my phone and he's not talking to me and the guy he's chasing planted a bomb and it totally changed everything." She looked behind her, tracking Wolfe's movements. Betraying Wolfe's trust right now seemed like a bad idea, but this was all going so wrong so fast.

"A bomb? Is everyone okay?" Brigid asked, her Irish accent deepening.

"Yeah, and I'm sure Angus knows more than I do right now, so definitely call him," Dana said, which was the truth. "Then call me and tell me everything Wolfe isn't, if I can't get it out of him. Which I will. But call me anyway."

The sound of typing came over the line. "What do you want saved?" Brigid asked.

"All of it," Dana burst out. "Don't listen to him. He's way off, and I don't want to lose any of my stuff."

More typing sounded. "I'll save all of your pictures, but there's no reason to save GPS or any of that data, is there?"

"Well, no." Dana craned her neck to watch Wolfe pumping gas, his gaze not wavering from the gas tank. "I guess that's okay, and I don't have any articles or story drafts in the cloud or anything."

Brigid typed faster, the sound rhythmic. "Well, he obviously thinks you're in danger and wants you to be untraceable. You should probably find out why."

Dana's legs shook. "I'll ask him, but so far, he's not talking to me." That Gary Rockcliff had found them and planted a bomb was scary as hell, and she could understand that Wolfe was spooked. Or pissed. Or both. She couldn't read him.

"Angus said that Roscoe is with you. What's his mood? He reads the guys pretty well," Brigid said.

Dana glanced down at the snoring dog. "He's sleeping, but he's hungover."

"Oh. Then he won't be much help until tomorrow." Brigid kept typing.

This might be a mistake, but she couldn't let Wolfe take on the lunatic by himself. "Have the team go to Wolfe's house and check out his office. Look at the evidence board he has set up." She was betraying his confidence, and her voice shook. He might hate her, but he'd still be alive.

"Evidence board?" Brigid asked.

"Yes," Dana whispered.

Wolfe replaced the gas nozzle and then opened his door, holding out his hand. "Phone."

Dana faltered and handed him his phone, trying to read his expression, but it was like trying to get through a stone wall with no cracks.

"Hey," Wolfe said into the phone. "Do me a favor and tell Force to be ready. Bye." He tore his phone apart and beat it into pieces on the ground before tossing it away. He glanced at the dog and retook his seat, shutting his door and driving out of the area. "Seat belt."

Oh, he did not.

She crossed her arms. "No."

He checked left and then pulled onto the quiet road. "Belt. Now."

"Fuck. You."

His gaze lifted from the pavement to the sky before he yanked the wheel to the right and pulled off the road. Slowly, deliberately, he put the vehicle in park and partially turned to face her. No words. Just burning topaz eyes and a jaw that was solid rock.

The saliva in her mouth dried up as she faced him, her stomach cramping. The area around her solar plexus ached, making breathing difficult, which she tried to hide. Anticipation ripped through her, tossing her into a fight-or-flight mode. She really wanted to flee.

He reminded her of a cougar that had gotten its leg stuck in a trap near the river one time, snarling and furious before the vet arrived to free him.

She cleared her throat. Once and again, searching for anger, but all she could find was bewildered concern. "I want to help," she said.

"You will. For now, put on your damn seat belt." He didn't move.

She remained still. He'd just sworn, so she was getting some kind of reaction out of him. "How am I going to help?"

"We'll discuss it on the way."

Okay, so much for concern. Finally, her temper was shoving through the fear, and she let it have free rein. "Not a chance, buddy. You tell me right now what's going on, or I'm getting out of this truck." She didn't have to stick around for this.

"You won't make it."

She wasn't a violent person, but smacking him in the nose was starting to have appeal. "Since you're trying to pretty much hide me, I'm guessing that Rock has a way to trace me? Or that he wants to?"

"I don't want to put my hands on you, Dana, but I will. Secure your seat belt."

"You already put your hands on me last night," she retorted. "You want to go? Oh, we'll go. Bring it on."

He blinked. Finally. "What?"

Now he was paying attention and actually seeing her instead of going through the motions. She put both her hands up, fists ready. "You want to use hands and be all threatening, then you can bring it on. I may not draw first blood, but you're gonna hurt."

He shook his head like a dog splashed with water. "Have you lost your mind?"

Yes. One hundred percent she had freaking lost her mind. But at least he was talking to her now, and if she had to act like a lunatic to get through to him, then she would. "You obviously are spoiling for a fight, so let's go, big man. Show me how tough you are."

"You are about to get spanked."

Okay. She had not expected that one. She drew back slightly. Well, all in or all out. "Maybe you'll get spanked." She launched herself at him, swinging one leg over him and landing to straddle him, her hands clamping on his face. The steering wheel dug into her back, so she shimmied even closer. Then she kissed him, full on the mouth, pressing as hard as she could.

He pulled her away by her ponytail. "What. Are. You. Doing?"

She panted, her mind spinning, her instincts misfiring. "Is that a gun in your pocket or are you just really happy I jumped on your lap?"

"Jesus. It's a gun." He yanked the gun free and settled it on the dash.

She gyrated against his pelvis. "I think you might have another one in there." Even now, he felt pretty good beneath her.

His mouth opened and then closed like a landed carp. "You are fucking crazy."

"I wasn't until I started dating you," she blurted, trying to defend herself. "Before you, I was totally normal. Ate healthy, worked out, never challenged a guy twice my size to a brawl."

"We are not dating."

"The hell we're not." She softened her hold on his face. "After last night, we are so totally dating." Was that what had been happening? "You're being a jackass to push me away? To make me go on my way and leave you alone?"

His head drew back. "I am not being a jackass."

The dog farted loudly from the back seat.

"See? Even the dog thinks you're being a jackass." She was feeling a little ridiculous, because if he didn't want her, she'd just acted a total fool. But he'd definitely been all in the night before; he wanted her. Yeah. That had to be the truth. "You can be all robotic and act like a moron, but I'm not going on my way."

He breathed out, for the first time in hours looking like her Wolfe. "How did I lose control so quickly?"

"Oh, honey," she murmured, caressing his whiskered jaw. "I'm not sure you ever really had control, you know?" She leaned in and kissed him again, her heart thumping when he finally kissed her back. "Now. Let's start at the beginning. Rock obviously found me and planted that bomb and now you're afraid that he's coming after me?"

"Yes, and we're calling him Gary now. He doesn't deserve a nickname." Wolfe's big chest filled with air and then deflated.

Now they were getting somewhere. "How did he find you?" she asked.

Oops. Wrong question. Wolfe's eyes got all narrow again. "He didn't find me. He found you."

She grimaced. "Oh."

He released her ponytail and cupped her entire neck. "He killed Candy, and he said he's coming after you next if I don't stop tracking him. By the way, I'm pretty sure he's dating Theresa Rhodes."

She shivered.

She'd put her entire family in danger. Her stomach revolted, and she had to swallow several times to keep from throwing up. "Well, okay then."

"Even if I stop, he'll still come after you," Wolfe said, feeling so strong and solid beneath her. "He can't help himself. He'll wait and watch and then strike. You're being locked down while I go after him. It's nonnegotiable."

She coughed out a laugh. "So your plan is to tick me off, drive me back to town, drop me in a safe house, and then go take him out?"

Wolfe lifted one shoulder in a shrug, nearly dislodging her. "Kind of. I wasn't trying to tick you off, but I was so angry, *am* so angry, that it's hard to talk. I'm trying. You kind of have the plan right. Except we're going to stop at the next grocery store without cameras, ditch the truck, steal another vehicle, and then drive back home. I can't be sure that Rock, I mean Gary, didn't leave a tracker somewhere on this truck."

"Oh." It seemed he had it all planned out. "I'm for the idea of stealing a car, but I hope we get this truck back sometime, if possible. I like it." Her stomach felt hollow, and she tried to hide the terror clawing through her. "I'm not hiding in a safe house when I can help track him. I'm a good journalist, Wolfe."

"We're dating, right?"

The world brightened. "Right. We are dating." It was nice to have him back.

"Then one of my jobs is to protect you, wouldn't you agree?" His thumb rubbed beneath her jaw.

The trap he'd set was a neat one, but she wasn't born yesterday. "I think it's my job to protect you, too."

"You can do that by staying safe." He leaned in, his nose touching hers. "I want to make you happy, and I don't want to be a jackass, but I am locking you down. Period."

Chapter Thirty-Two

The Ramcharger Wolfe had hot-wired hadn't been kept in very good shape. Roscoe glared at him from the hollowed-out back seat. "You shouldn't have combined different alcohols last night," Wolfe muttered. "It's your fault you're feeling poorly."

Roscoe tossed his head and lay down on the exposed floor.

Dana stared out the window, her body appearing more relaxed than earlier even though she was still giving him the silent treatment. Although he could understand why she didn't want to go into protective custody, he wasn't going to budge on the matter. He didn't like making her unhappy, but he'd like it a whole lot less if she ended up dead.

She might also be a little peeved that he'd been so grumpy this morning; he couldn't blame her. As soon as they got a little closer to the office building, he'd buy her one of the sweet lattes she loved. It was the least he could do.

They'd had fast food for lunch and dinner, but neither he nor Dana had eaten much. Roscoe had gone to town with the burgers, though.

They drew closer to the office, and he went through his favorite drive-through, buying drinks for the entire group, even though it was after supper time. He even bought a couple for the new puzzle lady and the British chap, just in case they were in the office. If not, he'd save the drinks for later tonight.

He pulled up to the office, noting the number of cars. "Looks like everyone is here."

"Uh-huh," Dana said, turning pink.

He didn't want her to feel uncomfortable, so he enfolded her hand with his. "Listen. I'd like to get this settled here and now, before we go inside." Arguing in front of everyone else just wasn't his style.

"I'm not arguing with you, Wolfe." She curled her fingers through his.

His trapezoids relaxed marginally. "Okay. Good." It was nice when she decided to be agreeable and make things easy for him. "I appreciate it."

"Well, don't. I'm not arguing because I'm not going into hiding. That would make me not only a crappy journalist but a rotten friend to Candy. She deserves better." Dana tilted her head in a purely challenging way.

He didn't want to tick her off again, but he wasn't going to relent. "Let's go inside."

"Sure." She removed her hand and opened her door.

He did the same, helping Roscoe over the seat. The dog landed on the pavement and immediately ran over to the trees to take care of business. He might have puked a bit, too. "I told you a burger on a hungover stomach wasn't a great idea," Wolfe called. At least for a dog.

Roscoe barked back and quickly returned, looking spritelier.

Wolfe surveyed the parked vehicles. "Why is everyone working on a Sunday?"

"How should I know?" She pressed her hands to her

hips. "I'm going to say, once again, that you should have your entire team after Gary."

"Not a chance." He turned and strode to the front door, opening it for her. Sometimes things were so clear he truly didn't understand how everybody else got it wrong. The elevator was a little tight with Roscoe in it, or maybe it was the anger coming off Dana that made the harrowing ride uncomfortable. He tried to think of a way to gain her cooperation without being too bossy.

Nothing came to mind.

The door opened and he gestured her inside after the dog.

Brigid, her red hair wild around her head, immediately emerged from case room two and rushed over to the dog, dropping to her knees for a full hug around the German shepherd's thick neck. "I've missed you." Her voice was muffled in the fur. Then she stood and made a beeline for Wolfe. "I've missed you, too."

He took the full impact hug, lifting the latte tray out of the way, and patted her small back, smiling at how her dark red hair seemed to brighten the dismal room. Or maybe it was her Irish brogue. "You make this place a home, Bridge." His feelings toward her were as brotherly as they were toward Nari, and no way was he letting his disastrous life touch her.

Her face softened. "Oh, Wolfe. You're a sweetie." Then she turned to Dana for a quick hug. "Let's grab lunch tomorrow if we get the chance. I want to hear all about the wedding and Roscoe's adventures."

Dana's face lost its pinched look for the first time that day. "That sounds lovely."

"She won't be here," Wolfe said bluntly.

Dana's brows narrowed into a V and her jaw jutted out.

Wolfe looked around the vacant room. "Where is everybody? The cars are all here."

Brigid took his arm. "We're all in case room two, and we've been waiting for you."

He didn't have time for another case, but he let Brigid lead them past the hub of desks, carefully balancing the large latte tray. Everyone was in the room. His entire team with case file folders, filled yellow legal pads, and pens all over the table.

Raider stood and held out a hand. "It's good to see you, brother."

"Welcome back." Wolfe set the tray on the table, needing to get this done with so he could move on to killing Gary. "I brought some for everyone."

Angus Force sat at the head of the battered conference table, next to Malcolm West. Pippa, his girlfriend, sat next to him, with a tray of goodies in front of her. Wolfe's mouth watered at seeing the chocolate chip cookies. Raider and Brigid reclaimed seats on the other side of the table, next to Nari, Jethro Hanson, and Serena Johnson. Even Agent Millicent Frost, her bobbed hair streaked with blue this time, sat over in the corner petting Kat. Frost consulted sometimes with the team and had all sorts of interesting gadgets to play with.

Wolfe eyed the two remaining chairs and pulled one out for Dana. "It looks like we're gearing up for an op." His blood started to hum, and he sat, reaching over to dispense lattes. Good thing he'd bought extra so Frost could have one.

"We are on op," Force confirmed, not touching his latte. He leaned to the side and kicked the door shut.

Wolfe looked up at the screen covering the whiteboard that extended across the entire northern wall. "Did we miss a presentation?"

"Yes, but that's okay." Wolfe nodded to Malcolm, who

stretched over and released the screen so it rolled up to the ceiling.

Wolfe caught his breath. The entire board from his home office had been moved and mounted to the wall in place of the other board. The picture of Gary Rockcliff stared right at him. His blood chilled. "What the hell?" he breathed.

"Oh," Dana murmured, noting her additions to the board. Wolfe turned toward her, and she held up a hand. "I'm sorry, but I'd do it again to keep you safe," she said quickly. She fidgeted as the tension cascaded off Wolfe as if he were a countdown timer about to explode.

"You directed them to my office?" he gritted out.

She nodded, unable to swallow over the lump in her throat.

Several of the people in the room watched him warily, but Angus Force looked downright pissed off.

"You broke into my house," Wolfe said slowly, his chin lowering.

"You gave us all keys," Angus shot back, the muscles in his arms bunching. For the showdown, he'd worn a black T-shirt with dark cargo pants and had a knife sheath strapped to his thigh.

"I didn't think you'd go through my office." Wolfe's chest widened.

Nari leaned forward. "You two look like a couple of silverback gorillas about to fight for dominance. Stop metaphorically beating your chests."

Wolfe's nostrils flared. "I don't want dominance. I just want to be left alone to do what needs to be done."

Brigid sipped her latte. "This is an intervention, Wolfe."

His head whipped toward her. "Intervention? I'm the last guy here who needs that. Start with Force."

"He's next," Brigid said easily, her accent lilting around the room. "You're now. You're an excellent strategic planner, and you know, intellectually, that a team is better than a lone wolf. For lack of a better term." Her smile was sweet and unrelenting at the same time.

Wolfe started to get up.

Angus leaned forward, his eyes a glittering river-bottom green. "We're a team, Wolfe. Get your head out of your ass and start working with us, because you don't want to work against us."

Dana winced, catching the same expression on Nari's face. That probably wasn't the best approach with an angry Clarence Wolfe. Even so, she remained quiet, drinking her latte, letting somebody else argue with the stubborn male for a while, considering she was no doubt seriously in the doghouse with him.

Nari twisted her latte around in her hands. "We care about you, Wolfe. We're family, and when there's trouble, family sticks together."

That got to him. There wasn't much of a visual clue, but Dana could feel the change in his body next to her. He turned toward Nari, and his voice softened. "I've lost enough family, doc. You don't know this guy—if he finds out about any of you, he'll take great pleasure in killing the people I care about."

Angus spoke before Nari could. "What the fuck do you think we've been doing the last twenty-four hours?"

Nari huffed out a breath. "Angus, just shut up for a moment."

A collective gasp ran around the room. Nari never lost her cool. It was totally inappropriate, considering the tension surrounding her, but Dana coughed away a chuckle.

Angus drew up short. "Did you just tell me to shut up?"

"Yes." Nari reached for Wolfe's hand and grabbed it. "We've been working on your case, so the cat is out of the bag, as they say. I've called in favors and received every record and file on this guy, and I've studied all night. I do know Gary Rockcliff."

Wolfe's brows drew down in a way that was deadly. And kind of sexy. "What do you mean, you know him?" He forced the words out in rapid staccato.

Nari's calm expression didn't alter. "He's a narcissist who suffers from a personality disorder, more psychopathic than sociopathic, who tells himself he's killing people for a desirable end result, but in truth, he enjoys the killing. He's calculating and methodical, and he likes the risk involved with using explosives, but he's still careful in the planning of an event."

Angus sat back in his seat. "He has a need to prove he's smarter and better than everyone else, and since you survived his attack in Afghanistan, he's going to become obsessed with you, if he hasn't already."

Sometimes Dana forgot Angus had been an FBI profiler before retiring and then returning to work for the HDD to lead this ragtag group.

"Exactly," Wolfe said. "He's obsessed with me, and he thinks this is a game. He'd love to extend it as long as possible, and that means targeting people around me before working his way to me. I'm starting to understand how his mind works."

Angus nodded. "I think there are two reasons he's left you alone so far. The first is that he has been busy trafficking the heroin from Afghanistan that your team was working on finding, and the second reason is that he hasn't found you yet. Well, until yesterday."

Wolfe turned toward Angus. "Thanks for handling the feds."

Force just nodded.

"We're in this, Wolfe. It's too late to turn back now," Raider said, his dark hair slicked back. With his part-Japanese heritage, his intriguing face was sharp and strong—and at the moment determined.

Wolfe made another last-ditch effort and turned to Malcolm, apparently going for the throat. "You'd risk Pippa?" The sweet introvert wasn't even a government agent and had even less training than Dana, and that was saying something. She'd recently gotten free of a cult chasing her, and Mal was definitely overprotective.

"I'd risk myself," Pippa said quietly, her mahogany hair settling softly over her shoulders. Everything about Pippa was soft and kind, but there was a thread of steel in her. "For you, the same as you would for me."

Wolfe kept his focus on Malcolm.

"I'm already working on security." Mal slid his arm over Pippa's shoulders. "We have Millie planting sensors and cameras around our property, and since your house and ours are located at the end of a cul-de-sac, we're trying to figure out if we can privatize that area and put up a gate."

"A gate?" Wolfe snapped. "You think a gate on the road will stop Rock?"

"Along with the sensors and cameras everywhere else," Mal said mildly.

Raider nodded. "I've looked into buying the three parcels on the other side of the cul-de-sac, so we own it all. Made an offer earlier this morning."

Nari angled to the side. "I'd like to buy one of those, if the price is right."

"It will be," Raider said.

Brigid took Raider's hand. "I'm still doing a deep dive on Albert Nelson, and his aliases, in addition to one on Frank Spanek. I've found connections and locations for you to follow up on. If we can find Spanek, he should be able to lead us to Theresa Rhodes, and from her to Gary Rockcliff."

Serena leaned forward, mascara on one of her eyes. Had she forgotten the other one? "I've decoded all of the pages, and I can give you everything Candy Folks had found for her story. She did a great job of tying everyone together. Theresa Rhodes used her companies to channel drugs. Nelson and his partner Spanek handled distribution for her. There's a note on a big shipment coming, but that's all Candy had dug up."

"Probably Gary Rockcliff's." Mal nodded. "My contacts should get back to us tomorrow about the heroin. Raider, Force, and Jethro have reached out to their contacts in the DEA, MI6, and CIA. Among the three of us, we should be able to locate the heroin, since it was such a big shipment. Hopefully."

Nari set her cup down. "If you want to really hit Gary Rockcliff, take the drugs. That'll expedite everything."

Wolfe looked around the room.

Dana caught the second he realized he wasn't alone and that the group would never let that happen. His shoulders relaxed and his breath exhaled slowly.

"Well. I, ah—" Wolfe stumbled for words.

"Ditto," Force said, reaching for a pad of paper. "Now. Let's get to work."

Chapter Thirty-Three

Angus Force reached into his bottom drawer and drew out a bottle of Jack, pouring a healthy shot into the too-sweet latte he'd just warmed up in the microwave. His team worked at various places around the aged basement office space, and he had just finished compiling a complete profile of Gary Rockcliff. What a nutjob. A talented, dangerous, psychotic nutjob.

Roscoe had abandoned him hours ago to follow Pippa around the office and beg for treats. The kitten was probably in Nari's office, where a bowl of kibble was always full.

A rap echoed on his door, and Jethro entered without waiting for an invite. "If this op goes wrong, you're going to have to put Clarence Wolfe down," he said mildly, drawing out a chair and sitting.

"I'm aware," Force said, nudging the bottle across his paper-and-manila-file-folder-riddled desk.

Jethro waved off the booze. "I'm still on a sugar high from that latte earlier. Does he always bring treats like that?"

"Yep. Probably fulfills some need to keep other people happy and safe." Angus couldn't help but profile the people around him, although he didn't like to get too involved if they didn't need help. "Stress and dangerous ops have kept the team from gaining weight, but if things ever calm down around here, we'll have to institute some sort of exercise program."

Jethro's eyebrows rose. "Do you believe things will calm down?"

"No, Jet. I really don't." Angus had no intention of stopping his search for Lassiter, and once he buried that bastard in the ground for good, he'd retire again to his cabin in the woods with his issue-riddled dog to fish and drink.

Jethro angled his head to read the top of one of the file folders. "We have not yet had an opportunity to discuss the fact that Lassiter might very well be deceased. Have you exhumed the body?"

"The body was supposedly cremated and the ashes spread somewhere." Of course, Angus had thought of that. "Before you ask, the executor of the will was a woman named Bali Sandaniz, who was the housekeeper that helped to raise Lassiter. She died of natural causes last year."

"You sure?" Intelligence shown in the Brit's eyes.

"Yeah. Read the autopsy report myself." The woman had been nearly ninety with several stints already in her heart. "I don't think good old Henry Wayne Lassiter would've killed his mother figure. She tried to protect him from arrest, putting herself in jeopardy at the time, and he seemed to have a sense of loyalty to her." The guy wasn't able to empathize or really feel emotions, but he had felt some sort of allegiance to Bali.

"I can assist you with this current case, but there's nothing for me to do on the Lassiter case unless he strikes again and drafts those love notes to you," Jethro said quietly, kicking out his legs and crossing his loafers at the ankles.

"I appreciate the help for now." Everything inside

Angus knew his nemesis was out there somewhere, and soon Jethro would have plenty to do. He looked at Jethro, who wore a short-sleeved button-down with a brown belt. "You look like a college professor." Except for his eyes. The eyes always told the whole story.

"I am a college professor," Jet said.

Angus tipped back his Jack and sugar. "Have you found the reason for good or evil yet?"

"No."

Angus should've taken a few moments to test Jethro's temperature and make sure he was up to another round with Lassiter, but his obsession always took over before he remembered those around him. "Been able to balance the scales yet?"

"Those scales will never be balanced, mate." Jethro's jaw clenched and then relaxed. "You know the why of what I do what I do now, but even you have no clue what I've done. I suppose you can profile me without the details, but don't ever assume you know the depths to which I swam in service to Queen and country."

"Gaining PhDs in philosophy isn't going to help you understand true evil," Angus said softly.

"You do not know that to be true. You can't beat something until you understand it," Jethro said.

Wolfe poked his head into the room. "Just told Mal and Raider that I remembered something Gary said earlier. Something about being in the heroin game for the long haul. The expression caught me off guard at the time, but I've been mulling it over."

It was good Wolfe was finally okay with the team approach. Angus twirled a silver pen on his desk. "Long term with heroin?" His mind rapidly went through options.

"Best bet?" Jethro said. "For more of a cash payout, much more, he'd possibly be having it cut with fentanyl.

It's cheaper, smaller, lighter, and easier to smuggle into this country."

Wolfe straightened. "Doesn't that kill people? I mean, even more than pure heroin?"

"You won't find pure heroin anywhere these days," Jethro said. "It's cut with something, and fentanyl is the newest thing." He reached for his phone and texted something rapidly. "If I wanted heroin cut, it'd be in Mexico before coming across the border."

Wolfe slowly nodded. "That fits with Theresa Rhodes's distribution channels, according to Candy's notes."

Force reached for a manila file folder. "That would explain why Gary Rockcliff isn't coming at you full force yet. He's busy for the time being." Force looked up, his green eyes tired. "But he can't stay away from you completely, so don't take a deep breath."

"I stopped breathing the second I realized Dana wouldn't go into protective custody." Wolfe shut the door, disappearing behind it.

Jethro blew out air. "That chap has it bad. Are you sure this isn't going to blow up in your face?"

"No." Angus was holding on as tight as he could without forcing everyone on a vacation to the middle of an island somewhere. "I don't see an alternative to the current plan, though."

The door opened again, and Brigid stood there, her red hair messy and a dot of whipped cream on her upper lip. "I found Frank Spanek. He's in an apartment building thirty minutes out of D.C. right now. Surveillance from a store across the street caught him entering the building two hours ago."

Angus pushed back from his desk. "Let's go."

* * *

Dana watched as Wolfe attached a Velcro gun holster to his right leg before tightening a worn bulletproof vest across his abs. Force tossed him his HDD badge, and he clipped it to his hip. "It feels weird being all official for this," he said.

Force tucked an extra clip in his jacket. "I know. We need to bring Spanek in, and we can hold him here for the night, but we'll need to take him to headquarters tomorrow. Or maybe the next day."

"I'll wait here to interview him," Nari said, her shoulders slumped beneath her silk blouse.

"No," Force said, bending to strap a sheathed knife to his calf beneath his jeans. "It's after one in the morning. Go home and get some sleep. You can interview Spanek tomorrow. "I'd like for him to sweat it out a little in our interrogation room, anyway."

The elevator door opened, and Millie Frost carried in a cardboard box, which she set down in the center hub before drawing out a metal box. "Everyone, turn off your cell phones and hand them over."

Dana perked up. "I can't." She scowled at Wolfe. "Mine was stomped to bits."

He shrugged. "GPS is a killer, baby."

She tried to growl, but it sounded more like a tired mewl.

Raider tossed his phone in the box. "Are you sure you don't want me on this?"

"We've got it," Force returned easily. "You and Brigid take care of the vehicle Wolfe stole on your way home, yeah? Wipe it down and leave it somewhere without cameras so it'll be found easy."

"Sure thing," Brigid said, gently setting her phone in the metal box.

Mal took Pippa's phone and put it with his in the box. "I'll take Pippa, Dana, Roscoe, and Kat back to the bungalows, if you're sure you don't want me to provide backup."

Everyone wanted in on the action, didn't they? Dana's heart warmed even as Wolfe's body tensed. No doubt he was already worrying about somebody getting hurt or killed.

"We've got Spanek, but thanks," Wolfe said, his nostrils flaring.

Jethro hesitated near the box.

"You too, 007," Millie ordered.

Force nodded.

Jethro sighed and put his phone in, stepping aside so Serena could do the same.

Force slipped his phone in the box, looking inside. "Good, Millicent. Yours is here. What now?"

She closed the metal box and locked it. "I'll get your data off for each of you; contacts, pictures, and so on. Then I'll destroy these." She gingerly set it inside the cardboard box and drew out a basket of black phones. "These are burners. Each is already programmed with everyone else's numbers, and you're listed there by the last letter of your first name, except for Dana. Since she and Pippa both end with A, Dana is Y in your phones." She handed out the innocuous devices. "Your number is on the back in case you want to give it to family or friends, but be careful there. They can be hacked, even if you can't."

Dana accepted her phone. She felt like she'd dropped into a spy novel. "Is this really all necessary?"

"Yes," Wolfe said shortly.

All righty then.

Milly dropped the now empty basket back in the box. "Also, for anybody who has navigation or a service like

OnStar on your vehicle, find something new to drive in the interim."

Brigid leaned against Raider, circles beneath her eyes. "It was easy to find Pippa through the property records of her house. Same with Malcolm and Wolfe." She rubbed her eyes. "I created a series of dummy corporations and transactions, dating them back a while, to muddy the waters and transfer ownership. That should help, but the record will always be there, so be alert."

Wow. Dana tilted her head. She wanted to learn how to research like that. When things calmed down, she was definitely taking Brigid to lunch.

Brigid looked at the rest of the group. "You're all easily found via your rental agreements. The best I could do was create new renters and file those online, hoping the owners don't take too close a look."

"Sounds good," Force said, patting Roscoe's head when he lumbered in.

Brigid shook her head at Wolfe. "The fake residence you set up in the abandoned cabin an hour from your real house is too obvious. Rock will know it's a trap, so I transferred it out of your name, to a corporation, to another corporation and then another. He'll be able to find the place, but it'll take some work."

Wolfe frowned.

Nari partially turned. "Is the place wired, Wolfe?"

"No. Figured I'd stay there until Gary made a move," Wolfe said. "But now we're giving him a target-rich environment, so he won't come for me first. The cabin is useless."

He had a cabin? Maybe they could fix it up when all of this was over—if they survived and managed to stay together. So far, they'd fought more than kissed, although the kisses had been spectacular. Dana tried to hide a yawn behind her hand.

"I'll walk you out to Mal's rig." Wolfe held out a hand, his back-to-business expression firmly in place.

She sighed and took it. Dating him sure took a lot of patience and energy.

Chapter Thirty-Four

Wolfe loosened his arms, surprised at the tension coursing through him as he tugged down the brim of his baseball cap. He'd been on more ops than he could count, but he couldn't let go of the dread in his gut on this one.

"Calm down, man." Force walked beside him on the quiet residential street, his hands at his sides, a similar cap covering his head. "Mal will make sure nothing happens to Dana."

"Rock, I mean Gary, might just blow up Mal's house," Wolfe growled.

Force shook his head, swerving around a fire hydrant on the sidewalk. "No. He won't want to make that much of a splash yet. He's going to pick your friends off one by one and prolong what he considers the game." He kicked a couple of rocks out of his way, ducking beneath the boughs of a leafy tree. "From what he said to you, he's got something else going on right now, and it's probably the heroin. Once that's taken care of, he will come."

"You think he was buying himself some time?" Wolfe asked.

Force nodded. "Yeah. You spent all day fighting with Dana about protective custody, and if you'd succeeded, you would've spent at least the next day or two making sure the arrangements were up to snuff and getting her to cooperate."

Yeah, that did make sense. "So you think she's safe?"

"I wouldn't go that far. Rockcliff is crazy, and from the autopsy report on Candy Folks, he likes to kill. Gets off on it. That kind of a compulsion won't be tamped down for long."

Wolfe's hand clenched into a fist. "Don't sugarcoat it."

"I wouldn't. You need full truth, and I expect the same." Force turned the corner onto a street that still had people mingling at this early hour. Closed businesses lined one side and apartment buildings the other. They were brick buildings with established trees; many held pots of flowers or plants on the wide balconies.

Wolfe scouted the area. "Brigid disengaged the cameras across the street?"

"Yep. Did it remotely, which I understand isn't easy but was possible because of the systems involved." Force turned onto a pebbled stone walkway, passed through a wrought-iron gate and strode between wings of the building to the front entrance, which was secured by a mesh security screened door in front of another locked door. "Should've brought Jethro. He can pick any lock."

That professor was becoming more interesting by the second. "We're official," Wolfe reminded him.

"Kind of, anyway." Force nodded. "Before we go in, what are you prepared to do to make Spanek give up Theresa Rhodes?"

Wolfe stilled. "Anything I need to do. Is that a problem?"

"Nope. Just want to know before we go in." Force pressed the button for the manager. Twice.

"What?" a cranky male with a Middle Eastern accent barked through the speaker.

"Homeland Defense Department," Force said. "Come and open the doors. Now."

The guy spouted a stream of Pashto, the grumbling getting creative.

Wolfe leaned toward the speaker and spoke a Pashto greeting, apologizing for the late disturbance and promising that they'd be gone soon.

The guy stopped complaining and then the speaker went dead.

Force nodded. "Nice. What language was that?"

"Pashto. I learned it in Afghanistan." Wolfe rolled his neck and looked down at his shiny badge. "I keep forgetting we have badges."

The door opened, and a potbellied man in a white tank top, his thick hair messy, shoved open the door. "What do you want?"

"We'd like to visit the occupant in apartment 3D," Force said pleasantly. "Would you mind letting us in?"

"Got a warrant?" the guy asked.

Wolfe put on his most pleasant expression. "We do not, but we could get one if necessary." That was a total lie unless they wanted their HDD handlers to know what they were working on. "We just want to speak to the tenant and won't cause any more disturbance."

The guy looked him up and down. "You were the one speaking Pashto?"

"Oh, oke," Wolfe said in Pashto.

The man stepped back. *"Sam da."*

Wolfe nudged Force. "He said okay." They moved into a dimly lit welcome area with a couple of tables and chairs set to one side.

The man shut and relocked the door. "I am not opening his door for you."

"We'll take it from here," Wolfe said. "Manana," he

added, thanking the super and striding for the stairwell next to the elevator. He climbed up to the third floor and pushed open the heavy door. "Did you bring handcuffs?"

"Zip ties," Force said, on his six. "After we're done talking to Spanek, we'll need to put him into protective custody if he gives up information on Theresa Rhodes and Gary Rockcliff. We'll have to go completely official at that point, just so you know."

One of the many reasons Wolfe hadn't wanted to involve the team. "Understood," he said, reaching the door to 3D, a clean wooden door whitewashed to a shabby-chic look like the rest of the doors down the hall. He pulled leather gloves from his jacket to cover his hands while Force did the same. "I prefer boot to knocking. Any argument?"

"Nope. Kick ahead." Force paused and reached for the doorknob, which twisted easily. He looked over his shoulder at Wolfe. "That's not good."

Wolfe shook his head, adrenaline surging through his veins and sharpening his senses. "I go low."

Force silently pushed the door open to reveal darkness. "Go," he mouthed.

Wolfe shot inside, his gun already out and pointed, Force behind him and to the right. No sound, no movement. Just darkness and a smell that hit him harder than a right cross. He coughed out almost silently, his eyes watering. Metal, blood, and death. Ripped flesh had its own scent.

Force shut the door and flipped on the light to reveal the living room. "Holy fuck."

Blood splatter coated the walls, the floor, and even parts of the ceiling. One nude body, a male, hung halfway across the sofa, his face partially turned toward them, his visible eye bloody in death.

Wolfe swallowed down puke. "That's Spanek." The guy was barely recognizable from his photo with cuts all over his face and body, some deep, some surface. He stepped over still fresh pools of blood, shutting down all emotion to partially turn and look through the barely open doorway to what had been the master bedroom. "Jesus," he breathed at seeing the dead woman inside.

Force approached from his left and looked past him. "Any idea who she is?"

"No. Must've been with Spanek when Rock got here." Gary had gone to town on her face with more cuts than Wolfe could count, and that didn't take into account the swelling and bruising. A purplish hand mark marred her neck. She was nude, spread-eagled, and definitely dead. Blood pooled all around her, soaking through the bedclothes.

"Okay." Force exhaled loudly, no doubt trying to stay in control. "Let's gather what information we can and get out of here before calling it in." He nudged the door open with his gloved hand.

Something clicked.

Wolfe stiffened, grabbed Force by the arms and started running for the exit. "Go!" They hit the doorway just as a wave of heat smashed into them, throwing them into the wall on the other side of the hall. Wolfe impacted headfirst and dropped, smoke filling his lungs.

"Force," he croaked. Then darkness claimed him, cold and empty.

Thrumming pain and swirling lights jerked Wolfe from the darkness. He freaked, striking out, finding himself on a stretcher being carried through the heated night.

"Whoa. Take it easy, big guy," said a male voice.

"Get the hell off me." Wolfe shoved his legs to the side and pushed away from the stretcher, landing on his feet.

His head spun. He couldn't see anything and furiously wiped at his eyes until they cleared. His stomach heaved, and he bent over, losing what dinner he still had left.

Sounds roared in. Sirens, boots running, people over radios talking. What had happened?

He lifted his head and focused on Angus Force sitting in the back of a nearby ambulance, an oxygen mask covering his nose and a blanket around his shoulders.

Force tugged the mask off, his face layered in soot. "You covered me with your body, asshole." He tossed off the blanket and struggled to step down.

"Wait," the same voice said as before. "We'll bring him to you." A tightly muscled paramedic who looked about eighteen shot an arm beneath Wolfe's shoulders and helped him up. "Let's at least check out your head." He assisted Wolfe over to sit by Force, grunting on the way.

Pain burrowed through Wolfe's solar plexus, and his ears rang, but he sat by Force as firefighters and police personnel ran around. "How bad are you hurt?"

"Not as bad as you. Don't ever do that again." Force leaned to the side and coughed hard enough to dislodge a lung.

The paramedic ducked and pointed a penlight into Wolfe's eyes.

Agony pierced his brain. Wolfe slapped the penlight away. "I'm fine. Go make sure there aren't other wounded." The blast had been fairly localized, it seemed, so hopefully nobody else had been injured. "Guess Gary wanted to sanitize the crime scene." He coughed, trying not to cry when his ribs protested vehemently.

Force groaned. "Yeah. He's probably tying off loose ends and appeasing his need to kill on the way to you. Frank Spanek didn't have a chance."

Wolfe's head would fall off if he tried to turn it, so he

didn't move. The image of the dead woman flashed across his mind. "Have you ever seen something like that?"

"Yeah, unfortunately," Force grunted. "I've chased my share of serial murderers, and more than a couple of them were really sick jerks." He glanced toward the building and then stiffened. "Ah, fuck."

Wolfe's eyeballs wanted to roll from his head, but he looked up anyway to see their HDD handlers maneuvering around firefighting equipment and emergency personnel to reach them. "Can I just shoot them?"

"Too many witnesses," Force said, the sound strained.

Agent Kurt Fields reached them first, his normal limp more pronounced than usual. Soot dotted the time-worn brown suit that went perfectly with his shaggy brown hair and beard, streaked with gray. He was in his late fifties and gave Wolfe the impression that he just wanted to retire. "You guys okay?"

"Great," Force growled.

Agent Tom Rutherford, careful of his expensive, shiny shoes, stepped over a hose to reach them, his thousand-dollar navy-blue suit as out of place in the crime scene as a ballet dancer would've been. Somehow, soot didn't mar his smooth blond hair or his angled face. His blue eyes narrowed. "What has your crazy unit done now?"

Wolfe swallowed ash and grit, trying to wet his mouth so he could speak. "Your nose healed nicely." He hadn't seen the agent since Raider had broken his nose and given him two black eyes.

Rutherford's head lifted. "This is going to shut you down for good. Now, what happened?"

Wolfe tried to make a fist, just in case he should break Rutherford's nose again, but his fingers weren't working properly. The ringing kept buzzing between his ears, and his vision wavered again.

Force remained slouched against the stretcher, part of his left pant leg burned away. "We got a tip, an anonymous one, that the guy in 3D was trafficking heroin. The tip seemed sketchy, so we decided to check it out on the way home tonight and not bother you experts in the HDD until we had more information."

That did sound good, considering Spanek had been in the heroin game.

"That sounds like horseshit," Rutherford said, red tinging his ambitious cheekbones. "Did you have a warrant?"

"Didn't need one," Force said, wincing and pressing a hand to his rib cage. "We knocked on the door, politely asked to visit a guy named Frank Spanek in 3D and were granted access. We'd just reached the door when the world exploded."

"There are body parts," Fields said, reaching in his pocket for a piece of candy.

Yeah, there were probably a lot of body parts. "Wow. Really?" Wolfe asked. "We didn't make it inside." There was no need to involve these guys, especially since they'd drag Wolfe down to headquarters to answer a bunch of questions he had no intention of answering.

"You're coming downtown," Rutherford snapped.

"Nope." Force stepped down to the ground. He wavered, set a hand on the ambulance, and ducked his head, his eyes shutting and his lips pressed together as he rode out what looked like a tidal wave of pain. Finally, he straightened, his face stark white beneath his tan. "We're regrouping tonight and will be available tomorrow if you'd like to come by the office. Wolfe can bring lattes."

"You don't get sprinkles," Wolfe grunted. Could he climb down without passing out again?

Fields appraised him. "I think you two should seek medical attention." He crunched on the candy.

Wolfe pushed off the ambulance to stand, his legs shaking. "It's not my first concussion. We'll be okay." Pain howled through him, but he turned and limped toward the sidewalk with Force at his side.

"Do you think we're gonna make it all the way to my truck?" Force wheezed, when they were out of earshot.

"Don't have to," Wolfe groaned. "We just need to get out of their sight."

"Good plan."

Chapter Thirty-Five

A noise awakened Dana around dawn, and she immediately sat up in Wolfe's bed, going on full alert.

"It's me," Wolfe whispered from the other room.

She turned and fumbled for the lamp on the bed table, illuminating the bedroom. "Where have you been?" she whispered back, even though nobody else was in the house.

He limped through the door, grimacing as if every step was agony.

She took one look at him and grabbed her throat, her head dropping forward as she stared. "What happened?" Soot mixed with blood on the side of his face, and parts of his clothing appeared to have been on fire. She hastened to him, careful not to touch anywhere. "You need a doctor."

"I need a shower." He stumbled into the bathroom, pausing near the sink to sway in place. Moonlight streamed through the skylight high above, illuminating his injuries.

She braced her feet so she could catch him if needed. "Wolfe." She didn't know what else to say. Was he still mad at her? Should she apologize?

He reached for the hem of his shirt and then moaned.

"Let me." Skirting him, she gently pulled up his ruined shirt, wincing at the bruises already forming across his inflexible chest. Smoke and soot tickled her nose, and she sneezed.

"Bless you." His head dropped, and debris fell from his hair.

"Thanks." She needed to talk him into seeing a doctor. "Is Angus all right?"

Wolfe deftly removed the gun and holster from his thigh and set them on the counter. "Yeah, he's okay. Busted up a little bit, but he'll be fine in a couple of days. Maybe by tomorrow."

That was good. "How bad is your head?" She released the button of his jeans and unzipped them, sliding them down his legs with as much care as she could. "Oh. Your boots." Her fingers clumsy, she untied them and held on to the first one, which had to be a size sixteen. "Step out."

He did, not making a sound. Even so, his pain was palpable.

She helped him with the other boot and then out of the jeans and boxer-briefs. Even those had a burn hole along the side. "Were you in a fire?"

"Bomb." He turned and reached into the shower to turn the knob. Steam rose. "Give me a minute, okay?"

She faltered. "You'll need help in the shower."

"No. I just need a minute. You and I have a discussion coming, and I'm not ready." His gaze held both pain and what looked like anger? "I could use about a hundred aspirin and a warm brandy, if you're looking for something to do."

"Okay." She understood the need to gather oneself after an ordeal and ducked to retrieve his discarded clothing.

He lumbered into the dark-tiled shower, his usual grace gone. "Throw those away, would you? I don't want to look at them again."

It was a good thing, because the clothes were ruined.

She hurried from the bathroom, threw away the clothing, and then warmed some brandy for him over the stove and heated a casserole from Pippa in the microwave. It was a healthy chicken, veggie, and noodle recipe that she made just for Wolfe, apparently.

The sky started to lighten outside. She wrung her hands and looked for something to do. Roscoe's bowl was full, as was Kat's, and both animals were sleeping on the sofa. Roscoe looked her way, apparently decided all was okay, and went back to sleep.

The microwave beeped and she took out the food before pouring the brandy into a tumbler. Then she fetched a glass of water from the fridge dispenser to place by the casserole along with the utensils. There was something else. Oh yeah. She reached for the closest cupboard and took out a bottle of aspirin to put by the plate.

Should she check on him? She didn't want to overstep or tick him off any more than she already had. Betraying him to his team and then challenging him to a fight in the truck on the way home was as forward as she wanted to get. For now.

The AC hummed to life just as he walked into the kitchen wearing just his black sweats, his gait slow. His broad chest was bruised, but there were no cuts or burns visible. He paused upon seeing the table, his eyes unreadable. "You didn't have to do this."

She chuckled, the sound strained, and sat. "Do what? I just warmed up a couple of things. Please sit down." Before he fell down.

He sat and reached for the brandy first, taking a big gulp. Then he swallowed four aspirin. "Those should kick in soon."

Her fingers itched to touch him and make sure he was all right. "You might need something stronger."

"No. That was fine." He looked at her, and the bruising on his jaw, combined with his scar, made him look like a deadly avenger. "I'll be better after a little sleep." Taking his fork, he ate about half of the casserole on the plate.

She let him eat in peace and then finally couldn't stand it any longer. Fear sensitized her skin, and she shivered from the cool air. "You said there was a bomb. Could you tell me a little more?"

His lips twitched. "I must really look like hell if you've decided to be that polite."

"I'm always polite," she said, giving in and placing her hand over his warm wrist. "Tell me what happened."

"We got to Frank's apartment, and he was dead inside along with a woman. Probably just some very unlucky woman in the wrong place at definitely the wrong time." Wolfe spoke slowly and deliberately.

Dana's temples ached and she reached for the aspirin, taking two and washing them down with Wolfe's water. "What aren't you telling me?" Oh, he'd definitely keep facts from her to protect her, and she didn't have time for that.

"We got inside, saw the bodies, and heard a click. Made it to the door, then boom." He planted both hands on the table and forced himself to stand. "That's it. Now come to bed."

The food, booze, and painkiller helped to dull the physical soreness, except for the spasm that kept attacking Wolfe's lower back. He groaned like an old man when he fell into the bed.

Dana cleaned up the small mess in the kitchen and quickly returned with an ice pack for him.

Warmth, the good kind, tumbled through him. "You don't need to fuss. I'll be fine."

"I want to fuss." She pulled the sheet and covers away from him and rested the pack on the left side of his rib cage. "This is the darkest bruise. Are you sure no ribs are broken?"

"I'm sure. Feels different from this." A couple might be cracked, but he didn't have time to worry about that. The ice chilled the bruise, easing some of the discomfort. "Come to bed, Dana."

She finished checking out his chest, abdomen, and legs. "How does your backside look?"

"You can admire it later." His eyebrows rose. "I mean, unless you want to get busy now."

Her instant grin healed him faster than the ice. "I appreciate the sentiment, but you had trouble just walking in here. I'd hate to tax you."

Oh, she had not just said that. He tried to lever himself up on an elbow. "I won't be taxed. Let's go."

"No." She said the word firmly and then settled the sheet over him, dragging the blanket and comforter off the end of the bed. "You don't need this weight on you, and it's hot, anyway." She extinguished the light and moved around to ease beneath the sheet with him. Snuggling closer, she rested her hand softly on his solar plexus. "Where does it hurt?"

Everywhere. "I'm fine now." He gingerly settled an arm around her, comforting himself with the scent of orange blossoms.

"Okay." She drew circles lightly across his skin, brushing his upper chest and over his clavicle. "How mad are you at me?"

It was a good question. While he understood her reasoning, he didn't like her going behind his back. "I'm not sure, and I don't want to deal with it right now." He didn't push her hand away, enjoying this sweet and adorable side of her, even though they had a difficult discussion coming when he regained his strength.

"Fine." She kept her hand over his heart and stopped moving. "I'll wait a while and then get you a new ice pack."

He planted his hand over hers, feeling his steady heartbeat through both. "You go to sleep." He'd never had anybody indulge him like this, and it was oddly appealing.

"I'm going to take care of you, Wolfe." Her minty breath brushed his jaw.

"That's my job." The woman kept getting their roles mixed up. "I take care of you. Remember?"

She kissed his neck. "We take care of each other."

"I don't get you." He shut his eyelids, letting his body slowly relax. If there was any trouble, Roscoe would awaken him.

"Nobody has ever fussed over you?" Her voice was soft and sleepy, but she seemed determined to chat.

He thought back through the years. "Not really. Grams was a good woman, but frail by the time she took us in, so we looked out for her. My sister was just a kid when we lost her, but she was always sweet to me." He'd do anything to bring her back, but that wasn't going to happen. "Then I was in the service, and there's not much coddling there."

Dana rubbed her cheek against his collarbone, her skin feeling like silk. "What about women? You've dated, I'm sure."

"Sure." He'd always liked women and sex, and he'd had a girlfriend or two through the years. "My job always got in the way, and they usually moved on. I understood." Wait. Was this the talking about old relationships part of dating? He'd never really gotten into that part, but he'd give it a shot. "What about you?"

"I've dated but never really gotten serious. Most people are kind of boring, and my job has also taken me away a lot." She nipped his earlobe. "You are not boring."

"I appreciate that." He paused, almost asking if Mike had called again, but then remembered that he'd destroyed her phone. The crime scene filtered through his mind, and he held Dana closer, remembering the dead woman on the bed. "At some point in the near future, you're gonna have to let me take care of you." He turned his head, ignoring the pain that flared inside his brain, and pressed a kiss to the top of her head.

"That's what you're doing."

"No." He'd given in earlier, but now he'd seen firsthand what Gary liked to do for fun. However, Wolfe had learned that bossing Dana around only resulted in her challenging him to a boxing match, and at the moment, she'd probably win. So he tried for logic, which certainly wasn't his strong suit. "You said we were dating, right?"

"Yes." She cuddled closer.

"You know me, better than I've let anybody else know me." The words were coming more slowly as sleep tried to draw him in, but this was important.

She sighed and settled against him. "I know."

The aspirin, ice, and woman were having a calming effect, and his heart rate slowed. "Then you understand, whether you like it or not, that I'll do everything I have to in order to keep you safe. Even piss you off."

"I don't think—"

He cut her off before he dropped into sleep against his will. "You do think and you do know. Make sure that you really want this and you really want me, because I've never had anything or anybody that was just mine." The words poured out of him with no filter, because his energy was gone. "There are consequences to being with me, whether you like it or not. Sleep on it and let me know where we stand in the morning." His words might've slurred on the end.

"Wolfe, I don't want to argue with an injured man." Her yawn cracked her jaw.

"There's no argument." He kissed her forehead. "Some things just are. Tell me you get me so we can sleep and heal." He tightened his hold.

"Fine. I get you." She buried her nose in his neck. "I can decide now and not wait until we wake up. I do really want this, but you need to know me, too."

"Fair enough."

She kissed his jaw, snuggled down, and was asleep in seconds.

Wolfe followed her into dreamland, hoping she really did understand him. He'd allowed his life and this relationship to enter the fuzzy gray zone where he wasn't sure what was happening, and that had to end now. The crime scene had proven that.

It was time to hunt.

Chapter Thirty-Six

Tuesday morning landed with caramel-topped lattes for the entire crew. The unit had taken Monday off, but Wolfe had slept most of the day away, healing. By the time the morning arrived, Dana was stretched thin, wondering when Wolfe would want to have that discussion. Or rather, that fight.

Dana led Roscoe into the basement offices with Wolfe carrying the trays of lattes. She wanted to get going on work and tried not to champ at the bit to get back on this story and take down Theresa Rhodes and Gary Rockcliff for Candy.

She grabbed two lattes and hustled to case room one, where Serena was waiting. "Sorry about the delay." They'd talked on their burner phones that morning. "Wolfe insisted on getting drinks." She handed one over to the cryptologist.

"Thanks." Serena gestured to the notes on the board. "There you go. They're all deciphered, although it looks like some sort of shorthand that she intended to expand when she wrote the story. A lot of it doesn't make sense to me, but now I'm passing it on to you." She flipped her wrist over to read her watch. "I have to get to class. The summer school classes are some of my favorites, and I like the extra money in my checking account. Call me if you need me, and I'll be here."

Dana paused. "Thank you for doing this. Nobody else could have."

"I'm happy to help. Let me know if you have any more puzzles." Serena reached for her pens. "Want me to give any message to Jethro? He's teaching today, too."

Hmm. Did Serena want an excuse to talk to Jethro? Dana racked her brain for a response. "I don't have anything specific, but I think he left a couple of books on Malcolm's desk. Would you return those?" At least it was a fairly decent excuse for dropping by his office.

"Sure. No problem." Serena skipped out.

Dana turned her attention to the deciphered notes, catching the sporadic connections. If each page dealt with a single subject, it would've been easy. But Candy had jumped around, as usual. Dana started with the page on Frank Spanek and read through his aliases, his arrests, and his known associates, moving on to Albert Nelson and then to Theresa Rhodes. The connection was clear, as Serena had detailed the other day.

She then moved to the page on Afghanistan, and her interest was piqued. Though Candy didn't have Rock's name anywhere, she had a nice timeline showing the theft and movement of the heroin, even posting several questions about an inside man from the military making it all happen.

Man, Candy had been good at her job. How odd that her story on women entrepreneurs connected to Wolfe's investigation of Gary stealing the heroin. Life was strange sometimes.

Malcolm stepped inside at some point. "Hey. The HDD handlers are asking us each to go be interviewed about our team and a bunch of bull . . . crap. We're only going to be able to hold them off for a few days or so. We'll meet up this afternoon or tomorrow morning to prepare."

Great. Dana knew the HDD wanted to shut down the team.

"Okay. Thanks." Right now, she needed to finish this project before she started worrying about lying to federal agents. Did it matter if she was working for federal agents? Probably not. She stepped to the side to read the page featuring Albert Nelson, which included how to reach him, his Captive affiliation, and several other connections. She'd start researching the names and see if Brigid was up to conducting some deep dives.

After a couple of hours, Dana finished making her own notes, came up with a plan to conduct more research, and wondered if anybody had thought to order lunch.

Angus Force appeared in the doorway. "How's it going with the deciphered notes?"

Dana partially turned, her gaze caught by the mottled bruises down the side of Angus's face. "Ouch. Are you all right?"

"I'm fine." A bruise over the entire right side of his face, giving him a black eye, belied the words, although his tone strongly suggested she agree with him.

She had enough to worry about with Wolfe's injuries and wasn't about to argue with Angus Force as well. "Candy did some incredible research." Dana turned back to the papers taped to the board. "However, she wouldn't use a complete sentence to save her life. These papers are more like lists and phrases, just to keep her straight and organized. We need to follow the trail she left."

Angus prodded a bruise on his neck. "Sounds good. Anything interesting so far?"

"Yes." She pointed to the page about Albert. "As you already know, Candy discovered that Nelson and Spanek were drug traffickers, and they worked with Theresa Rhodes and another partner, whom I'm assuming is Gary Rock-cliff. There are also a number of places listed, and I'm not sure what those mean." She pursed her lips. "The town of Culiacán is starred in two places."

"Culiacán?" Angus drew abreast of her and studied the document. "Nice job, Dana." He quickly strode out of the room.

"Wait a second." Dana jogged after him. "What did you just figure out?"

Angus reached Wolfe's desk. "We have a problem."

Wolfe looked at Dana and then focused on Angus. "Define problem."

Mal and Raider looked up from their desks, while Brigid and Nari emerged from their offices.

Angus planted a hand on his ribs and took a shuddering breath. "Dana has been looking at the journalist's decoded notes, and it looks like Culiacán is the place in Mexico."

"Oh." Wolfe ground a palm into his left eye. "It wouldn't be Culiacán itself, but areas in the mountains that are used for production. There are many labs there, so it would make sense that Gary chose that locale to process the heroin. We can reach out to our contacts—one of them should be able to pinpoint where the action is right now."

"That's not the problem," Angus said quietly.

Dana stepped closer to Wolfe, her mind spinning. "What's the problem?"

"Access," Wolfe said, reaching for his burner phone. "I can get in."

Angus shook his head and dropped a hand on Wolfe's shoulder. "No way can you go in alone. These labs have decent security, and one soldier alone is too dangerous."

What the heck was going on? "I'll go with you," Dana blurted out.

Angus looked over his shoulder. "You know how to parachute out of a military transport in the dead of night?"

Her mouth shut. Angus had been FBI, Raider and Nari HDD, and Malcolm an undercover police detective. They were all trained and dangerous, but Wolfe was the only one with special-teams experience and knowledge of parachuting, and she had no doubt she didn't know half of his military background. "You are not going alone," she said, putting her hands on her hips.

"We're not even close to worrying about that," he said, his phone paused on the way to his ear. "The plan is to destroy Gary's heroin so he'll come after me, tracking me to the cabin that Brigid kind of hid from him. But first, everyone needs to reach out to their contacts to locate the right lab. Brigid? You have to have friends in satellite surveillance."

"No, but Raider does," Brigid said. "I bet Millie Frost has connections there, too."

Wolfe barked more orders, and everyone set off to reach out to anybody who might have relevant information. Angus shut his office door, calling in favors.

Dana hesitated, reaching out for Wolfe's arm. "You can't go by yourself."

He patted her hand, the bruises on his face standing out starkly. "Honey? What do you think I did in the military?"

Close to midnight, Wolfe paced around the conference room table, studying the map taped over his board. It had taken all day, but they'd been able to piece together the information they needed. "It has to be in that hilly region."

Angus nodded. "All of my contacts confirm that." He pointed to the rough terrain. "The other side has been raided lately, so my bet would be right here." He used a permanent marker to circle an area next to a large hill. "Satellite imagery confirms the heat and power numbers are what we're looking for."

Wolfe shook out his numb ankle. It hadn't been right since the explosion the other night.

Angus lobbed the pen onto the table, where it bounced once and then rolled a couple of inches. "All right. Everyone else has gone home to get a good night's sleep. Let's do the same, and we'll plan the op tomorrow."

"Good plan." Wolfe wanted to get home to Dana, since she'd left hours earlier with Malcolm.

Force leaned against the table, lines cutting into the sides of his mouth. "I don't have transport in, Wolfe. My connections don't include military helicopters."

"Mine do." Wolfe had already made the call. "It'll be a HAHO jump. I still have some good contacts in the military, and we'll bill it as a training exercise." After this, he was definitely out of favors.

"You're not going alone," Angus said.

Wolfe's chest hurt. "My team is dead, Force. I can't ask anybody currently with the military to break code and do it, and I'm not close enough to anybody discharged to ask. It's just me, and that's okay."

"Jethro is going with you," Force said, widening his stance as if expecting a fight.

Wolfe frowned. "I don't know that guy well enough to work with him on this kind of op."

"I do," Force said. "Jethro was MI6 and knows how to jump."

"He's a professor now, so jumping isn't in his plan. Why he left MI6, I don't care. But he's out, and from what I've seen, he wants to stay out." Wolfe wasn't putting his life in the hands of a guy he didn't trust.

Force limped around the table and switched off the

light, heading into the main hub area. "He has no problem blowing up a drug facility, so long as you make sure civilians are nowhere around."

"You already talked to him," Wolfe drawled.

"Yep, and he has a contact that can help extract you two if you don't get killed." Force whistled for the dog, who came running from Nari's office, a pink high heel in his mouth. "Damn it." Force yanked the shoe free and turned it over to reveal bite marks. "How did you get this?"

Roscoe sat and panted happily.

Wolfe paused. "What the hell is Roscoe still doing here? I told Dana to take him with her."

"Guess she's not the obedient type," Force returned.

Oh, that was going to change. Wolfe scooped Kat up from the top of his desk. "It's too hot to wear a jacket, buddy, so there's no pocket for you to ride in." He set the kitten on his shoulder.

His older burner phone buzzed from his back. He stiffened and pulled it out, giving a nod to Force.

Force's eyes lit with interest.

Wolfe set the phone on his desk and pressed the speaker button. "Gary. I thought we were done."

Silence crackled for a couple of moments. "As did I, my friend. Imagine my surprise at seeing you show up at Mr. Frank Spanek's residence."

Nails scraped over Wolfe's skin. Had there been a camera in Frank's apartment? He hadn't had time to conduct a thorough search before the bomb had detonated. "I don't know what you're talking about." Maybe Gary was just on a fishing expedition.

"Yeah, you do. I have to tell you, the blue hat wasn't for you."

Damn. Wolfe had been wearing a blue baseball cap. "I really don't know what you're talking about."

"Who was your friend? His face was hidden by a cap, too." Gary's background was silent as usual, giving no clue as to his whereabouts.

"I don't have any friends," Wolfe retorted, jerking his head when the kitten sneezed in his ear.

Gary chuckled. "Oh, I'm your friend. So is Dana. How is the lovely Dana?"

"You're not my friend." Wolfe eyed Force, who motioned for him to keep Gary talking. "With both Nelson and Spanek dead, you're going to have a difficult time moving the heroin, right? It was a mistake to take them both out."

"I've got it covered," Gary drawled.

Wolfe ground his back teeth together. "You know the entire government is looking for you, right? They have been since the fiasco in Afghanistan. Some pretty powerful people are not happy you tried to blow up a nice country club."

"I'm pretty good at staying under the radar," Gary said, sounding unconcerned.

Wolfe's ribs ached, and his temper threatened to blow. "I wish you had the balls to meet up with me. Just the two of us."

"What fun would that be? Death should be slow and erotic." There was a shuffling sound as Gary apparently moved around.

Wolfe angled his head, trying to hear better. There had to be background noise somewhere. The more he got Gary to talk, the better Force could profile him. Images of the crime scene wouldn't leave him alone, so he went in that direction. "Was death slow and erotic for the woman in Frank's apartment?"

"It was beautiful," Gary breathed. "She wasn't as tough as the journalist, but she made it worth my time."

Wolfe scrubbed his hands across his eyes. "There was a lot of blood. How did you keep them quiet?"

Gary was quiet as if remembering. "Gags do wonders. Frank didn't take long, so he didn't get a chance to make too much noise. The woman? Well, now. She didn't seem to enjoy the gag as much as I did."

Wolfe wanted to hurl. "Who was the woman?" As far as he knew, the police hadn't made an identification yet.

"She worked with Frank and her name started with a B. Or maybe a P. Her name didn't really matter to me."

Wolfe wanted to reach through the phone and rip out Gary's jugular. "Tell me you have some regret for killing them. For killing our team, the men who trusted you."

Gary clicked his tongue. "Wolfe, you just don't get it. I'm going to have fun with Dana, a lot of it, and I'm not going to have a touch of regret there, either." He ended the call.

Wolfe turned fully toward Force, fire in his belly, yet careful not to dislodge the kitten. "Well?"

Force slowly nodded. "Yeah. He's ape-shit crazy."

Chapter Thirty-Seven

Dana had spent the afternoon tangled in the disaster Wolfe was planning, trying to figure a way out. When Mal had offered her a ride home, she'd jumped at the chance, wanting some time to think. Instead, she'd been stewing. Finally, around midnight, she'd gone to bed with anger instead of concern heating her.

A while later, the front door opened, and Wolfe's heavy footsteps echoed through the living room to the bedroom.

She sat up and turned on the lamp. "Do you make that noise on purpose?"

He lounged in the doorway, his broad shoulders taking up all the available space, his expression unreadable. "Huh?"

"The stomping." She hugged her knees to her chest. "I know you can move silently, so do you make noise on purpose?"

"Yes."

That made sense. She was trying to find the right words to persuade him to avoid the suicide mission, so it took her a heartbeat to realize he was staring at her without smiling. Her head tilted before her thoughts caught up. Oh. Was it time to fight? "What's your problem?"

"My problem?" he repeated, his tone silky.

She blinked, her central nervous system reacting to him automatically. "Yes."

"My problem is that I gave you explicit instructions to keep Roscoe with you at all times, especially if I am not around." The corded muscles in his neck actually bulged beneath the bruises. "You failed to keep Roscoe with you and came home alone."

"Oh please," she muttered.

He drew himself up as if she'd punched him. "You purposely ignored the rules."

Rules? Had he just said rules? "Yes, I did." Her chin lifted and she met his gaze without flinching. "Roscoe was having a good time playing in Nari's office, and I let him be."

Wolfe tucked his thumbs in his jeans pockets in an inexplicably threatening move. "That's not it, and you know it."

Saying *nuh-uh* would just sound juvenile. She took a deep breath, wishing she was wearing jeans instead of a pale yellow baby-doll teddy. "You do not know what was in my mind at the time."

"I know exactly what was in your mind." He remained patiently in place, watching her. "You're ticked I'm going on that mission, and you decided to play by your own rules. Teach me a lesson."

"No," she denied. Okay, maybe. Roscoe was having a good time with the bone in Nari's office, and Dana might've had a *so there* moment. "I don't see how you can be irritated when you won't listen to me."

"You're digging a hole, baby."

Her lungs felt like she'd swallowed a space heater. She tried to swallow over the lump in her throat, acutely aware she was out of her depth. "Fine, but that was only part of it. Roscoe really was having fun." She scrambled out of the bed and stood to face him, no longer hiding. "I don't want you to parachute drop into some hills crawling with armed criminals all alone."

"Okay."

"Wait—what?"

His gaze wandered over her baby doll to her bare feet and up her long legs, pausing at her breasts, then returning to her face. "Jethro is going with me."

Her entire body heated at his look. "Wait. The British professor?" she shrieked.

He winced. "Lower the decibels, would you?"

"Oh, you're gonna get kicked." It was too bad she didn't have on boots.

Wolfe's gaze heated. "First, if Force trusts him, then I trust him. He's former MI6, and apparently he knows his stuff." He held up a hand when she started to argue. "Second, this is what I do. I'm good at it, and I will come back."

"And third?" she snapped, her ears turning hot. Very.

"Third? This is *not* what you do, so you will follow all directions until I take out the guy who wants to take us out. It's simple. Yes, you're a good journalist. Yes, I understand that your job entails some danger, which I will try to lessen. But this maniac after us, after you, is coming because of me. That makes this my op."

God, he was sexy when he got all bossy while trying to sound reasonable. "When does it get to be my op?" she asked.

"Next time. Maybe." He didn't sound convincing.

She drew in air. "Is this when we discuss my telling your team about your murder board?"

He crossed his arms, and those impressive muscles flexed. "Well, now. I was pissed about that, but turns out that was nowhere near as irritating as you leaving Roscoe at the office and putting yourself in danger."

She was a fair person, so she gave him the truth. "I'm not sorry I told the team, because I want to protect you, too. As for Roscoe, he was fine and I was fine with Mal next door, so maybe you should just relax."

"Relax?"

The way he said it sent shivers down her body. She tried to say something, anything, to lessen her challenge, but words died in her throat.

He watched her, his expression knowing. "Are you about done being a brat?"

It was only a semi-fair question. "If I'm not?"

He straightened. "You're not gonna like the answer to that question."

Her chin lifted. "Are you done being bossy?"

"You're also not gonna like the answer to that question."

She cleared her throat. "I don't want to fight with you."

"Are you in or out with this relationship?" His deep tone wound through the silent night.

She blinked, caution pouring through her. What a surprising question at the moment. "I'm in."

"Then it's my way, Dana. No compromise when it comes to safety so long as Rock is on the loose and gunning for us. Either you tell me you understand that, or I'll make sure you understand that."

Now her mouth gaped open. "Is that a threat?" Her temper stirred.

"It's a fact. Tell me you get me." He moved toward her then, sleek and sure, his grace obviously back in place.

"Oh, I get you, but I'm not saying I agree." She lifted her chin, her body rioting at his nearness.

"You'll let me handle danger from now on. I like your

sleepwear." He slid his thumbs beneath both straps and drew them down her arms.

"It's called a baby doll," she said, desire flashing hot and bright inside her. Fast.

"It's pretty." He yanked the soft material down to her waist, his former gentleness gone. "But not as pretty as you."

Her nipples hardened beneath his gaze, her breasts feeling heavy. Needy. "I'm mad at you."

"You're not mad. You're scared." He flattened his hands over her shoulders and caressed down both arms and back up, twisting his fingers and brushing her nipples.

A jolt shot through her, and her legs wobbled. "You're *insightful* now?"

"I've always been insightful. Now I'm choosing to share my observations with you." He lifted her, tossing her easily back onto the bed.

She fell back on her elbows, her breasts bare, her tiny yellow panties hardly covering her. "You probably think this authoritarian thing you have going on is sexy."

He ripped his shirt over his head. "Never gave it a thought."

Her mouth watered. All right. Now that was sexy. Hard, smooth, sleek lines—the scarred body of a warrior sporting fresh bruises.

His gaze devoured her, giving her a sense of feminine power. "You're getting all of me, Dana."

"It's about time," she said, meaning it.

Wolfe kicked off his boots and jeans, wanting to get his mouth on that tiny yellow scrap of material. How he could go so quickly from pissed off to amused to irritated to turned on was a complete mystery, and the only answer was Dana Mulberry. She was going to drive him crazy, or crazier than he already was, and he was all in. Fully nude, he grabbed a condom from the bed table, and tossed it on the bed.

Lust coursed through him like a forest fire out of control. He forced himself to go slow and enjoy her, wrapping his hands around her small ankles and then gliding them up her calves, over her knees, along her thighs. Dipping his head, he nibbled her hip bone, wandering across her abdomen to the other hip.

She held her breath, her abdomen tight.

He grinned and planted his mouth right where they both wanted it, sucking hard.

She cried out and arched against him, her clit safely in his mouth. He released her and then tore the panties off with his teeth, returning to what was rapidly becoming his favorite treat. She was wet and ready, but his control wasn't firmly in place, so he wanted her wetter and more ready.

He slipped one finger inside her, and her body sucked him in, surrounding him with wet heat. His groan was heartfelt. Desire sparked down his spine to land in his balls. He licked her again, inserting another finger, giving her enough pressure to drive her nuts and drawing out her pleasure until she couldn't take any more.

She gyrated against him, making incoherent noises. "Wolfe. Please."

He crisscrossed his fingers inside her, reached up and lightly pinched one nipple, then sucked her clit back into his mouth. She flew apart against him, mewling, impressive waves taking her body. He eased her down, smiled at her soft mumbling, and then stood.

She made another sound, a sweet one, when he rolled on the condom. Then she reached for him.

The sight of her doing so, of her wanting him, accepting

him, would stay with him forever. He grasped her now pliable thighs and widened them, sliding his knees onto the bed.

He gripped her hips, his fingers extending across her ass and his thumbs tucked into her hipbones, lifting her lower half off the bed. "Wrap your legs around me," he ordered.

She did so, balancing her weight on her shoulders, her sunshine-colored hair spread out on his bed and her butt in the air. He kept her gaze, pressing against her entrance, slowly and surely penetrating her. Pulsating wet heat surrounded him, stretching and easing as he kept pushing, his balls drawing up tight.

Finally, he'd completely impaled her, groin to groin. Hunger filled her luminous eyes. She was open and vulnerable to him, but the feet pressing into his back held strength. "You okay?" he asked. "Your shoulders and neck?"

"I'm perfect," she whispered, so beautiful it hurt to look at her.

Yeah. She was. He tightened his grip, enjoyed the widening of her eyes, and then pulled out to power back inside her. She gasped and tightened around him, her hands digging into the comforter.

Oh yeah. She was ready.

So he let himself go. Hard and fast, he hammered into her, holding tight to her hips and pulling her in to meet his thrusts. Her breasts bounced and he watched, entranced.

She tossed her head on the comforter, her neck straining, the bedclothes bunching up around her. "Wolfe," she gasped, her internal walls clinching him in a hold so fierce his eyes nearly rolled back into his head. "More. Give me all of you."

He gave her more, driving fast, the sound of flesh against flesh mixing with their panting breaths.

A fusillade of sparks rioted through his abdomen, making him swell.

He reached between them and stroked her swollen clit, pressing at the last second and watching her go over. Her eyes glazed, her body tightened, and she cried out, thrusting her head and gripping him so hard he'd never get free.

Her orgasm lasted forever, pulling him farther inside and caressing his hard length. Finally, she subsided, her body going lax.

His control, what was left, snapped. He pounded harder, holding her right where he wanted her, the feelings too powerful to bear. Live coils unwound in him, and he exploded, the climax splintering him for a moment into nothingness. He came back to the moment in a second of pure release, holding her tightly against him, even his legs trembling.

His head dropped, and he panted, his heart clobbering his bruised ribs. He felt no pain.

Slowly, he withdrew and set her gently on the bed, turning to take care of the condom. His heart was filled with her, and the idea of anything happening to her made his hands shake as he returned to the bed and turned her over onto her stomach.

"What are you doing?" she asked, her body limp, her voice muffled and content.

"Taking care of you." He straddled her, careful to keep his weight off her, and reached down to knead her neck.

She moaned, her little butt wiggling against him as she snuggled into place. He gritted his teeth to keep from taking her again so soon. "A massage?" she mumbled.

"You were on your shoulders," he said, working out a couple of knots. "I don't want you to be sore tomorrow."

She chuckled, and her smooth body moved against him again. "Oh, I'm going to be sore, but it's a good sore." She sighed and brought her hands in to rest beneath her cheek. "This is nice, Wolfe."

Nice. That was him. He brushed her hair out of the way and leaned over to kiss the nape of her neck. "I just want you ready for round two." By the end of the night, there'd be no question that she belonged to him.

Chapter Thirty-Eight

Dana couldn't think of another argument to change Wolfe's mind as she sat in the Deep Ops office after several hours of mission planning, the afternoon heat heavy in the room. Or rather, of listening to several hours of mission planning. He was in control and definitely sexy as he outlined the mission parameters, but man, she didn't want him to go.

"This sounds really dangerous." She looked at the map in front of the conference room, her body nicely sore from the previous night.

Jethro looked over from the end of the table, where he was poring over some documents. "It'll be fine. Wolfe and I have both done this before."

Wolfe nodded, studying satellite images of the hills he planned to parachute into from way too high.

Jethro stood. "We need to leave in five minutes to catch the military transport." With a nod to her, he exited the conference room, shutting the door and leaving them alone.

"Please be careful and promise you'll come back," Dana said.

Wolfe put the papers down and reached for her, settling her on his lap with an easy strength that zinged butterflies through her abdomen. "I promise I'll be careful and will return."

She played with his dark shirt. "I understand how you'll get into the hills, but I didn't quite catch how you were gonna get out."

"Well, if all goes well, a friend of Jethro's in a helicopter is going to get us out of there."

She bit her lip, searching for the right words. "I trust you to come back."

He tugged her ponytail back and kissed her neck. Then he lifted his head, his dark gaze serious. "The second Gary gets wind that we've blown up his heroin, he's gonna be out for blood. So I need you to stay with my team and Roscoe until I get back. Promise me."

"I promise." She kissed him, marveling at the firmness of his mouth. "I'll miss you." His plan was to return to D.C., and then go to the cabin he'd rented to wait for Gary to show. In other words, he would use himself as bait and keep her safely away from danger. "This plan had better work."

"It will." Wolfe kissed her, going deep and taking possession. Then he stood and placed her on her feet. "Try not to do anything dangerous until I get back." He kissed her again and then turned, striding out of the room and heading straight for the elevator with Jethro. Seconds later, they were gone.

She pressed her lips together to keep from calling him back. They could never live normal lives with Gary out there waiting to strike, so she understood Wolfe's need to get this mission behind them. Roscoe padded in as if sensing she needed support, and she dropped to the chair to hug him, burying her face in his fur.

Pippa came in afterward with a tray of cupcakes. "I

bake when I get nervous, and so, here." She slid the tray across the table.

Dana straightened her back. Enough wallowing and giving in to fear. Sugar was another matter. She took a cupcake and bit into it, smiling at the delicious blend of vanilla and nutmeg. "This is amazing," she said around a mouthful.

"Thanks." Pippa took a vacated seat, today wearing skinny jeans and marvelous brown boots. Her mahogany hair tumbled down her back, and her pretty eyes were relaxed but concerned. "How are you doing?"

Dana gulped down the rest of the cupcake. "I'm eating my feelings."

Pippa laughed and reached for a white frosted cupcake. "I'll eat some feelings, too."

Roscoe yipped.

"No," Dana said. "No more sugar for you." He'd snuck two cookies earlier in the day and then had danced spastically for about fifteen minutes before dropping into a loud snooze. She played with a pen on the table to keep from reaching for another treat. "How are you and Malcolm doing?" she asked.

"Fantastic, although he's a little on edge with this op. Like the rest of us." Pippa finished her cupcake and brushed crumbs off her jeans. She stood. "I have to get some stuff finished, so I'll let you get back to work. We need a spa day when this is all over, and I'll look for a good one and make the arrangements." She patted Dana's shoulder and left.

Dana smiled. "Thanks." Pippa was one of the nicest people she'd ever met. Drawing her laptop across the table, she started typing her article, beginning with Candy's disappearance. She was freelance now, and she wouldn't sell the story until Wolfe was safe and it was over, but she could start now. It'd probably be a three-part article when she was finished, and she'd put Candy's byline first.

She got lost in writing, taking her time, petting the dog every once in a while.

When the elevator dinged outside, she grew still, her hands halting on the keyboard. What time was it, anyway? Her stomach growled. Must be around supper time.

Nari soon entered with Dr. Georgetown in tow. "Look who we have." She winked at Dana and then gracefully exited, shutting the door behind herself.

Heat climbed into Dana's face. "Oh. I totally forgot about the follow-up blood tests. Wolfe isn't here right now."

Today the doctor wore red plaid shorts and a bright blue shirt with a peacock above the left pocket. "I was golfing today, so it was no problem to stop by." He dropped his worn doctor's bag on the table and drew out a syringe still hygienically sealed and wrapped in a container. "How are you feeling?"

"Fine," Dana said. "No aftereffects from the drugs."

"That's what Wolfe said. I've been checking in with him daily, and he has reported on you as well." The doctor drew a rubber band thingy from his bag. "I just want to make sure the drugs have cleared your system and all is well. Does that work for you?"

She held out her arm, laying it on the table. "Sure."

The doctor wrapped the rubber around her vein and tapped a few times before using a wipe to clean her arm. "This is going to pinch." He smoothly inserted the needle and drew blood into the attached vial.

Dana looked away from the blood to keep from throwing up.

The doctor watched the vial fill. "There we go. Isn't it nice that life has calmed down a little?"

Her mouth gaped open. Oh, the poor guy had no clue.

* * *

Wolfe hated leaving Dana, but he had to finish this game of cat and mouse with Gary. The only way to draw out the bastard was to really piss him off, and destroying the drugs he'd trafficked to Mexico was an excellent way to do that. Then they could finally end this thing.

He led Jethro to the C-130 on the airstrip and was met immediately by his military contact, Cathy Roberts, as she crossed around.

"Cathy." He hugged her and then turned her to meet Jethro. "Professor Jethro Hanson, please meet Colonel Cathy Roberts."

They shook hands. Cathy looked good with her black hair cut short and her back ramrod straight. "You guys ready for our training exercise?" She used her fingers to make air quotes. "It'll take us nine hours or so to get there. You have a ride out?"

"Affirmative," Wolfe said.

"Well. I want to check out this bus, too." She smiled and turned to run to the front of the plane, where another pilot waited.

Jethro's eyebrows rose.

"What?" Wolfe asked, looking around. Oh. Cathy was a surprise? "She's one of the best pilots I've ever known, and she has also commanded in various positions throughout AFSOC. She's phenomenal, man."

Jethro nodded, and they settled into seats across from each other, falling asleep the minute the plane rose into the air.

Wolfe awoke to darkness, cold seeping into gear that Cathy had generously provided for them. It was the good stuff, too. He'd brought his own guns and knives—ones he knew well.

Jethro stretched awake, looking as relaxed as if he was settling in for a night of football, except for his alert eyes. He glanced at his watch, nodded, and reached for the tank to breathe pure oxygen for forty-five minutes to flush the hydrogen from his body

Wolfe did the same, breathing deep.

At about forty minutes, Cathy turned and gave them the sign. Wolfe stood and suited up with Jethro's help and then did the same for the Brit. They each had a small oxygen tank, compasses, and GPS devices. When the green light came on, he moved to the back door of the plane, which opened. He checked his gear again, gave the sign, and then jumped out.

The wind grabbed him, and he waited several seconds before pulling the rip cord. In a HAHO, a high-altitude high-opening jump, he felt in control. Cold wind batted at him, and he finished counting and aimed. An image of Dana filtered through his thoughts, but he pushed it aside, focusing only on right here and right now.

The Brit followed him.

Flimsy clouds surrounded him, and he glanced at the compass, breathing the oxygen. They were right on track. Cathy had somehow acquired good explosives for this training mission as well. He coasted down for quite a while, adjusting his course easily, eventually landing near a rocky hill and running to slow down. Then he unclipped the chute and wrapped it up as Jethro did the same, looking for a place to hide them.

Jethro stashed them behind some rocks before jogging up. "Nice jump. We're about two miles from target."

Wolfe ditched the oxygen. "You up to a jog?"

"Affirmative."

Wolfe checked his pack and silent radio before reading his compass. He freed the binoculars Cathy had provided, scouting the area, looking for heat signatures. Nothing close. So he replaced them, swung his pack to his back, and started jogging up the hill, keeping alert for any sounds.

Jethro easily kept pace, and he'd been an expert on the jump. Wolfe should probably find out more about this guy when he got the chance.

They reached the top of the first hill and kept running, going for about twenty minutes until they came to another hill. This one was guarded by two guys with machine guns.

Wolfe motioned for Jethro, who nodded. Wolfe took the one on the left and Jethro the right, dropping them with no shots fired. They were both unconscious, so Wolfe tied their hands and feet before dragging them out of sight.

Jethro slapped duct tape over their mouths, stood, and jogged back toward the hill. When they reached the top of the one they wanted, Wolfe crouched down and pulled out his binoculars. He pointed. "There." Adrenaline percolated throughout his veins, providing focus and a buzz that would help keep him alive.

A patrol of two men walked by what looked like an entrance into the adjacent hill.

Jethro watched them go. "Hello, underground lab."

"I hope our intel is good." Wolfe was fine destroying any drug lab, but this had better be the one working with Gary. The combined sources of the Deep Ops teams were good, and more than a couple had directed him here.

It was around two in the morning and wouldn't be dark for long. The lab was probably as empty as it was gonna get. "Let's clear it," Wolfe said, shimmying down the hill.

Jethro followed suit. They reached the bottom and crouched, running full bore for the metal door set into the rock. He counted to three and opened it.

Wolfe darted inside, gun sweeping. Nothing. Empty corridor, cold and wet.

Jethro shut the door. "Let's move, mate."

Wolfe took point, inching down the corridor and drawing on his mask to protect his lungs from any chemicals. He'd dealt with enough drugs in his system lately. They reached a lab that was empty but well stocked. Then another empty lab.

Voices came from up ahead, and he hurried, finally reaching a working lab. He motioned for Jethro to move past the entrance without being seen, and Jethro nodded.

Wolfe did the same, coming to a storage room. He forced open the door and sucked in air. Stacks and stacks and stacks of bagged heroin. Millions and millions of dollars' worth of the deadly opiate. He stepped inside and drew off his pack.

A guard appeared from the other side of the stack, starting and gasping, his body tensing. He lifted his weapon.

Chapter Thirty-Nine

Dana stretched out on Wolfe's sofa after a dinner of delicious beef Wellington with Pippa and Mal. If Mal didn't marry Pippa, Dana was going to. That woman could really cook. As if conjured by the thought, Pippa knocked on the back sliding door before stepping inside, holding a stack of glass containers in her hands.

"Hi," Dana said, standing. She couldn't eat anything else tonight—she was happily stuffed.

"Hey." Pippa moved to the fridge as if she'd done so a hundred times before. "I have leftovers and some goodies for the upcoming week." The stunning brunette took a moment to organize the rest of the fridge's contents as if she couldn't help herself.

Dana had followed her into the kitchen. "I kinda love you."

Pippa laughed, the sound free and happy. "Ditto."

Dana's friends were a small and select group, and it felt good to add Pippa to that number. Pippa was always nurturing Dana and Wolfe with food, and Dana wanted to reciprocate. What did Pippa need? A thought struck Dana, and she reached out for Pippa's hand. "I have an idea. As soon as all of this craziness is over, let's get hold of my sister Katie."

Pippa tilted her head. "Okay?"

"Yeah. She's a shoe buyer for Neiman's. We can either take a weekend and go visit her, or we can talk her into bringing a boatload of samples here." It was well known that Pippa loved boots. She also suffered from social anxiety but was branching out more these days.

Pippa's eyes lit up like those of a kitten seeing its first goldfish. She grabbed Dana's other hand. "A buyer for *Neiman's*?"

"Yes," Dana said, laughing. "It kills her that I'd rather wear tennis shoes than anything else, but she's gonna love you."

Pippa impulsively pulled Dana in for a hug in a rare show of trust. "Oh, thank you. I can't wait. Can you imagine seeing the next line before it's public?"

Dana wasn't sure what a line was, but she hugged her new friend back anyway.

The slider opened and Malcolm, looking ripped and dangerous, paused outside. "Um, what's the hugging about?"

Pippa released Dana and turned, actually hopping once. "Dana's sister is a buyer for Neiman's, and she can bring the *next season's* samples here sometime. Can you believe it?"

Mal's strong eyebrows rose. "I, ah, I don't know what that means."

"Shoes, boots, sandals," Pippa said, moving excitedly toward him. "All here, all new. All mine."

Mal's eyes softened and he reached out to touch her face. "That sounds great. Although, isn't there a limit to how many pairs of boots one set of feet can wear?"

"No," Pippa and Dana said in unison.

Mal chuckled. "I'll trust you on that." He tugged Pippa outside, the obvious gentleness in contrast with his dangerous appearance. He drew Pippa close and pressed a kiss to her temple, while unobtrusively scouting the area to each side of the house, no doubt looking for problems.

Dana could just sigh in happiness at the love between the two. They'd certainly earned it after Malcolm had been shot while undercover and Pippa had escaped from a dangerous cult. It was nice to see them relaxed and not looking over their shoulders constantly.

Well, except when they were watching for Gary Rockcliff. He was a threat to the entire team. Thank goodness everyone was involved in the case now. The unit members had some definite quirks, but they got things done when they worked together. The intervention with Wolfe had been a little tense, but there had been something sweet and caring about it.

Mal turned serious, zeroing his focus in on her. "Are you sure you don't want to stay with us? We have a guest room, and both animals are welcome, too."

"I'm sure," Dana said. She'd probably be up all night writing and worrying about Wolfe, anyway. "Thanks for dinner, and the goodies. I'll see you two tomorrow morning before we head in to work." They still had to discuss the interviews with HDD, but she just couldn't worry about one more thing right now.

Mal nodded. "Okay, but lock the door and set the alarm right after we leave. The sensors and cameras aren't up around the properties yet, because Agent Frost had to special order all of it. Got it?"

"Yep." Most of the Deep Ops guys were pretty bossy, weren't they? In fact, so was Nari when it came to her meetings and Brigid when it came to her computer room or anything to do with the Internet. They should rename themselves the Bossy Bunch instead of Deep Ops. Dana chuckled and moved to shut and lock the door.

Dinner and talking with Pippa had been a nice distraction, but her stomach still hurt and her shoulders felt as if she'd had them tensed for days. Nothing would help that but Wolfe getting home safely. She turned back as Roscoe padded in from the bedroom, stretching after a nap. He headed for the back door. "Need to go out, huh?" She opened the door and let him bound out, watching him chase his tail around the backyard as darkness slowly began to descend.

Then Kat came out of nowhere, also wanting to go outside. He had a litter box in the laundry room, but he seemed to prefer the outdoors, so she let him wander out and sniff the grass, following Roscoe. The humidity hung low and heavy as she stepped out on the deck and sat on the stairs, shutting the door so as not to cool the outside, as her dad would've said.

She took a deep breath, looking out at the fence that enclosed the two backyards together. Beyond the fence was a trail and acres of forest, teeming with wildlife. How in the world was Millie Frost going to set sensors and cameras everywhere? It seemed impossible, especially since Wolfe and Pippa owned forty acres between them. Their bungalows were at the end of a long country road with forested land across from them.

The quiet countryside reminded Dana of home, and she leaned back against the glass, trying to relax. The animals played, chasing each other, Kat halfheartedly swiping at Roscoe's nose.

She let them goof off for a while until they both looked too hot, and then she called them in. "It's going to cool off someday," she said, standing and shutting the door to securely lock it before setting the alarm.

Both animals headed for their bowls of food. The AC brushed her skin, and she shivered at the contrast with the heat.

She might as well get back to work. Instead of using the home office, she spread her notes across the kitchen table and started typing on her laptop, feeling cozy with the animals in the house and Mal and Pippa next door. Her thoughts kept returning to Wolfe, and she hoped Jethro was as good at backup as Angus had promised.

Her burner phone buzzed, and she scrambled for it. Maybe it was Wolfe. "Hello?"

"Hi, Dana. It's Dr. Georgetown."

Oh. She'd forgotten all about the doctor. "Hi. Is everything okay with my blood?" Had there been something else in the drug cocktail? She'd kept her worry under wraps, but it'd be nice to have confirmation that some bizarre disease or germ wasn't crawling through her system.

"I just wanted to let you know that everything is normal and I didn't find any trace of those drugs or anything odd in your blood. Well, Donald didn't find anything. He did the actual tests." The doctor sneezed several times.

"Bless you," Dana said.

"Thanks." The sound of papers shuffling came over the line. "I'll need to test Wolfe's blood, just to make sure, when he's available. Have him call me."

Dana took a sip of her water. "I will. Hopefully soon."

The doctor cleared his throat. "There is one more thing. I'd rather tell you this in person, but Donald and I are going on holiday tomorrow, so over the phone will have to do."

Dana stopped breathing.

"Dana? We found a significant amount of hCG in your blood."

Dana's mouth opened, but no sound came out. She tried

again, clearing her throat. "I, ah, you, um, is it possible to have hCG and not be pregnant?"

"Probably not, hon." He was quiet, letting her digest the news. "We can talk about options, if you like."

"No. Thanks." Her body went numb, and she stared at Roscoe, who'd turned from his food to watch her. "I appreciate your calling." She didn't hear much of what else the doctor said before she hung up. Something about prenatal vitamins and rest.

She'd had a feeling. Oh, she'd shoved it down with logic and statistics and distractions, but deep down, she'd had an odd feeling about that night with Wolfe that she couldn't explain.

Roscoe, sensing her emotions, lumbered across the kitchen and set his jaw on her knee.

Thoughts and feelings bombarded her. A baby. Wolfe's baby. They'd just started dating and a psychotic killer was hunting them. They'd been drugged and not in their right minds when having unprotected sex. A little girl with Wolfe's startling bourbon-colored eyes and her gift for writing. Or a little boy with Wolfe's face and her eyes.

Wolfe had mentioned maybe dating her when this was all over. He'd never talked about a future. It was way early in the pregnancy, and most things went wrong in the first trimester. She hadn't even missed a period yet. Most folks didn't announce until after three months just in case something went wrong. Would Wolfe want a baby? She wasn't ready, but she was pregnant, so she'd have to get ready.

It was impossible to grab on to just one thought.

Except that Wolfe was somewhere in a remote part of a different country surrounded by killers with guns while trying to bomb a building full of heroin. There with only one man for backup, an unclear plan for extraction, and an uncertainty about even the correct location of the drugs.

Plus, Wolfe was still wounded from the bomb explosion the other night. He might not be as quick as usual or even as strong. Sure, he was incredibly tough, but his ribs were bruised and he'd limped when he'd thought she wasn't watching him. At this very moment, he might be in extreme danger. He'd promised to come home, but sometimes things were out of one's hands, even Wolfe's. He could be getting shot at right now. Or maybe he was still parachuting from a high altitude, where so many things could go wrong.

She was pregnant and he didn't know it.

"Oh, Roscoe," she murmured. "This is huge."

Chapter Forty

Wolfe fired once, the suppressor on his weapon making barely a small pop. The guy went down fast and quiet.

Jethro nodded, dropped his pack, and drew out several devices. He moved to the back of the room, placing bombs as he went, starting the timers for three minutes. Wolfe set one near the doorway, gave Jethro a signal, and dodged back into the corridor.

The timing was good for this op; there were few people inside the facility. The second it exploded, he and Jet would have to run. It was impossible to see how many insurgents were crawling the hills, but they'd deal with that next. He hustled down to the end of the corridor, setting a device and engaging the timer.

Jet met him and they moved back the way they'd come, guns first.

Wolfe reached the occupied lab and stood in the doorway while Jethro covered the corridor. He briefly lifted his mask so everyone could hear him clearly. "You have four minutes to vacate this building before it explodes."

Several of the techs, dressed in white with masks covering their faces, looked up from their equipment.

Wolfe looked for threats, but saw no guards. Maybe they stayed mainly outside. He tried again. *"Hay explosives*

*en esta instalación que detonarán en menos de cuatro
minutos. Sal de aquí y corre tan lejos como puedas. Ahora!"*
he yelled.

A woman to the far left gasped, and the group scrambled
for the door.

"There you go," Jethro said through his own mask.

Wolfe nodded, turned, and started to run to get out
before the techs. He emerged first into the night. Bullets
zinged by his head, and he ducked and rolled, coming up
firing toward the bursts.

Jethro did the same, and the gunfire stopped.

Wolfe scrambled up and started running away from the
underground lab.

The sounds of people screaming orders and scrambling
away filled the night, along with more gunfire. Wolfe ran
in a zigzag pattern, heading between scraggly trees and
climbing the next hill.

Gunfire erupted, and he turned to return fire, adrenaline
bursting through him.

Jethro grunted in pain and went down.

Wolfe skidded to a stop and ducked low, reaching his
friend. "How bad?" His voice was muffled through the
mask.

"Bad." Jethro clutched his bleeding right thigh.

Shit. Wolfe grabbed Jethro by the shoulders and yanked
him around a tree, propping him up. Then he dropped his
pack, grasping the knife from his sheath and slicing up
Jet's pants leg, cutting the material away.

He peered down to look via moonlight, not wanting to
give away their position.

The scent of blood and dirt filled his nostrils.

Jethro looked down at his leg, his mask safely in place.
"Bugger."

"Looks like ankle, calf, above knee, and thigh," Wolfe

said, calculating the blood loss. It was a burst of bullets. There was nothing like an AK-47 to mess up a body—old school.

He dug in his pack and drew out QuikClot to wrap around each of the wounds. Jethro bit his lip but didn't make a sound, his body tense with pain.

A man came around the nearest tree, caught sight of them, and quickly lifted his weapon.

Wolfe partially turned and threw the knife, penetrating the guy's neck. The man dropped his gun, grabbed the knife handle, and fell forward to land on his face, his legs kicking out.

Jethro grunted, his face looking pale, even in the darkness.

Wolfe padded each wound and tied them tight, wrapping material from his first aid pack around each one.

Jethro shook his head. "I can't run, mate."

"I'm aware." Wolfe stood and replaced his pack. Shouting came from the hill to the right, and three armed men scaled the top, running toward them.

Wolfe leaped to the nearest tree, ducking and dodging for a better angle. "Go flat."

Jethro instantly complied, sliding down, his gun out and ready.

Wolfe levered himself up, aimed, and squeezed the trigger three times. The men fell fast, one of them getting off a shot that spit up dust next to Wolfe.

Gunfire erupted from the opposite direction, throwing twigs and rocks all around him.

Shit. Jethro was exposed, even flat on the ground.

Wolfe ducked his head and launched into motion, weaving to avoid the rain of bullets. He reached Jethro, clamped his hands around Jet's good ankle, dropped his shoulder to the ground, rolled and twisted, hitting his knees and coming up to his feet with Jethro over his shoulder, one arm manacled around Jet's calf and the other on his forearm.

The man's muscled weight bore down on Wolfe and he grunted, running for the distant trees and the one hill that didn't hold anybody shooting at them.

Yet.

A soldier ran toward them from the side, shooting erratically. Jethro lifted himself up from his position on Wolfe's shoulders, and fired rapidly, dropping the guy.

Wolfe grunted and held on, his grip sliding to Jethro's thigh as the Brit twisted and fired three more shots in the same direction.

Grunts and cries of pain echoed back.

Wolfe's ribs cracked together and projected pain throughout his body. He sucked it in, let pain take him, and shoved sensation away, ignoring the agony. He kept a tight hold on Jethro, running up another hill, along a ravine and then over yet another hill, through a series of trees, and over rocks that kept dropping beneath his feet to another ravine below.

Jethro held tight, not making a sound.

Impressive.

Wolfe kept running, his boots barely finding purchase. He glanced at his compass and switched directions a couple of times because of the terrain. Blood slid over his arm, and he glanced down to see what he thought was Jethro's good arm bleeding. "You shot in the arm, too?" Wolfe growled.

"No. Just a scratch," Jethro whispered back, his voice low with pain.

Pain was good. It meant that Jet still had feeling in the limb, which boded well. If they got out of here. The moon shone down, lighting Wolfe's way; the stars were brilliant above them. He took an angled approach to descending the next hill, running along a gully and frightening a couple of iguanas into the rocks.

An explosion sounded behind them, and Wolfe ducked, riding out the waves. Fire billowed, along with smoke, into the sky, lighting the entire area.

Screams and more gunfire started pattering in every direction but not directly at them. What was everyone shooting at? Particles started falling, and he pressed his mask closer to protect his lungs from what might be pure heroin.

He saw an opening and took a barely there trail between two rocks up yet another hill, digging his feet in to keep moving. This one was more of a mountain, but he kept climbing, finally reaching the top with his breath panting out painfully. He looked down at a small field where a camouflage-painted helicopter waited quietly.

Movement sounded behind him.

Not good. He started to run again, this time letting gravity take control as bullets pinged the rocks around them.

The entire crew showed up too early for work the next morning. Angus Force tapped his fingers against his desk, his concentration splintered. The Jack Daniels in his bottom drawer beckoned to him. A soft knock on the door had him looking gratefully up. "Come in." He lost his eagerness when Nari clip-clopped her way inside and shut the door. Today the shrink had dressed in a black pencil skirt with a soft purple blouse that made her skin almost translucent. Her black hair hung naturally around her slim shoulders, and concern glowed in her midnight dark eyes. "I don't want to talk, Nari."

She lifted a perfectly painted pink nail. "I'm not here to talk you into therapy."

He gestured toward one of the two rickety chairs on the other side of his dented desk. "Have a seat." He might as well make use of her since she was there. "How is the team doing?"

"Not well." She crossed her legs, and he fought a groan at the graceful movement. "Malcolm is staring at his phone, Brigid is yelling at her computers, Raider is silent in case room two, Dana looks like she was hit by a bus, and Roscoe keeps trying to filch whipped cream from everyone."

Sounded like a normal day to him. "I assume Pippa is at home working?" The woman did some sort of online accounting and seemed to keep busy.

"Yeah, with Kat." Nari's small nostrils flared as she breathed deep and slowly let the air out. "Shouldn't we have heard something from Wolfe and Jethro by now?"

Yes. Angus schooled his face to show no emotion. "No, maybe not. Keep in mind that anything might've altered their plan."

"Like getting shot?" Nari asked.

"Don't borrow trouble." That was his job. There was an edge in his voice that crept in any time he talked with the shrink. She worked for HDD and not him. "I'm sure you've been in contact with our HDD handlers, and I know they want to interview us. What have you told them?"

She flushed. "I've been avoiding their calls, too. We need to pull the entire team together and come up with a reason you two were at Frank Spanek's apartment right when it blew up."

Wait a second. She'd been avoiding them, too? He never could judge her allegiances easily, but now wasn't the time to try to figure her out. He reached for the plain coffee he'd bought on the way in to work, not having to hide it since

Wolfe was out of the office. "We received an anonymous tip that Frank Spanek was trafficking heroin, which, incidentally, was actually true."

Nari bounced her shiny black high heel on the leg that was crossed. "How did we receive this tip?"

Good question. Phone records could be tracked. "Letter sent here. Wolfe took it to the apartment."

Her pink lips pursed. "Ah. So it was blown up in the explosion?"

"Exactly." It didn't matter if the HDD handlers believed the Deep Ops team had been out of line; it mattered that they couldn't prove it. That bobbing foot and slender ankle were going to drive him crazy.

"All right. I don't suppose we took a copy of the letter, as protocol would more than likely dictate?" she asked.

He shrugged. "Oops. Guess we missed that one." Why the hell hadn't Wolfe or Jethro called in? He didn't have a way to reach them through official channels, and he didn't want to get them in trouble by trying. But if they didn't make contact by that night, he would have to do something.

A sharp rap echoed on the door and Brigid yanked it open, her red hair wild around her face. "Satellite imagery confirms an explosion in the hills outside of Culiacán last night. It took me all day to hack into the—"

Angus held up a hand. "Don't want to know and really don't want the shrink to know."

Both women shot him a look that made his head ache.

Angus ignored their irritation. "Did you see anything else?"

Brigid shook her head. "The satellite I accessed recorded the explosion because it was so bright in the night sky, but I couldn't get much more detail than that. There is some chatter across governmental lines, but so far, nobody is claiming responsibility."

Somebody would. Didn't matter who.

Brigid hesitated in the doorway. "Shouldn't we have heard something directly by now?"

"Not necessarily," Angus said. The team had to remain calm and focused, so he hid his own concern. "If they didn't get out by daylight, they probably went underground until they could execute their exit strategy." He didn't like this, but there wasn't a damn thing he could do right now. Except keep Dana Mulberry safe until Wolfe returned. "Check on Dana, would you? She looked a little pale this morning." The woman was probably terrified for Wolfe. It didn't take a profiler to see that something was going on between those two.

Brigid nodded and tossed the mail his way. "Just came in." Then she turned to head toward the hub of desks.

Nari wetted her lips. "Are you adding new members to the team? If so, we need to do it officially."

That prim and proper voice kept Angus up at night, so he glowered. "No. Serena, Millicent, and Jethro are acting as consultants to the team. We don't need to deal with the red tape of HDD personnel policies."

Nari's eyebrows rose. "They might want to get paid at some point."

"I can pay them as consultants," Angus said, taking another shot of his coffee. Maybe he should put a little sugar in it. Huh. Wolfe was ruining him. "Your job is to shrink heads and report back to HDD that we're on the straight and narrow. Worrying about consultants is outside your purview."

She stood, all grace and class. "Could you go one day without being a total butthead?"

He nearly choked on his coffee but quickly regained his composure. "No."

She rolled her eyes and exited the office.

Grunting, he ripped open the mail, tossing the junk into the trash. He lifted the last one, a cream-colored envelope, and sliced it open. A handwritten note dropped out.

The world went silent. Electricity jolted from his head through his extremities in a dangerous rush of sparking heat.

His hand shook as he smoothed the paper to read the two words on the paper. *Miss Me?*

The handwriting, he knew well.

Sound rushed back in as fast as it had disappeared. Lassiter was finally making a move. Force had known that the bastard was still alive. Evil had its own presence. Okay. He'd start tracking, really hunting, the serial killer right away.

Then he turned his attention back to his too silent burner phone.

Where the hell were his men?

Chapter Forty-One

After a full day of working and getting nothing done, Dana smoothed her hands down her jeans, sitting at Wolfe's desk in the bullpen of the HDD offices, with Roscoe munching on the side of her tennis shoe. She looked down. "It's like you're addicted." Or maybe she'd spilled whipped cream from her latte on her shoe. Yeah, that was probably more likely.

The office was too quiet. The place seemed empty without Wolfe. He didn't talk much, but he seemed to fill a room with his presence.

Malcolm worked quietly next to her, glancing at his phone every once in a while.

She wanted to reassure him that Wolfe was fine and would call in soon, but considering it was nearly dinnertime, and they hadn't received any notice, the words kept choking in her throat.

The elevator protested, thunked, ground gears, and then opened.

"Ah, shit," Mal said, leaning back in his chair.

At the sound, Angus and Raider emerged from case room two, their expressions identically irritated. Angus had been off all day, but so had everyone else.

Agents Fields and Rutherford hurried off the elevator

as if afraid the doors were going to close on them, which was entirely possible.

Rutherford took the lead, his perfectly coiffed hair gleaming in the yellow fluorescent lights. Did he use mousse or some other product? Dana would love to get that kind of volume. "Why the hell aren't any of your phones working?" Rutherford asked, looking out of place in the dingy office with his smooth, shiny gray suit and polished loafers.

Dana winced. Hadn't anybody told the agents about the burner phones? Probably not. She kept silent, figuring Angus could handle the HDD guys.

But it was Nari who spoke first, stepping out of her tiny closet office. "We've been busy working on all the case files you dumped on us last week."

Oh, good point. Dana had forgotten those case files, as had everyone else, as far as she could tell. Roscoe abandoned her shoe and stood, turning around and positioning himself between her and the agents. Ah, that was sweet. She reached out and scratched him between the ears, calming him. His butt dropped and he sat, his focus still remaining on what he must consider a threat.

Fields kept his gaze on the dog. Sharp man.

Rutherford wasn't that smart. He looked at Angus, his stance belligerent. "I've requested to interview your team, and I'm tired of waiting for you to cooperate with the people paying your salary. So, we're going to conduct said interviews right here and right now." He angled his neck and looked beyond the elevator. "I believe there are a couple of interrogation rooms in this dump?"

Dana's burner phone buzzed, and she jumped, scrambling for it on the desk and knocking over a cup of pens. "Hello? Hello?" she said frantically, pressing it to her ear.

"Hi, baby." Wolfe's voice came through strong.

Her entire body went limp, sagging in relief so strong she almost started crying. "Are you all right?"

"I'm fine, but Jethro is having surgery on his leg right now. Sorry about the delay calling, but we got pinned down for quite a while and then had to take evasive measures. It was all quiet until we landed at the Fort Sam Houston hospital early this evening." Wolfe sounded strong and sure. Alive and well.

Dana pressed a hand instinctively against her abdomen and looked up to see everyone watching her intently. Wolfe was on a secret mission, and she instantly tried to sound nonchalant. "I'm glad to hear that," she said.

Wolfe was quiet for a moment. "Are you all right?"

"Yeah, just working away in the office with everybody." She smiled and Rutherford's eyes narrowed.

"Is there somebody present you can't speak freely in front of?" Wolfe's voice had turned all business.

She forced a laugh. "Yeah. Definitely."

"Dangerous?"

"No. Annoying like the summer weather." She wasn't good at this subterfuge crap.

He sighed. "Fields and Rutherford."

"Yes, that would be a lot of fun, Mom. I can't wait," Dana said, getting into the act.

Malcolm snorted quietly next to her.

"You're not very good at this, sweetheart," Wolfe murmured, making her smile wider in response. "When you can talk, tell Force that Jet took a couple to the leg and might have shattered an ankle. Surgery will take a few hours."

"Yeah, Mom, I like the blue shoes," Dana replied.

Wolfe chuckled. "Stop talking and just nod. I want to speak with Jethro's doctor. Then I'm going to hop a transport in about two hours. That'll get me home six hours from now, and I can't wait to put my mouth on you."

Her answer strangled in her throat, so she followed his directions and just nodded, her face warming from her neck to her forehead. Wolfe disengaged the call, so Dana waited a sec, said good-bye to the silence, and put her phone on her desk.

"Your mother?" Agent Fields asked dryly.

She cleared her throat and reached to pet Roscoe again.

Force strode out of his office toward the agents, and Roscoe stood again, his fur rising along his back. "Down, boy," Force murmured, pausing by the dog. "Here's the deal. We're in the middle of a couple of those cases you shoved down our throats, and we don't have time to chat today." He looked over his shoulder at Brigid, who finally peeked out of her computer room. "Bridge? Would you create a schedule for everybody on the team to meet with these fine gentlemen—starting on Monday after we clear these cases?"

Rutherford's patrician features darkened, and he stepped forward, stopping only when Roscoe growled a clear warning.

Fields sighed. "We need a better handle on what caused the explosion the other night."

Force shrugged. "I'm no expert on explosions. We received an anonymous letter here at the office, didn't really think it was true, and went to check out Frank Spanek just to make sure. Got there, knocked on the door, and the world pretty much volcanoed around us."

"Where's the letter?" Rutherford asked softly.

Dana listened intently. If this was the story, she wanted to remember it. Although, apparently, she wasn't very good at playing this game.

Force winced. "It must've gotten caught in the fire. I haven't seen it."

"That's handy," Fields said, reaching into his pocket for a green sucker, unwrapping it and sticking it in his mouth.

"Not really," Force countered, resting his hand on the vibrating dog. "I don't know anything about the explosion other than it hurt to hit the wall on the other side of the hallway. Might've been motion activated, on a timer, or even detonated from afar. I really have no idea."

Fields studied the assembled group. "All right. The rest of your team can wait until Monday, but you and Clarence Wolfe need to be interviewed today."

Force turned on his heel. "You can interview me in my office. Wolfe is running errands, and you're welcome to wait for him, but it might be a while."

Rutherford looked around the small group. "I'd advise you all to remember that lying to federal agents is a felony, and I would love to prosecute every single one of you."

Force halted at his office. "It's now or never, gentlemen. I have a hot yoga class in an hour."

Raider coughed out a laugh.

The two agents strode through the space, giving the dog a wide berth.

Malcolm waited until the door had closed before standing. "Let's get out of here before they change their minds."

Dana nodded, packed up her belongings, and jogged toward the elevator with the rest of the group, including Roscoe. Kat had stayed home with Pippa for the day, so she didn't have to worry about him. Once outside the building, Roscoe seemed as happy as she did to get away from the office, jumping into Mal's truck with a wag of his tail.

They shared companionable silence on the way home, and Pippa had dinner waiting at Mal's house.

"I love her," Dana said, taking a deep breath of the fragrant air and preceding Mal into his home.

"So do I," Mal said, smiling.

They had a wonderful dinner of chicken and rice before Dana yawned and decided to take both Kat and Roscoe home. She had another baby doll to wear to bed, this one a sexy black, and she wanted to get ready for Wolfe, so she walked between the backyards, with Malcolm watching her. Maybe Wolfe had some candles somewhere so she could make it more of a romantic night.

Daylight was fading, but not the oppressive heat when she opened the door, entered the alarm, and breathed in the cool air inside. She moved to the fridge for a glass of wine, remembering at the last second that she couldn't drink. Kat sprawled across the table, sleeping, and Roscoe conducted a quick survey of the house, hitting every room.

Should she tell Wolfe about the pregnancy tonight or wait until the morning, after, well, welcoming him home the right way? Excitement flushed through her.

Roscoe returned to her and sniffed at the door.

"Why didn't you go while we walked over?" She sighed, punched in the code, and opened the door. The dog bounded out. She laughed, watching him play. He was so sweet to check out the house before relieving himself outside. What kind of training did he have, or was that just instinct?

He stopped cold in the middle of the yard and spun around, looking at her.

"Roscoe?" She stepped near the slider. What was wrong with him?

Silent as death, a man twisted off the roof, hands on the eaves, and swung inside. He hit her with his legs, knocking her several feet back to land on her butt. Pain ripped up her back to her neck, and she slid across the floor, striking the lower part of the kitchen counters.

Roscoe bunched and ran full bore at the intruder, impacting him and shoving them both inside. Roscoe slashed with his teeth and growled, furiously going for the guy's neck.

The man covered his face, fighting back, and reached for a gun at his waist.

"Roscoe!" Dana scrambled up and jumped for the duo, but the man turned and fired. The gun barely made a sound. It had to have had a silencer. The dog yelped, spittle flying from his mouth.

Roscoe stopped, his eyes wide, then fell back, blood spurting from his side.

The man stood and slid the door closed, turning to face her. He slowly dropped a backpack to the floor.

Gary Rockcliff.

Chapter Forty-Two

Dana cried out and dropped to her knees, reaching for Roscoe. His eyes had shut, and blood poured from above his belly. She frantically turned and ransacked the second drawer for a towel to press against the wound. The dog didn't move.

She looked up, her body going numb.

Gary Rockcliff stared down at her, the barrel of the gun pointed at her head. "It's time for us to go."

She shook her head, pressing the towel against Roscoe's fur, the blood welling up between her fingers. "You're crazy. How could you shoot a dog?"

Kat jumped to all fours, arched his back, and hissed at Gary from the table.

Gary pointed the gun at the kitten.

"No!" Dana exploded, jumping for Kat, snatching him up, and shoving him into the small pantry. She shut the door, leaning against it, her nerves misfiring from adrenaline and terror.

Gary pointed the gun at the unmoving dog. "Come here, Dana, or I'll shoot him again."

She rapidly thought through her options, glancing between Gary and the dog. "I don't understand what you want." Wasn't there a knife in the drawer by the oven? She had to get over there somehow.

"You will." Gary was as tall as Wolfe and as broad across the chest, but his eyes showed a madness that made the bile rise in Dana's throat. He'd dressed in all black and had a knife visibly strapped to his thigh. "Here's the plan. We go out one of the windows to the east, away from that other house, and then we quietly walk through the forest to the vehicle I have waiting."

"Is that how you got here?" Dana panted.

"More or less." Gary stepped toward her, his hand steady on the weapon. "I was on that roof forever, waiting for you."

She shook her head, frantically seeking a way out. "Wolfe will kill you for this."

Gary chuckled, the sound scratchy. "Oh, you have no idea what he'll want to kill me for, but you will soon."

Her stomach dropped, and her hands shook.

Without warning, Gary grabbed her and yanked her in front of him to face the backyard, pressing the gun to her head. She shrieked, fought his hold, and then subsided when the cold metal cut into her skin. She blinked several times, looking out at the darkened night through the slight reflection in the sliding glass door. Outside, Malcolm stood, a rifle in his hands.

Gary angled himself behind her. "Do you think he could hit me and not you through this glass?"

"Yes." Her lip trembled.

Malcolm took several steps back, the fury in his eyes evident even across the distance.

"Guess not," Gary said, pushing her toward the sliding glass door. "This changes our plans, now doesn't it?" He shoved harder with the gun, and she winced. "Draw the blinds shut. Now."

Roscoe whimpered behind her. "Let me put him outside," Dana said. Then Malcolm could get the dog some help.

"No." Gary sighed. "Here's the deal. You shut these blinds, or I'm going to shoot you in the knee. It won't kill you, but it'll hurt like hell, and you won't even get a chance to run. Don't you at least want a chance to run?" he crooned, dropping his head to whisper in her ear.

The thought of the baby inside her nearly dropped her to the floor. She had to stay alive. Malcolm knew Gary was there; he'd get the rest of the team. All she had to do was stay alive. "Okay." She drew the blinds closed, instantly feeling cut off as Malcolm disappeared.

Gary nudged her toward the keypad. "Engage the alarm."

She punched in the code and then pushed him. "It's locked and we're secured. Will you please let me put the dog out on the front porch? Malcolm is out back, so I can do it without him seeing." She had to save Roscoe. Maybe she'd get a chance to run, too.

"No." Gary maneuvered them to the living room and shoved her onto the sofa. "You move, and I'll shoot you." His smile revealed one too-long canine. "In the knee, of course. We want time to play, don't we?"

She looked around the room for something to use as a weapon if the chance arose, but there was nothing. How could she get through to him? She thought back to a television show she'd watched a while ago, trying to concentrate. "You saw me at the golf course the other day, right?"

Gary lifted the blinds to check the darkened road. "Yeah."

"I was there with my family." She remembered an investigator on the show telling people to personalize themselves to bad guys. "I have three sisters. Do you have any?"

"No."

Tires screeched outside. Gary nodded. "Backup has arrived. That was quick—must've been in the neighborhood." He let the blinds fall back together and turned to face her, looking like one solid lump of muscle.

It couldn't be Wolfe outside. He'd probably just be landing, and the airstrip was at least thirty minutes away. Dana sat on the edge of the sofa, her body tense and ready if an opportunity came. "I'm a journalist because I like to write." She tried to look into the kitchen but could only see Roscoe's motionless tail. Her eyes filled and she batted emotion away. "Articles right now, but like most journalists, I've thought about writing a book. Maybe some sort of young adult novel with an element of science fiction."

Gary's bushy eyebrows rose. "Dana? Do you think my getting to know you is going to help somehow?"

"It can't hurt," she said. "Why don't we talk and get to know each other?"

He stared at her chest. "I want to know two things about you. First, how loud can you scream, and second, is your blood sweet or spicy tasting?"

Something buzzed, and he reached in one of his many pockets for a small phone. "It's about time," he muttered, lifting it to his ear while also pointing the gun back at her. "Where the hell have you been?"

If she could get into the bedroom, she could lock the door and run for the window. She stiffened.

He shook his head and dropped the aim of the gun to her leg. Then he frowned, his nostrils widening. "What are you saying to me?"

Dread slammed into Dana.

Gary focused on her, his eyes hardening. "All of it? Are you sure?" He swallowed and red infused his thick neck. "I'm going to kill you when I find you. Just so you know." He clicked off, his face frighteningly intense. "Well. I guess we know where Wolfe is." He tucked the phone back into the pocket and reached for a wickedly sharp-looking knife. "We should get started."

Wolfe swung open the helicopter door and jumped from the military transport, his mind on Dana. Maybe she'd wear that yellow baby-doll thing again if he asked nicely, after he'd taken a shower and gotten out of this black mission clothing. He stopped cold at the sight of Brigid waiting for him next to a souped-up sports car. Her Irish green eyes swallowed up her pale face. He reached her in seconds. "What's happened?"

Her teeth chattered. "Gary Rockcliff is at your place right now." She'd barely gotten the words out before he ran around and dropped into the driver's seat. She opened the passenger door and sat, securing her seat belt as he ignited the engine and spun away from the tarmac.

"Tell me everything," Wolfe ordered, opening up the throttle, his hands cold on the steering wheel. Fury threatened to take him, and he tamped it down, only to be assaulted by a great wave of fear. His body bunched as if he'd taken a blow, and he wrestled all feeling into nothingness. "Brigid?"

She swallowed, her hands pressing against the dash when he took a corner too fast. "Raider, Nari, and I were having a late dinner when Mal called and said Gary was inside your house with Dana. Angus was already on his way to Mal's for some reason, so he got there quickly.

Raider and Nari took his truck to go cover the house as well, and I borrowed Nari's car to pick you up."

"How long has he had her?" Wolfe asked, his chest pounding.

"Thirty minutes or so. Raider and Nari should be there by now." Tears filled Brigid's eyes. "She'll be okay."

Wolfe drove faster, winging between other cars and driving on the shoulder when necessary. "His plan must have been to kidnap her, and Malcolm ruined that. He'll be pissed off to have his plans changed." He barely missed a motorcycle rider but sped up again anyway.

"Mal thinks Roscoe has been shot," Brigid whispered.

Wolfe tightened his hold on the steering wheel and punched the gas pedal to the floor. "You have a phone?"

"Yes." She fumbled for her burner.

"Call Force." He'd be there by now and was the planner on most operations.

She speed-dialed and pressed the speaker button.

"Force," Angus answered.

"It's Wolfe. Give me a status," he ordered, taking a corner on two wheels and barreling down the country road.

Brigid yelped and grabbed the handle above her window, keeping the phone held out toward him so he could hear.

"It's a shit show," Force affirmed. "Rockcliff is inside with Dana and has the blinds drawn. More than likely has the alarm engaged as well. Just a sec." A pounding erupted, and then he was back. "We're keeping him occupied as much as possible, but it's not going to last long. He knows you're coming, and he'll want you to find a mess."

A mess. As in, Dana bloody and dead.

Damn it. Rock no doubt knew about the explosion of his lab, and now he'd want revenge. Possibly, he wouldn't have anything to lose. "How did he find her?"

"Dunno," Force gritted out.

Okay. Think, damn it. "He'll be expecting me to knock down the front door." Wolfe cut through a field, risking the undercarriage of the vehicle.

"Yeah. What are you thinking?" Force asked as more pounding echoed through the line.

"What are you doing?" Wolfe asked, swerving to avoid a downed tree trunk. Where had that come from?

"We're approaching from different entry points, keeping him looking for us. He fired out of the bedroom window a few minutes ago." Force yelled something that Wolfe couldn't make out. "I don't want anybody without combat training here. Mal sent Pippa off with the truck. Brigid? You get in with Pippa and get clear. Okay?"

Brigid shook her head. "No. I'll be nearby in case somebody gets hurt and needs a ride to the hospital."

Force sighed. "That's exactly what Pippa said. I have no doubt she's at the edge of the lane right now, disregarding Mal's orders. And mine."

Wolfe didn't have time to worry about it. "I'm approaching from the north right now and will park and run so Gary doesn't hear another vehicle. I don't want him to know I'm there until I'm in front of him." He looked at a very pale Brigid. "How do I disengage just one area of my alarm without going to the panel? Like one window?"

They hit a bump, and she dropped the phone onto her lap. "You need to go to the panel or disable the sensor somehow. Where is the panel?"

"It's in the garage, hidden behind a false wall." A plan started to form in his head, and he took a turn into the forest, stopping when there wasn't any more room for the car to maneuver. "We're about half a mile away, and I'm going to run from here." He secured her phone and opened his door. "You stay here or retreat the way we came and meet us on the road. But stay away from the house. Yeah?"

"Okay." She scooted over to the driver's seat. "Good luck, Wolfe."

"Thanks." He turned and ran through the forest, his boots pounding, his ribs feeling as if they were cracking open, one at a time. Images of Dana propelled him faster, his lungs struggling with this newest fight.

Gulping, he circled around the trees to the side of his house, crab-walking between the trees and crouching against his fence, pressing speed dial on his phone.

"Force."

Wolfe ducked down lower, swearing at the clear night. It was hot and humid with no cloud cover. "Here's my plan." He slowly laid it out, finishing with, "So, I go in first, and then you guys breach from every direction." Hopefully shock and awe would throw Gary for just enough time.

Force was quiet. "That's crazy."

Wolfe closed his eyes against a wave of terror at what Dana was going through. "It's all we've got."

Chapter Forty-Three

Dana fought against the ropes binding her wrists as she sat on the sofa. She instinctively knew that telling Rock she was pregnant would be a mistake. "You're going to get us both killed," she said.

He finished attaching some weird putty to the front door and added a piece of metal to it, tweaking something with his back to her. "Yeah, but think how beautiful the blast will be." He smoothly moved to the front window, his pack in hand. "I've never felt the heat of a blast, you know. Sure, I've set a bunch and watched everything disintegrate, but I've never *felt* that."

God, he was crazy.

Kat howled from the pantry, and Roscoe still hadn't moved.

Dana waited until Gary started affixing another device to the front window before edging closer to the table. He'd put the gun away after tying her hands, so now was her only chance.

"You move and I'll cut you," he said, not turning around. "I'm going to cut you anyway, but it'll happen sooner rather than later if you try to run." He looked over his shoulder, his now blank eyes freaking her out. "I wouldn't mind getting started, but I have a couple more windows to do first."

She gulped down fear. He'd already wired the back slider, the door to the garage, and the windows in the master bedroom and bathroom. The office was the only window left. "You don't have to do this. If you jump out of the office window, you can run and they won't chase you. They'll be worried about me." And Roscoe. She didn't want him to focus on the dog again, so she didn't mention him. "Just go, Gary. Live a new life or something."

He chuckled, finishing with the device. "Live a new life? Wolfe will never stop coming, and you know it." Snagging her bound hands, he pulled her off the sofa and shoved her toward the office. "This ends today."

She stumbled and then walked, trying to see if Roscoe was still breathing. Red matted his fur, and his eyes were closed. Was he moving? She couldn't tell.

Gary shoved her harder, and she fell into the office, landing on her side. Pain blew up her forearm, and she twisted, kicking out and trying to trip him. He sidestepped her and looked down. "That wasn't nice." Pulling his boot back, he kicked her in the thigh.

Agony exploded in her leg, and she cried out, her eyes filling.

Pounding came from the front door this time. Gary shook his head. "They think they're distracting me."

How could she let them know the place was wired? If she yelled, he'd be on her in a second, and he'd promised to cut out her tongue. But could she get enough of a warning out first? Probably not.

He grabbed her by the hair and lifted, shoving her into the desk chair. "Sit here and shut up for a minute." He patted her injured leg, and she gasped, leaning forward as the pain attacked her again. He laughed. "You're going to be fun. I can already tell." He reached in his pack, turned, and carefully set up another device.

Tears slid down her face and her nose started to run. She grabbed a tissue from the desk, struggling since her hands were bound. "How did you find me, anyway?" Telling him about herself hadn't helped, but maybe if he talked about himself, she could buy a little more time.

He finished with the device and zipped up the backpack. "Once I knew about you and had a couple of pictures of you and Wolfe from the wedding, it was easy. A quick search online, and your interview with Angus Force came up."

Oh yeah. After they'd caught the Senator, she'd immediately taped an interview with Force. "So you figured that I was working with Angus Force."

"No. I figured that Wolfe was working with Force, and you were dating Wolfe." Gary turned around and tossed his pack into the corner. "It was a surprise to see you leaving Force's office."

"You followed me from there?"

"Yes. I stayed far enough away that you wouldn't notice and then parked, running a few miles until I found these two bungalows. It took a couple of tries, to be honest." He looked around the room. "This area is too small."

She was going to puke, but she set the tissue down and smoothly grasped a blue pen. "Why did you kill Candy?"

He moved to the closet to open it. "Wolfe doesn't have any good sex toys, does he?"

Her stomach heaved. "No," she croaked.

"Shoot." Gary shut the closet door. "I killed Candy because she was yet another nosy bitch, like you, and she deserved to die. Like you," he added, almost as an afterthought.

"What about Theresa Rhodes? You must understand love."

He chuckled. "Love? No. Her mind impresses me, and she has a hell of a body as well as excellent contacts in the heroin trade." His gaze darkened. "Unfortunately, she's smart enough to have planted evidence that will hang me if she's ever harmed. Guess she thought I might kill her at some point."

Now that was terrifying. Dana tried again. "You must feel something for her."

"Sure, but she makes stupid mistakes." He shrugged. "Or maybe just untrained ones."

Dana swallowed. "Like hiring those two guys to shoot at me after the Captive party or hiring the two gangbangers to take me out after I identified my friend's body?" Her stomach lurched.

Approval filled Gary's eyes. "You are smart. Yeah. Hiring any of those morons was a stupid move, as was drugging both you and Wolfe. I made her regret those actions, if that helps. Well, for a while, anyway." He clapped his hands together. "She called off the gang hit afterward, not that that matters any longer. Let's go back into the living room. The couch is a good cream color that will soak up blood nicely." He reached for her hands.

She jumped up, striking the pen up into his jaw, using her legs for power. As the pen sank in, Gary stepped back, his eyes widening. Turning, she lunged through the doorway, going for a knife in the kitchen.

He caught her by the hair, yanking her back and throwing her against the wall. She impacted with her shoulder. The pen was still in his neck. She scrambled to her feet, her body shaking. He laughed and pulled the pen free, spurting blood. "I'm going to stab you with this, too." He grabbed her by the neck and threw her into the living room.

She landed on the sofa and bounced, turning and scrambling away from him, her back to the sofa's arm.

He pulled the knife from its sheath, blood dripping from his jaw.

She fell off the sofa, crawled around the coffee table, and backed away. Something shattered in the master bath.

Wolfe!

Gary must've realized at the same time. He jerked and lifted the knife, rushing at her, aiming for her neck.

Wolfe dropped from the skylight in the master bath, and his knife sheath hit the mirror, cracking it loudly. Damn it. He bunched his body and exploded through the bedroom, skidding into the living room as Gary rushed at Dana. He kicked off the wall and leaped to intercept him, shoving his hand between her neck and the knife.

The blade cut into Wolfe's palm, going through.

In one smooth motion, he twisted and pushed Dana out of the way. "Get out of here," he ordered, throwing his free elbow at Gary's head.

Gary yanked the knife free, and Wolfe hissed in pain as blood spurted from his hand. The phone was connected to his vest, and he leaned down to yell at Force. "Breach now."

"No," Dana cried, waving her hands. "Don't breach."

"Stand down," Wolfe ordered.

Gary punched him in the neck, and he saw stars. Grunting, he ducked his head and charged the asshole, hitting his midsection and lifting him. They came down hard, smashing the coffee table into bits of wood and glass. "Dana, get out of here," Wolfe yelled, punching and trying to block hits, rolling to the side and coming up on his feet.

"The place is wired. Every window and exit," she yelled, her bound hands waving wildly.

"Except the damn skylight," Gary bellowed. "You dick."

He had to stop the team. "We're wired. Got that?" Wolfe said into the phone.

"Affirmative," Force said. "You got this?"

"Yeah." Wolfe's left hand might never recover, and his strength was ebbing, but he wasn't going to let Dana down. He feinted and then kicked Gary in the face. Blood was already flowing from his neck, or rather, from beneath his jaw. "You okay, Dana?" Gary stabbed at him, and he blocked with his forearm to the handle, bending down to release his own knife.

"Yes." She ran into the kitchen and fumbled in some drawers. "Roscoe was shot. We have to get out of here."

Gary's eyes gleamed. "I guess it does come down to you and me." He twisted the weapon around in a reverse knife grip technique with the blade in. "I'm gonna kill you and then take my time with her."

"You talk too much." Wolfe swung with his knife, drew back, and side-kicked Gary in the ribs.

Something crunched.

Gary hissed and edged to the side, dodging and weaving, looking for a weakness. "It wasn't nice of you to blow up my heroin."

"I was bored and needed a hobby." Wolfe matched his movements.

Gary swiped with the knife, and Wolfe ducked, not seeing the punch to the temple coming. Gary landed the punch, and lightning exploded through Wolfe's head. He flew into the television set, smashing the screen. Gary rushed for him, and Wolfe pivoted and connected with an uppercut that ricocheted up his arm and down to his bruised ribs.

Gary's teeth snapped together and he went down, his shoulders hitting the ground. He used the ground to push off, flipping all the way over and landing on his feet.

Wolfe charged, blocking and striking, seeking to draw blood. He fought hard, methodically, countering every strike with one of his own. He refused to feel pain, looking for any opening. A kick to the knee caught him unaware, and he twisted, going down to his other knee.

Gary jump-kicked and nailed Wolfe's wrist; his knife went flying across the room.

"Wolfe!" Dana yelled.

He went from his knees to his feet, his hands out and ready. Gary attacked, knife slashing rapidly, steadily advancing. Wolfe blocked each slash, trying to protect his face and neck while sacrificing his forearms. Pain cut into him sharper than the blade.

Gary kicked him in the knee again, sending Wolfe onto the other one. Smiling with bloody teeth, Gary flipped the knife around, grabbed the handle and struck.

Wolfe drew on all of his strength, spun on his knee, launched up and side-kicked Gary in the ribs. Gary emitted a shocked *oof*, and bent over. Bellowing, Wolfe landed on his feet and instantly kicked up, catching the bastard beneath the jaw and throwing him across the room.

Gary yelled as he impacted the front window, which instantly exploded.

Wolfe turned away, but the blast hit him, blowing him into the kitchen, where he smashed the table into bits. His ears rang. He coughed out dust and chalk, rolling over to spit out blood. "Dana?" he gasped.

She was on her knees with the dog's head in her lap, protected from the blast. Tears slid in dirty rivulets down her face while debris fell on her. "We have to get you to a hospital."

Force came through the front window first, followed by the rest of the team, all with guns out.

Wolfe reached for a damaged kitchen chair and forced himself to his unsteady feet. He wavered and then stood. "I'm fine. Roscoe needs help."

Force dropped into a slide, reached the dog, and picked him up, running toward the broken window again. Malcolm followed him, while Raider reached Dana and helped her up.

"Gary?" she croaked.

"Dead," Raider affirmed. "Very." He looked over at Wolfe. "You need help walking?"

Wolfe shook his head, and it almost exploded faster than the window had. He wrapped a towel around his hand.

"You need a doctor," Raider said, shoving a shoulder beneath his arm while also keeping hold of Dana. "Let's get you to the hospital."

"No," Wolfe said, allowing Raider to help him to the front window. "If Dana's okay, I want to go to the vet's or wherever they took Roscoe."

"Me, too," Dana said, grabbing Wolfe's hand. "If you're sure."

"I'm sure." Wolfe winced and limped toward the sill. Roscoe hadn't looked good.

Chapter Forty-Four

Dana accepted the bottle of water from Pippa, and seated herself on the wide padded bench next to Wolfe at the Cottage Grove emergency veterinarian hospital. The Deep Ops team took up the entire small waiting room with Raider and Brigid in seats by the fish tank, Mal, Pippa, and Nari near the door, Serena and Millie on a couch by the wall. Angus paced back and forth at the reception desk, his face hard and unreachable. Kat was under Mal's chair, watching everything with wide eyes.

Wolfe's head was back against the wall, his legs were extended and crossed at the ankles, and his eyes were closed. Fresh bruises from his fight with Gary mingled with older bruises along his neck and face. He'd bandaged his hand.

"It has been two hours," Dana whispered, reaching out to rub his forearm. "Shouldn't they be done?"

His eyelids opened.

Something wet, very wet, covered her palm. She lifted her hand to see red. Bright red. "What in the world?"

Raider immediately approached and pulled up the black sleeves of Wolfe's military gear. Bloody gashes covered Wolfe's forearms.

Dana gasped. The black material had covered the cuts. "Why didn't you say anything?"

"I was worried about Roscoe. These aren't deep," he rumbled, seeming unconcerned.

Raider frowned. "You're losing too much blood, dumb ass." He reached for one of Wolfe's shoulders just as Malcolm crossed the room and grabbed the other. The two men hauled him up, giving him no choice. They pushed him around the receptionist desk.

"Hello?" Malcolm called. "We have a wolf here that needs stitches." They disappeared down the long hallway.

Dana stared at the blood on her hand and gagged. The room spun, so she closed her eyes, leaning back the way Wolfe had. She stayed in that position for at least thirty minutes, until she couldn't stand the blood on her hand any longer.

Glancing down, she saw that the liquid had started to dry, cracking on her skin. Sucking in air, she stood and hurried to the restroom to wash off her hand. She waited at the sink, trying to control her stomach. This night was too much. She started shaking and couldn't stop, her teeth chattering. Tears flowed down her dirty cheeks, and she coughed.

"Dana?" Wolfe called through the door.

"Wolfe," she said, trying to regain control between the two sinks.

He opened the door and walked in, his boots clomping on the small square tiles. His bare chest was mottled with bruises, and fresh bandages now covered his forearms and hand. "Whoa." He reached for her.

She swatted him away. "Don't. You just got stitches." Her shaking increased in force.

Wolfe partially turned his head. "I need a blanket," he bellowed. Then he lowered his chin and reached for her again, this time ignoring her slaps and plucking her off her feet. "You're going into shock."

She snuggled her face into his neck, breathing in his masculine scent. "I am not."

The door opened. "What's happening?" Malcolm asked, handing over what looked like a horse blanket.

"Need a minute," Wolfe said.

"Sure." Malcolm disappeared.

Wolfe swung around and strode toward the tile wall by the door, away from the stalls and sinks. He slid down to the floor, cradling her against his heated bare skin and covering her with the blanket that was rough but smelled fresh. "I want you to take deep breaths. In and out. Where are you?"

"In the bathroom," she said, taking in a deep breath.

"Where else are you?" Amusement tinged his voice this time.

Oh. "With you. Next to you." Surrounded by him, actually. "You're here and you're safe." She let his warmth seep through her skin and stop the shaking.

"That's right. I've got you. Understand?" He kissed her forehead, and he was solid and strong and powerful, even wounded.

She nodded. "I love you." He stiffened beneath her, and she winced, lifting her head to look in his eyes. "I know we're in the bathroom at a vet hospital, and we're all dirty and banged up, and this is the wrong place to say that. However, who knows what's going to happen next, so I wanted to say it right now."

His eyes warmed to that bourbon color she loved more than anything. "This is the perfect place. I love you, too."

She blushed. "You don't have to say it just because I did."

He nipped the top of her nose. "I'm saying it because I mean it. I've loved you since you attacked me with that umbrella in the woods at Hunter's house, but I didn't think I'd be around for long."

"I've loved you since that moment, too. Even though you owe me an umbrella." She wanted to find levity in the moment, but Roscoe's fate hung over them. "I mean, it's deeper now, but I've always felt something for you, even when you're driving me crazy."

"I think your crazy balances mine." He set his forehead against hers.

The door opened, and Raider stood there. "The nurse said the veterinarian wants to talk to everyone in a minute."

Dana's eyes filled. "The wound was bad, and he bled for so long." She didn't protest when Wolfe stood, still holding her, and carried her into the waiting room where everyone seemed to be holding their breath. Angus had grown still by the desk, his face pale, his eyes inscrutable.

Wolfe settled back onto the same bench, and when she tried to move off him, his hold tightened. She relaxed against his hard chest again.

The wait was excruciating. Finally, a female veterinarian in green scrubs walked into the room, her eyes weary. "Roscoe's family?"

"Yes," Nari said, standing and moving to Angus's side as if she could catch him should he fall. She set her hand on his arm.

The vet smiled. "It was a rough surgery to remove the bullet, but he's a tough one, and he hung in there pretty long. He's an impressive animal. He's going to need rest for a while, but I think he's going to be fine."

The relief made Dana dizzy. "He was so brave trying to defend me. You'd be proud, Angus."

"Can I see him?" Angus asked.

The vet looked around the room. "Just you. You can see him tonight, and everyone else can see him tomorrow. He needs rest, and I suggest you all do the same." Motioning, she led Angus behind the reception desk.

Wolfe stood with Dana. "Mal? We need a place to stay tonight."

"No problem," Mal said, standing and holding Pippa's hand. "We can deactivate the explosives at your place tomorrow."

Dana slipped her arm over Wolfe's shoulder and kissed a bruise on his jaw. She needed to tell him about the baby. "We have to talk," she whispered.

"We will." He kissed her, somehow walking out of the waiting room and into the heated night as he did so.

She sank into his kiss, feeling she was finally home. But what would he think about her being pregnant? He'd seemed open to the possibility of dating before, but his response had been more about protection than love.

This was different. This was everything.

Wolfe hurt from his big toe to the top of his head, but he'd never been happier. After a long, hot shower with Dana, who'd been uncharacteristically quiet, he slid into the large bed in Mal's guest room, and tugged her in with him. Was she still in shock? Or maybe she was regretting their conversation in the restroom, chalking it up to emotion. "What's going on, Dana?"

She turned toward him on the bed, looking adorable in a cami and short set she'd borrowed from Pippa. Her gaze stayed on his chest, and her breath emerged shallow.

"You're going to have a panic attack. Breathe deep." With one knuckle, he lifted her chin so he could look into her spectacular eyes. "Talk now. What's up?" He'd spend the rest of his life assuring her every day that he loved her, but he needed to know the problem so he could fix it.

She took a deep breath and pushed her blond hair over one shoulder. The scent of orange blossoms wafted toward him. "Okay. Here it is. I'm pregnant." A light pink suffused her face, and she plucked nervously at the bedspread.

He frowned. "It's only been a little over a week since we, ah, had unprotected sex."

She shifted her weight. "Dr. Georgetown did a blood test, and sometimes early results can be conclusive. The pregnancy hormone is in my blood."

He couldn't breathe. His chest expanded and filled, with light and excitement this time. "You're sure?" His voice shook.

She nodded. "Yeah. What do you think?"

His smile made his bruises ache, but he didn't care. "I think it's the best news in the entire world." Grabbing her hand, he started to inch off the bed.

She tugged back. "What are you doing?"

"We're going to get married." He'd have to borrow clothes from Malcolm, but they were close to the same size, so that was okay.

She laughed and clutched his wrist, trying to pull him back. "What are you talking about?"

He could just carry her. "I know it's fast, but let's go do it."

She sighed. "For the survivor benefits?"

"Of course." Now they were on the same page. Why wasn't she smiling? He ran through the last few minutes in his mind and then sat. "Oh." Sometimes he was a block-head. He slipped from the bed onto both knees, almost hiding a grimace at the pain. "Dana? I love you more than life. Will you marry me?"

Her lips twitched. "You mean it?"

"Yes."

"Yes." Her eyes lit up.

His heart pretty much burst. He stood and picked her up off the bed.

She shook her head. "Not right now, Wolfe."

He paused. They probably did need to wait until morning. "Oh. Okay." He set her back into bed and then followed. "We can sleep late and then go."

Her laughter was a balm to every ache he had. "Listen, Wolfe. This is way too soon. We are going to take our time, get to know each other more, and then make plans."

He rolled to his side, facing her. "I'm gonna marry you."

She smiled and caressed his jaw. "I know."

"You said you are gonna marry me." The feeling of her soft hand on him was distracting, but he needed to get this out.

"Yeah." She leaned in and kissed him.

"Why wait?" He wanted her and the babe to be his now, not sometime in the future.

She chuckled, scooting closer to him. "You make a good point, but I want the whole shebang. Wedding, dress, flowers, cake . . . you name it."

Oh yeah. Her family. "I guess I should talk to your dad, huh?"

Her chest hitched as she laughed again. "That's awfully old-fashioned, don't you think?"

"Yeah." He ran his palm along her flank to her hip. "I'll talk to him next weekend if I can get away. He said he wanted to take me fishing." He should probably buy her a ring, too. Maybe one of her sisters would help him get the right one. Her family was going to be his, too. He could handle that.

Between his team and now his new family, Clarence Wolfe had never been happier. "Thank you," he whispered.

Her eyes widened. "For what?"

"For everything." Because that's what she was—his everything.

Epilogue

Two weeks later

Dana munched contentedly on one of Pippa's special butternut cookies and then slipped a small piece to a rapidly healing Roscoe, who lay at a healing Jethro's feet in the middle hub at the office. Both males allowed everyone to shower them with attention, sweets, and admiration. The bandage had been taken off Roscoe's stomach, but Jethro's leg was in a full cast, resting on a pillow on Mal's desk.

Mal sat in his chair with Pippa planted happily on his lap.

Wolfe prowled in from the second case room, holding boxes of outdated materials from cases they'd put to bed; Angus Force was right behind him, his eyes more bloodshot than usual. The leader had been on a mission for two weeks, and he seemed more on edge than ever.

Wolfe cut him a look. "You going to tell us what's going on?"

Force shook his head. "Not yet. There isn't anything to tell." Even his voice sounded exhausted.

"I thought we were going to paint the floor or something today," Brigid said, emerging from her computer room with Raider on her heels and Kat in her hands.

Nari leaned against her doorjamb, eating a cookie. "I

thought that was the plan, too. We really need to brighten this place up." She looked around the dingy office. "We have some juice since we took down Rockcliff and Theresa Rhodes."

Theresa had been taken into custody shortly after Rock had died, and rumor had it she'd lawyered up quickly.

Wolfe set the boxes down and frowned, looking sexy and strong. "Dana? You can't be here if there are paint fumes. I hadn't realized that was the plan."

Pippa leaned to the side. "You're allergic to paint?"

"No, she's pregnant," Wolfe said.

Silence descended a second before pandemonium hit. There was a rush toward her, and then a lot of hugs, including a very gentle one from Angus Force. The sheer joy and congratulations of the team filled Dana, and she had to bat back tears.

Wolfe was still frowning. "Hadn't we told you guys that?"

Man, he was clueless sometimes.

"No." Angus gave him some sort of man hug, his expression lightening for a brief moment.

"Huh." Wolfe's eyes softened as he looked at her, making her feel powerful and so happy she almost ached. "We're getting married, too. She's got a lot of sisters and friends, so I'm probably going to need groomsmen. We'll figure it out later. I guess you guys would all look okay in a tux."

Okay? It'd be the best-looking groom's side ever.

"We're not painting today," Angus said, shoving a box over by the ones Wolfe had set down. "Nari is right that we have some juice now, so I called in a couple of favors."

The elevator protested, screeched, and then descended, opening to reveal Agent Millicent Frost, her hair streaked with blue, boxes in her hands.

Dana cocked her head to the side. "What's happening?"

Angus moved to help Millie with the boxes. "I've hired both you and Agent Frost as part of the Deep Ops team."

Dana's mouth opened and then closed. "I don't recall applying for a job." She liked being a journalist, but the idea of being a government agent, with all of those resources at her fingertips, was definitely appealing.

Wolfe nodded. "Agreed. She's pregnant."

"So what?" Dana asked, turning toward him. "Pregnant women work. I'll take the job, Angus."

"That was easy," Angus mumbled, his dimple flashing. "She'll be on desk duty like Brigid, Wolfe. We need their skills, without question."

Dana grinned. She'd give this a shot. If she wasn't happy, she'd go back to freelancing. It was nice to have options. While her big wolf figured out whether this was a good development or not, she walked to him and slid an arm around his waist, leaning into his strength.

He sighed, stirring her hair.

"Millie?" Raider asked. "You want to, ah, work *here*?"

Dana bit back a laugh. The office was depressing, that was for sure.

Millie nodded, her face a little pale. "I do, and a lot of cool gadgets come with me. I'm a trained agent, and I can also go undercover if necessary."

Dana was missing something, but now wasn't the time to ask. Was Millie okay?

Nari looked around the room. "We can get another desk."

"No need," Angus said. "There's actually another storage area beyond the two interrogation rooms—all we have to do is clear it out. It's a good space for gadgets and the like, and Millie says it's fine for her."

So they were all there on a Saturday to clean out the

storeroom. Made sense. Dana turned toward the hallway by the elevators, halting when Wolfe didn't allow her to move. She looked up at his rugged face. "Wolfe?"

"An old storage room is too dusty for you," he said, leaning down to press a kiss to her nose. "Plus, who knows what else we'll find there."

She sighed, going up on tiptoe to kiss him full on his firm mouth. "You're going to drive me crazy for the next eight months, aren't you?" It was nice to be protected, but he was a mite overbearing.

"No." He kissed her back, humming with enjoyment and then releasing her mouth.

She blinked, trying to remember what they'd been talking about, her body warm. "No?"

"Not for eight months. For forever." He grinned, looking happier than she'd ever seen him. "I've always indulged myself with sweets, Dana. You're the sweetest thing in my life, in any life, and I'm keeping you. I love you. Always."

"Always," she said, meaning it, her heart full.

For him.

Don't miss Rebecca Zanetti's Dark Protectors series!
Read on for an excerpt from

GUARDIAN'S GRACE

The vampire was late.

Grace Cooper twirled the straw in her half-finished ginger whiskey and tried to ignore the skunk smell wafting through the bar. Rather, the smell of pot, which two kids were smoking in the back corner by the lone pool table, seemingly uncaring that recreational use of marijuana was illegal in bars in Colorado. None of the few folks ambitiously drinking in the place paid them any heed.

Darkness had descended outside along with a blistering snowstorm, and the wind howled against the few windows in an effort to sneak inside. Mother Nature had decided on a brutal end to January, which might explain why so few patrons had ventured through the storm for cheap booze and a stereo system from the early nineties that only played Bon Jovi songs. "Runaway" was currently blasting at a slightly slower speed than she remembered.

Why in the world had the vamp wanted to meet in this dump?

The bartender, a sixty-something man wearing a ripped T-shirt, snow pants, and thick boots, tipped back a couple of shots of tequila as he wiped down the bar, ignoring everyone unless they approached him for more alcohol.

This was the closest she would come to Denver, where

she'd lived before going into a coma and then becoming an immortal mate. Well, kind of becoming one. She'd promised everyone, especially her sister, that she'd never return to Denver. But persistent questions kept her up at night; she had to know the truth. First, she had to survive for another week.

Grace turned her wrist, the healthy one, and read the time on her sports watch. She'd give Sebastian five more minutes.

The door opened, and wind blasted inside. A male wearing a baseball cap covered with snow kicked the door shut, looked around, and spotted her. He brushed snow off his long overcoat and strode toward her, his boots leaving a wet trail across the sawdust-covered floor. "Grace."

He was thinner than he'd looked in his picture. "Sebastian."

"I'm sorry I'm late." He pulled out the wooden chair across from her small table and sat, his eyes an odd bluish hue. "I can explain."

She held up her good hand, her temples starting to ache. "It doesn't matter. Do you have it?" She hoped a vial would get her through until she could see the one and only expert on her condition.

He kicked back. "Yeah, but I thought we could maybe come to another arrangement." With the hat bill low over his face, and the bar so dark, it was difficult to judge his age. Or rather, what his age appeared to be, considering he'd supplied proof through email that he was over two hundred years old. "What's the hurry? There's a storm out there." He spoke with a very slight lisp.

She tilted her head. The overcoat was odd. "Take off your hat." Adrenaline started to hum through her veins.

His chest puffed out. "There you go. I knew we'd get along." With a flourish, he whipped off the cap with black fingernails, revealing thick blond hair—and black eyeliner rimming his eyes.

She blinked. Once and then again, looking closer. Were those colored contacts? Like the ones kids wore for Halloween? Yep. "You have got to be kidding me." How in the world had he fooled her? She'd asked for documentation, although records could be falsified. She began to stand.

He grasped her good wrist and tugged her down, leaning toward her. He smelled like cheap beer and even cheaper cologne. This close, he appeared to be in his early twenties. "I promise I'll give you what you want. My blood is all yours after I take a taste of my own." He opened his mouth, showing fangs.

Fake ones.

Anger snapped through her. "I can't believe this." Yes, she was a complete moron. The risks she'd taken for this meeting had kept her up for nights. She jerked free and started to stand.

The front door burst open, and a mammoth blond male strode inside just as a commotion sounded from the rear exit on the other side of the bar. The kids by the pool table snuffed out the pot, backing away and plastering themselves against the sole dartboard, their eyes wide and their chests sunken.

She stopped breathing. Damn it. Grabbing her bag, she moved toward the restroom behind her and the window she'd already scoped out—just in case this assignation went south.

"Grace?" The voice came from near the back exit. The low, dark, accented tenor stopped her cold.

She slowly turned, her body flashing to full-on panic mode. It couldn't be. *No, no, no, no, no.*

Yep.

Adare stood there; the surprise on his face quickly

banked. The fury in his impossibly black eyes, however, glittered harsh and bright.

She edged backward.

"Donna even think it." In his anger, his Scottish brogue, the product of a distant time and place, broke free and strong. His black hair hung to his shoulders, dotted with snow that was quickly melting. For the raid, or whatever this was, he'd worn a jacket, cargo pants, and boots—all black and more than likely concealing various weapons.

"Holy shit," Sebastian muttered, standing and turning.

Grace nodded in agreement. If she could shove Sebastian toward Adare, she might be able to—

Adare's nostrils flared, and her body reacted, stopping her in her tracks. Then he started moving toward her, smooth and graceful, his six-foot-six height and broad chest making him look like the proverbial immovable object.

Sebastian swallowed loudly and backed to her side. "That guy is huge. Like huge, huge." He looked toward her, one fluorescent blue contact falling out of his eye. "What have you gotten me into?"

The lump in her throat nearly choked her. "Nothing. You're fine, but don't go around pretending to be something you're not. Trust me, Sebastian."

"Freddy," the kid croaked. "My name is Freddy. Not Sebastian. I thought that sounded more like a creature of the night."

The huge blond guy's mouth dropped open and then shut quickly.

Oh, this was so bad. She'd tried hard not to leave a trail. Fake name, fake email address, and she'd even moved around to use different library computers and IP addresses—in different towns. What kind of laws had she broken? As far as she knew, there weren't prisons for immortals, so what did that leave? Death for treason?

Not that she wasn't dying anyway.

The blond, his black eyes taking in the entire room, quickly stepped up to the bar and flashed a badge. "U.S. Government. We only want those two for federal crimes."

"Whew," one of the kids in the back sighed.

The bartender shrugged, still drying off a beer glass with a dirty towel. "Take 'em."

Freddy lifted his hands. "I haven't done anything. Really. The chick is nuts. She thought I was a vampire, and she wanted to buy blood, so I figured, why not? Freaky sex might be fun."

"Shut. Up." Adare manacled Freddy's neck with one hand, cutting off all sound. Without taking his gaze off Grace, he flicked his wrist and tossed Freddy toward the blond. "Nick? Take him, please."

The *please,* for some reason, sent shivers down Grace's back. Her legs weakened, but she lifted her chin, facing Adare. It had been nearly three years since they'd crossed paths, and he appeared even better looking than she remembered. Meaner and bigger, too. A pissed-off expression on him was normal, but this one was new. All heat and fury. "I'll get going, too," she said, taking another step back.

Nick caught Freddy and leaned to the side, holding the human like a rag doll. "Adare? Do you know this female?"

Adare slowly nodded, his focus stronger than any hold. "She's my mate."

"I am not," she retorted.

"Yes. You. Are." Adare's face was as impenetrable as rock, even as the words rolled out with that brogue.

Nick's light eyebrows rose. He looked around the bar, and apparently satisfied that nobody was going to attack, returned his focus to Adare. "What's your mate doing trying to buy vampire blood in Colorado?" he whispered.

It sounded ridiculous. Heat spread up Grace's chest to her face, causing her cheeks to pound.

Adare's gaze followed the heat, making her even warmer. "We're about to get an answer to that question." He held out one broad hand, no leniency on his hard face. "Let's do this somewhere else."

It was an order, not a question.

"No." She said it softly but with authority. The bond of their mating was almost gone, and he had no hold on her. He never would, which suited them both just fine. "This was obviously a mistake, so let's just go our separate ways."

His lids half-lowered, slowly and deliberately, the deadly predator at his core fully visible. Not many people disobeyed the dangerous hybrid, and no doubt a human female, one whose life he had saved, shouldn't even think about it. But she was no longer his responsibility, and she was done being lost.

"Grace." One word, said in that brogue, with a demand that was absolute.

If she could run, she would. Instead, her body froze, her heart thundering. "I know I goofed up here, and I won't do it again." The appeasing note in her voice ticked her off, but she wasn't up to a physical struggle right now. This disastrous meeting had taken weeks to set up, and she only had one week to go. "Let's just forget this and move on."

"Have you lost your mind?" He sounded more curious than angry.

Hope flared through her. "Yes, briefly. It happens." He'd never wanted anything to do with her, so giving him an out should work nicely. A simple apology—she tried to sound sincere—although she wanted to kick him in the shin instead. He'd always been a jackass, but there was no doubt he'd win any physical fight. Even at her best, which she wasn't close to right now, she couldn't take him. It was doubtful anybody could. "This whole thing was a mistake, and I'm sorry." She choked on the last word.

"Let's go." His hand was still out.

An electric shiver took her. "Adare, I don't think—"

"Exactly. You didn't think." A muscle ticked in his rugged jaw, revealing the effort his control was costing him. "Apparently that's something we need to discuss. At length."

Was that a threat? Yep. That was definitely a threat. "Not a chance," she snapped, drawing on anger to camouflage panic.

Nick turned to Freddy and shoved him toward the door. "We need to take this somewhere else," he muttered.

"Not me," Freddy said. "Really. This isn't my fault." He pushed back against Nick, his voice dropping to a whine. "I just wanted to get laid. Whatever she's into, I'm not a part of it. Please. Let me go."

Nick opened the door and propelled him into the snowstorm. The wind shrieked, blowing snow inside.

Adare grasped her upper arm. "Now."

She tugged free. "Absolutely not."

"I wasn't asking." For a big male, he moved surprisingly fast. He ducked his head, and within a heartbeat, she was over his shoulder, heading toward the door.

Her chin hit his lower back, and her stomach lurched, the alcohol she'd consumed stirring around. She pounded against his waist with her good hand, not close to stopping him. This was a disaster. Panic grabbed her, and she tried to struggle but could barely move. "Let me go. Now."

"Hold on to your strength, Grace. You're going to need it." With that, he took her into the storm.